Peter H. Reynolds and Fable

ZEBRAFISH

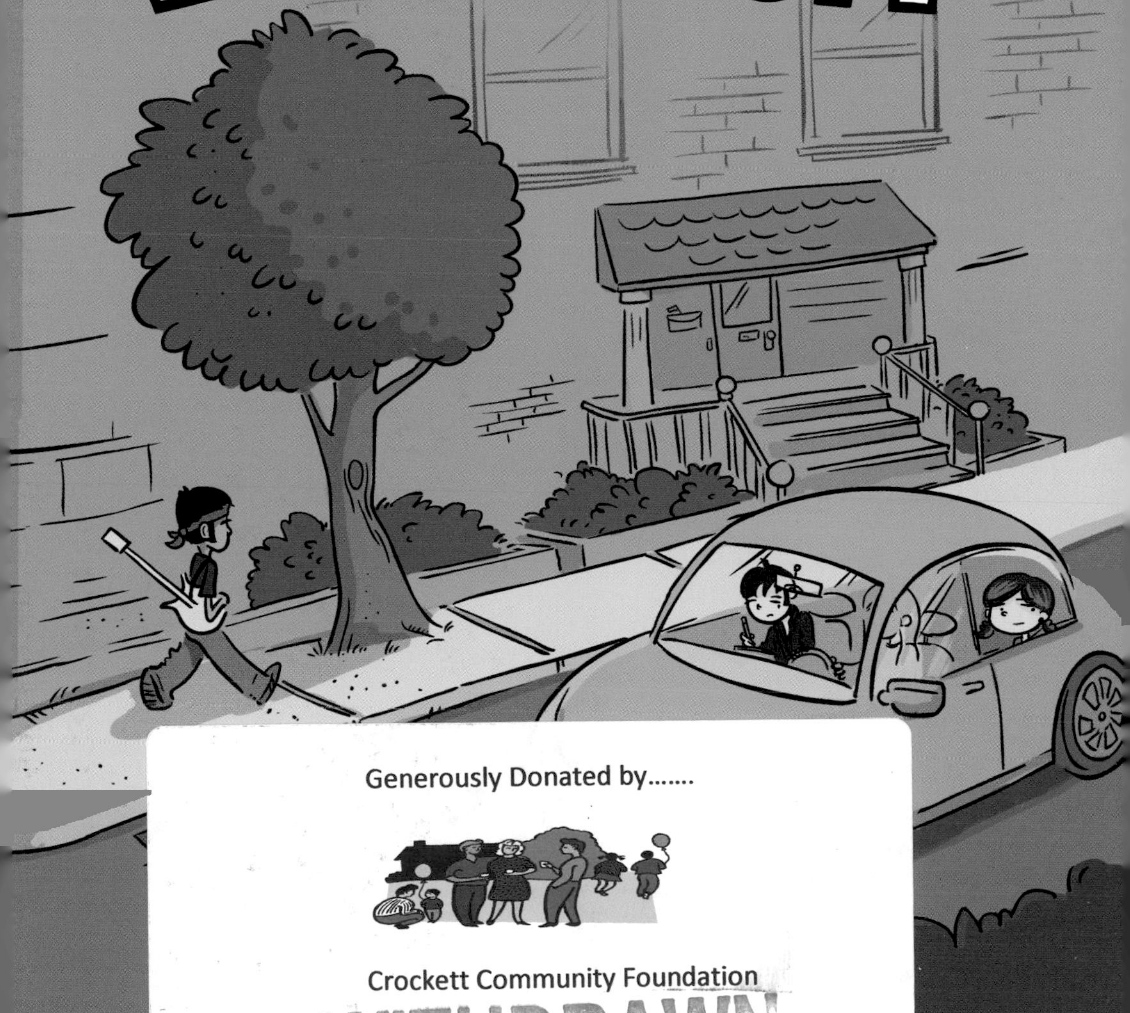

Written by Sharon Emerson
Drawn by Renée Kurilla

Atheneum Books for Young Readers
New York · London · Toronto · Sydney

ATHENEUM BOOKS FOR YOUNG READERS

An imprint of Simon & Schuster Children's Publishing Division
1230 Avenue of the Americas
New York, New York 10020

For information about special discounts for bulk purchases, please contact Simon & Schuster Special Sales at 1-866-506-1949 or business@simonandschuster.com.

The Simon & Schuster Speakers Bureau can bring authors to your live event. For more information or to book an event, contact the Simon & Schuster Speakers Bureau at 1-866-248-3049 or visit our website at www.simonspeakers.com.

Book design by FableVision, Inc.

The text for this book is set in AGaramondPro, ArialMT, Slappy, Times New Roman, space-cowboy.

The illustrations for this book are inked and colored digitally.

Manufactured in China
0210 WGL
First Edition
2 4 6 8 10 9 7 5 3 1

CIP data for this book is available from the Library of Congress.

ISBN 978-1-4169-9525-8

Contents

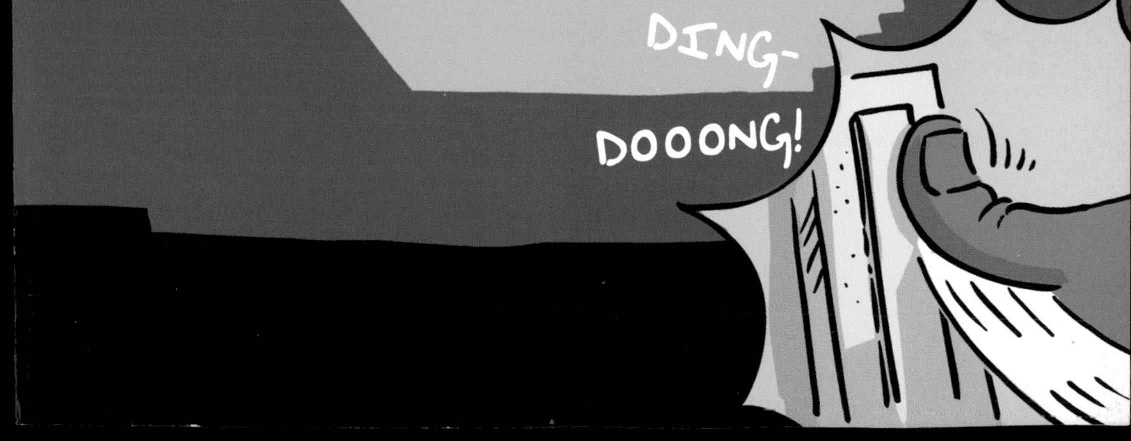

DING-
DOOONG!

Thank you

For the inspiration:
Dr. Dario Fauza
Dr. Richard White

For the challenge:
Gary Goldberger
Kate Cotter
Shelley Brown
Janet Cady
Caitlyn Dlouhy
Dan Potash

For the help:
Bob Flynn
Didi Mitova
Samantha Wilder Oliver
Keith Zulawnik

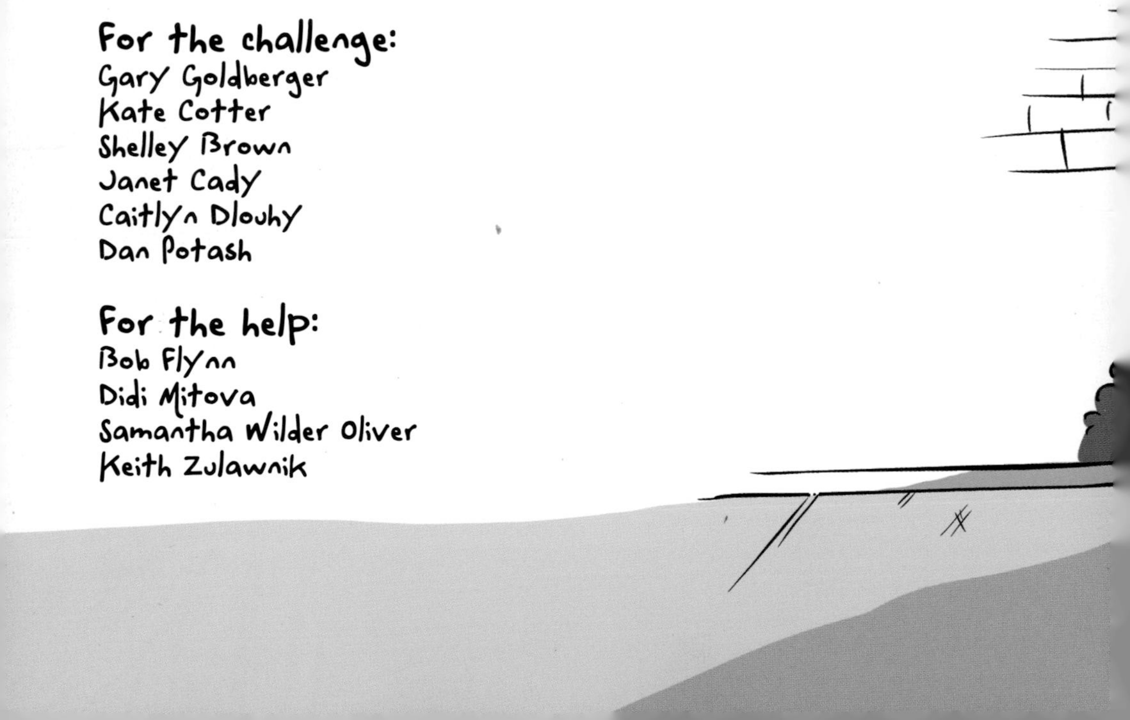

1. Family

Late June...

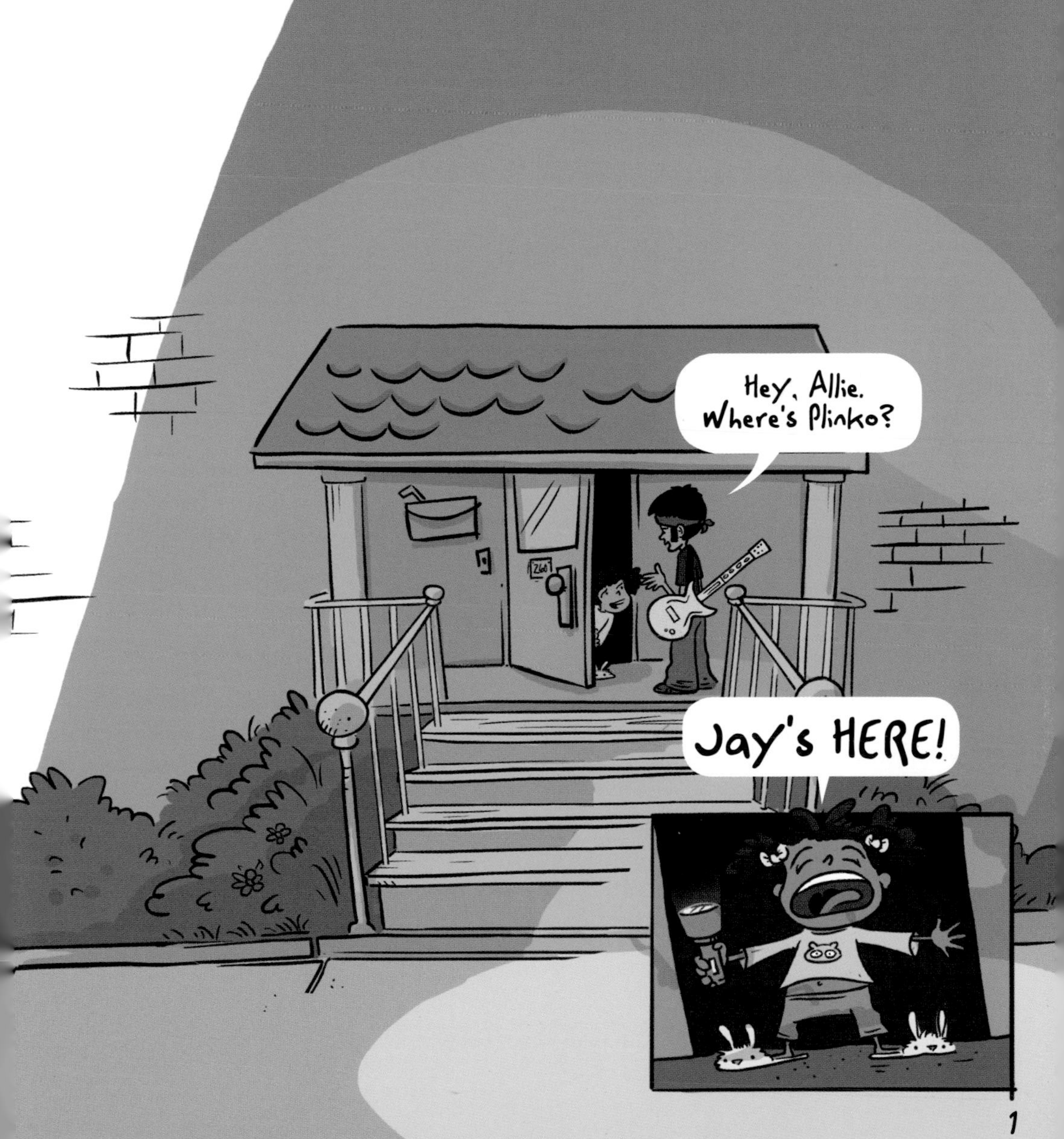
Hey, Allie. Where's Plinko?
Jay's HERE!

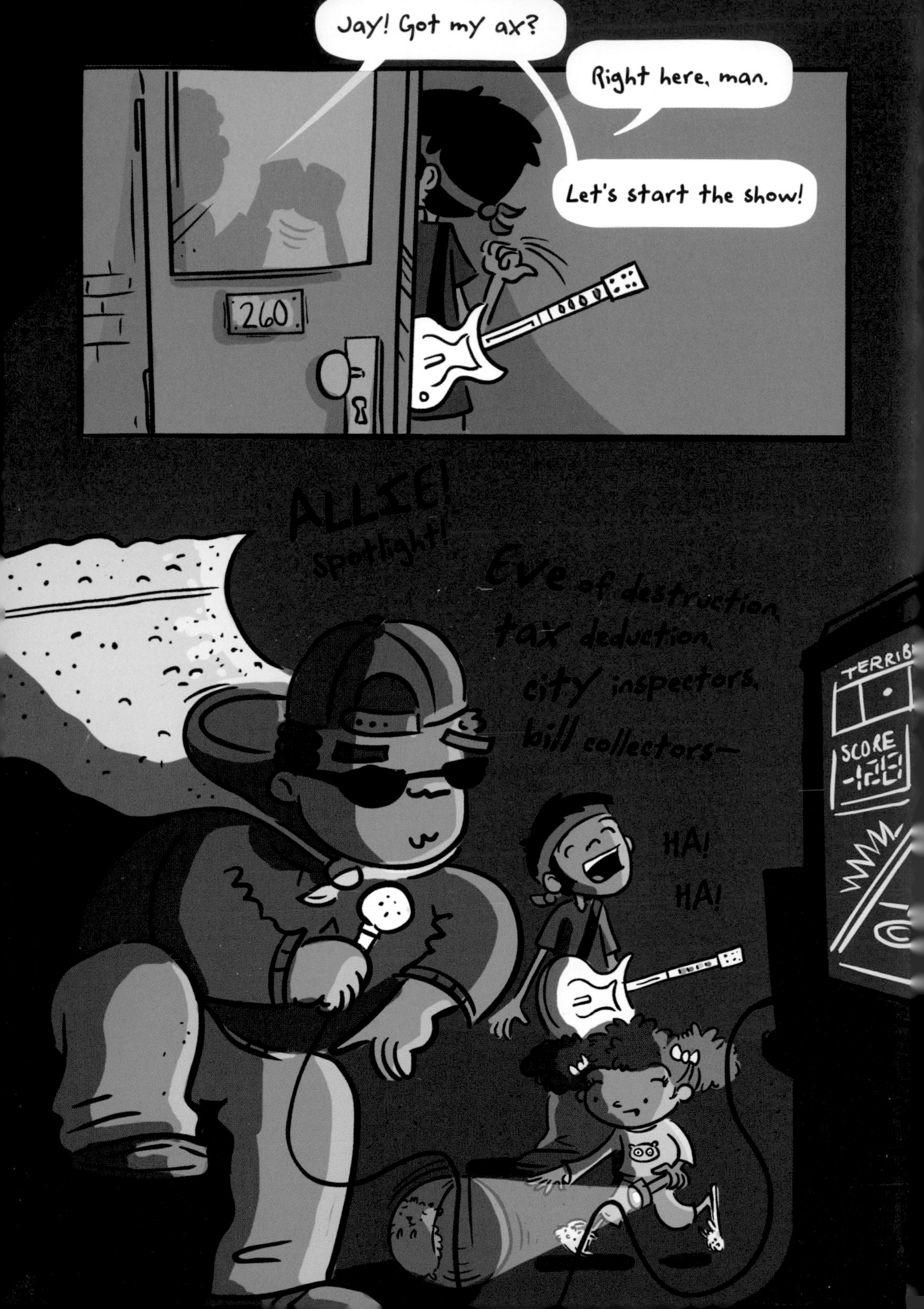
Jay! Got my ax?
Right here, man.
Let's start the show!
260
ALLIE! spotlight!
Eve of destruction, tax deduction, city inspectors, bill collectors—
HA! HA!
TERRIB
SCORE

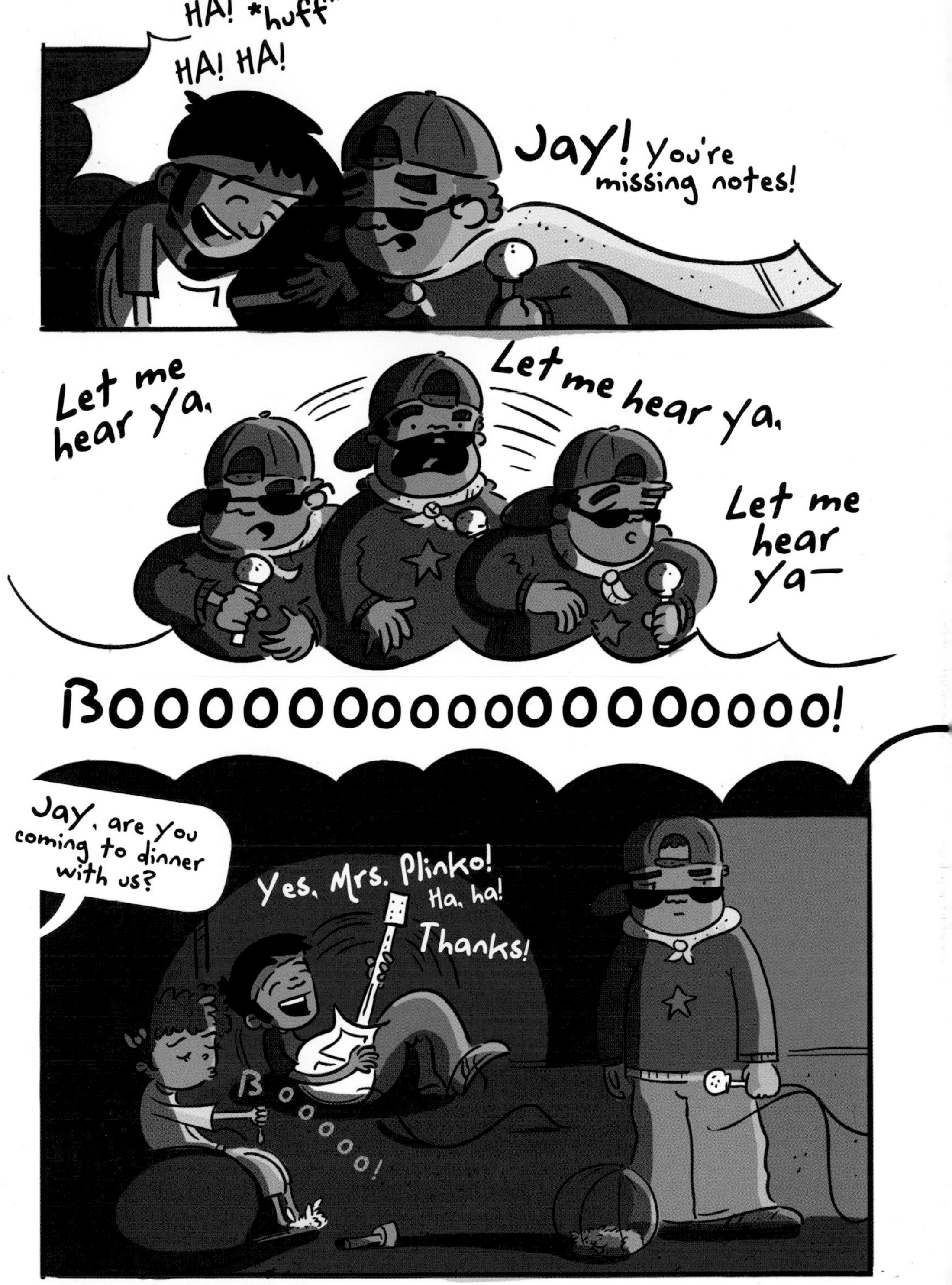
HA! *huff* HA! HA!
Jay! You're missing notes!
Let me hear ya.
Let me hear ya.
Let me hear ya—
BOOOOOOooooOOOOOOOOO!
Jay, are you coming to dinner with us?
Yes, Mrs. Plinko! Ha, ha! Thanks!
Boooooo!

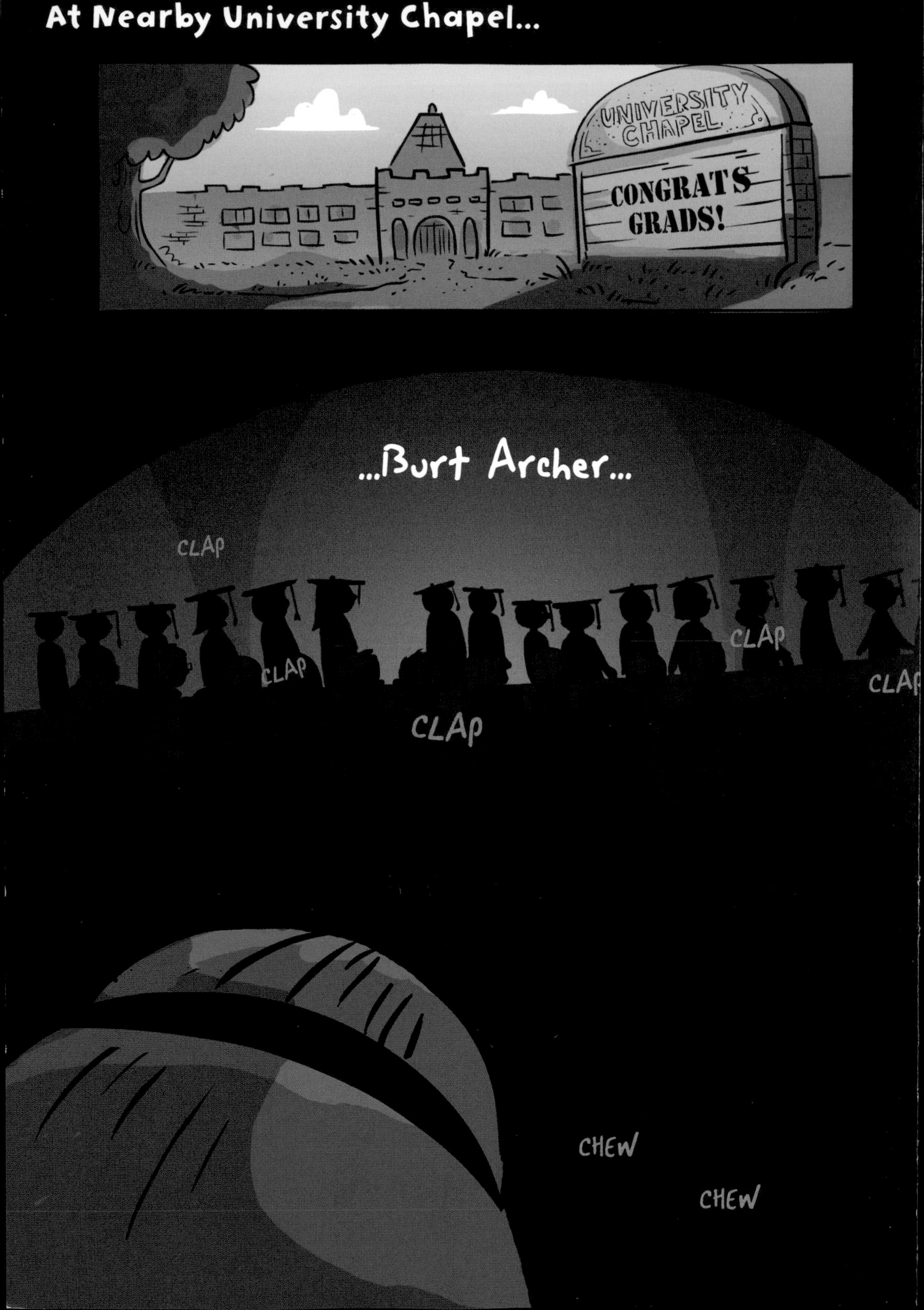
At Nearby University Chapel...
UNIVERSITY CHAPEL
CONGRATS GRADS!
...Burt Archer...
CLAP
CLAP
CLAP
CLAP
CLAP
CHEW
CHEW

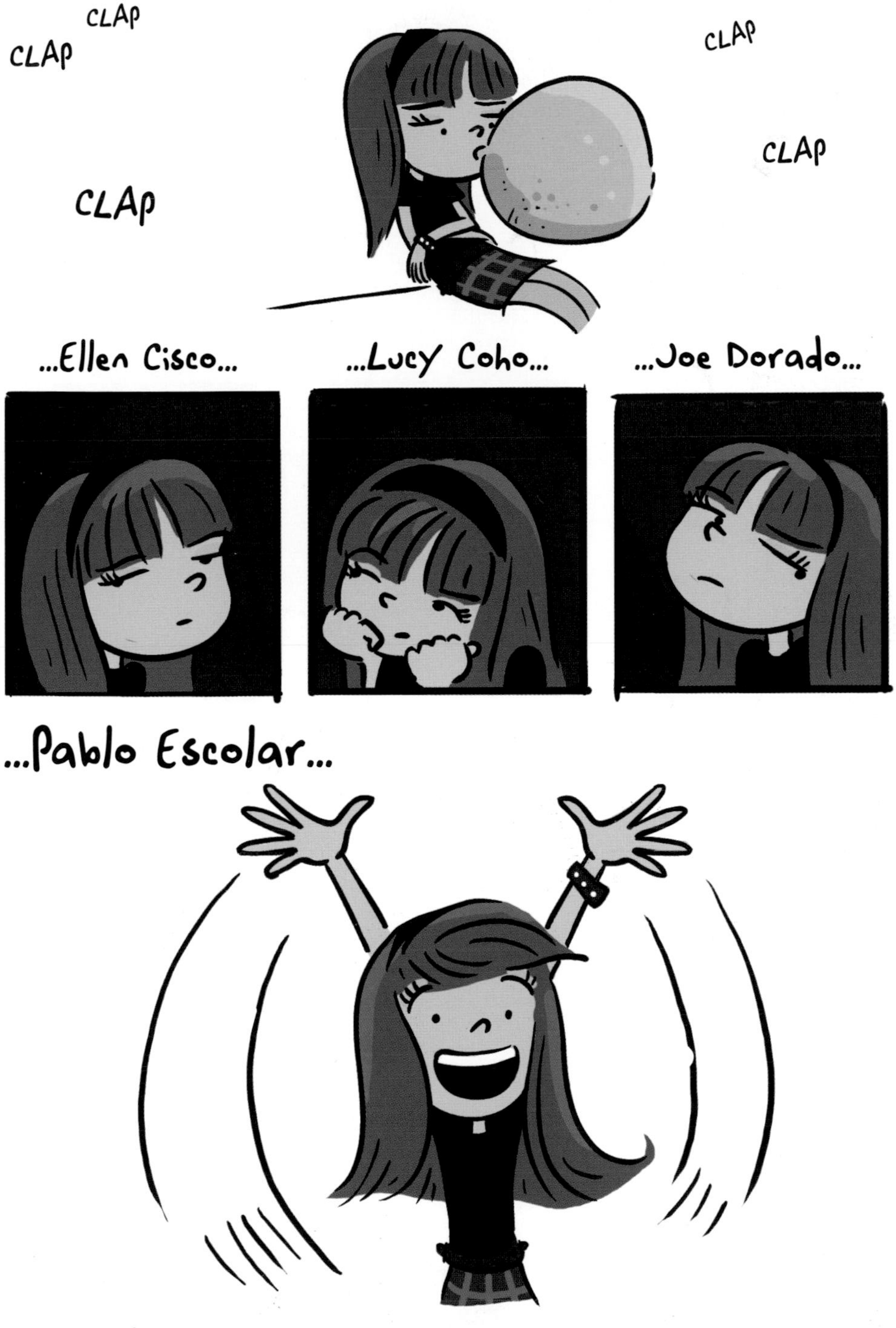
CLAP
CLAP
CLAP
CLAP
CLAP
...Ellen Cisco...
...Lucy Coho...
...Joe Dorado...
...Pablo Escolar...

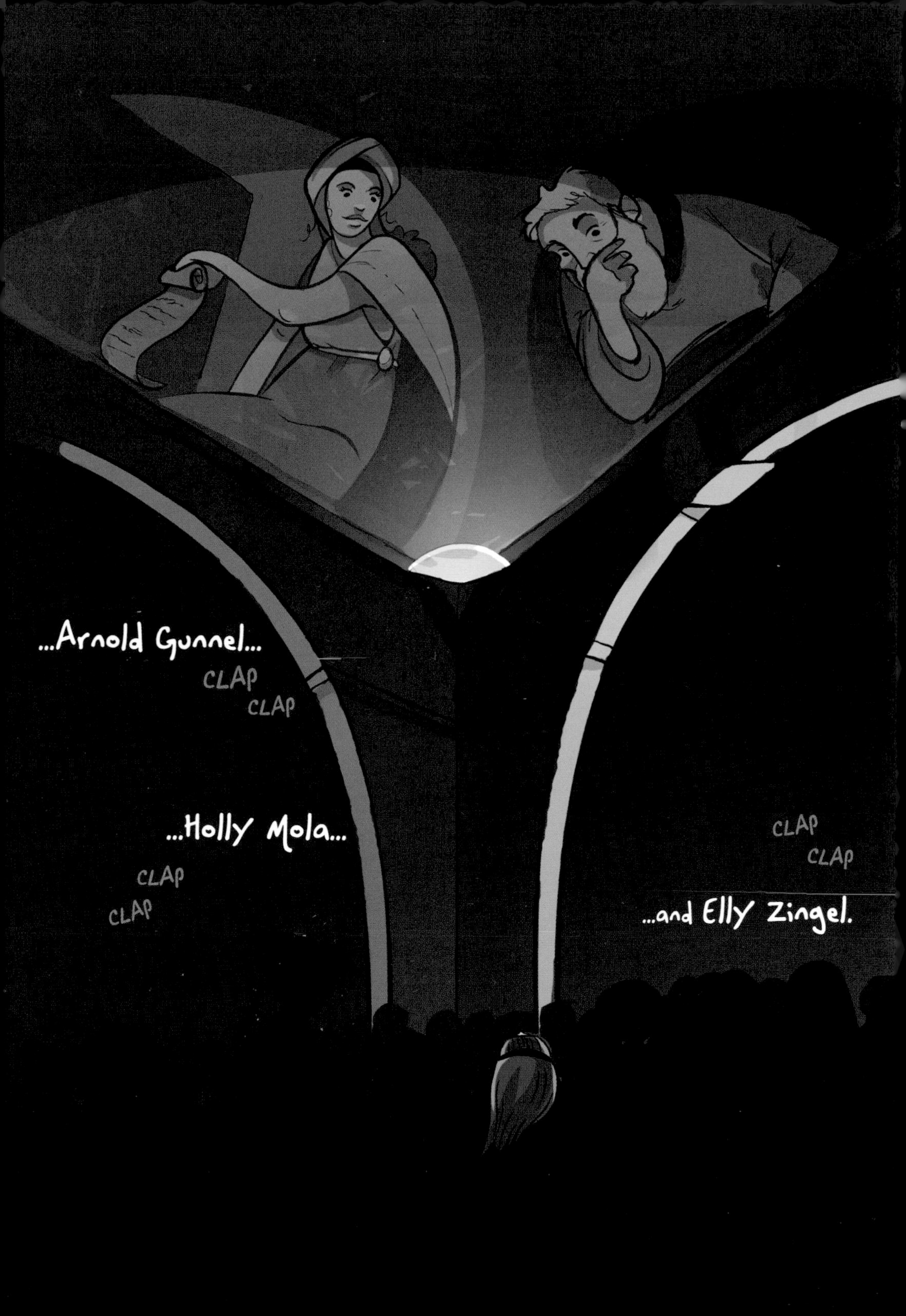
...Arnold Gunnel...
CLAP
CLAP
...Holly Mola...
CLAP
CLAP
CLAP
CLAP
...and Elly Zingel.

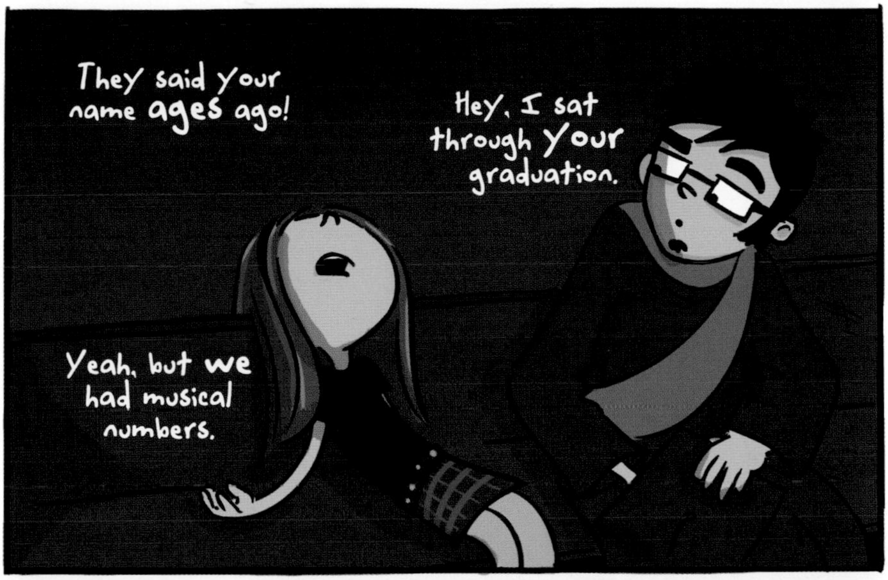
They said your name ages ago!
Hey, I sat through your graduation.
Yeah, but we had musical numbers.

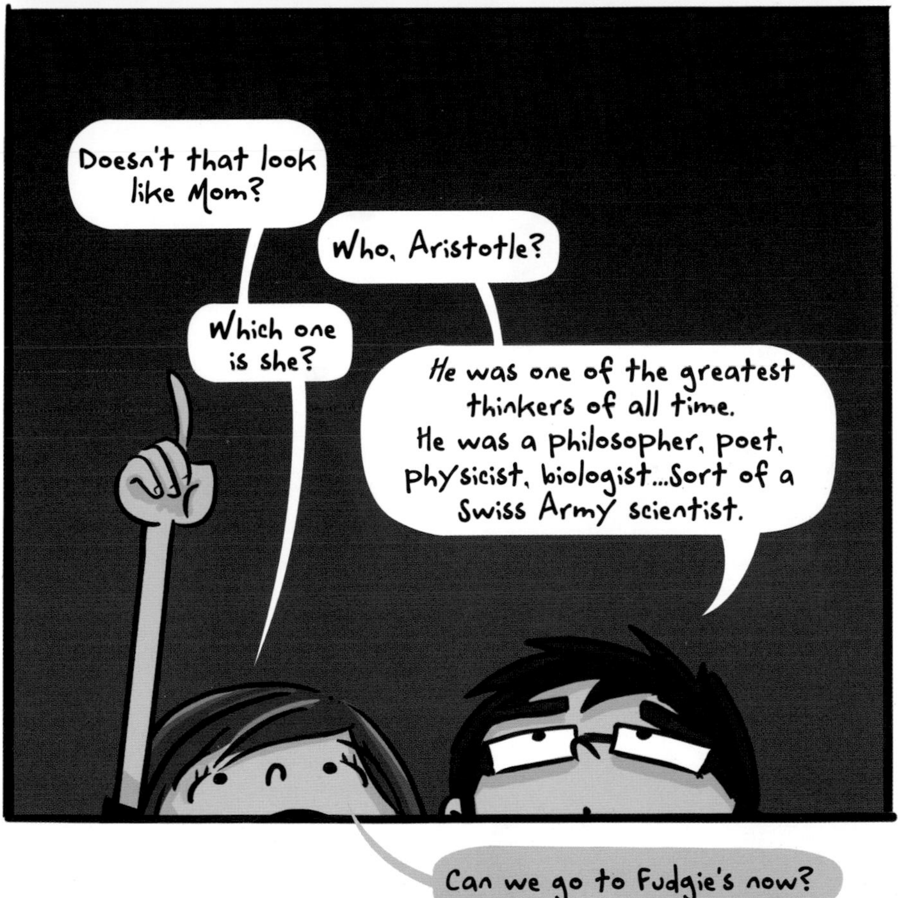
Doesn't that look like Mom?
Who, Aristotle?
Which one is she?
He was one of the greatest thinkers of all time. He was a philosopher, poet, physicist, biologist...Sort of a Swiss Army scientist.
Can we go to Fudgie's now?

Later...

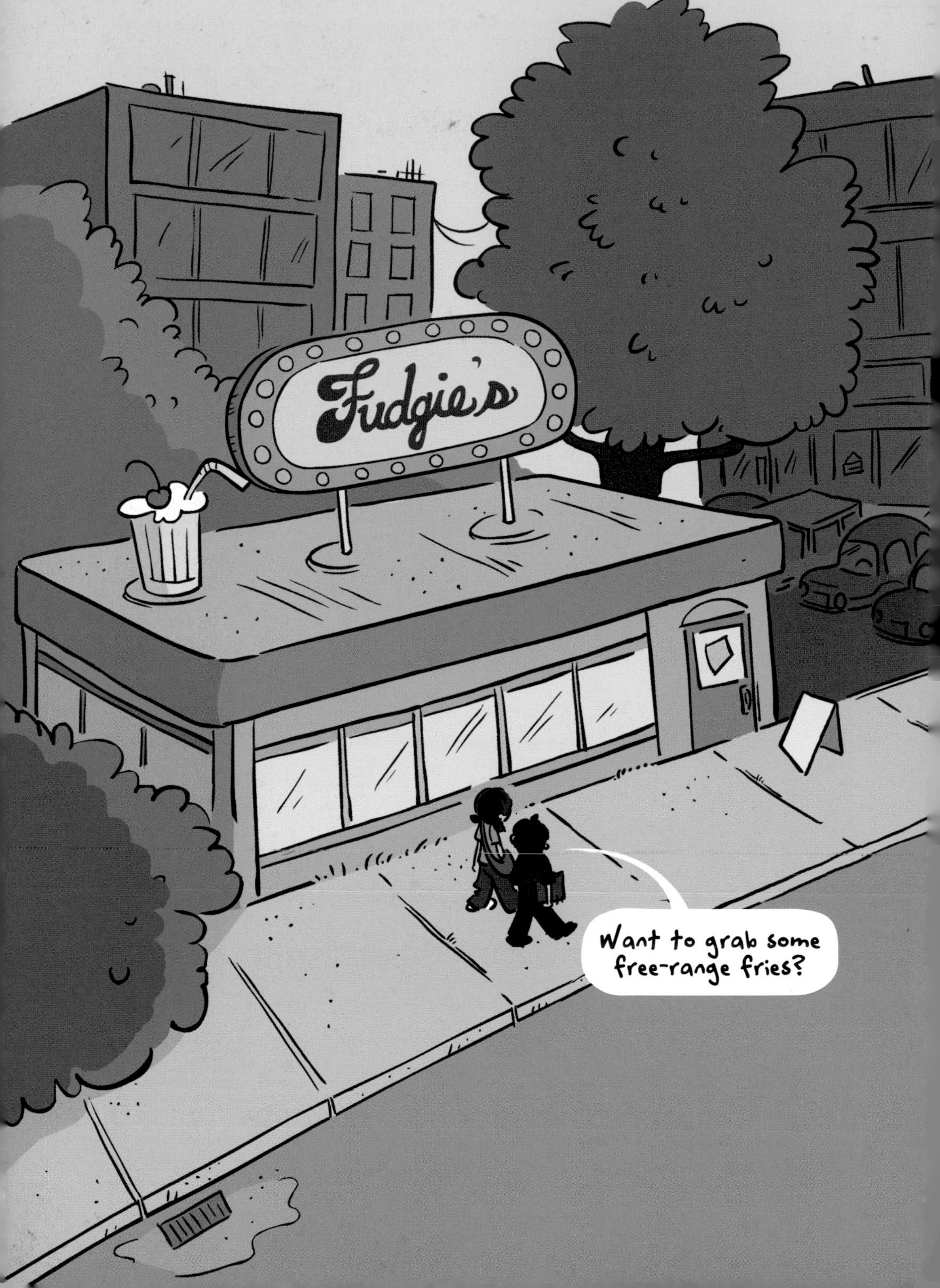
Fudgie's
Want to grab some free-range fries?

No time. Mom's on her way. Besides, I'm not even hungry...

...my stomach hurts.

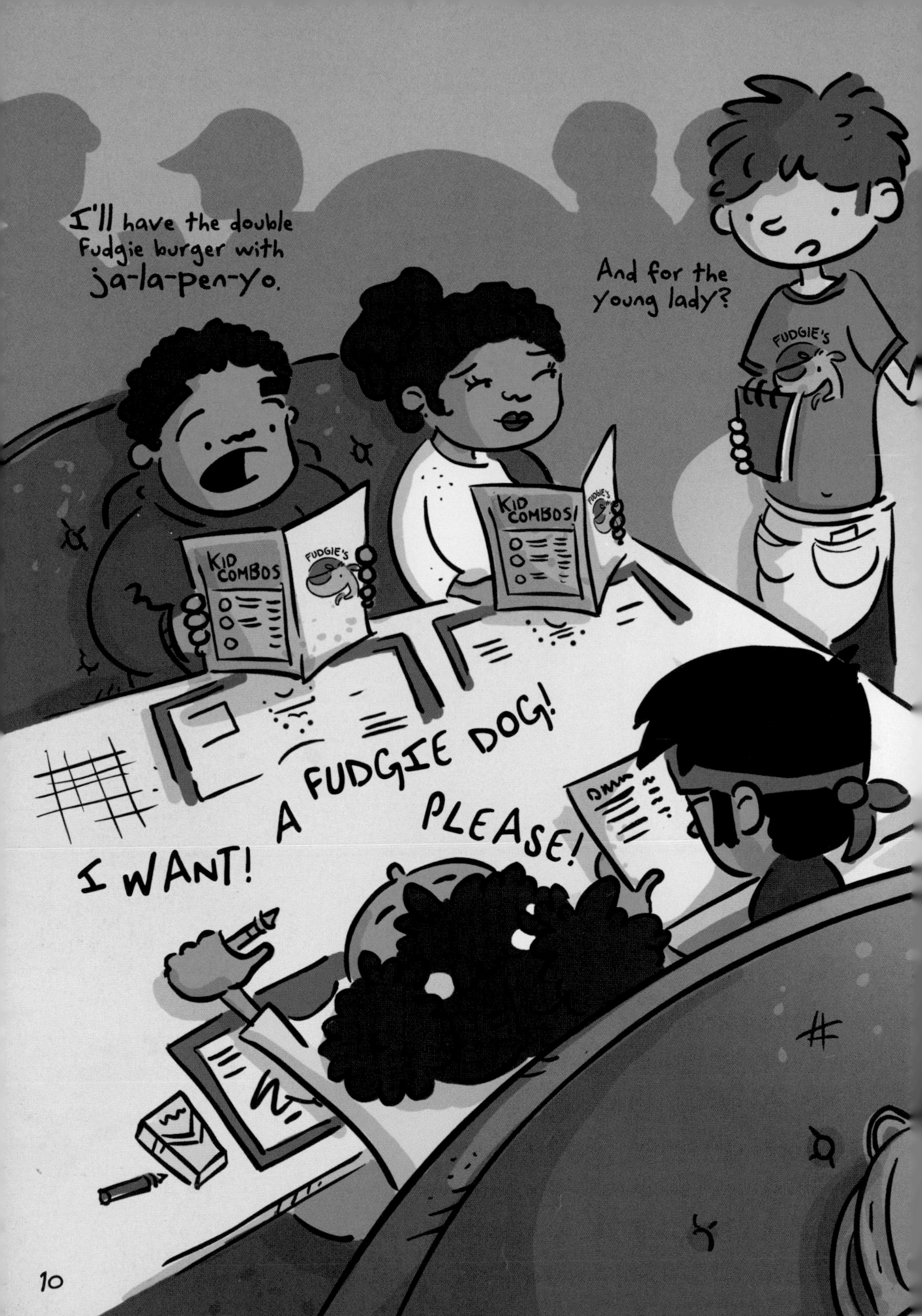
I'll have the double Fudgie burger with ja-la-pen-yo.
And for the young lady?
FUDGIE'S
KID COMBOS
FUDGIE'S
KID COMBOS!
I WANT! A FUDGIE DOG! PLEASE!

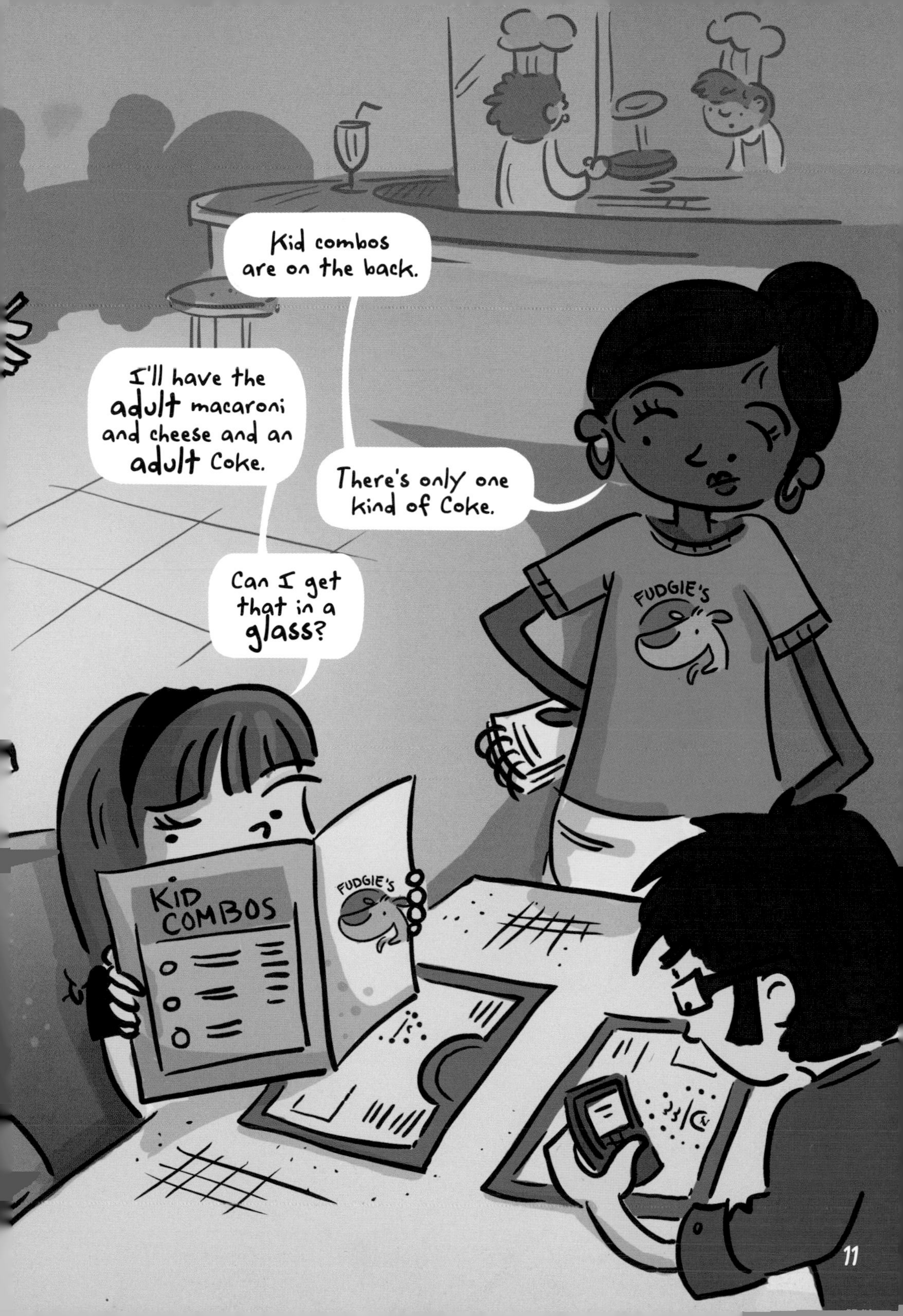
Kid combos are on the back.
I'll have the adult macaroni and cheese and an adult Coke.
There's only one kind of Coke.
Can I get that in a glass?
FUDGIE'S
KID COMBOS
FUDGIE'S

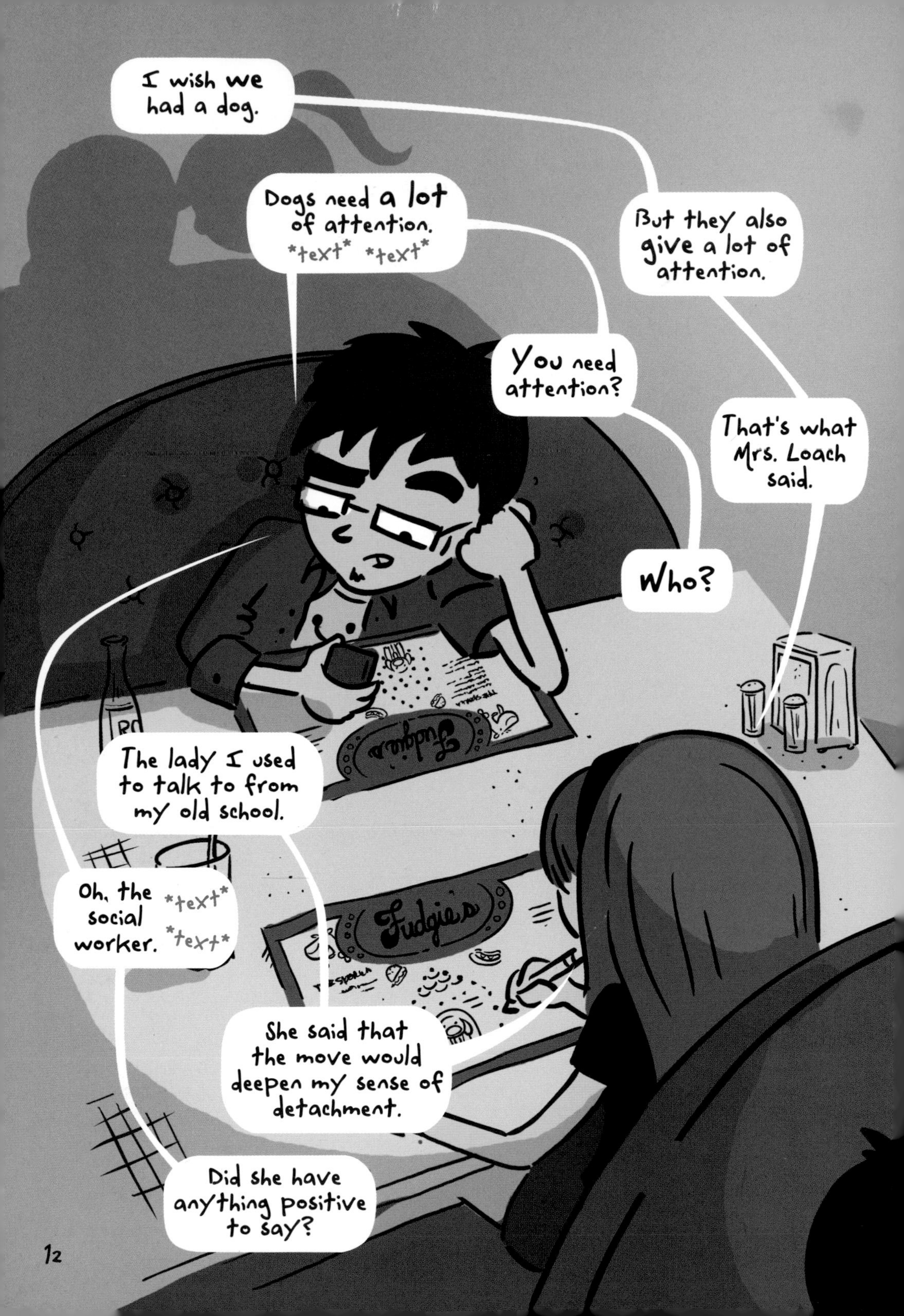

I wish we had a dog.
Dogs need a lot of attention. *text* *text*
But they also give a lot of attention.
You need attention?
That's what Mrs. Loach said.
Who?
The lady I used to talk to from my old school.
Oh, the social worker. *text* *text*
She said that the move would deepen my sense of detachment.
Did she have anything positive to say?

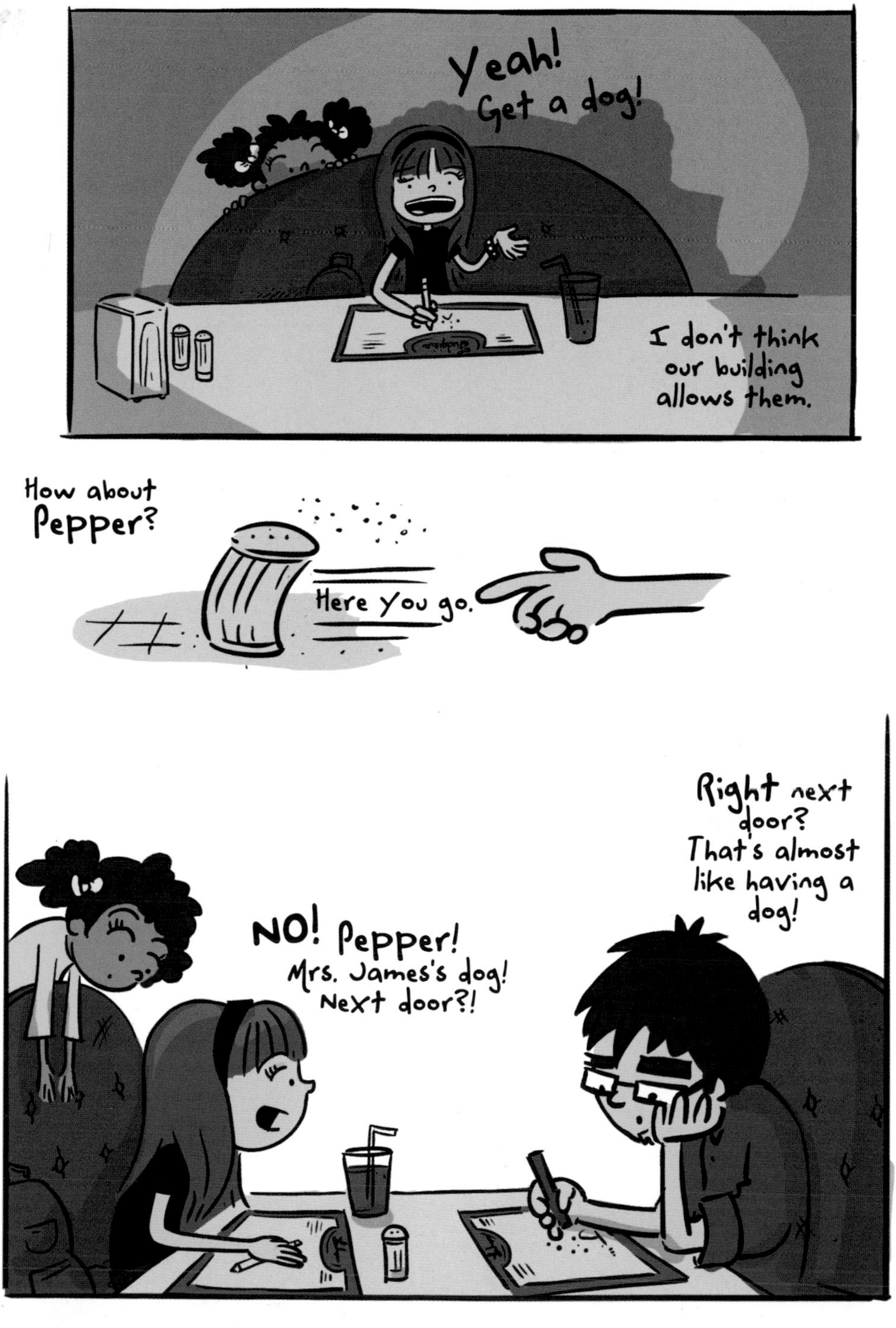
Yeah! Get a dog!
I don't think our building allows them.
How about Pepper?
Here you go.
NO! Pepper! Mrs. James's dog! Next door?!
Right next door? That's almost like having a dog!

The Next Day...

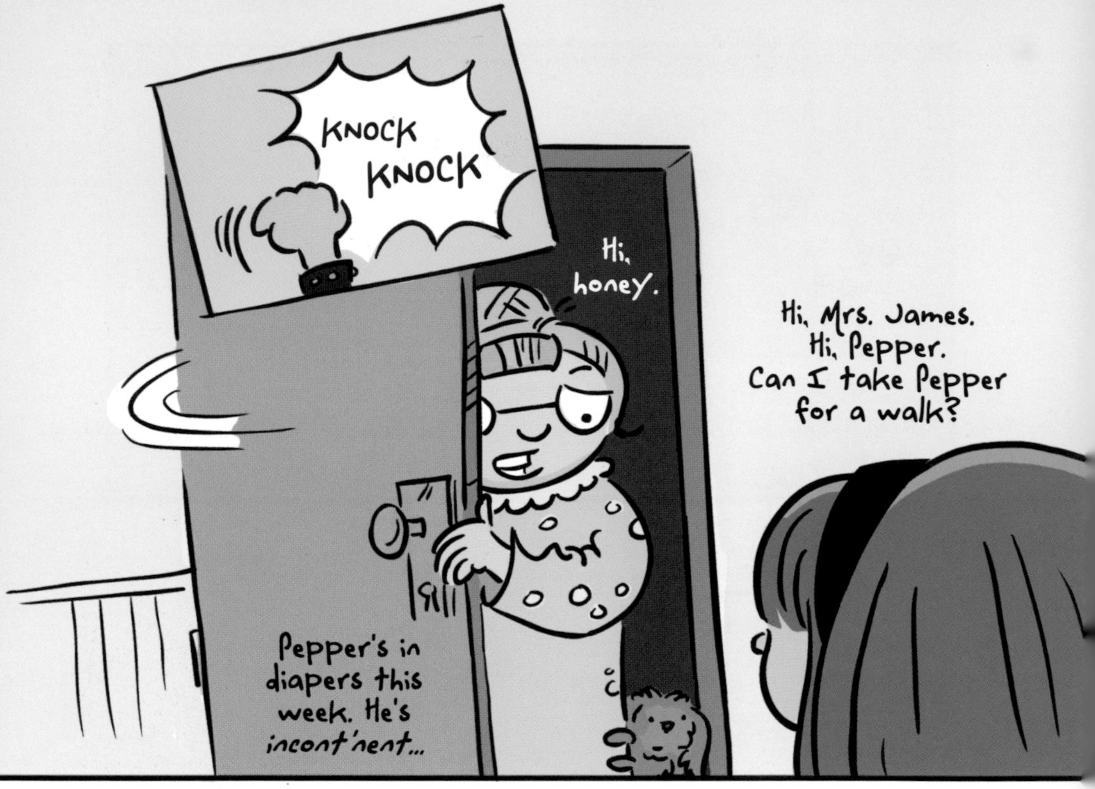
KNOCK KNOCK
Hi, honey.
Hi, Mrs. James. Hi, Pepper. Can I take Pepper for a walk?
Pepper's in diapers this week. He's *incont'nent*...

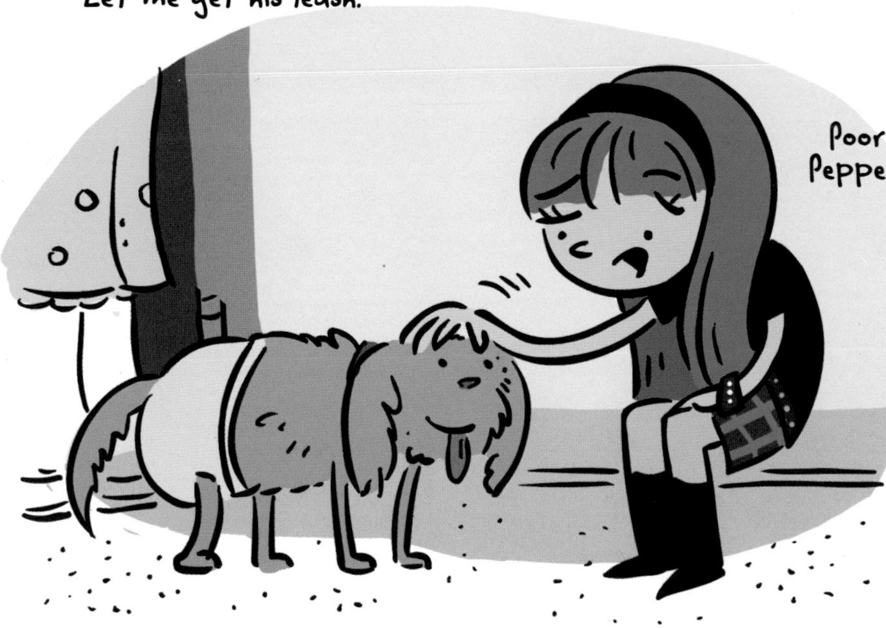
But...I s'pose he could use some fresh air. Let me get his leash.
Poor Pepper.

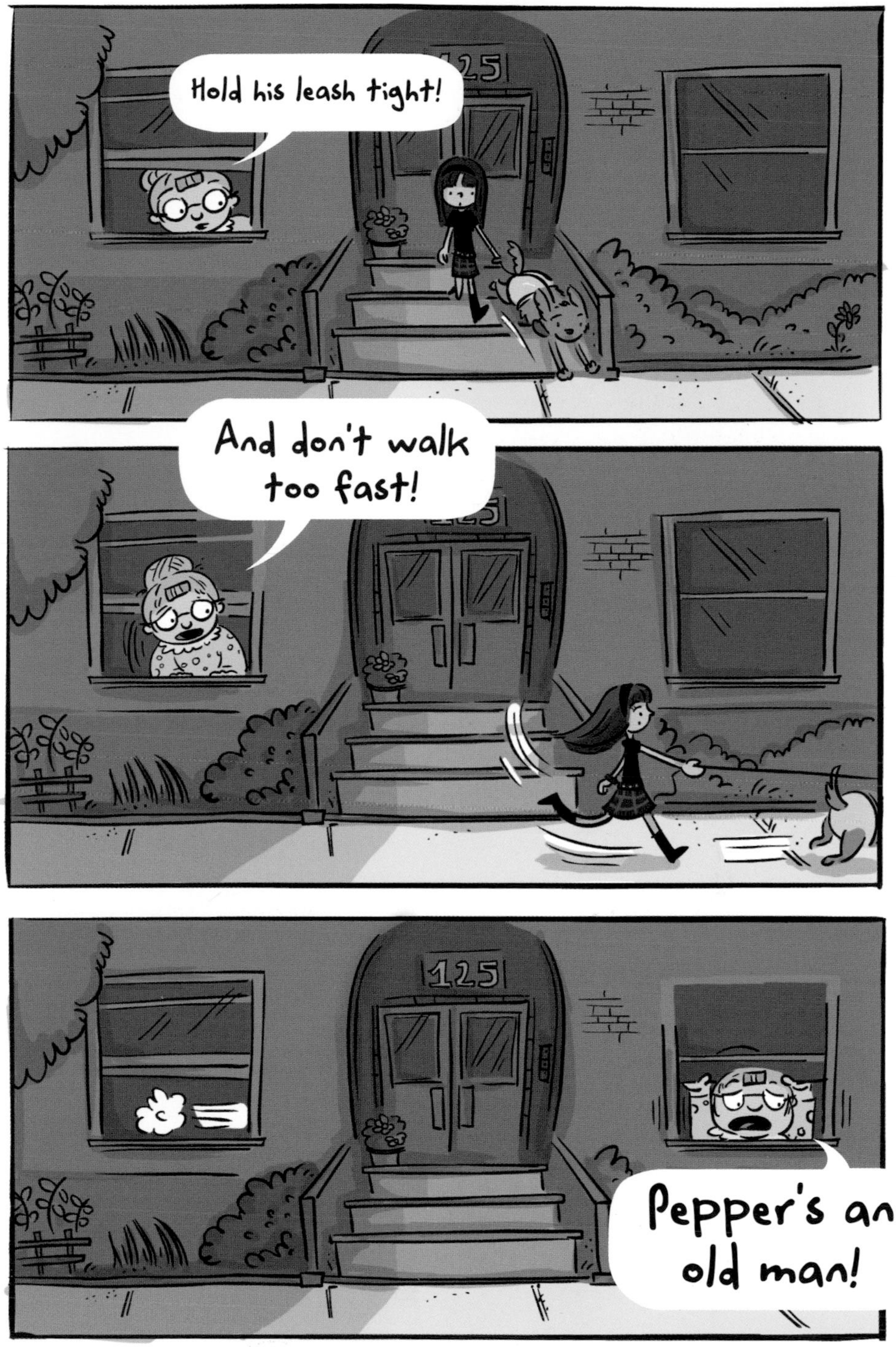
Hold his leash tight!
And don't walk too fast!
125
Pepper's an old man!

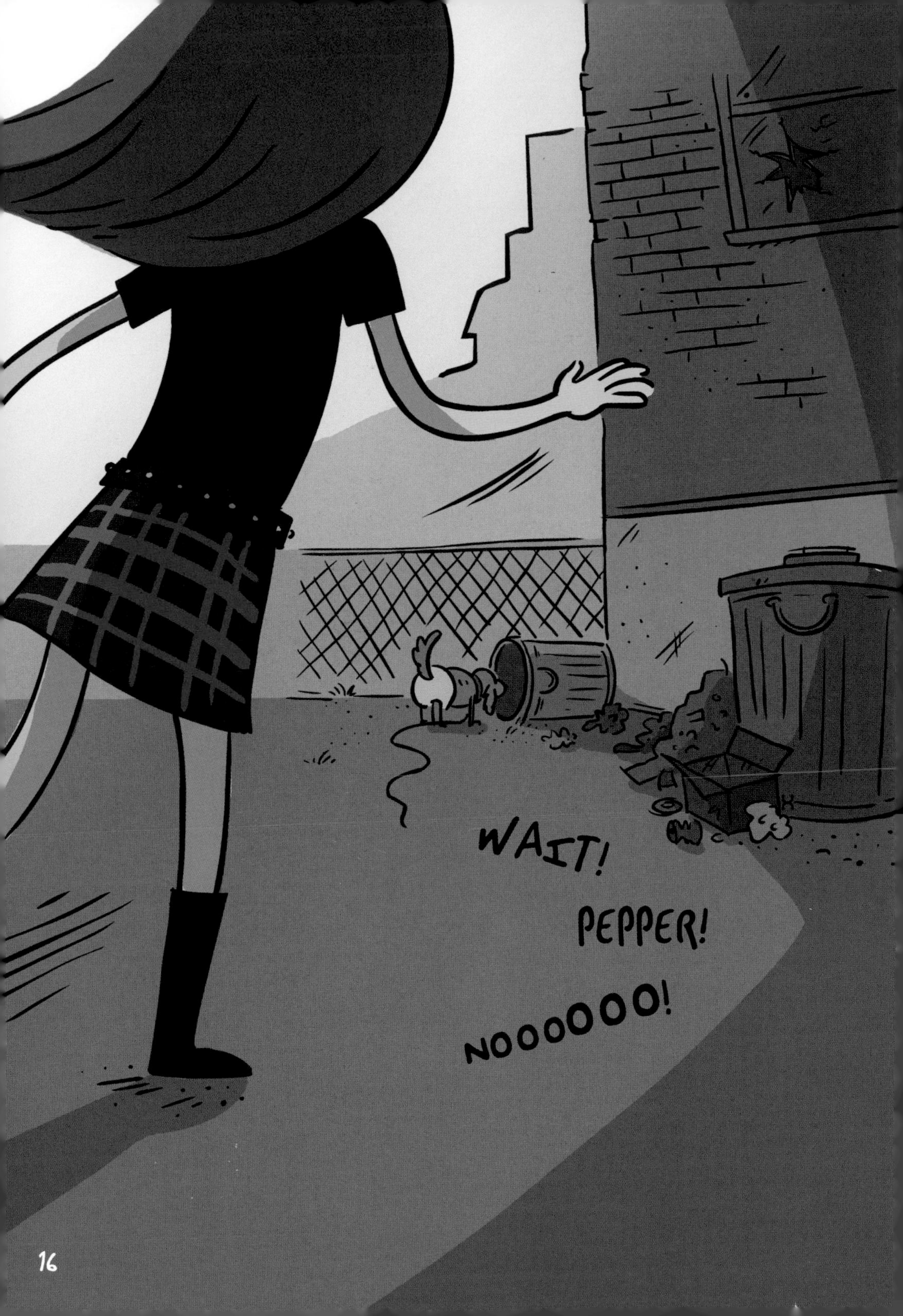
WAIT!
PEPPER!
NOOOOOO!

Don't! Eat! Trash!

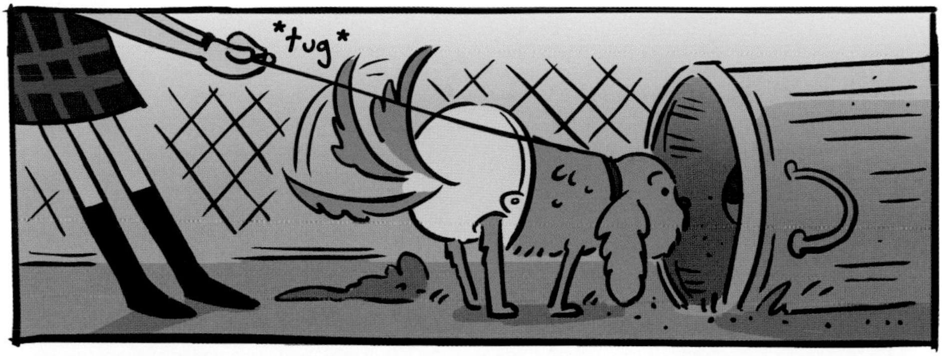
tug

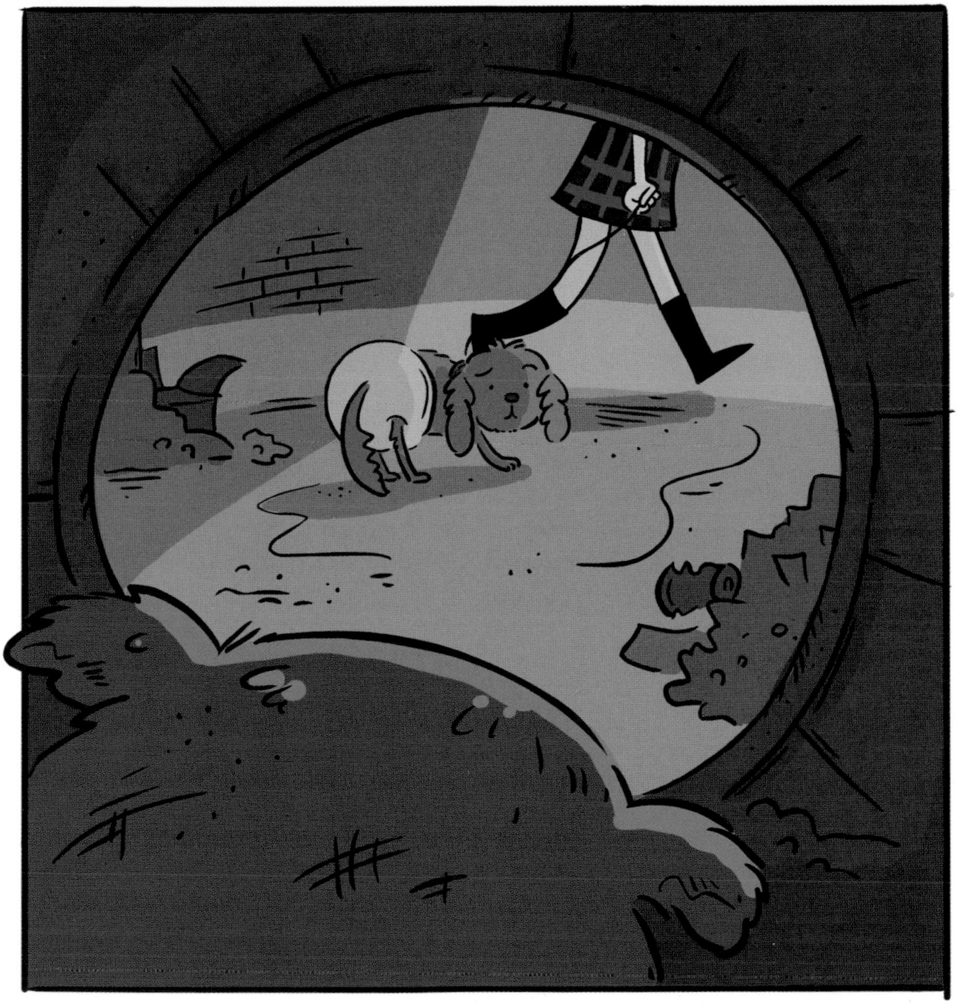

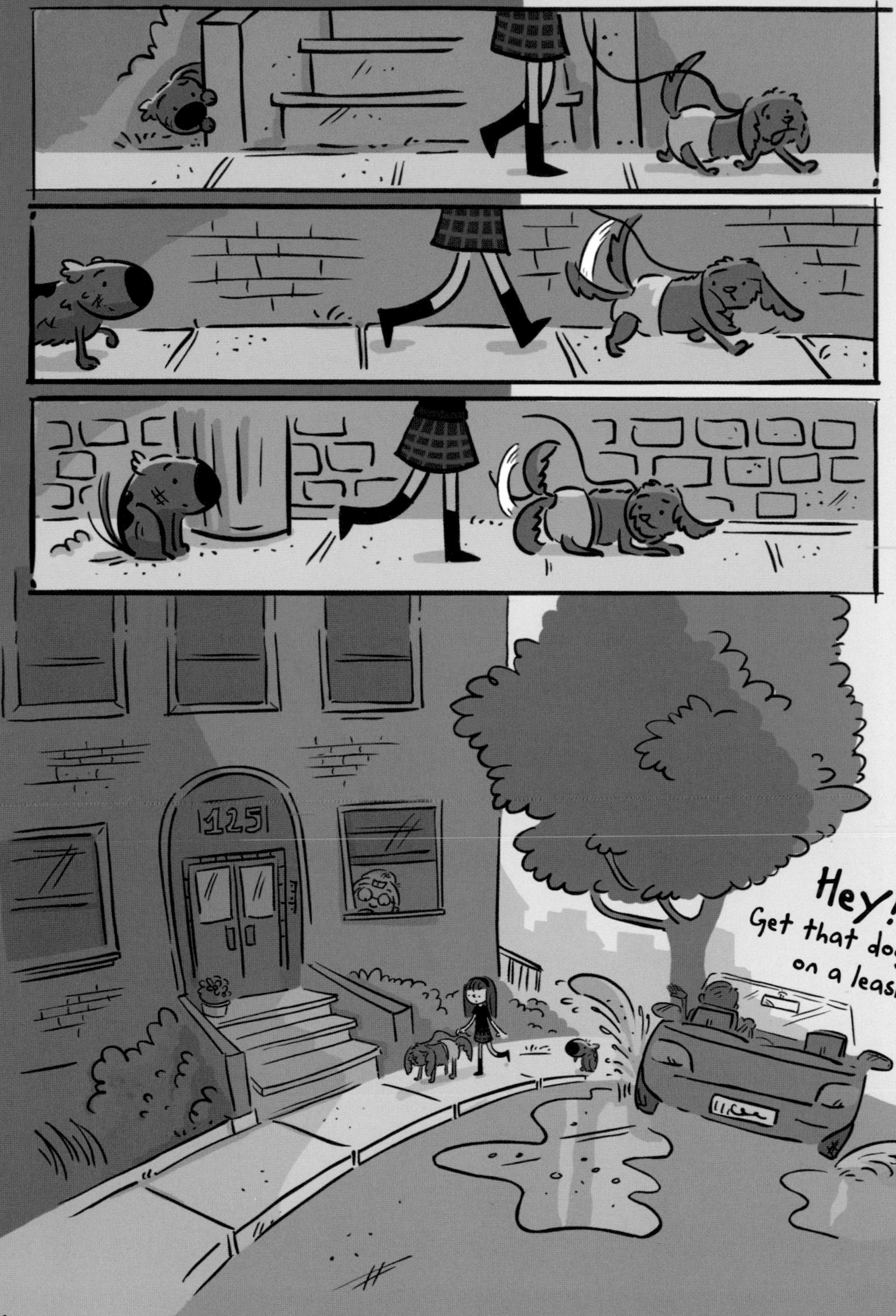
125
Hey! Get that dog on a leash!

Later, Upstairs...

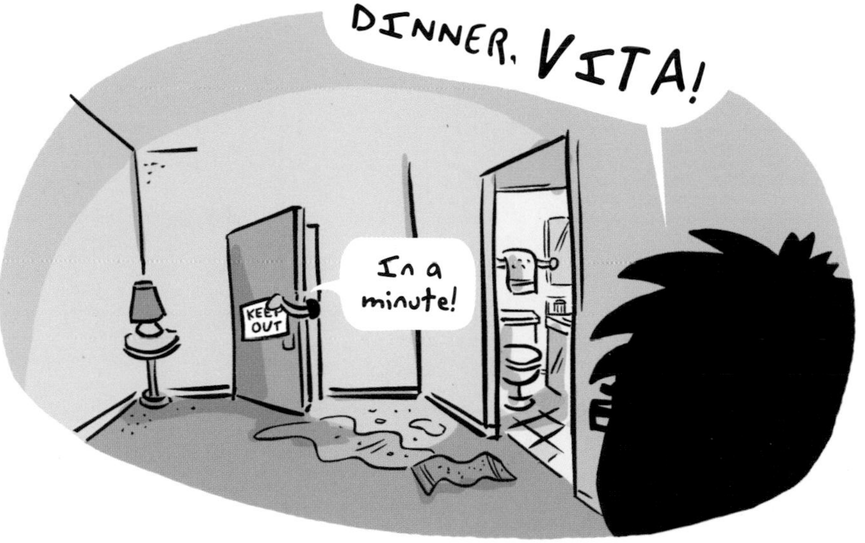
DINNER, VITA!
In a minute!
KEEP OUT

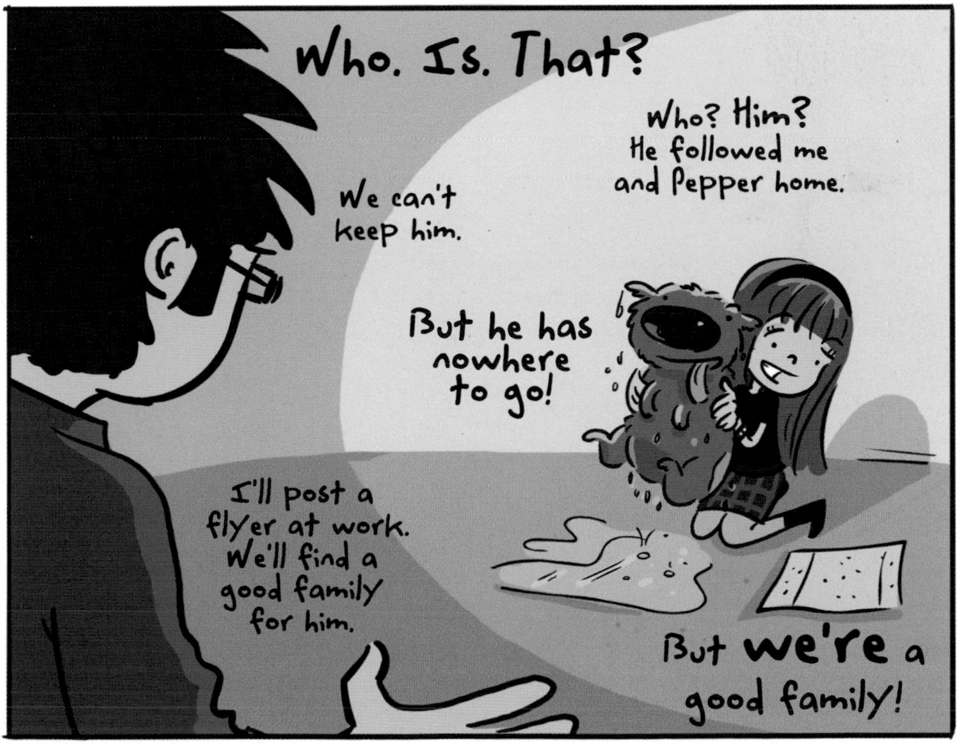
Who. Is. That?
Who? Him? He followed me and Pepper home.
We can't keep him.
But he has nowhere to go!
I'll post a flyer at work. We'll find a good family for him.
But we're a good family!

The Next Day...

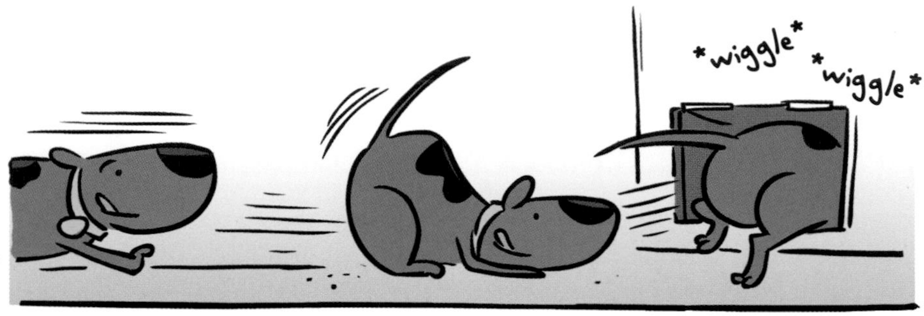

wiggle *wiggle*

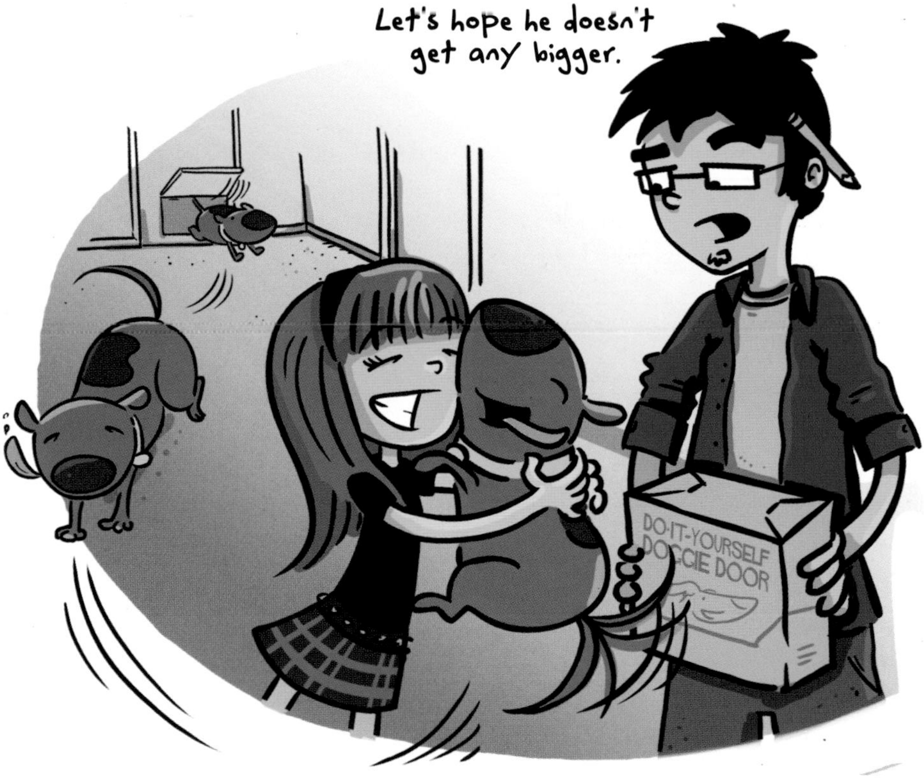

Let's hope he doesn't get any bigger.
DO-IT-YOURSELF DOGGIE DOOR

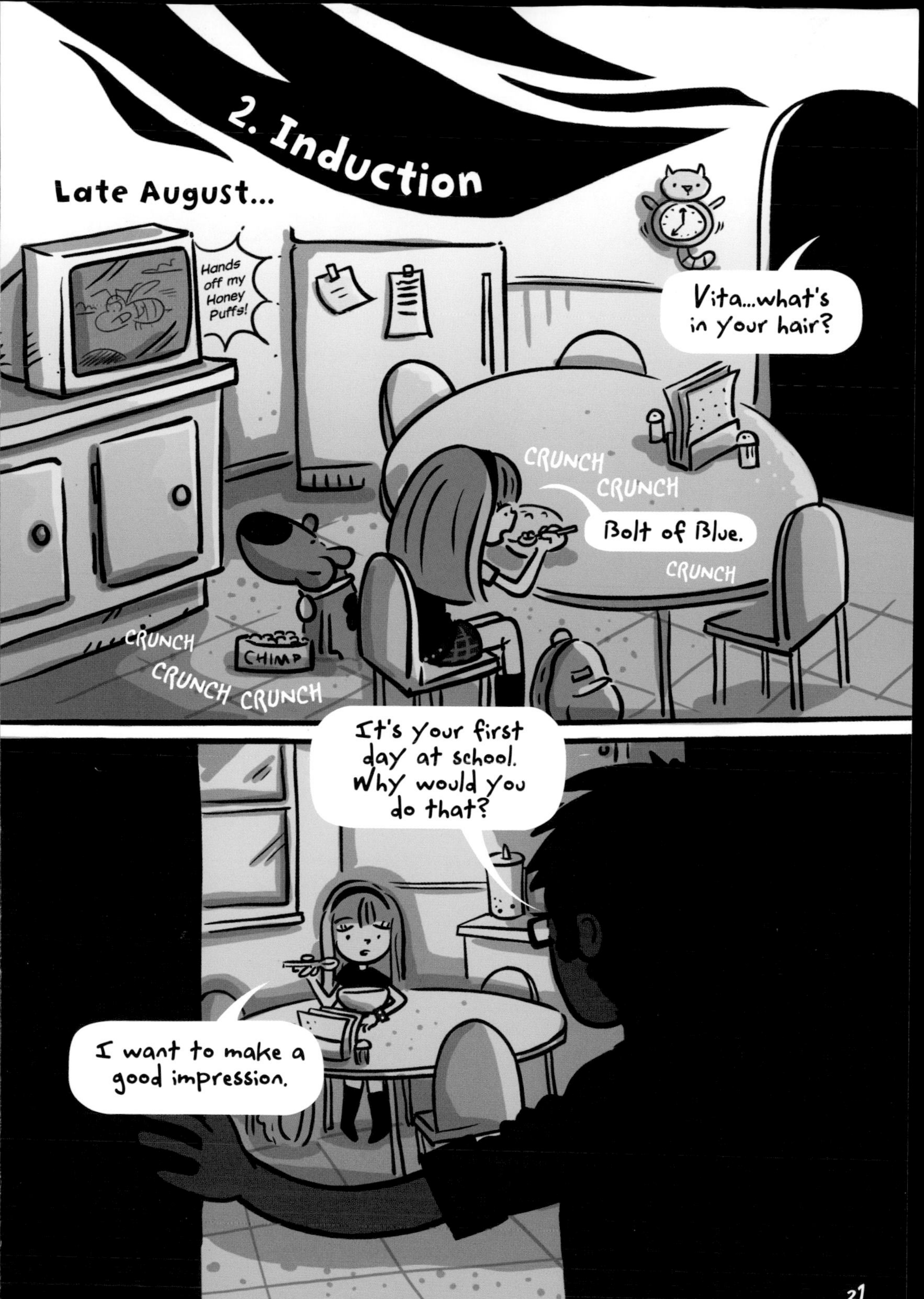
2. Induction
Late August...
Hands off my Honey Puffs!
Vita...what's in your hair?
CRUNCH
CRUNCH
Bolt of Blue.
CRUNCH
CHIMP
CRUNCH
CRUNCH CRUNCH
It's your first day at school. Why would you do that?
I want to make a good impression.

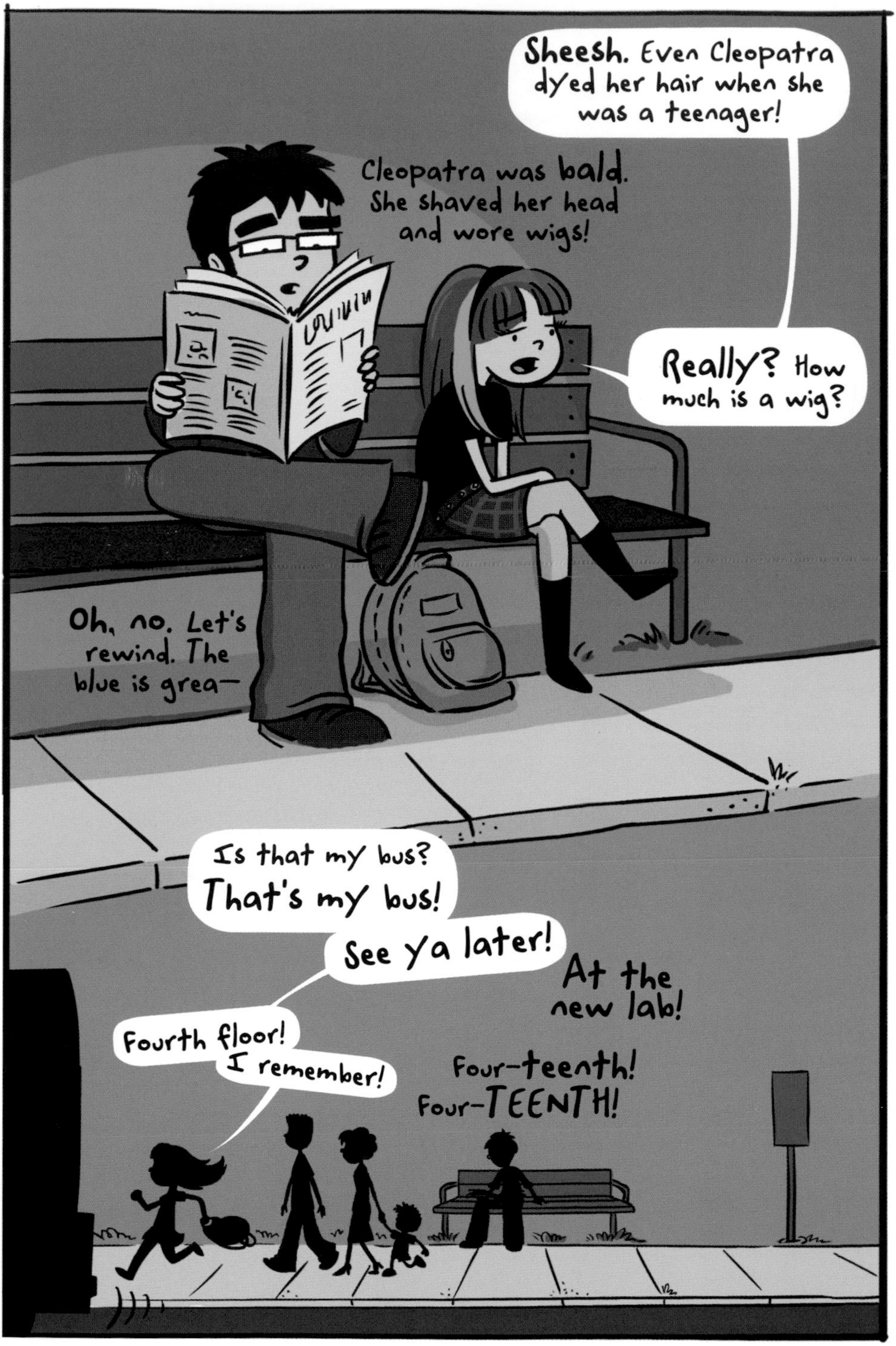

Sheesh. Even Cleopatra dyed her hair when she was a teenager!
Cleopatra was bald. She shaved her head and wore wigs!
Really? How much is a wig?
Oh, no. Let's rewind. The blue is grea—
Is that my bus? That's my bus!
See ya later!
At the new lab!
Fourth floor! I remember!
Four-teenth! Four-TEENTH!

Southside School...

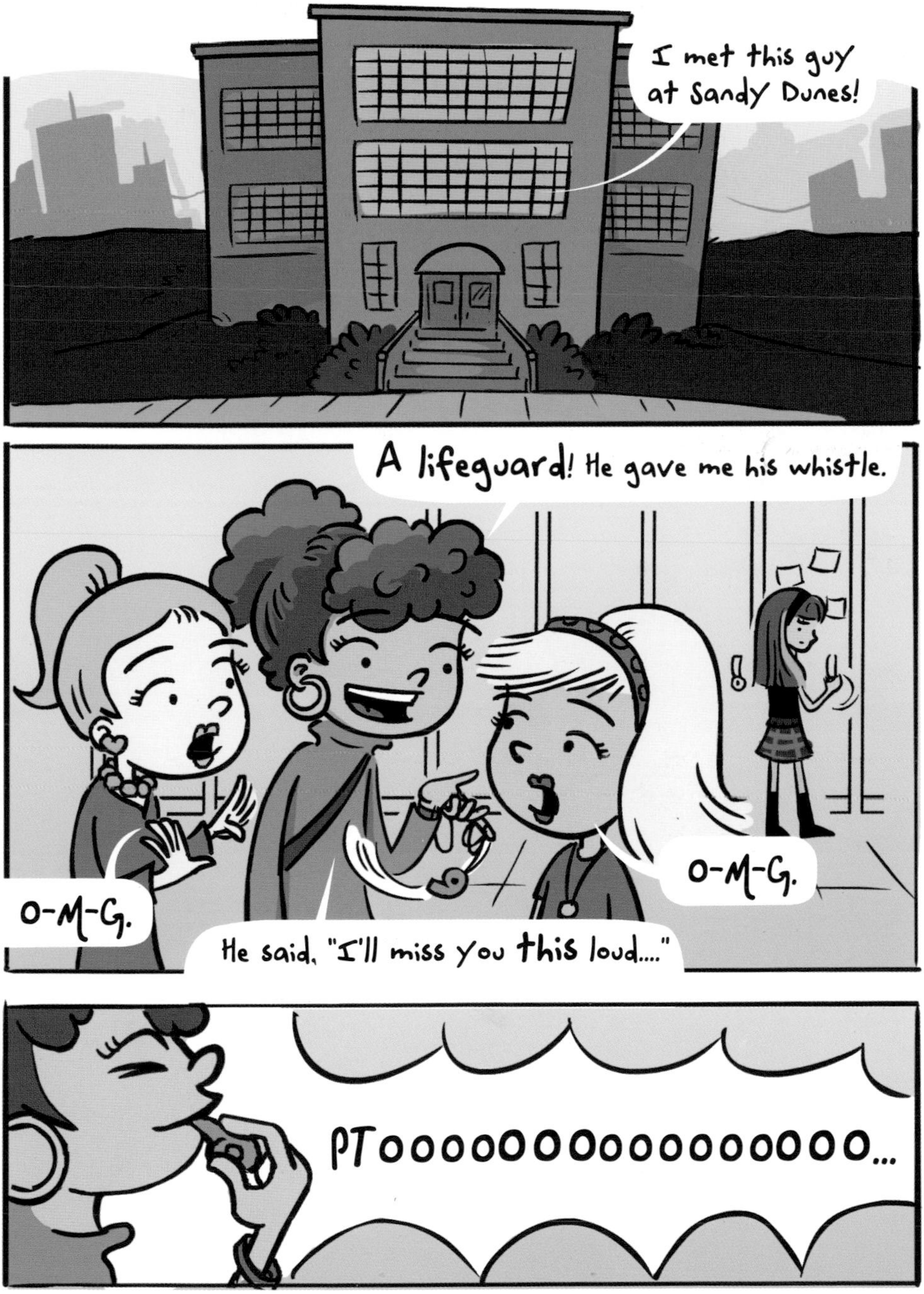
I met this guy at Sandy Dunes!
A lifeguard! He gave me his whistle.
O-M-G.
O-M-G.
He said, "I'll miss you this loud...."
PTooooOOOooooooooOO...

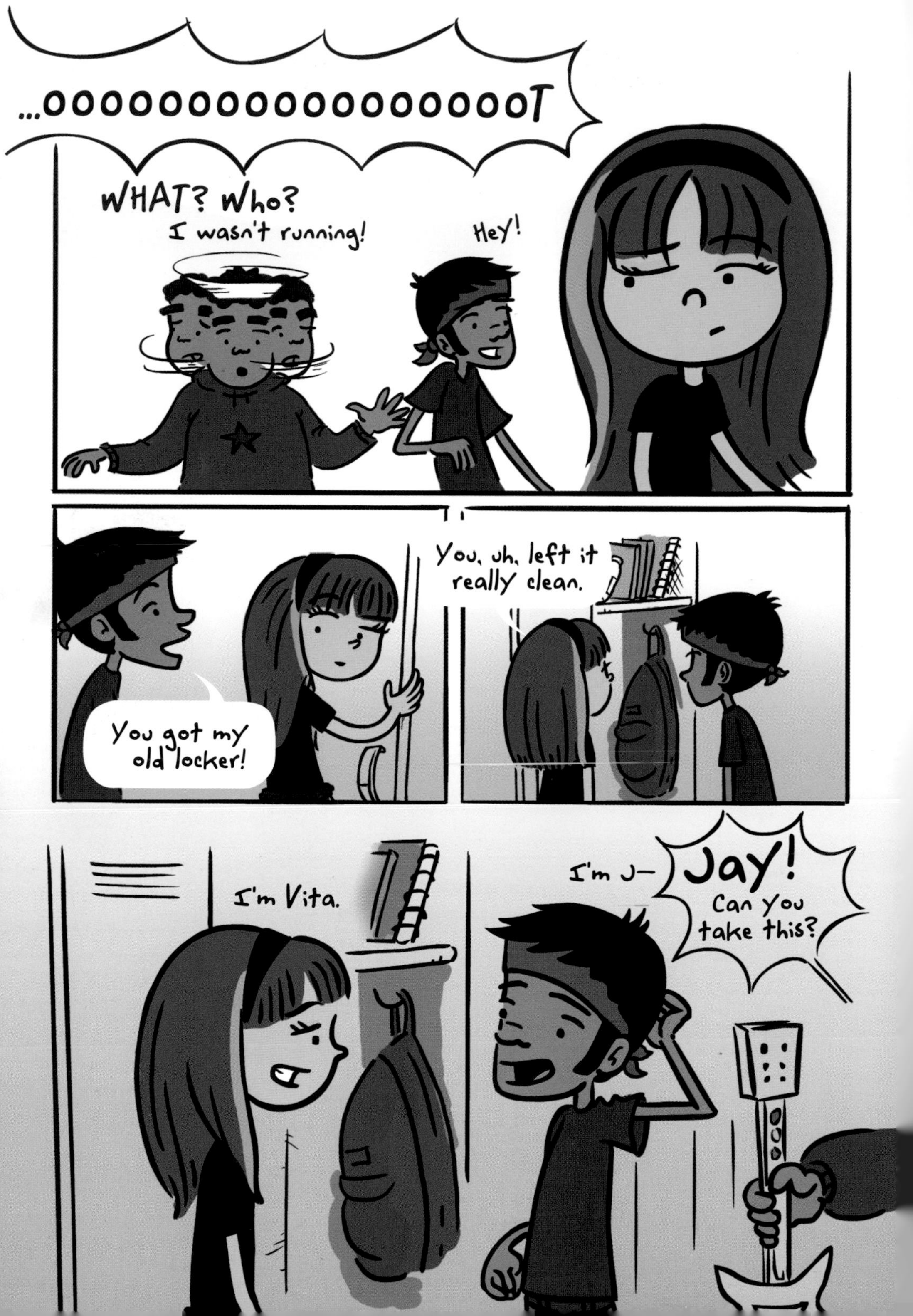
...OOOOOOOOOOOOOOOOOOOOT
WHAT? Who?
I wasn't running!
Hey!
You got my old locker!
You, uh, left it really clean.
I'm Vita.
I'm J—
JAY!
Can you take this?

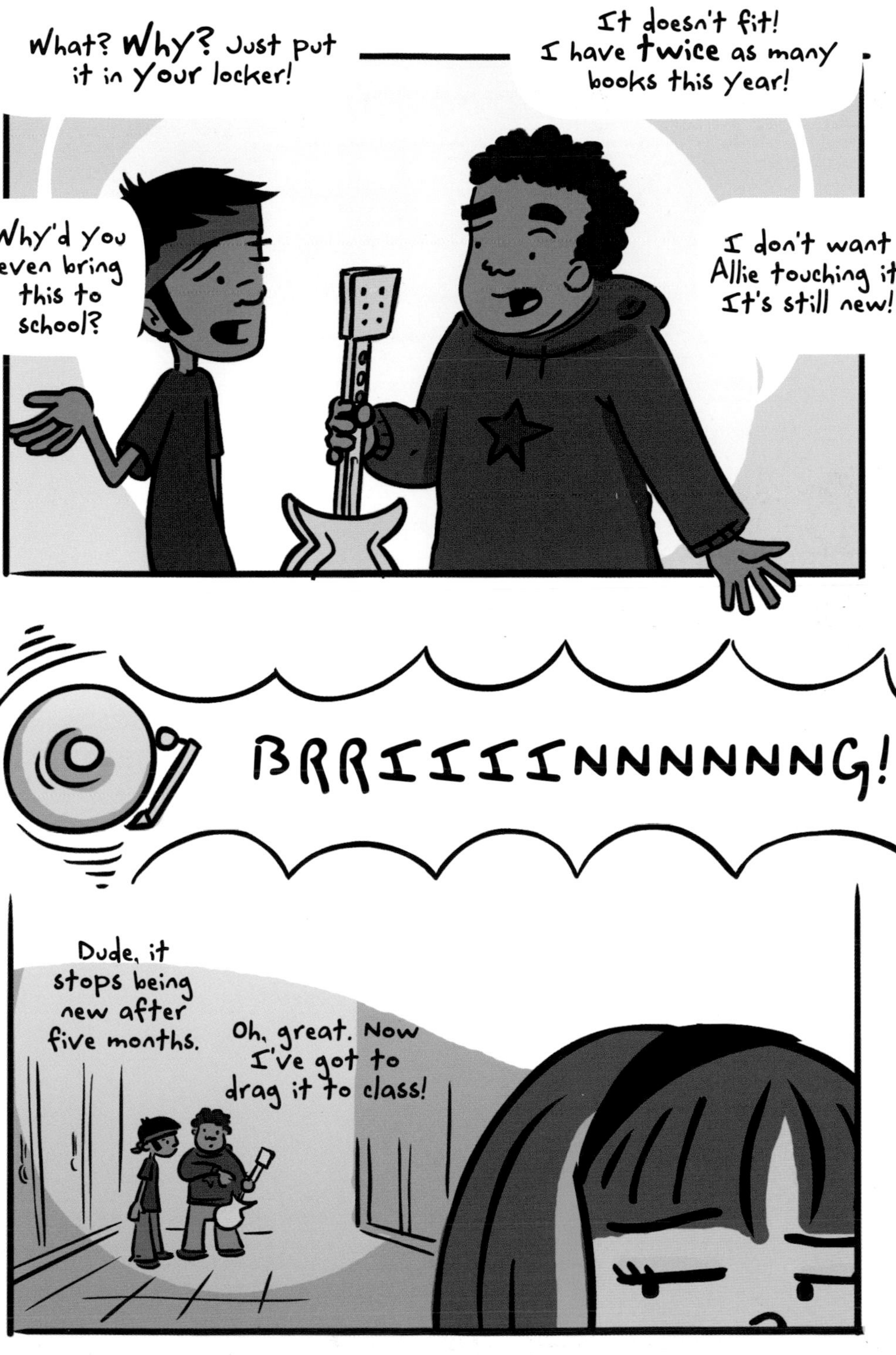
What? Why? Just put it in your locker!
It doesn't fit! I have twice as many books this year!
Why'd you even bring this to school?
I don't want Allie touching it. It's still new!
BRRIIIIINNNNNNG!
Dude, it stops being new after five months.
Oh, great. Now I've got to drag it to class!

After School...

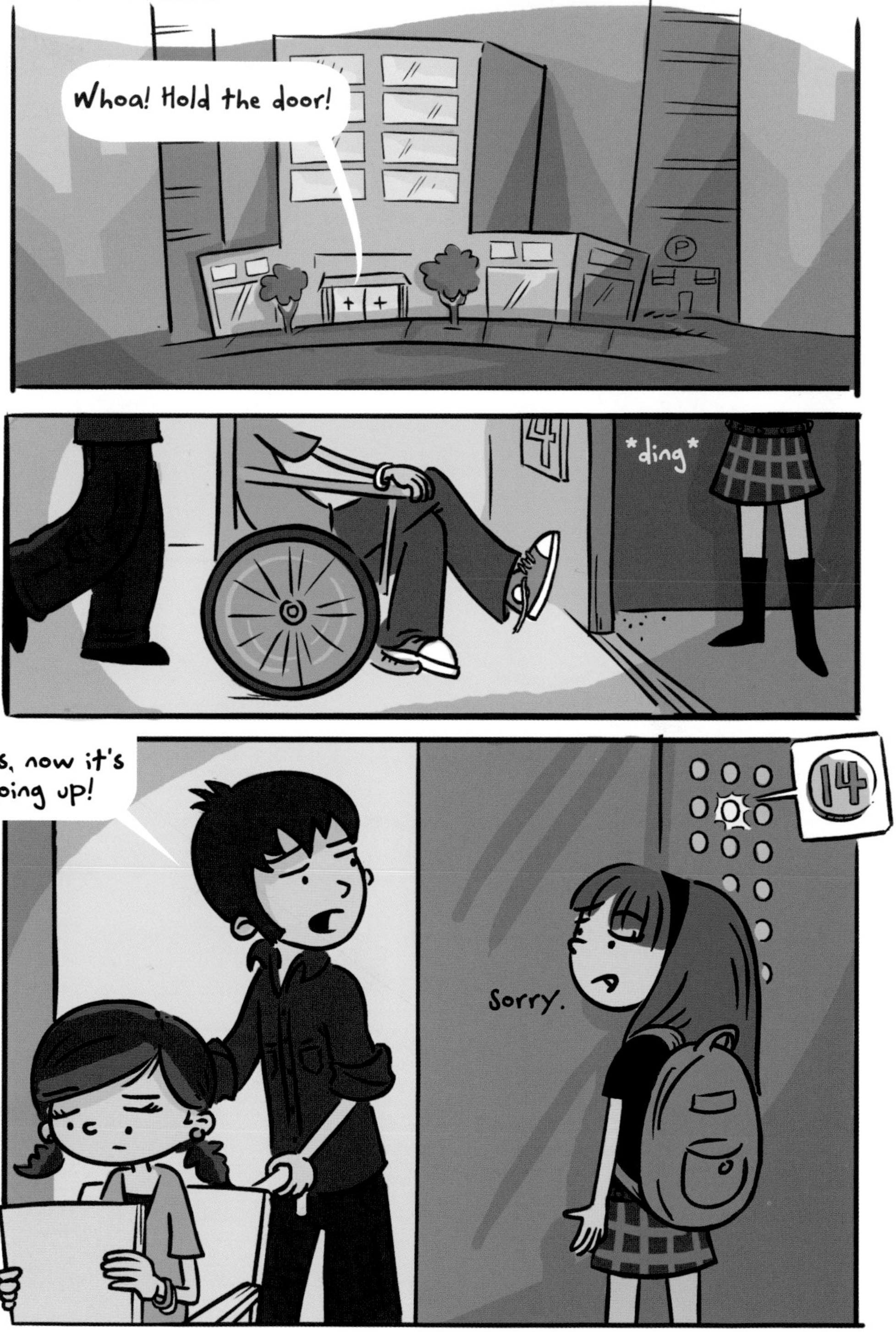
Whoa! Hold the door!
ding
Nuts, now it's going up!
14
Sorry.

The New Lab...

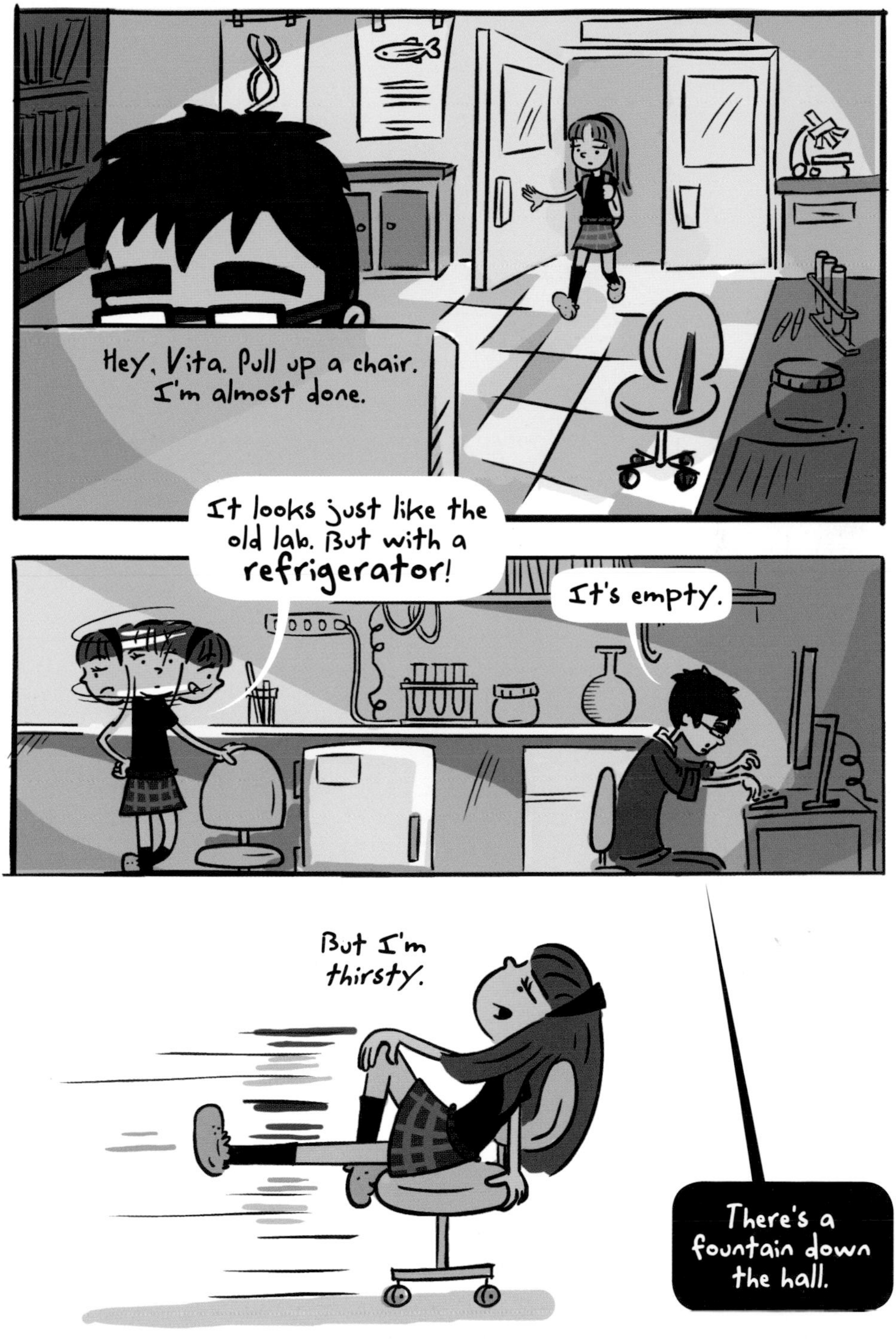

Hey, Vita. Pull up a chair. I'm almost done.
It looks just like the old lab. But with a **refrigerator**!
It's empty.
But I'm thirsty.
There's a fountain down the hall.

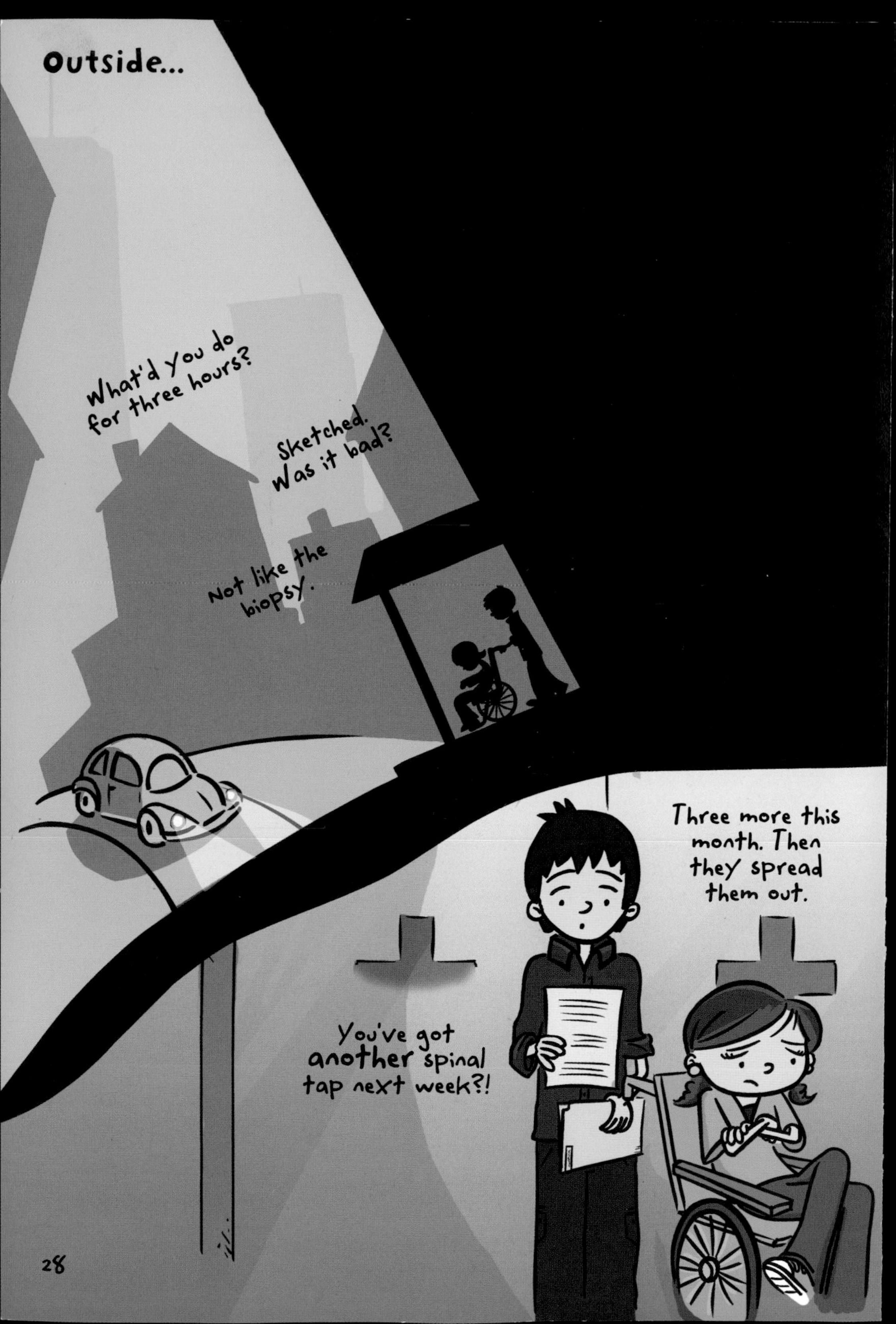
Outside...
What'd you do for three hours?
Sketched. Was it bad?
Not like the biopsy.
You've got **another** spinal tap next week?!
Three more this month. Then they spread them out.

3. Cause and Effect

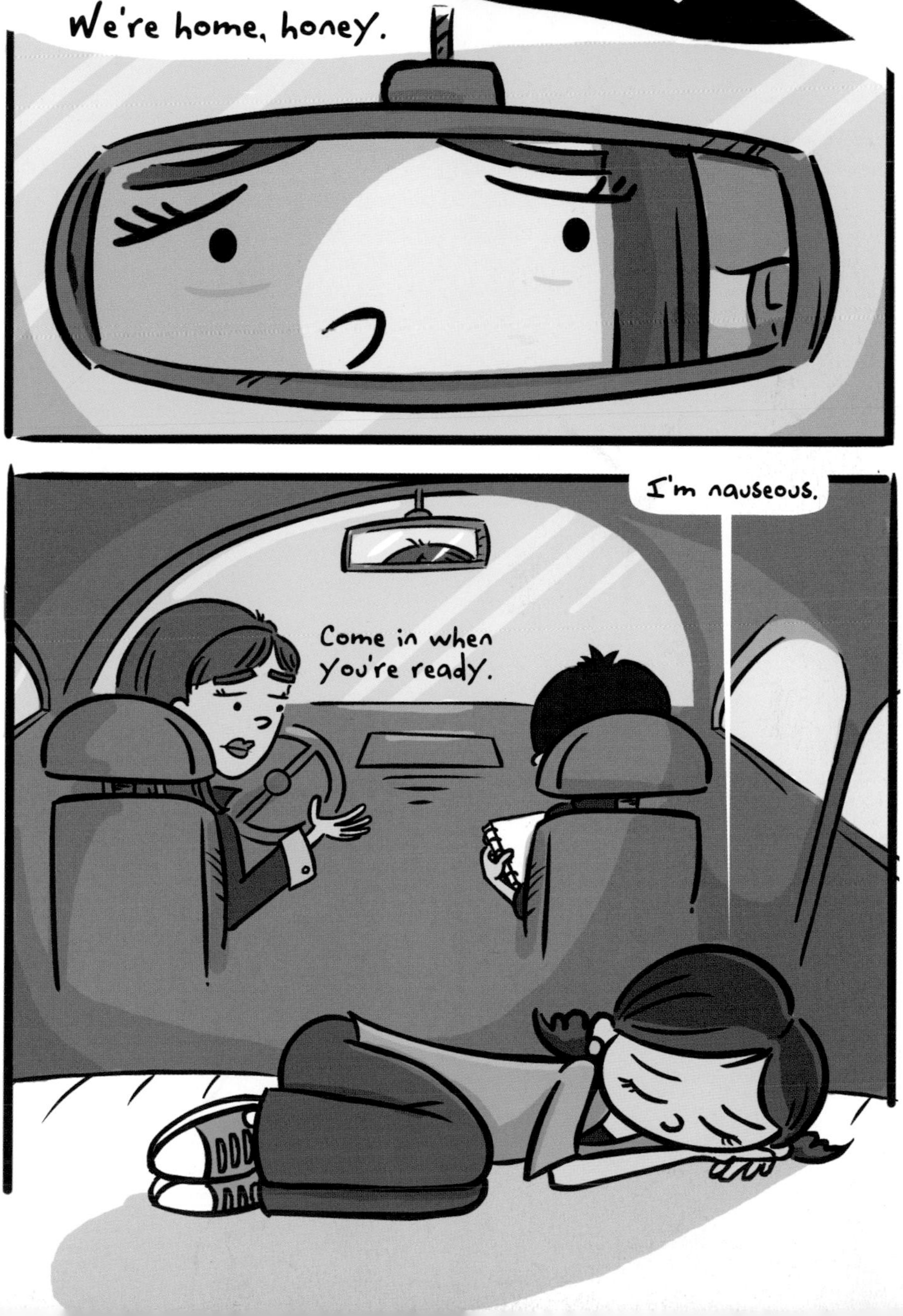
We're home, honey.
Come in when you're ready.
I'm nauseous.

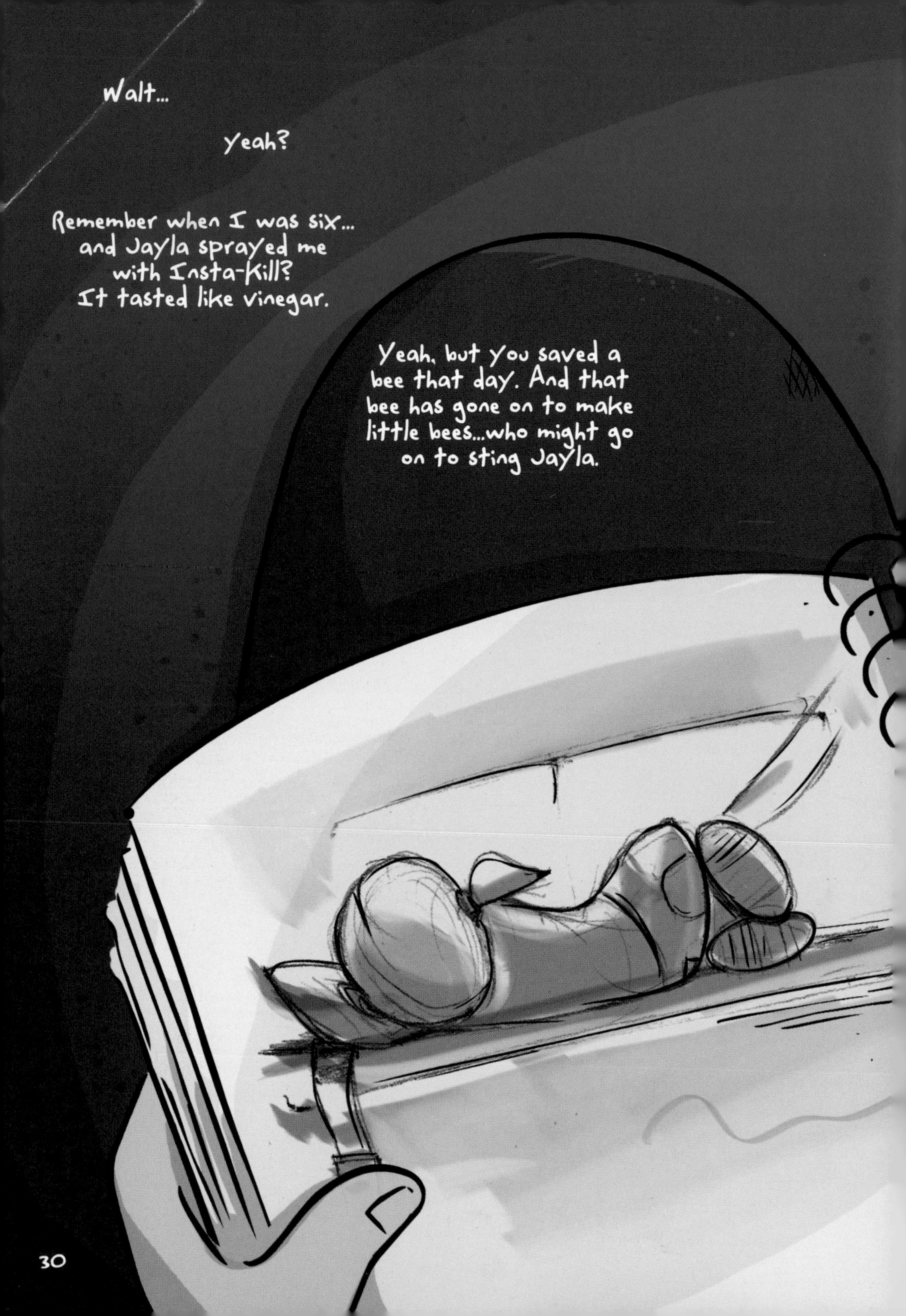
Walt...
Yeah?
Remember when I was six... and Jayla sprayed me with Insta-Kill? It tasted like vinegar.
Yeah, but you saved a bee that day. And that bee has gone on to make little bees...who might go on to sting Jayla.

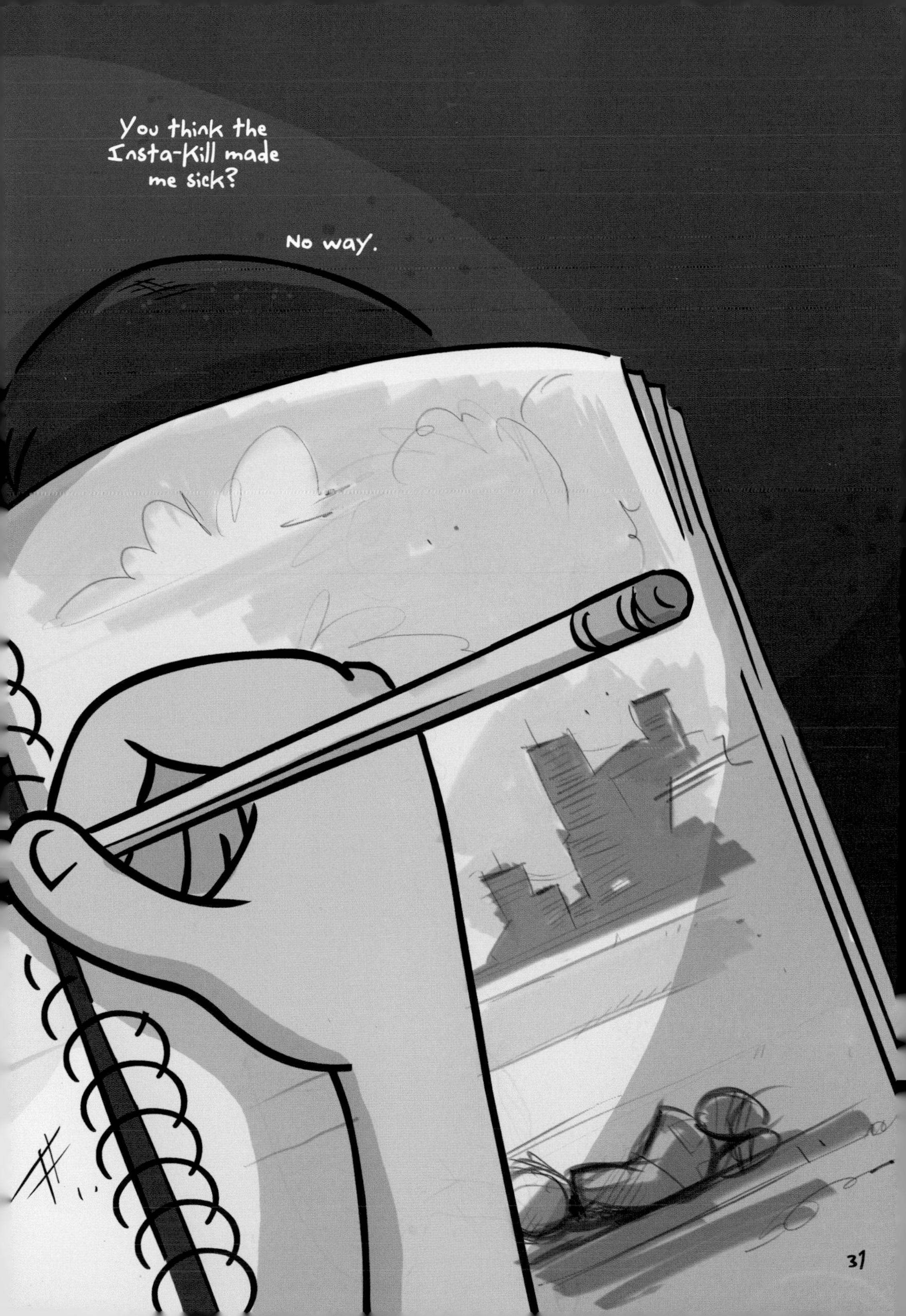
You think the Insta-Kill made me sick?
No way.

4. A Star Is Bored

Early September...

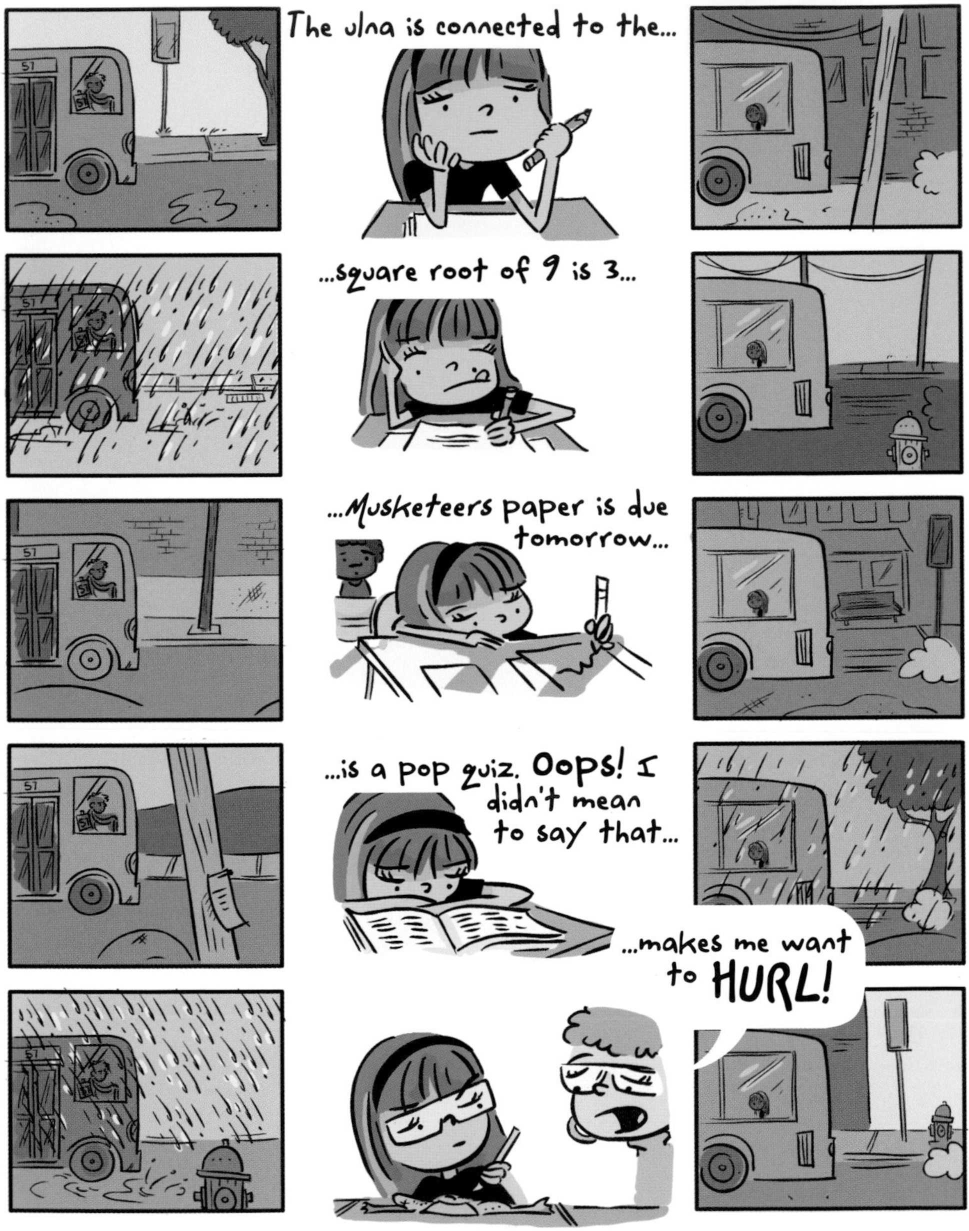

The ulna is connected to the...
...square root of 9 is 3...
...Musketeers paper is due tomorrow...
...is a pop quiz. Oops! I didn't mean to say that...
...makes me want to HURL!

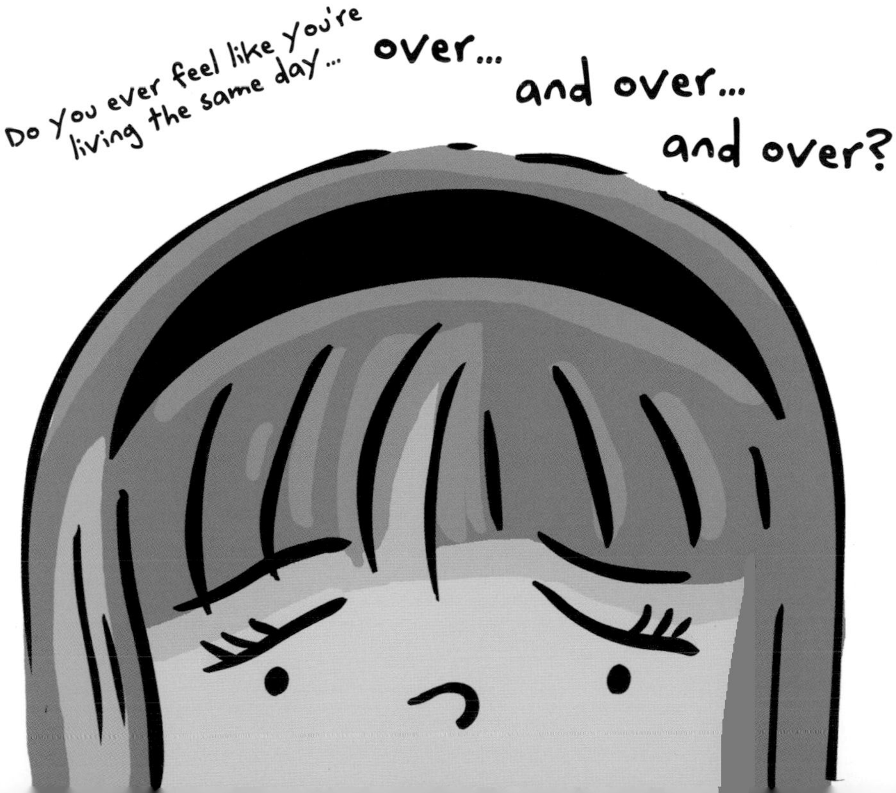
Do you ever feel like you're living the same day...
over...
and over...
and over?

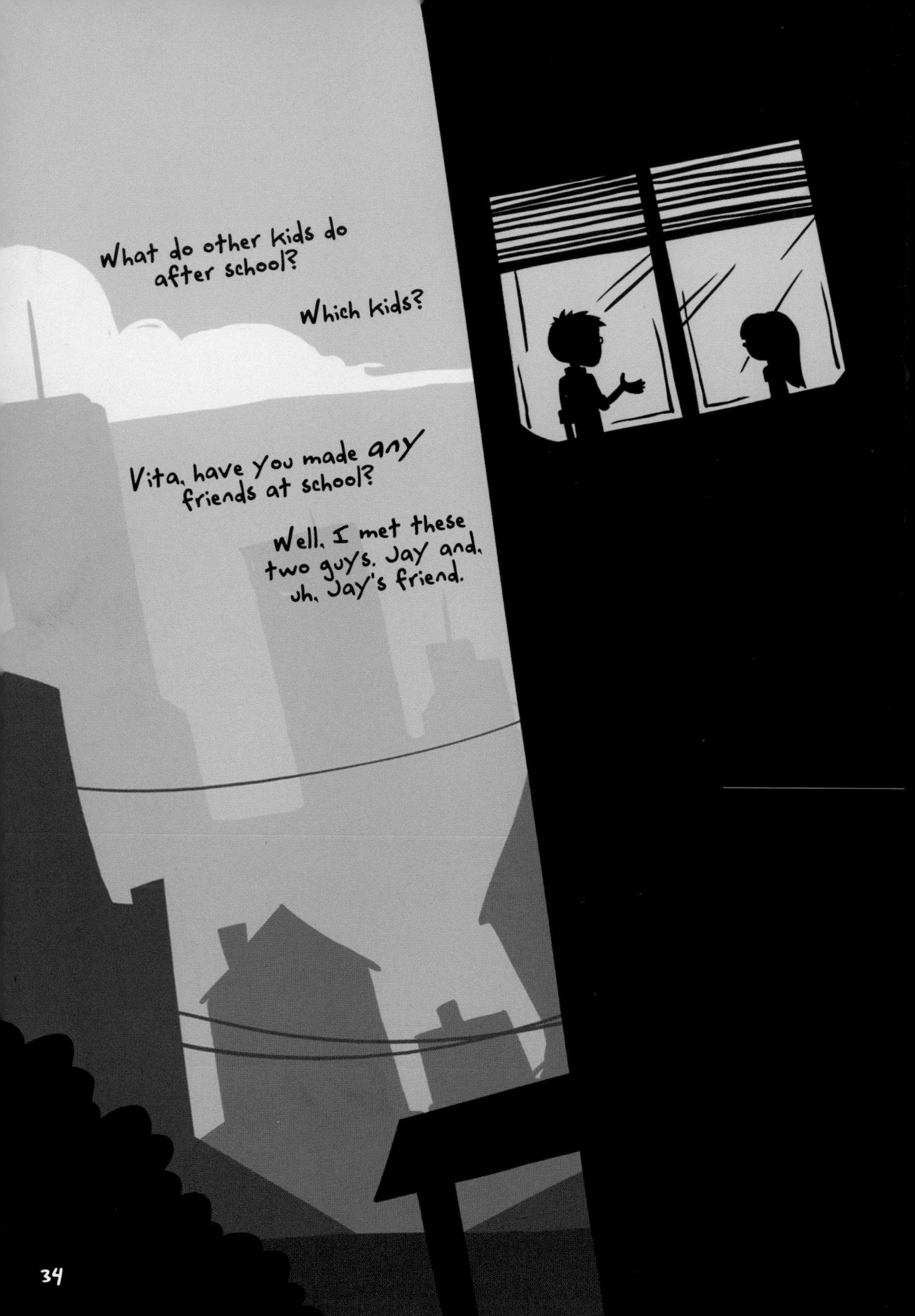
What do other kids do after school?
Which kids?
Vita, have you made any friends at school?
Well, I met these two guys. Jay and, uh, Jay's friend.

Later That Week...

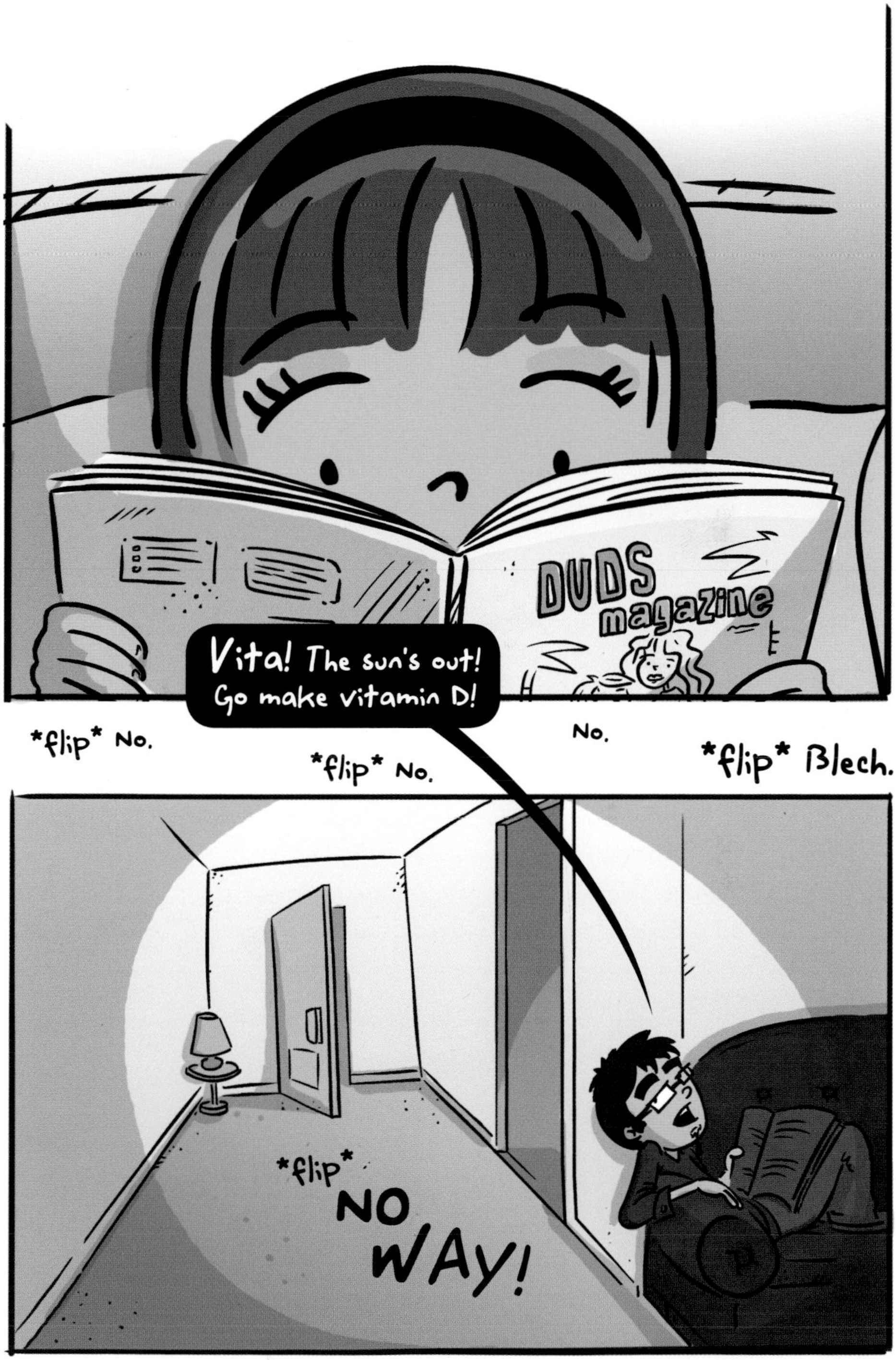
DUDS magazine
Vita! The sun's out! Go make vitamin D!
flip No.
flip No.
No.
flip Blech.
flip NO WAY!

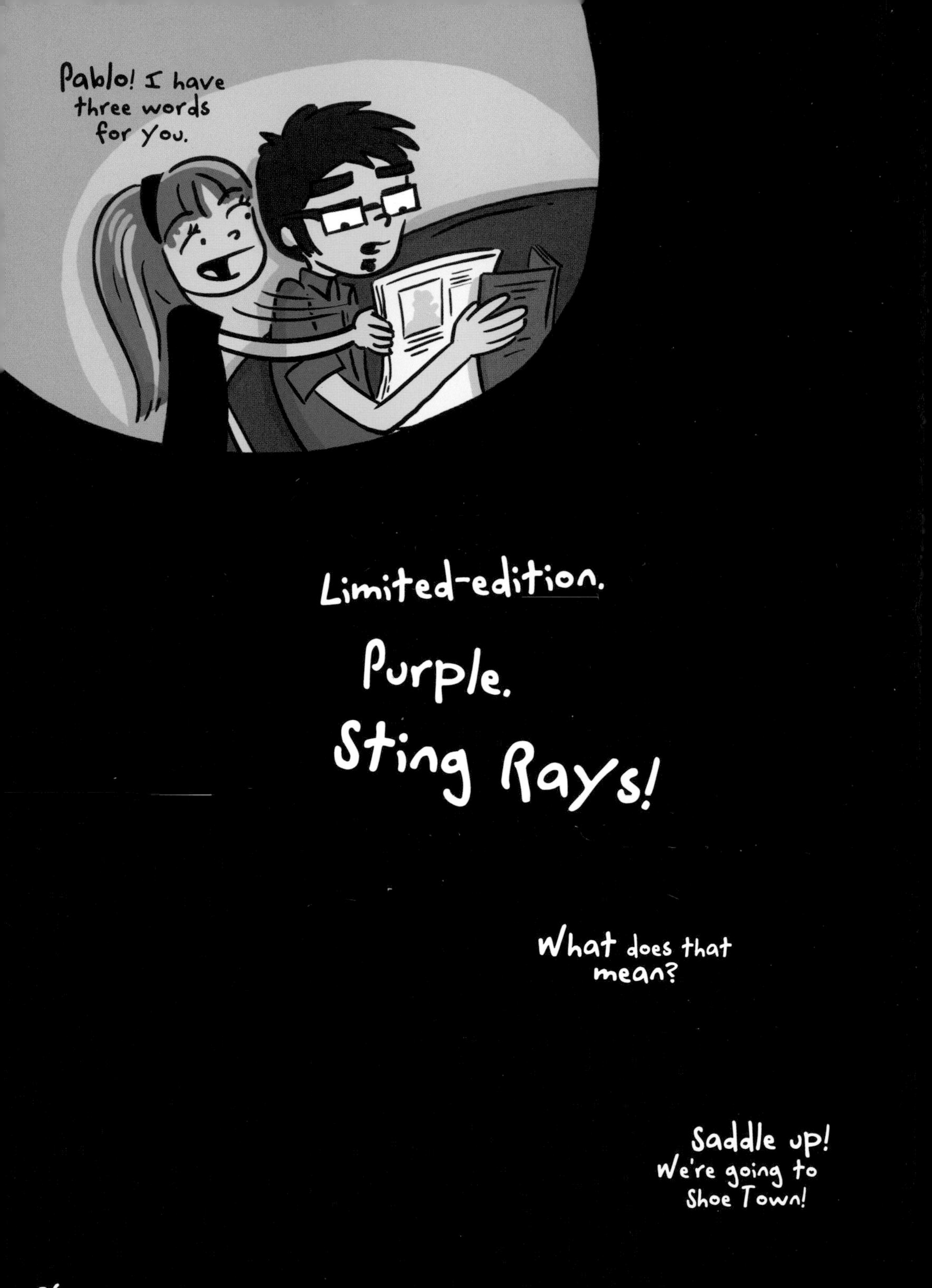
Pablo! I have three words for you.
Limited-edition.
Purple.
Sting Rays!
What does that mean?
Saddle up! We're going to Shoe Town!

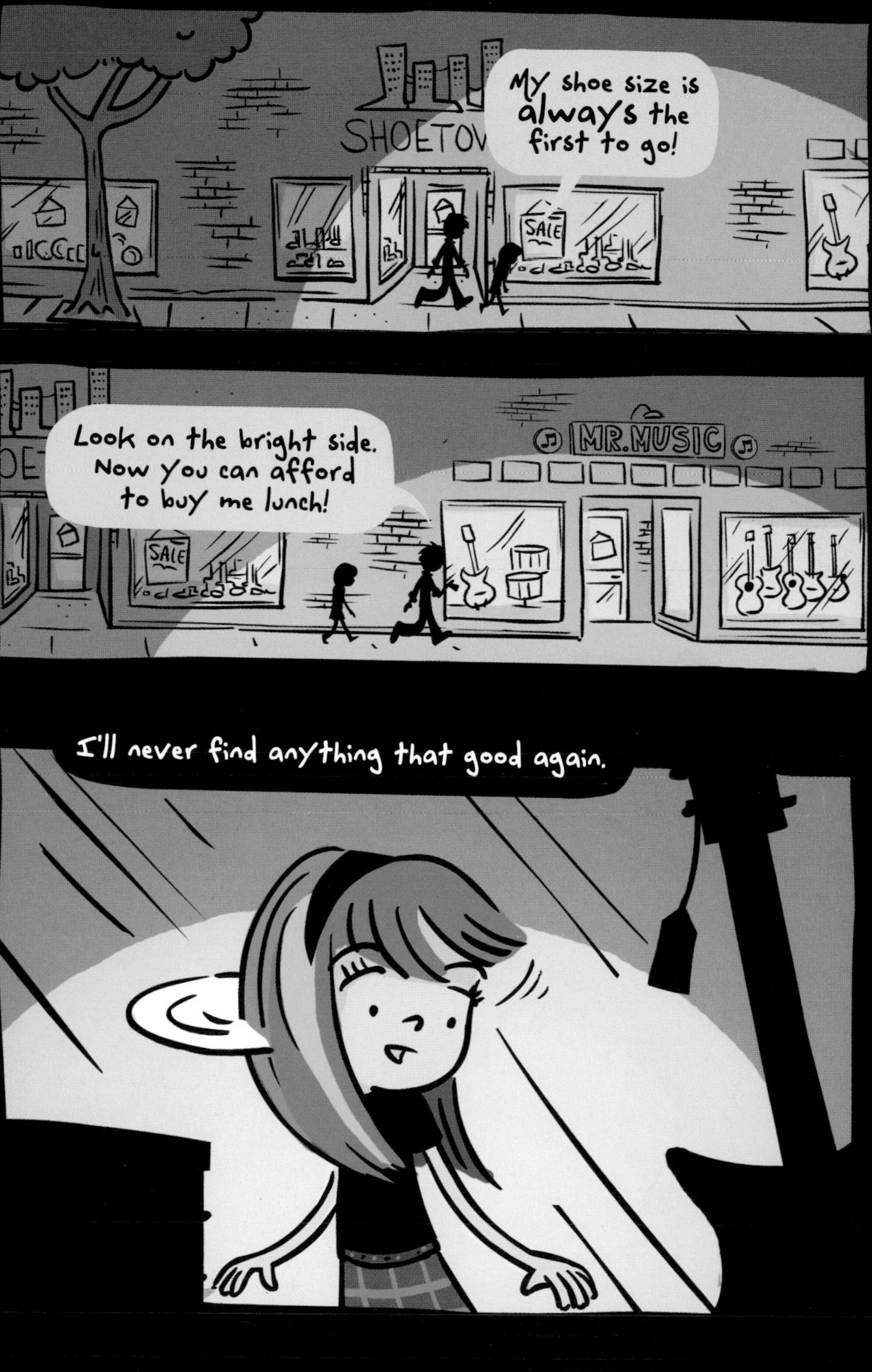
SHOETOW
My shoe size is always the first to go!
SALE
MR.MUSIC
SALE
Look on the bright side. Now you can afford to buy me lunch!
I'll never find anything that good again.

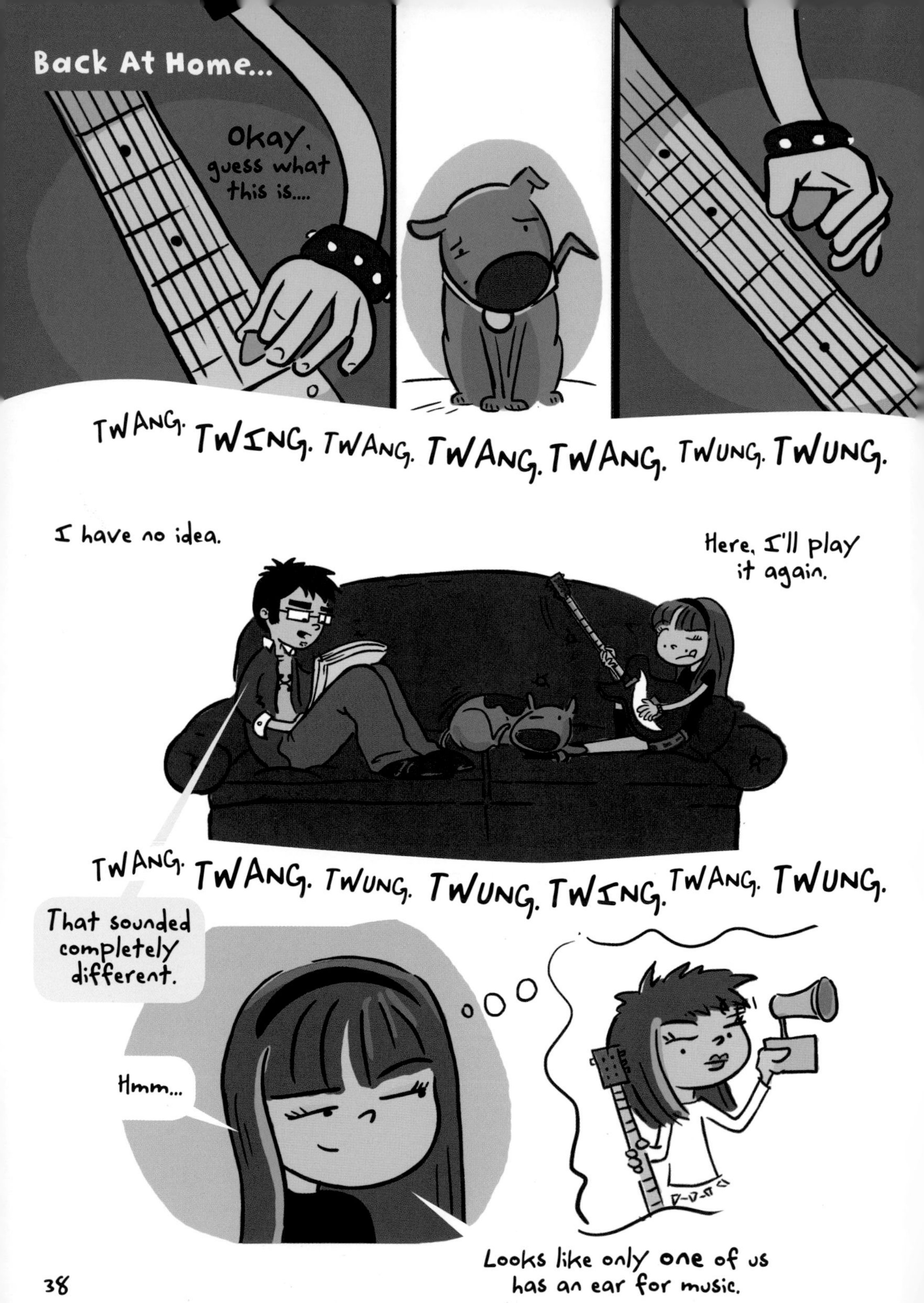
Back At Home...
Okay, guess what this is....
TWANG. TWING. TWANG. TWANG. TWANG. TWUNG. TWUNG.
I have no idea.
Here, I'll play it again.
TWANG. TWANG. TWUNG. TWUNG. TWING. TWANG. TWUNG.
That sounded completely different.
Hmm...
Looks like only one of us has an ear for music.

5. What's in a Name?

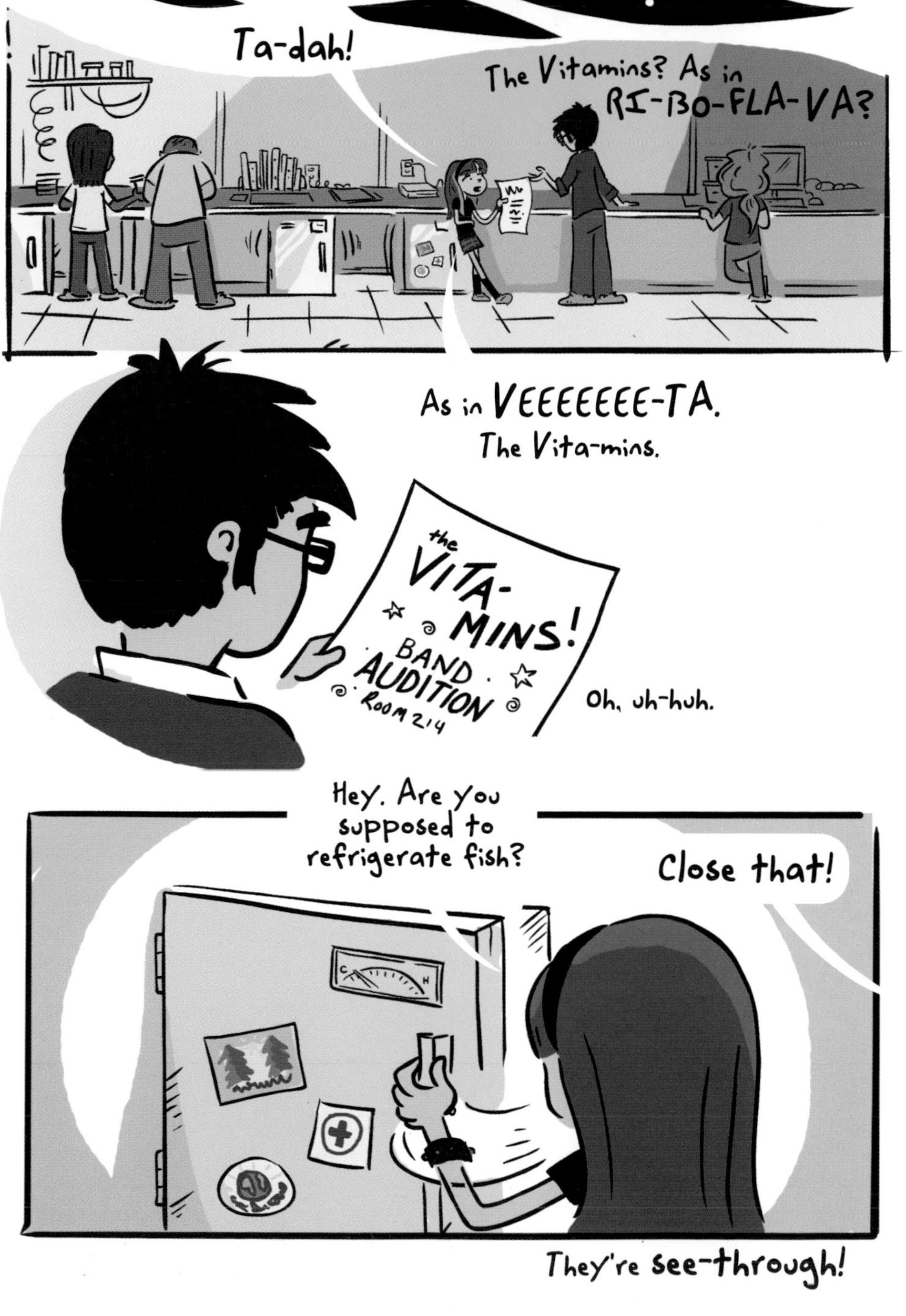

Ta-dah!
The Vitamins? As in RI-BO-FLA-VA?
As in VEEEEEEE-TA. The Vita-mins.
the VITA-MINS! BAND AUDITION ROOM 214
Oh, uh-huh.
Hey. Are you supposed to refrigerate fish?
Close that!
They're see-through!

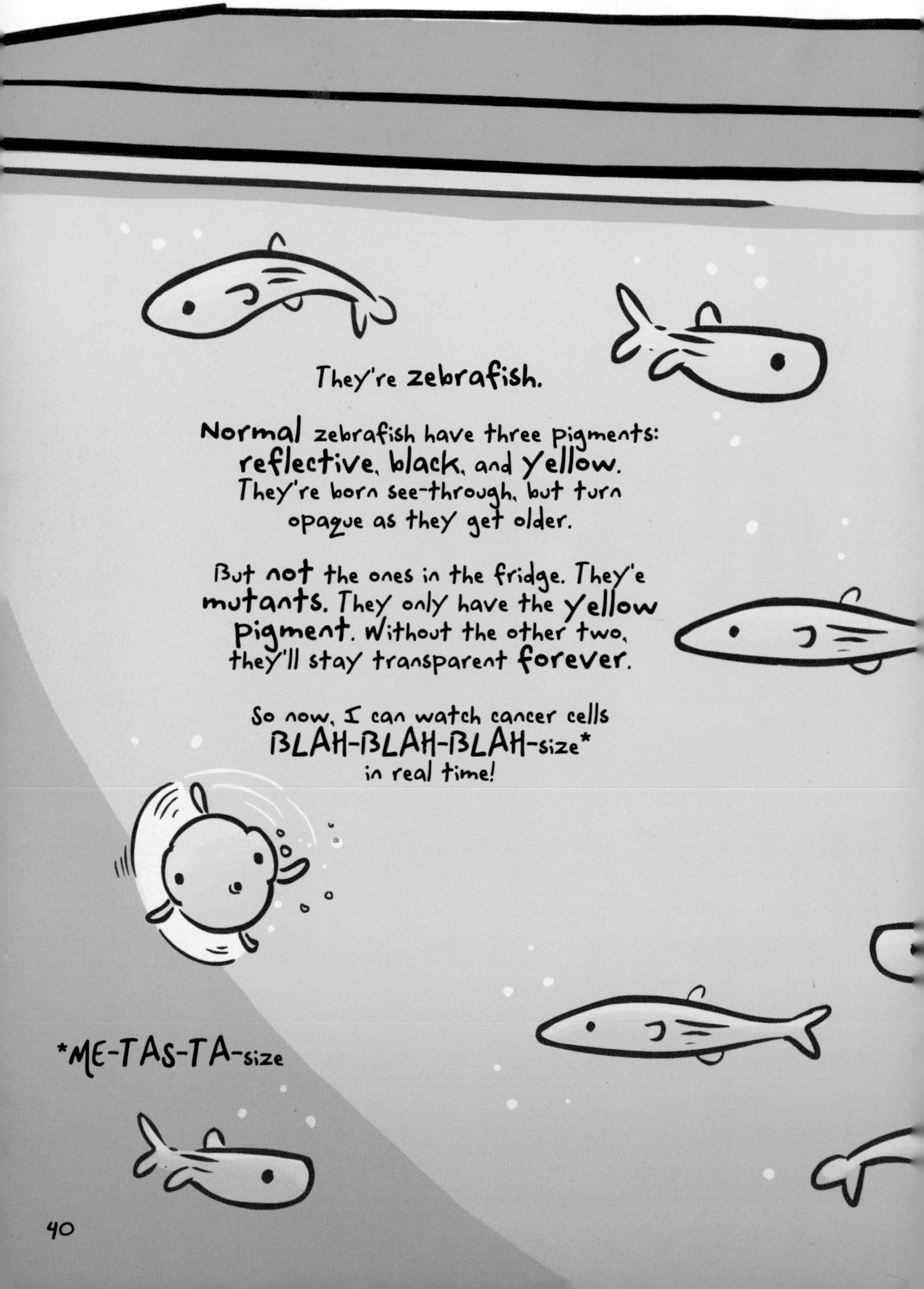
They're zebrafish.
Normal zebrafish have three pigments: reflective, black, and yellow. They're born see-through, but turn opaque as they get older.
But not the ones in the fridge. They'e mutants. They only have the yellow pigment. Without the other two, they'll stay transparent forever.
So now, I can watch cancer cells BLAH-BLAH-BLAH-size* in real time!
*ME-TAS-TA-size

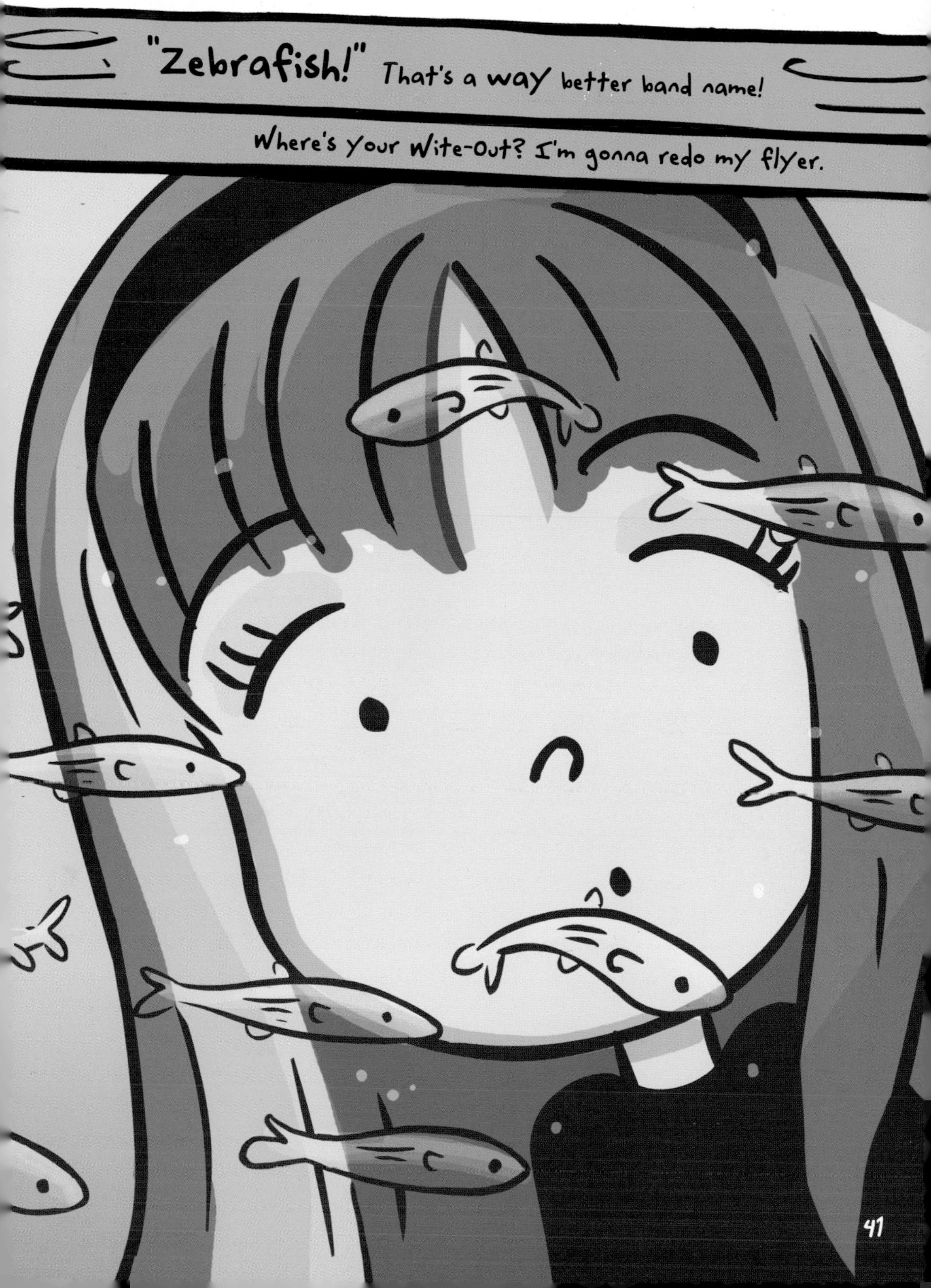
"Zebrafish!" That's a way better band name!
Where's your Wite-Out? I'm gonna redo my flyer.

6. Reentry

Late September...

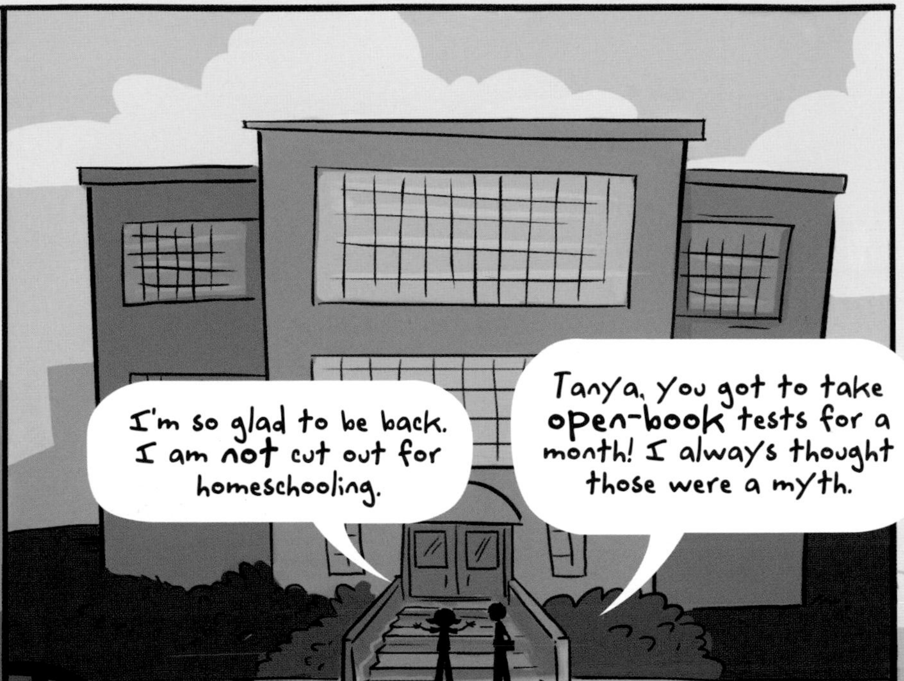
I'm so glad to be back. I am not cut out for homeschooling.
Tanya, you got to take open-book tests for a month! I always thought those were a myth.

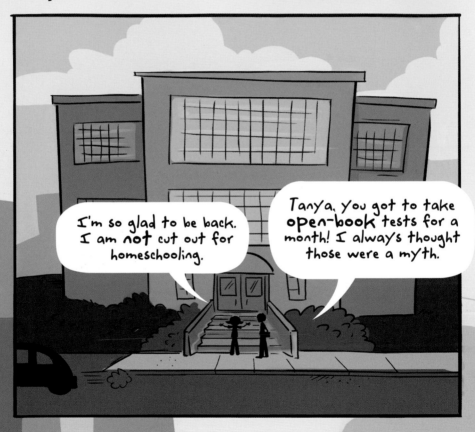

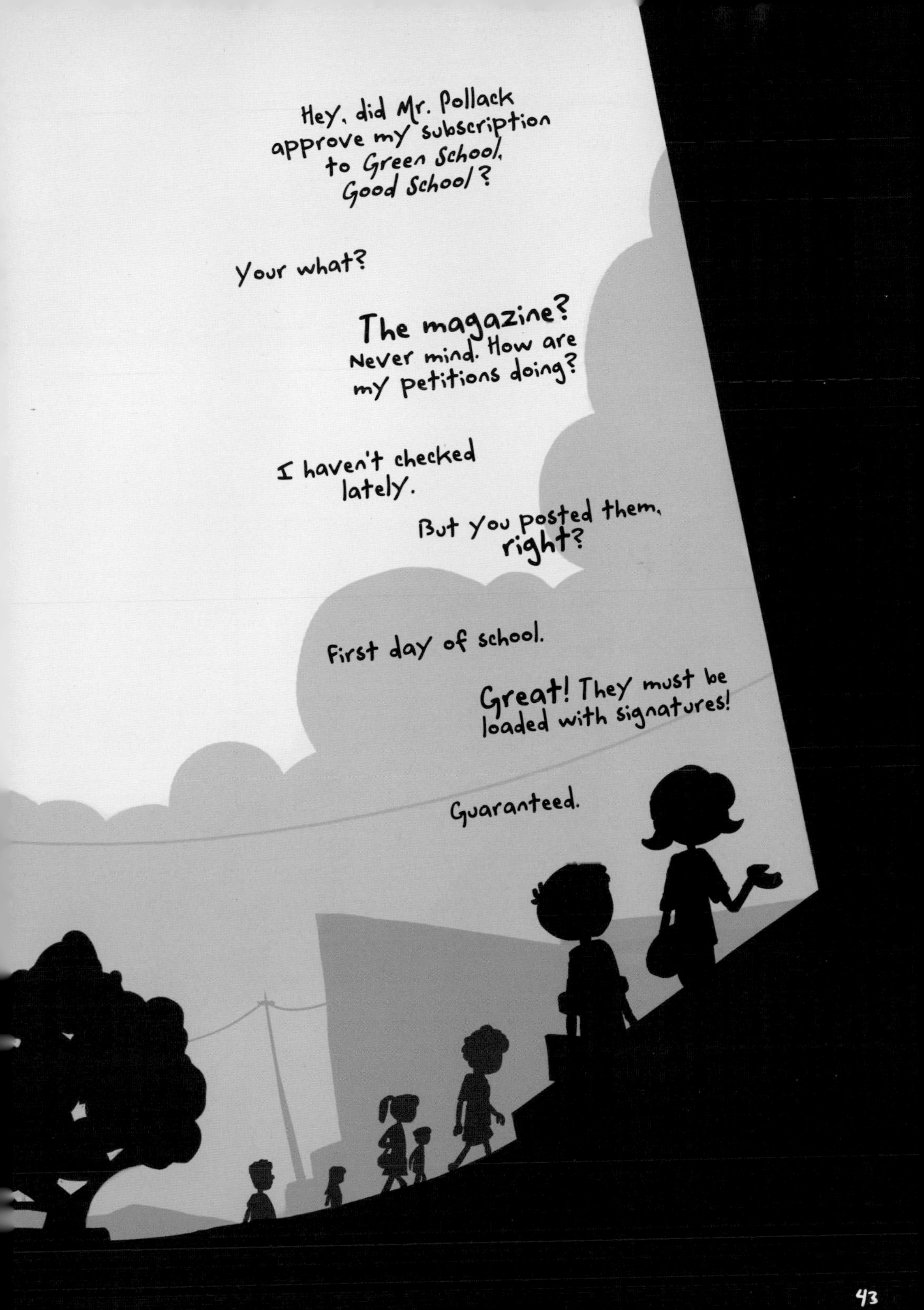
Hey, did Mr. Pollack approve my subscription to Green School, Good School?
Your what?
The magazine? Never mind. How are my petitions doing?
I haven't checked lately.
But you posted them, right?
First day of school.
Great! They must be loaded with signatures!
Guaranteed.

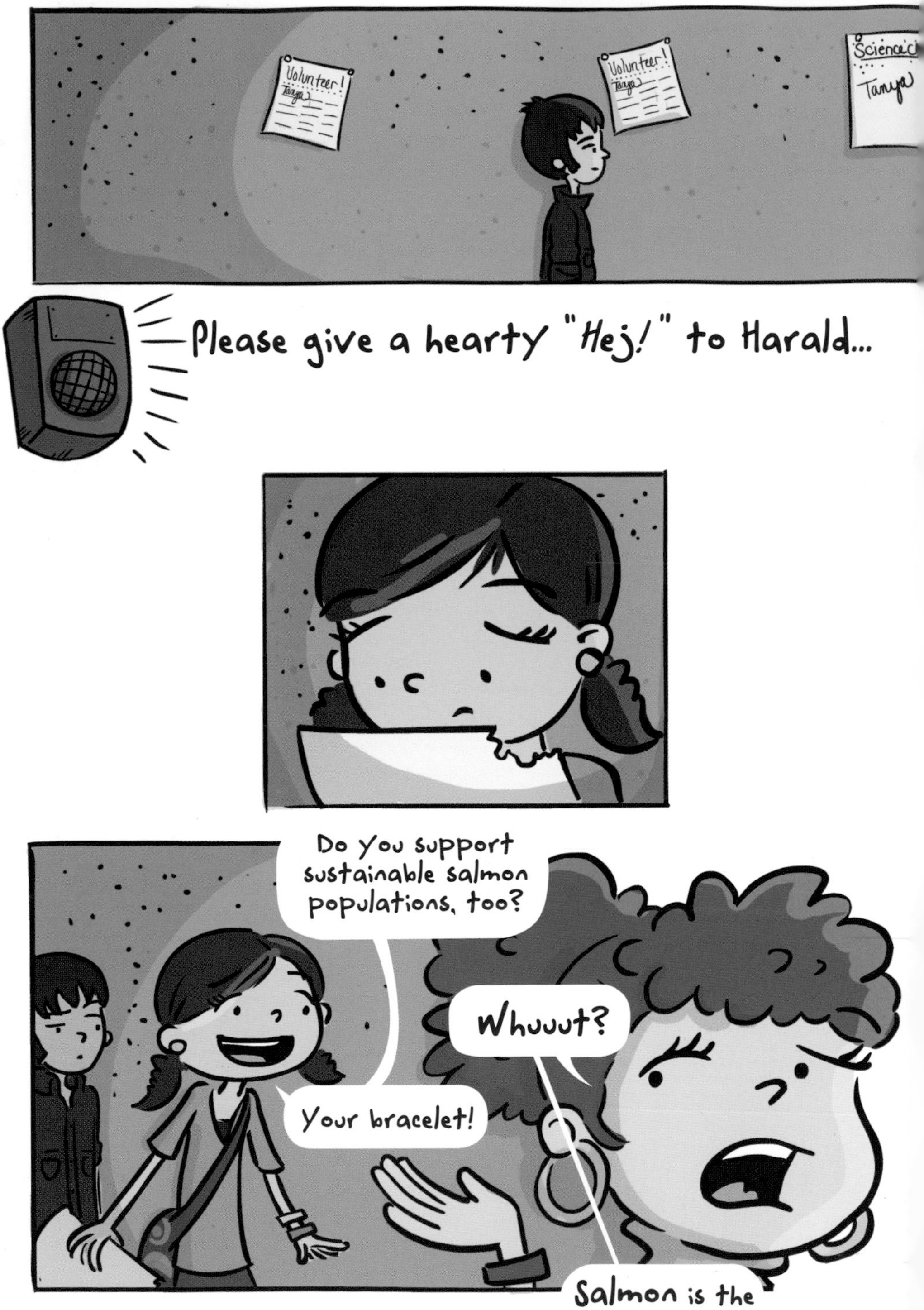
Volunteer!
Tanya
Volunteer!
Tanya
Tanya
Please give a hearty "Hej!" to Harald...
Do you support sustainable salmon populations, too?
Your bracelet!
Whuuut?
Salmon is the new orange.

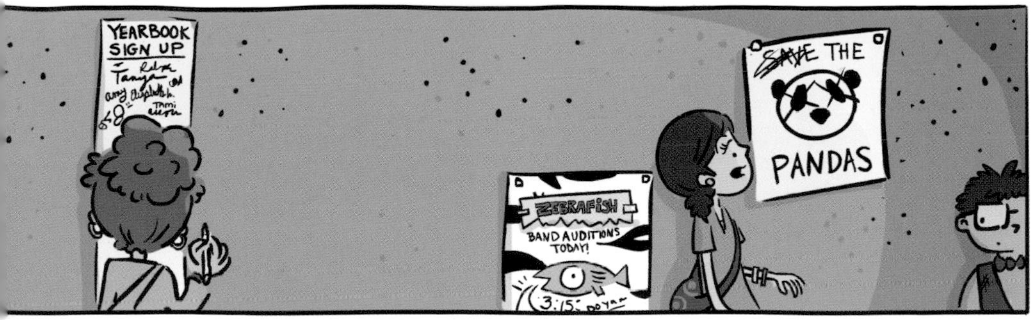
YEARBOOK SIGN UP
SAVE THE PANDAS
ZEBRAFISH
BAND AUDITIONS TODAY!

...our foreign-exchange student.

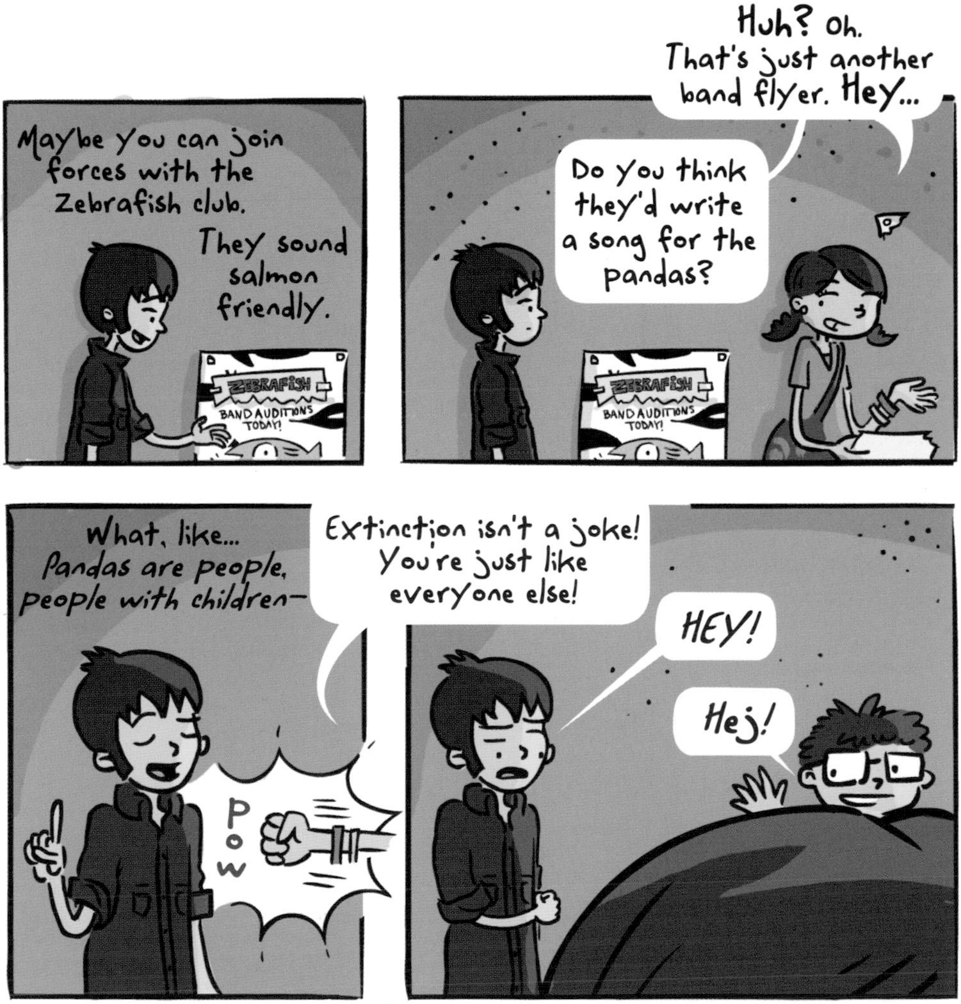
Maybe you can join forces with the Zebrafish club.
They sound salmon friendly.
ZEBRAFISH
BAND AUDITIONS TODAY!
Huh? Oh. That's just another band flyer. Hey...
Do you think they'd write a song for the pandas?
ZEBRAFISH
BAND AUDITIONS TODAY!
What, like... Pandas are people, people with children—
Extinction isn't a joke! You're just like everyone else!
POW
HEY!
Hej!

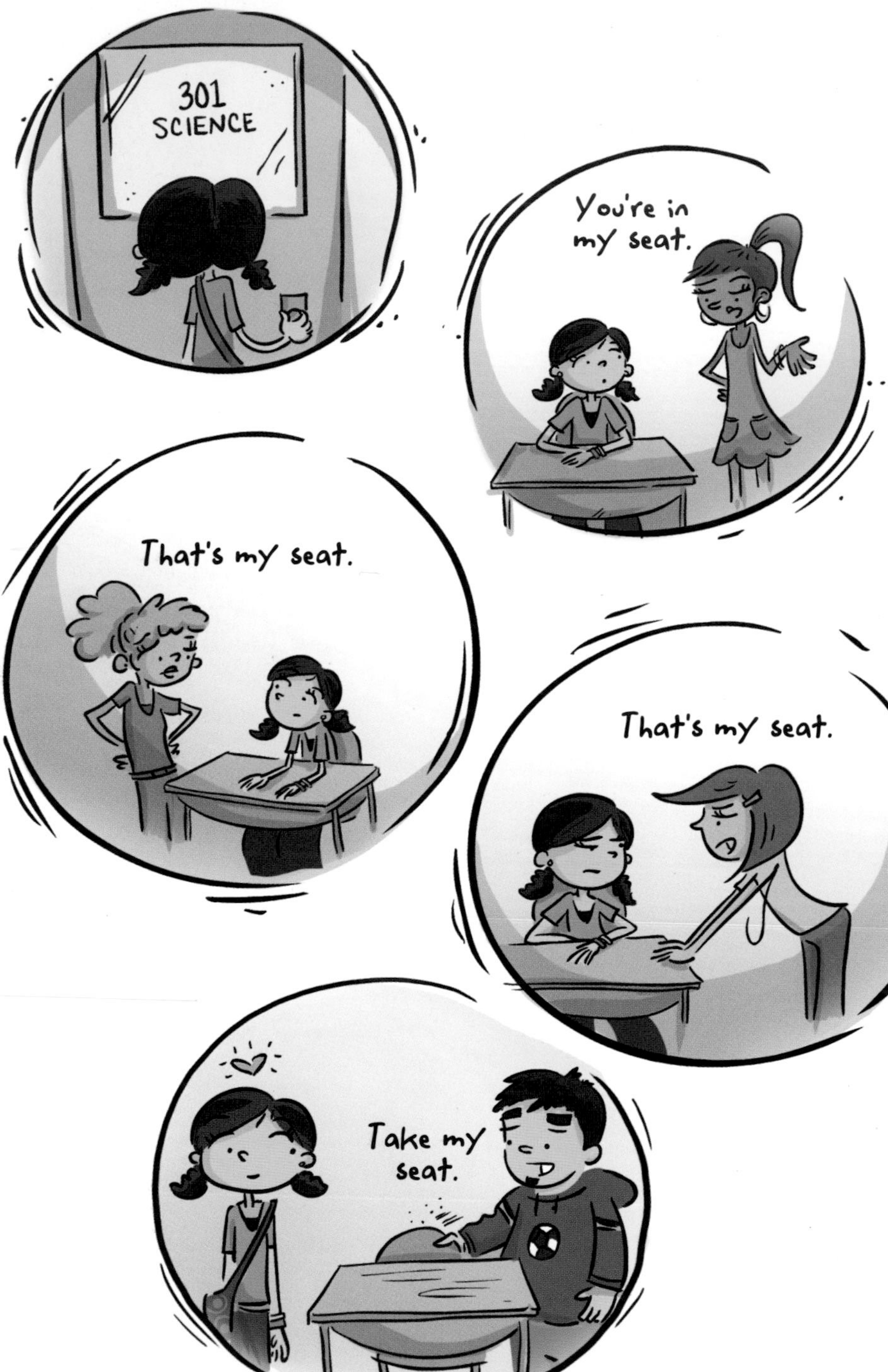
301
SCIENCE
You're in my seat.
That's my seat.
That's my seat.
Take my seat.

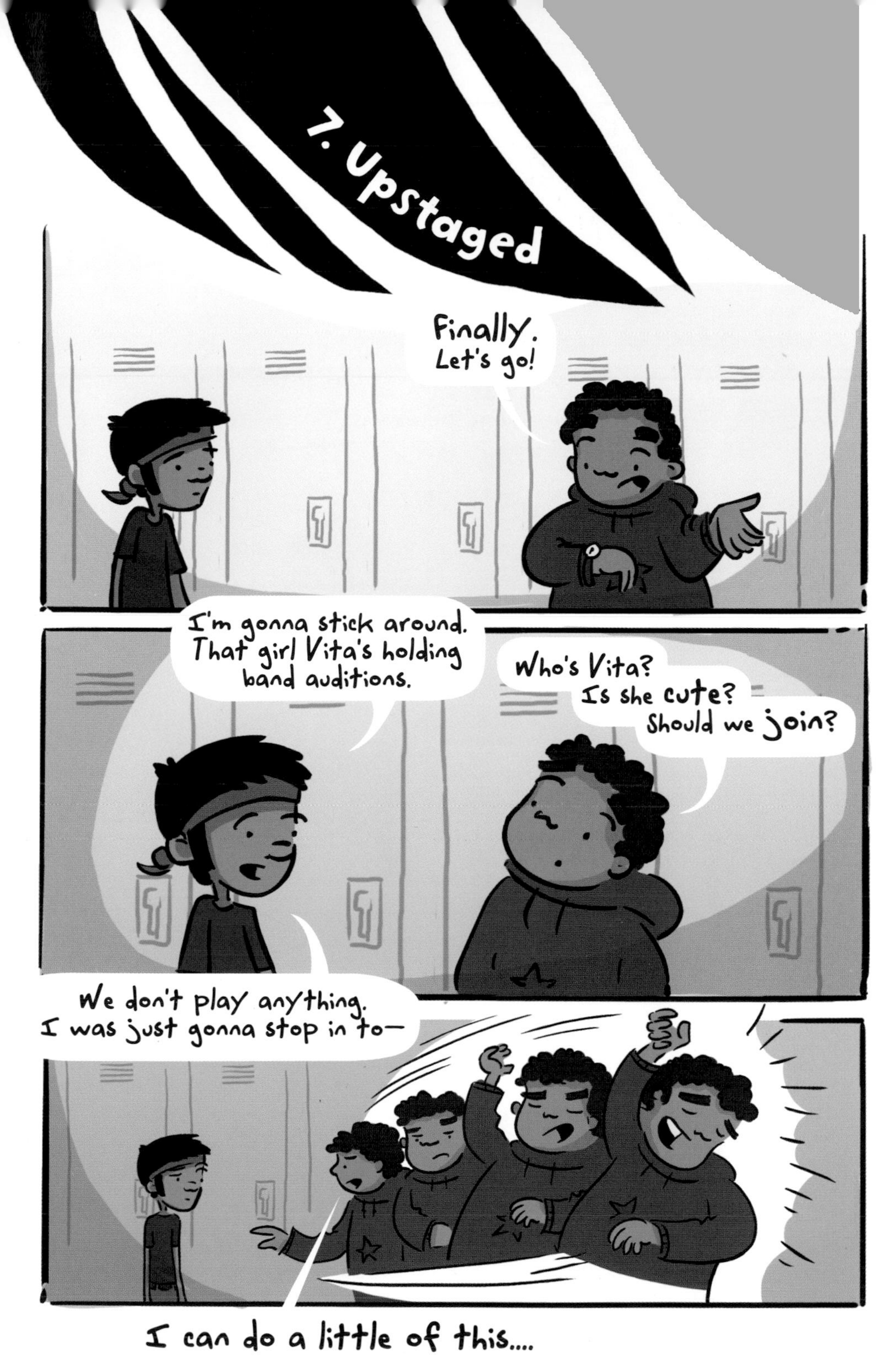
7. Upstaged
Finally. Let's go!
I'm gonna stick around. That girl Vita's holding band auditions.
Who's Vita? Is she cute? Should we join?
We don't play anything. I was just gonna stop in to—
I can do a little of this....

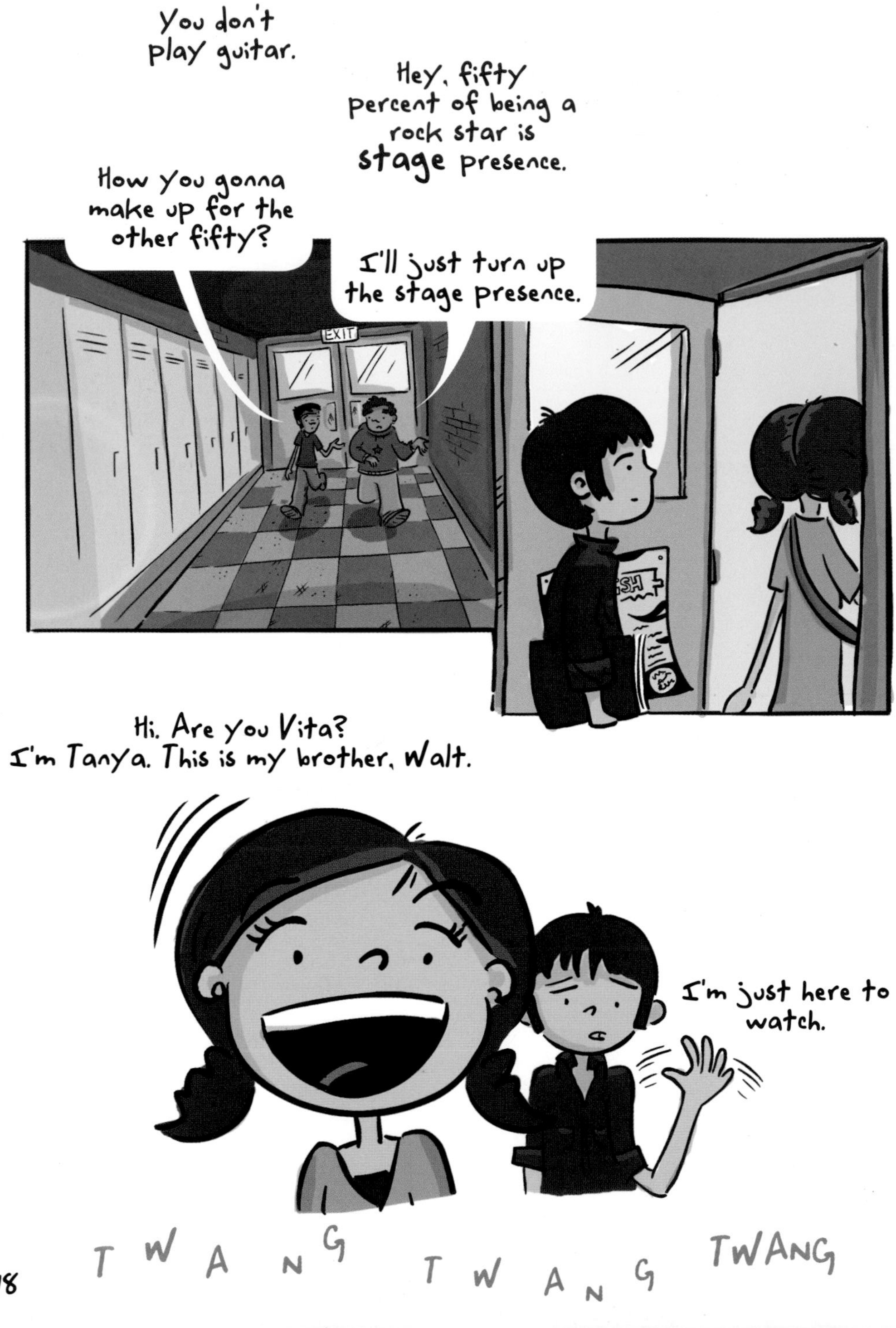

You don't play guitar.
Hey, fifty percent of being a rock star is stage presence.
How you gonna make up for the other fifty?
I'll just turn up the stage presence.
EXIT
Hi. Are you Vita? I'm Tanya. This is my brother, Walt.
I'm just here to watch.
TWANG TWANG TWANG

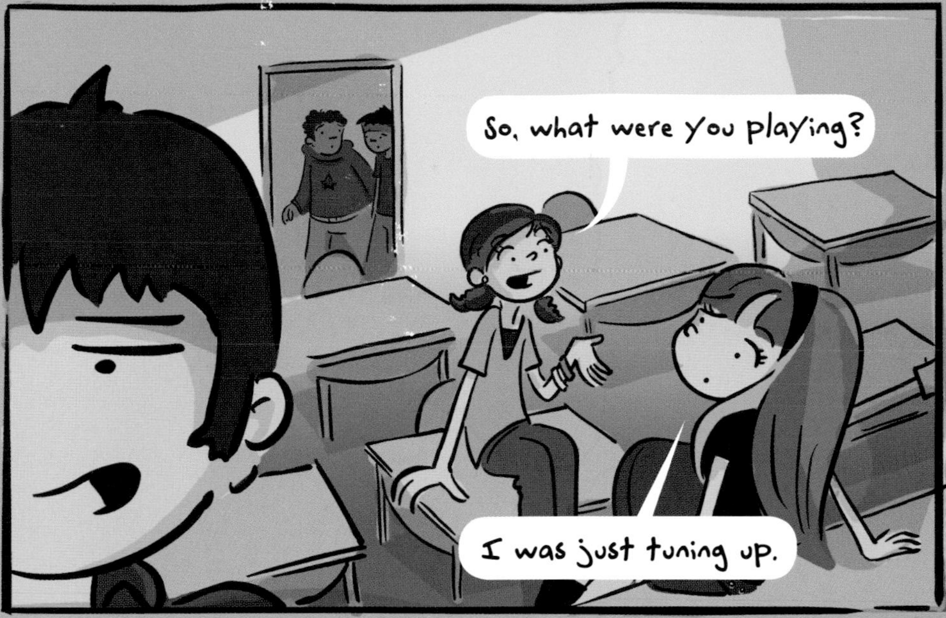
So, what were you playing?
I was just tuning up.

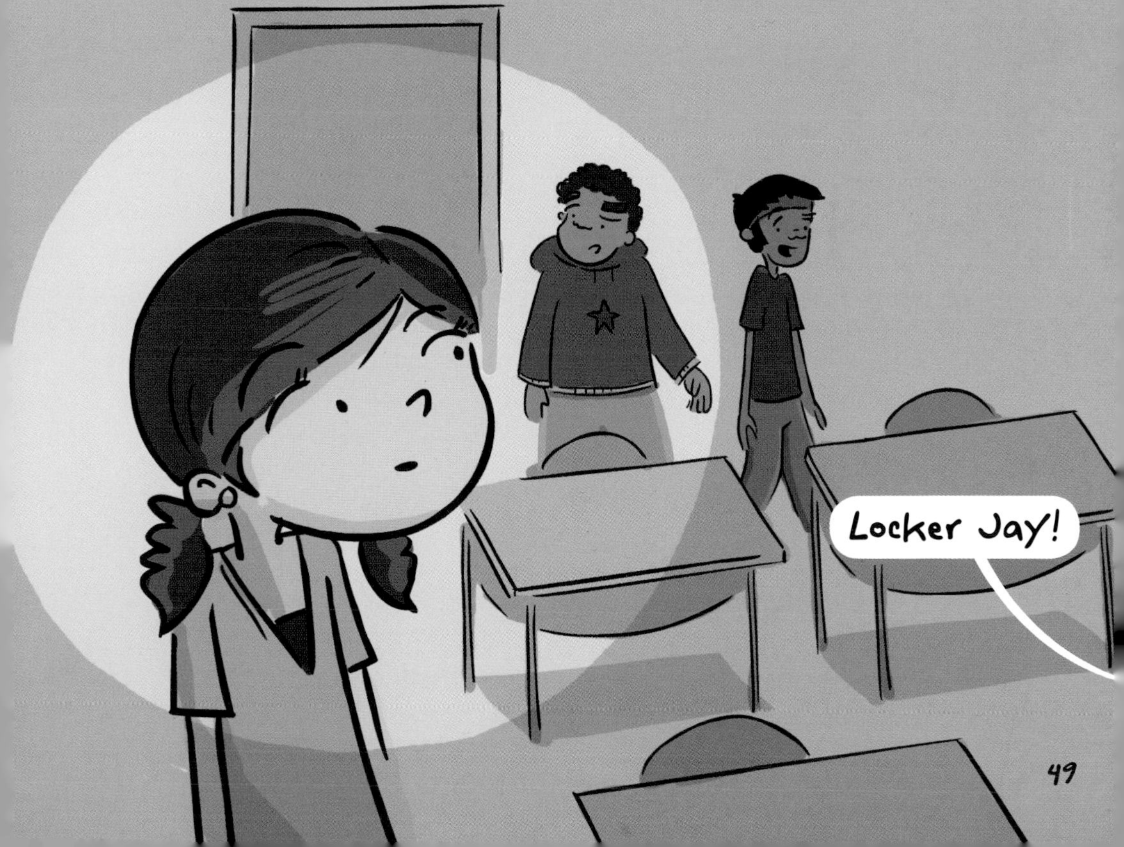
Locker Jay!

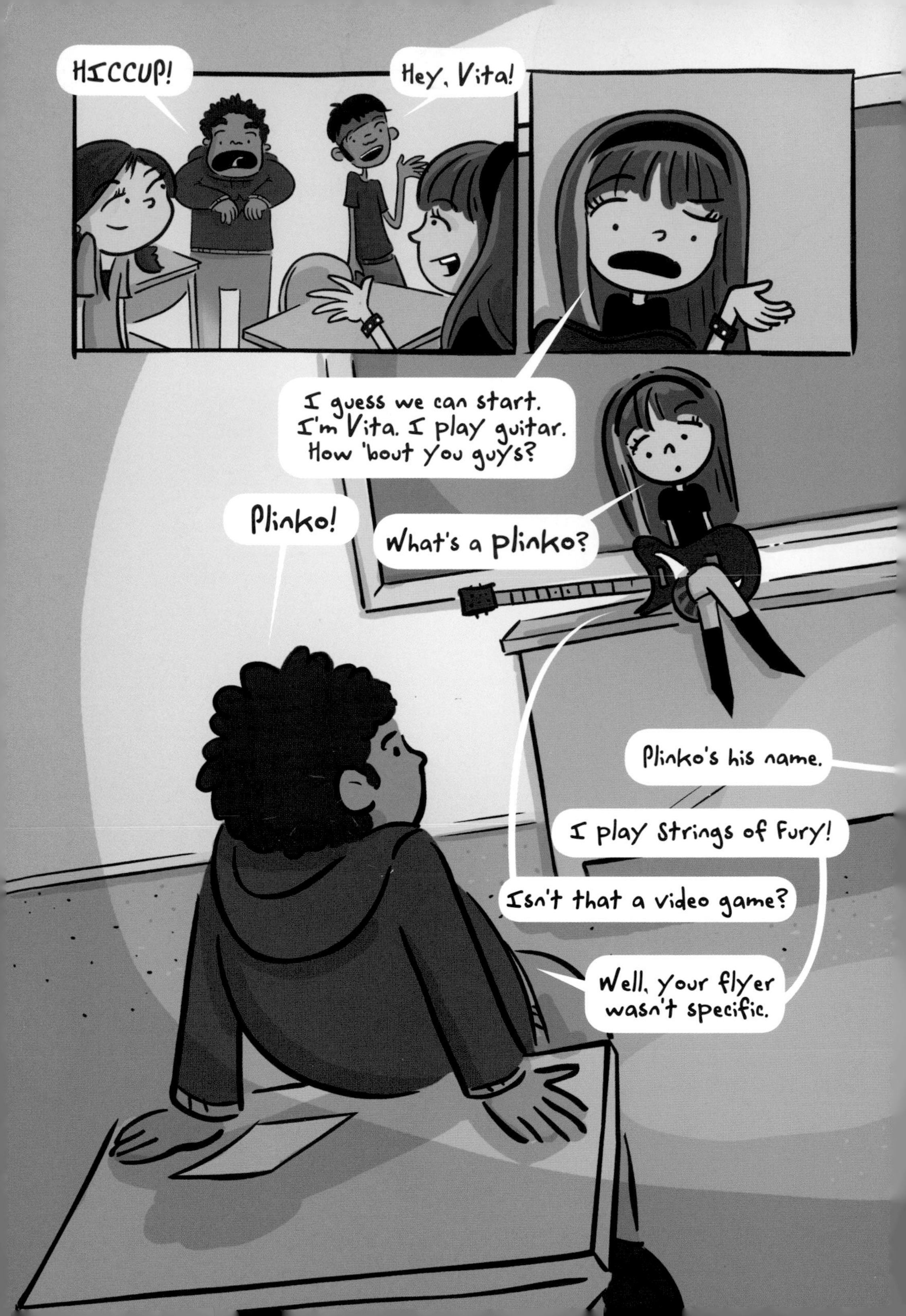
HICCUP!
Hey, Vita!
I guess we can start. I'm Vita. I play guitar. How 'bout you guys?
Plinko!
What's a plinko?
Plinko's his name.
I play Strings of Fury!
Isn't that a video game?
Well, your flyer wasn't specific.

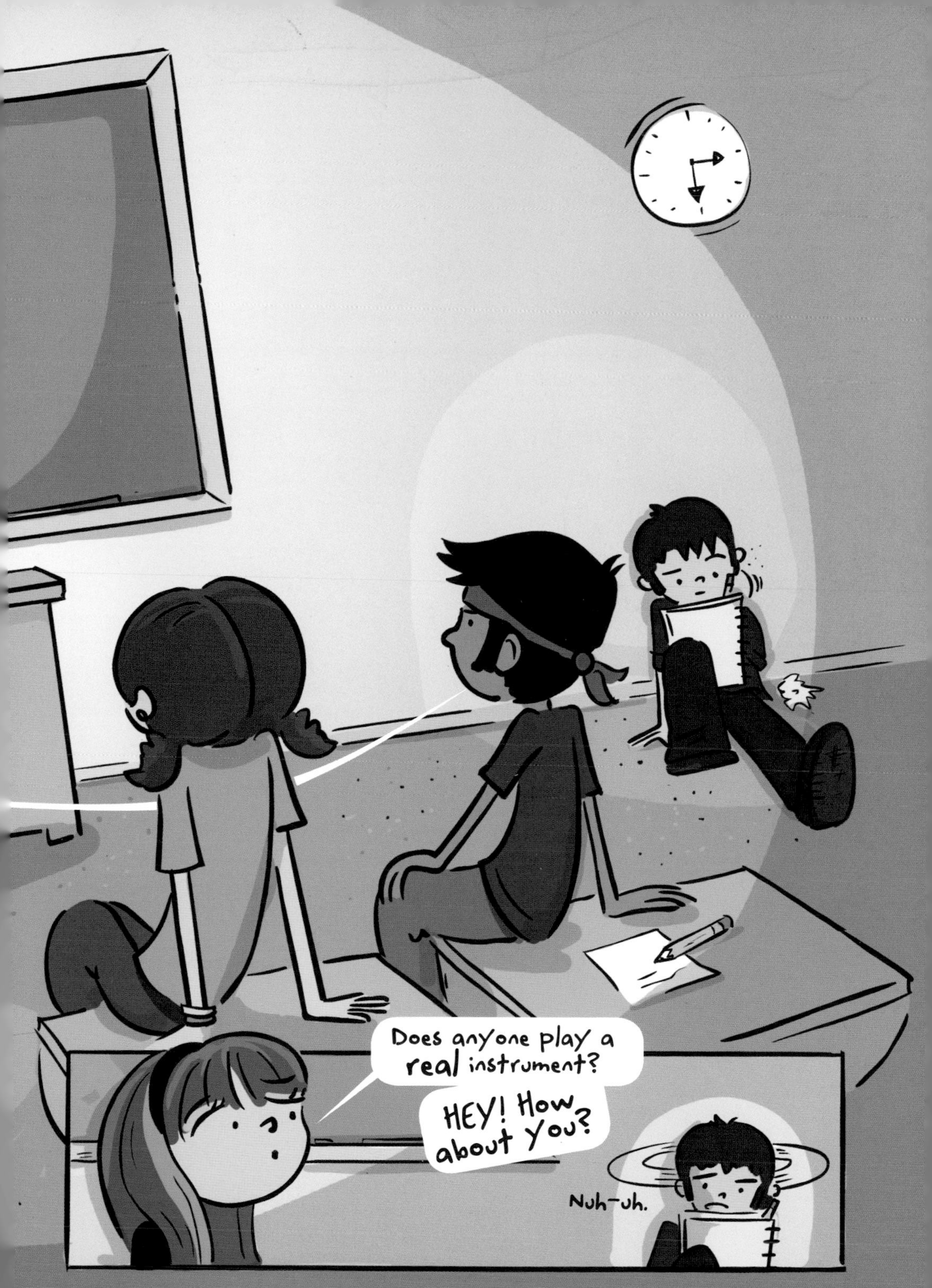
Does anyone play a real instrument?
HEY! How about you?
Nuh-uh.

That Night...

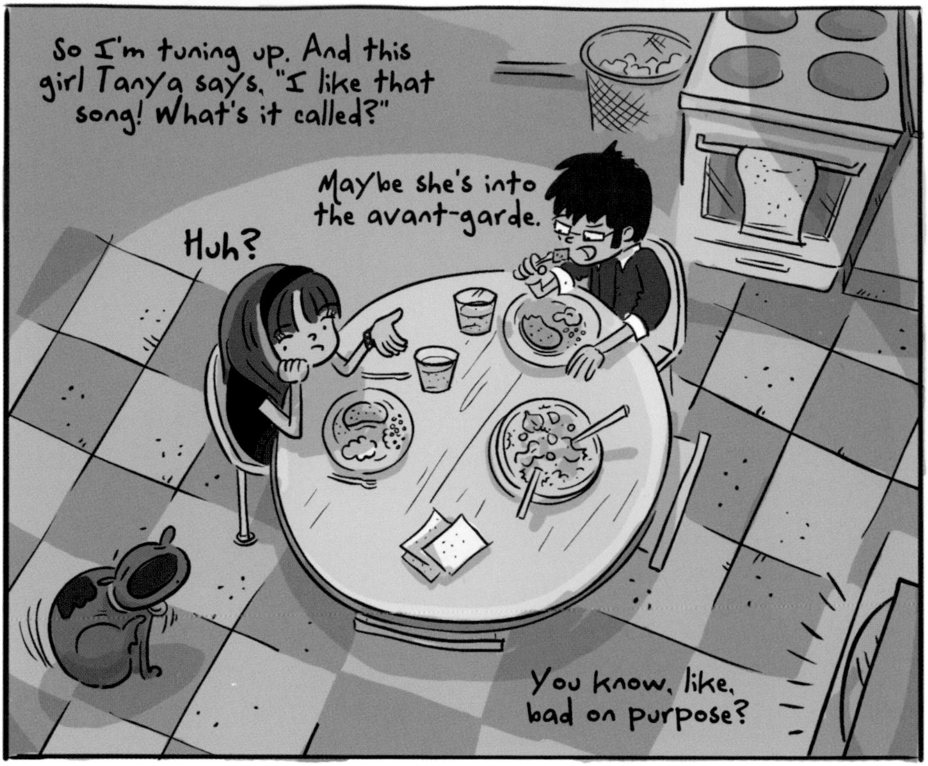
So I'm tuning up. And this girl Tanya says, "I like that song! What's it called?"
Maybe she's into the avant-garde.
Huh?
You know, like, bad on purpose?

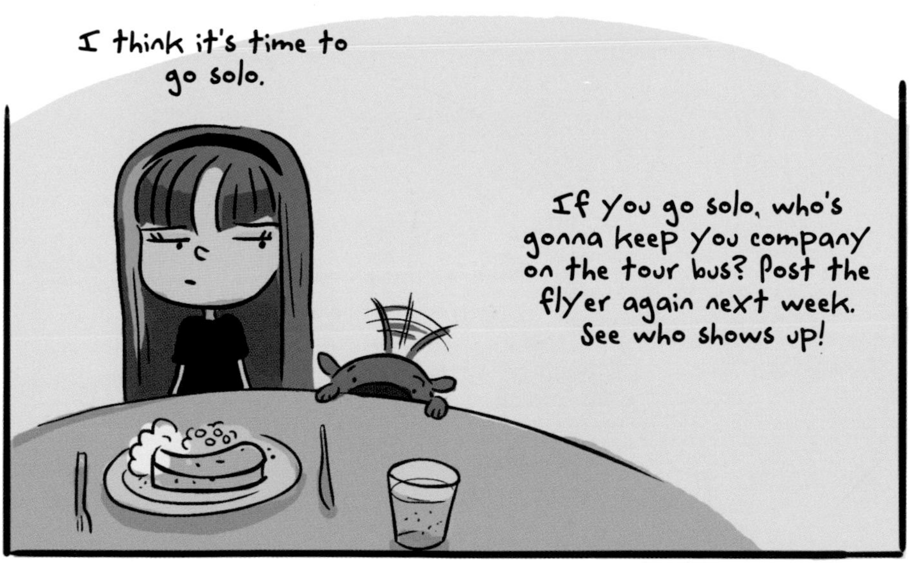
I think it's time to go solo.
If you go solo, who's gonna keep you company on the tour bus? Post the flyer again next week. See who shows up!

8. Take Two

One Week Later...

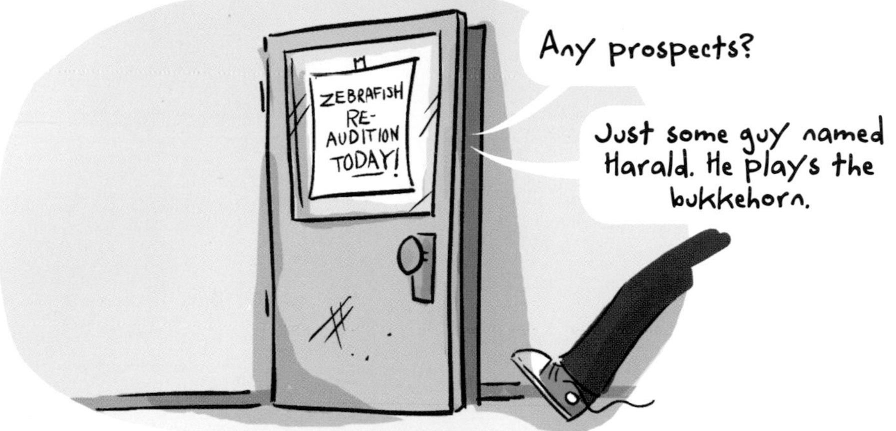
ZEBRAFISH RE-AUDITION TODAY!
Any prospects?
Just some guy named Harald. He plays the bukkehorn.

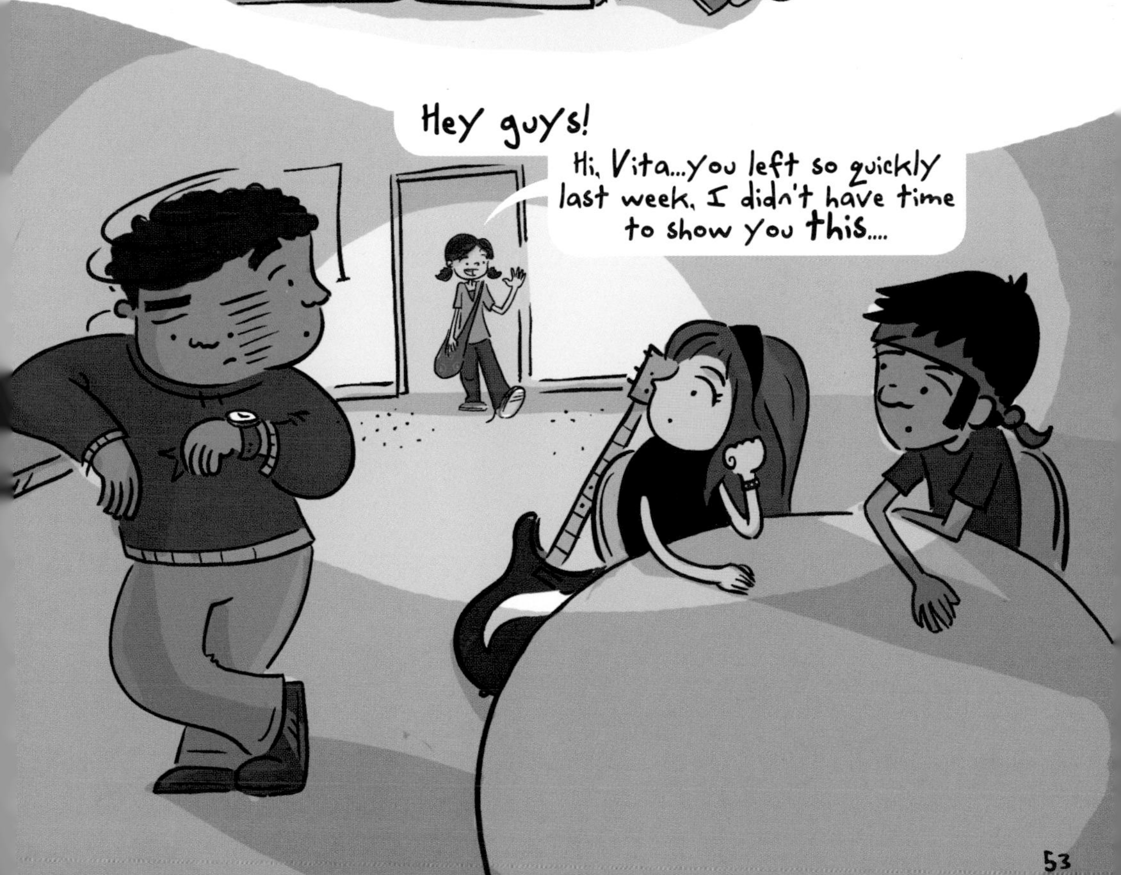
Hey guys!
Hi, Vita...you left so quickly last week, I didn't have time to show you this....

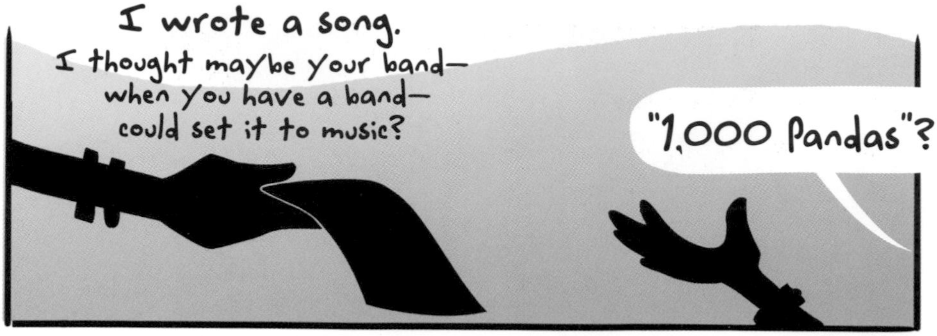
I wrote a song.
I thought maybe your band— when you have a band— could set it to music?
"1,000 Pandas"?

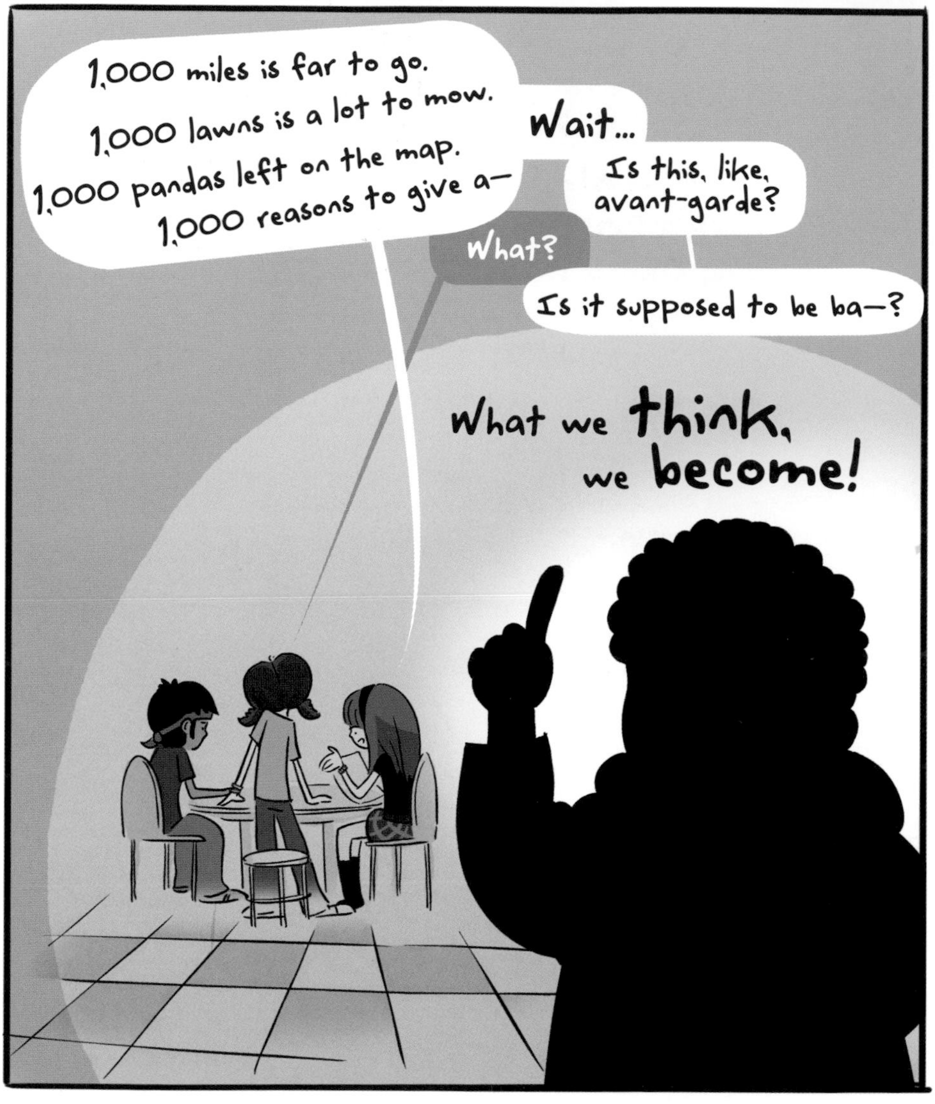
1,000 miles is far to go.
1,000 lawns is a lot to mow.
1,000 pandas left on the map.
1,000 reasons to give a—
Wait...
Is this, like, avant-garde?
What?
Is it supposed to be ba—?
What we think, we become!

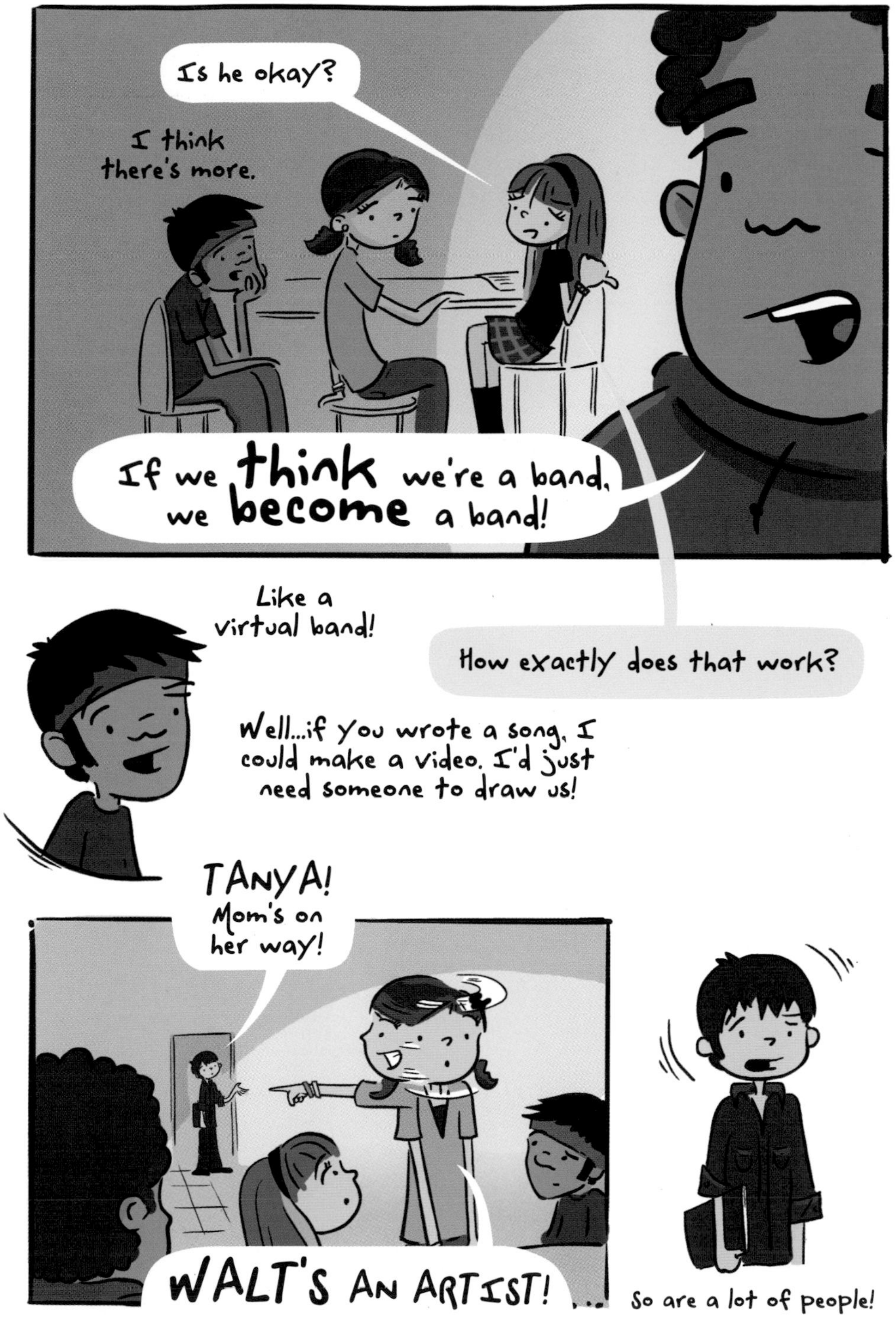
Is he okay?
I think there's more.
If we think we're a band, we become a band!
Like a virtual band!
How exactly does that work?
Well...if you wrote a song, I could make a video. I'd just need someone to draw us!
TANYA! Mom's on her way!
WALT'S AN ARTIST!
...
So are a lot of people!

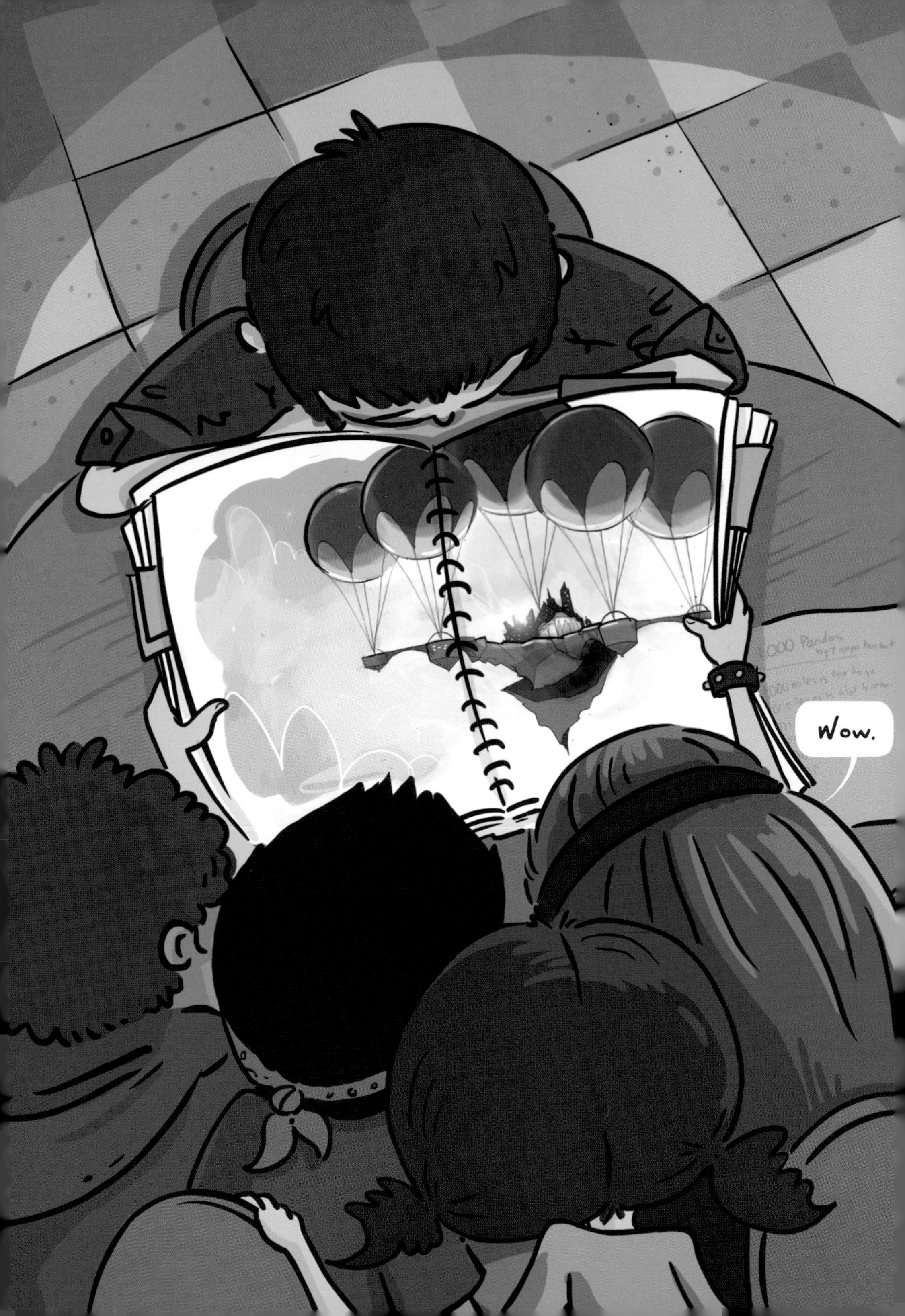
Wow.

9. Crushed

Days Later...

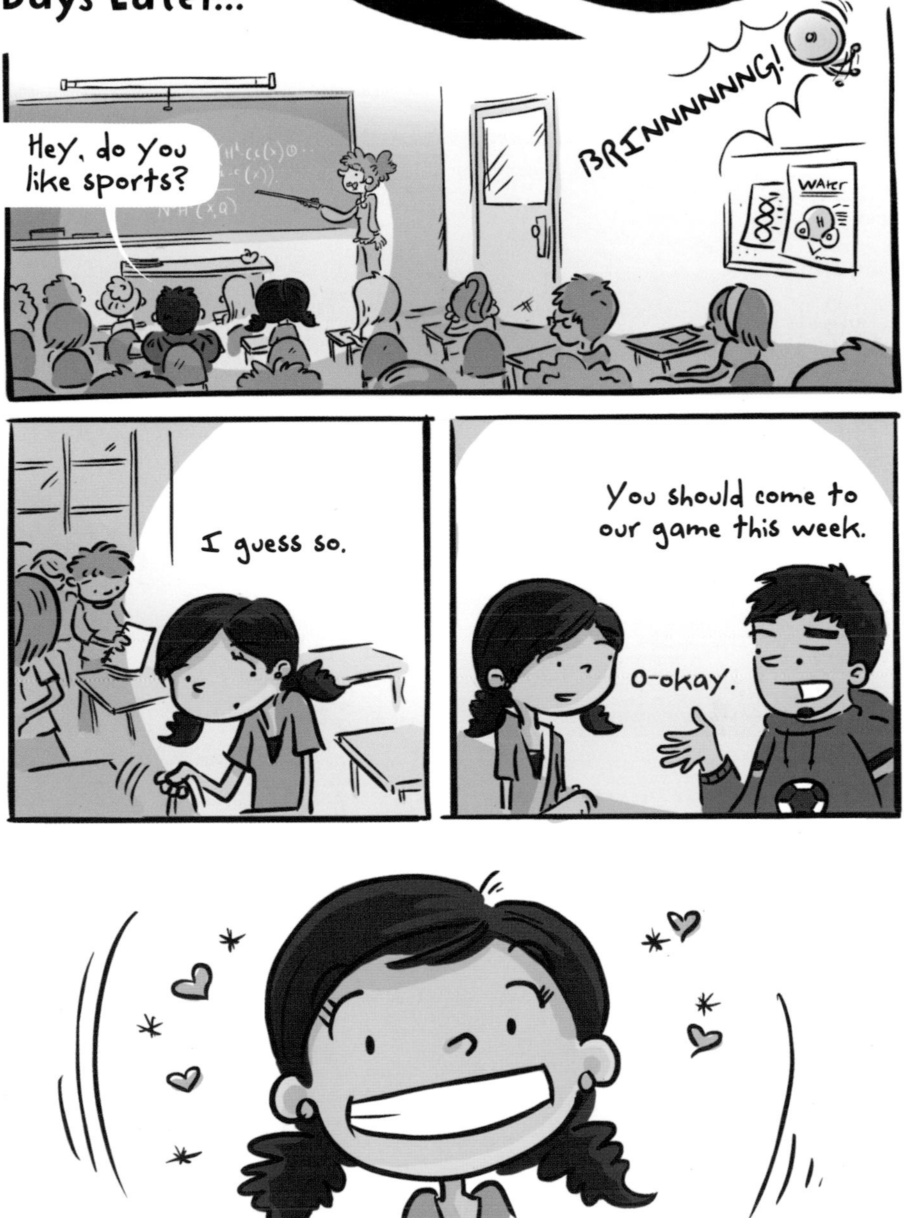

BRINNNNNNG!
Hey, do you like sports?
I guess so.
You should come to our game this week.
O-okay.

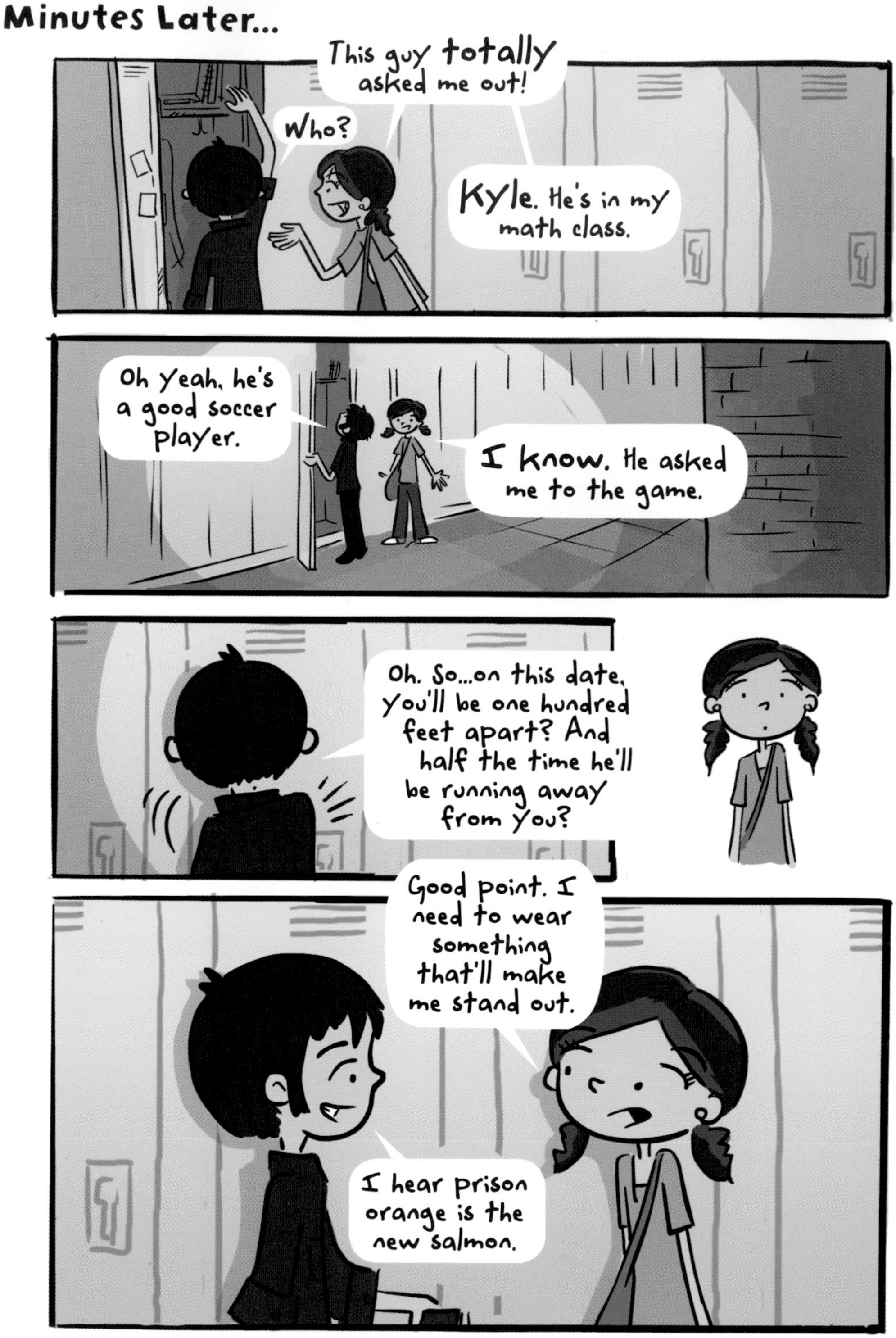
Minutes Later...
This guy totally asked me out!
Who?
Kyle. He's in my math class.
Oh yeah, he's a good soccer player.
I know. He asked me to the game.
Oh. So...on this date, you'll be one hundred feet apart? And half the time he'll be running away from you?
Good point. I need to wear something that'll make me stand out.
I hear prison orange is the new salmon.

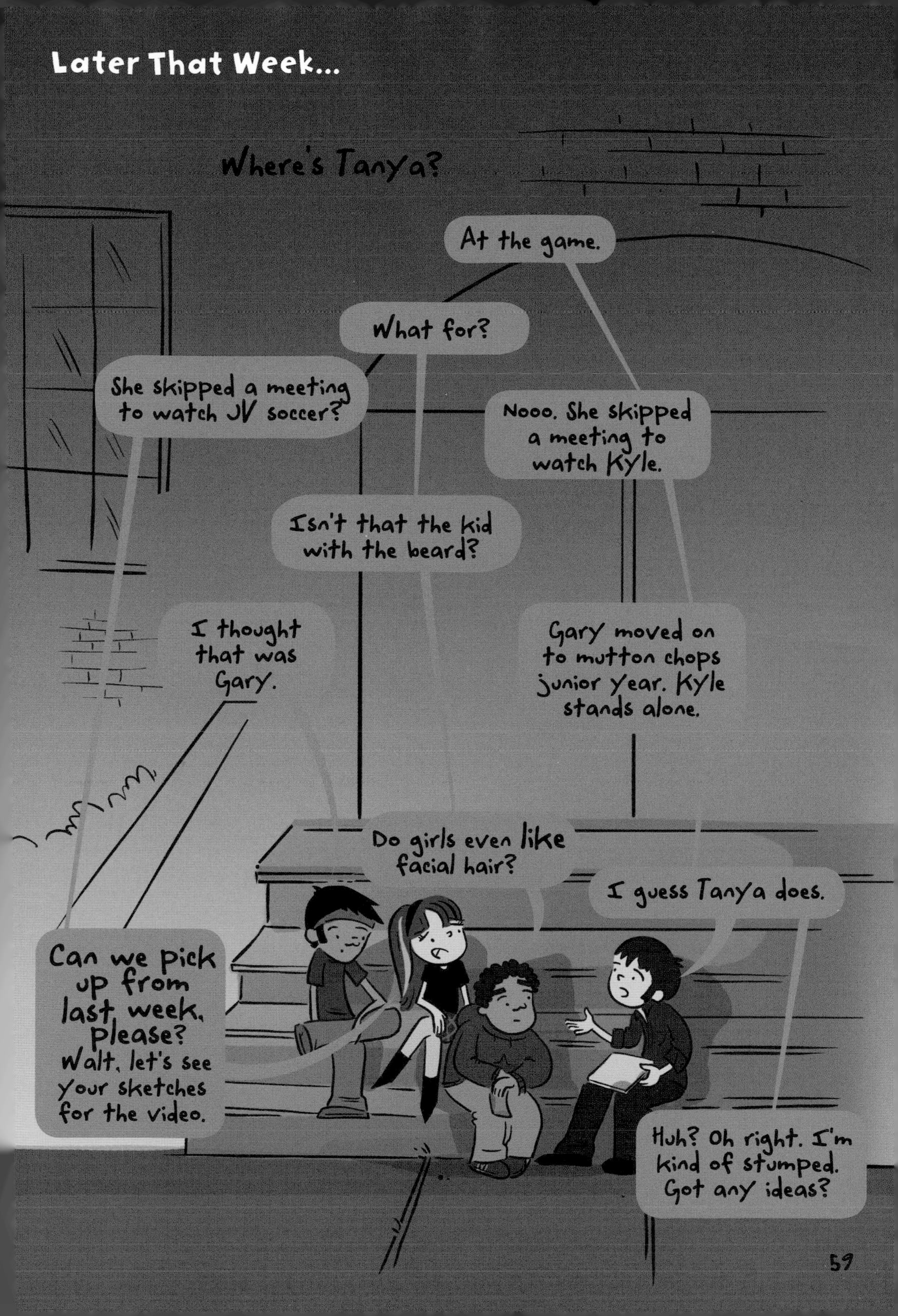
Later That Week...
Where's Tanya?
At the game.
What for?
She skipped a meeting to watch JV soccer?
Nooo. She skipped a meeting to watch Kyle.
Isn't that the kid with the beard?
I thought that was Gary.
Gary moved on to mutton chops junior year. Kyle stands alone.
Do girls even like facial hair?
I guess Tanya does.
Can we pick up from last week, please? Walt, let's see your sketches for the video.
Huh? Oh right. I'm kind of stumped. Got any ideas?

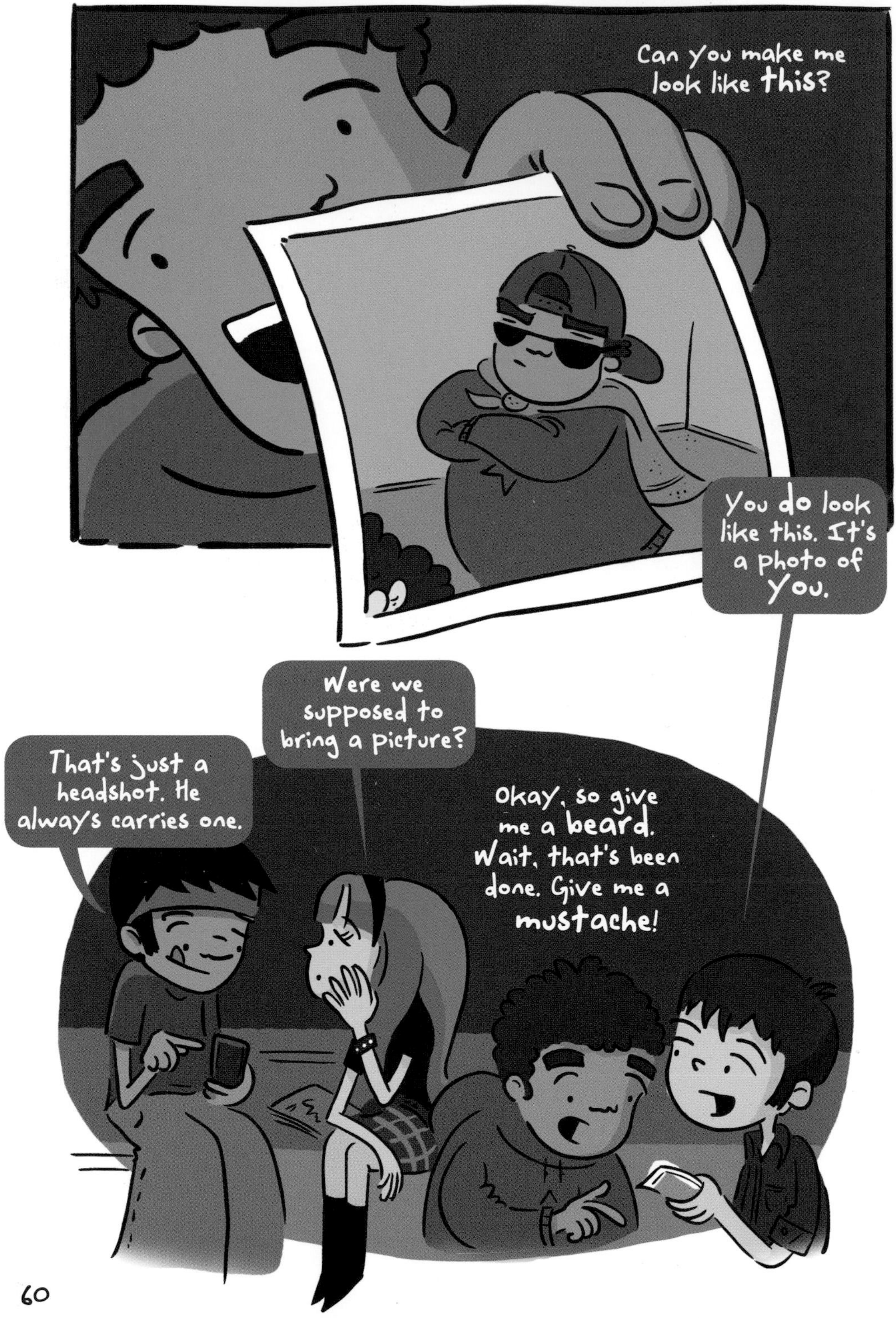
Can you make me look like this?
You do look like this. It's a photo of you.
Were we supposed to bring a picture?
That's just a headshot. He always carries one.
Okay, so give me a beard. Wait, that's been done. Give me a mustache!

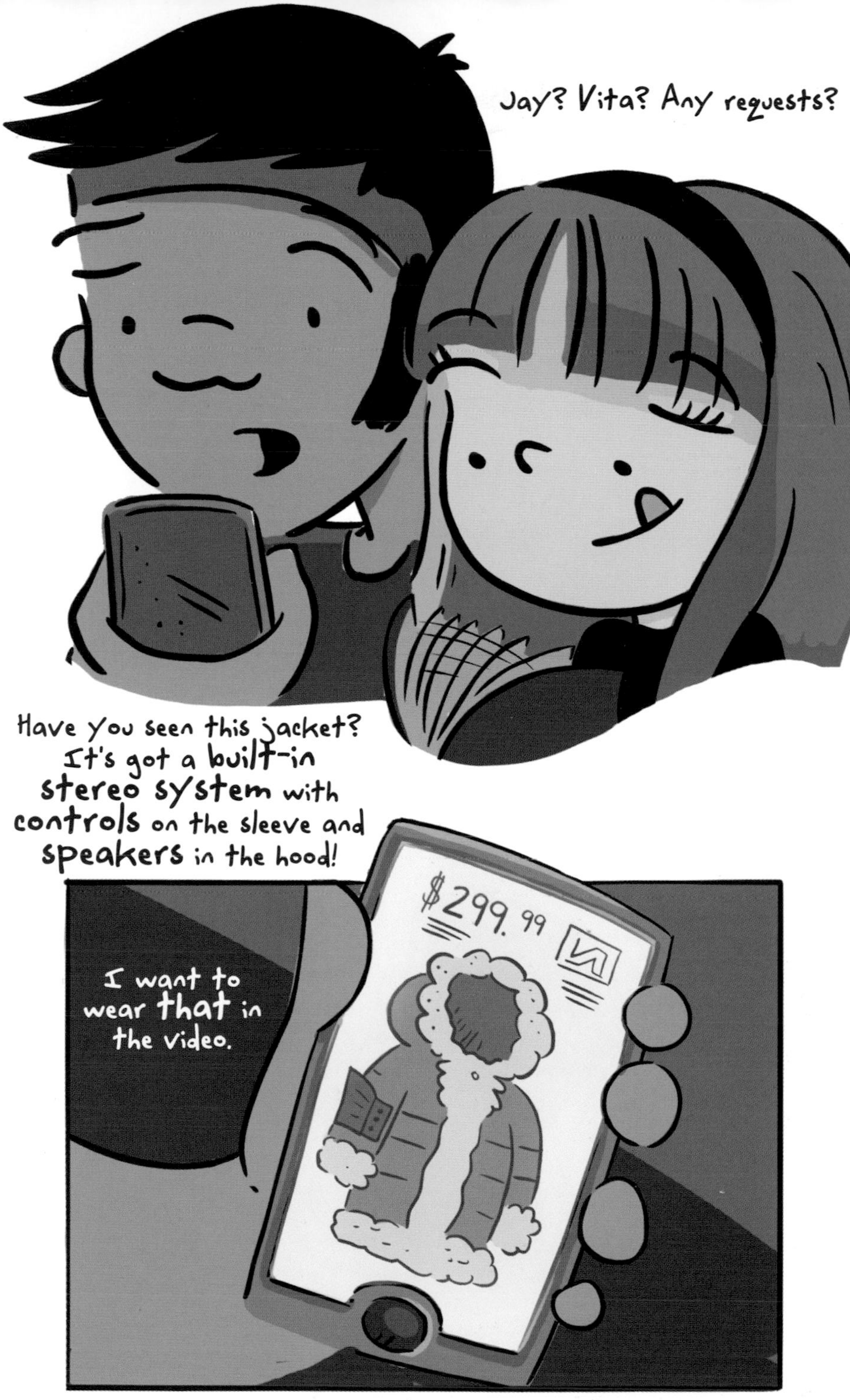
Jay? Vita? Any requests?
Have you seen this jacket? It's got a built-in stereo system with controls on the sleeve and speakers in the hood!
I want to wear that in the video.
$299.99

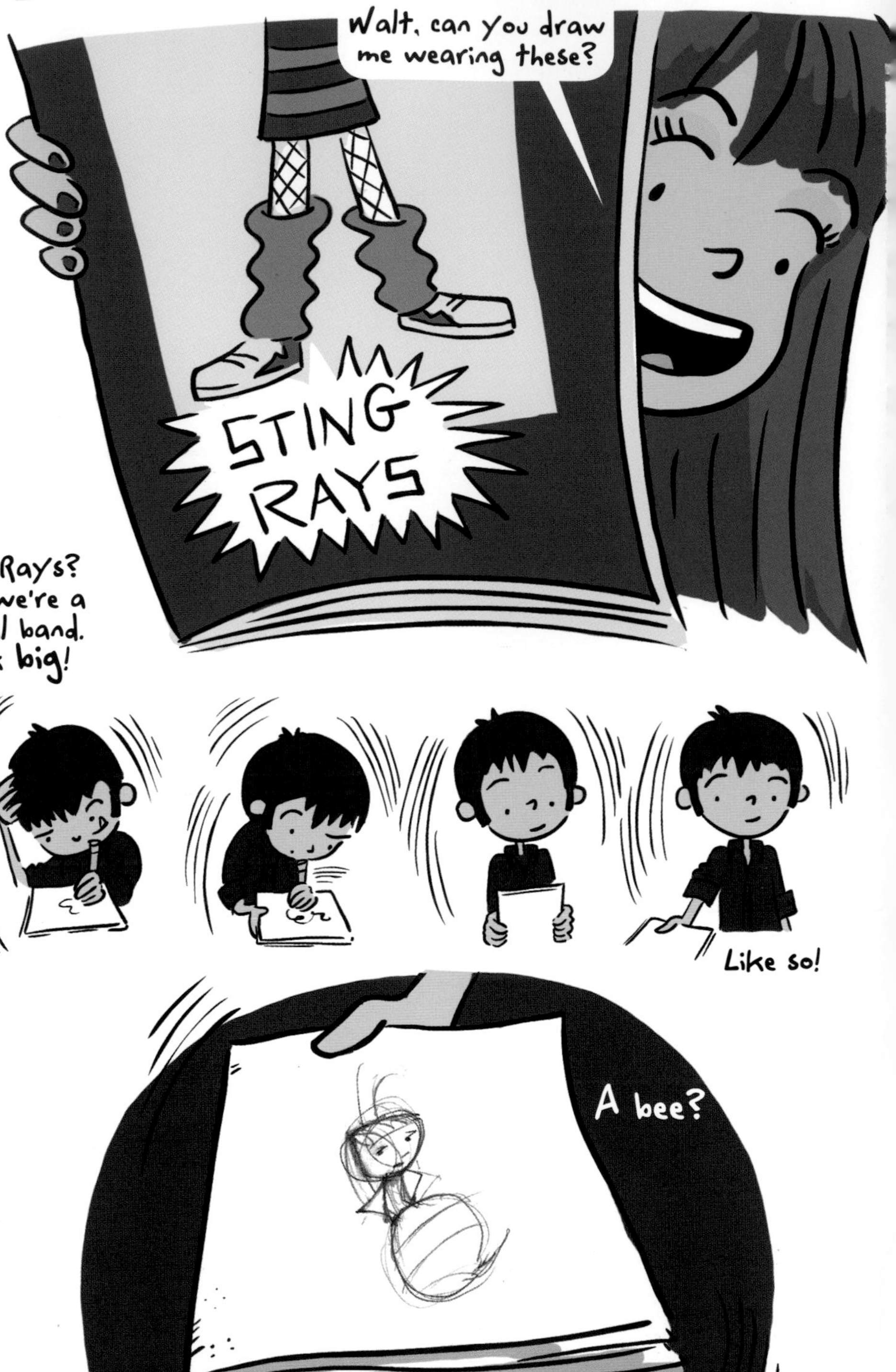
Walt, can you draw me wearing these?
STING RAYS
Sting Rays? Vita, we're a virtual band. Think **big**!
Like so!
A bee?

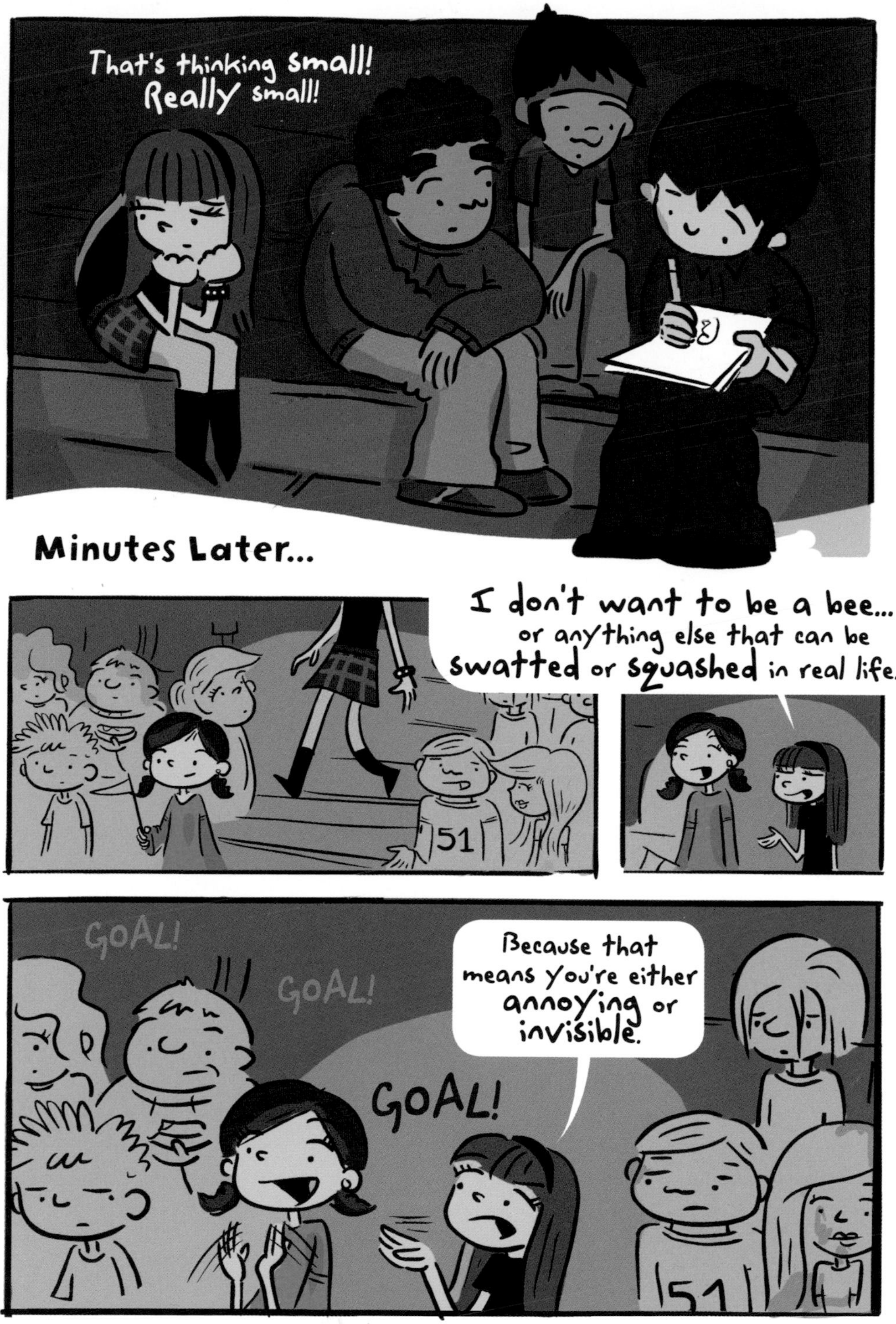
That's thinking small! Really small!
Minutes Later...
I don't want to be a bee... or anything else that can be swatted or squashed in real life....
51
GOAL!
GOAL!
GOAL!
Because that means you're either annoying or invisible.
51

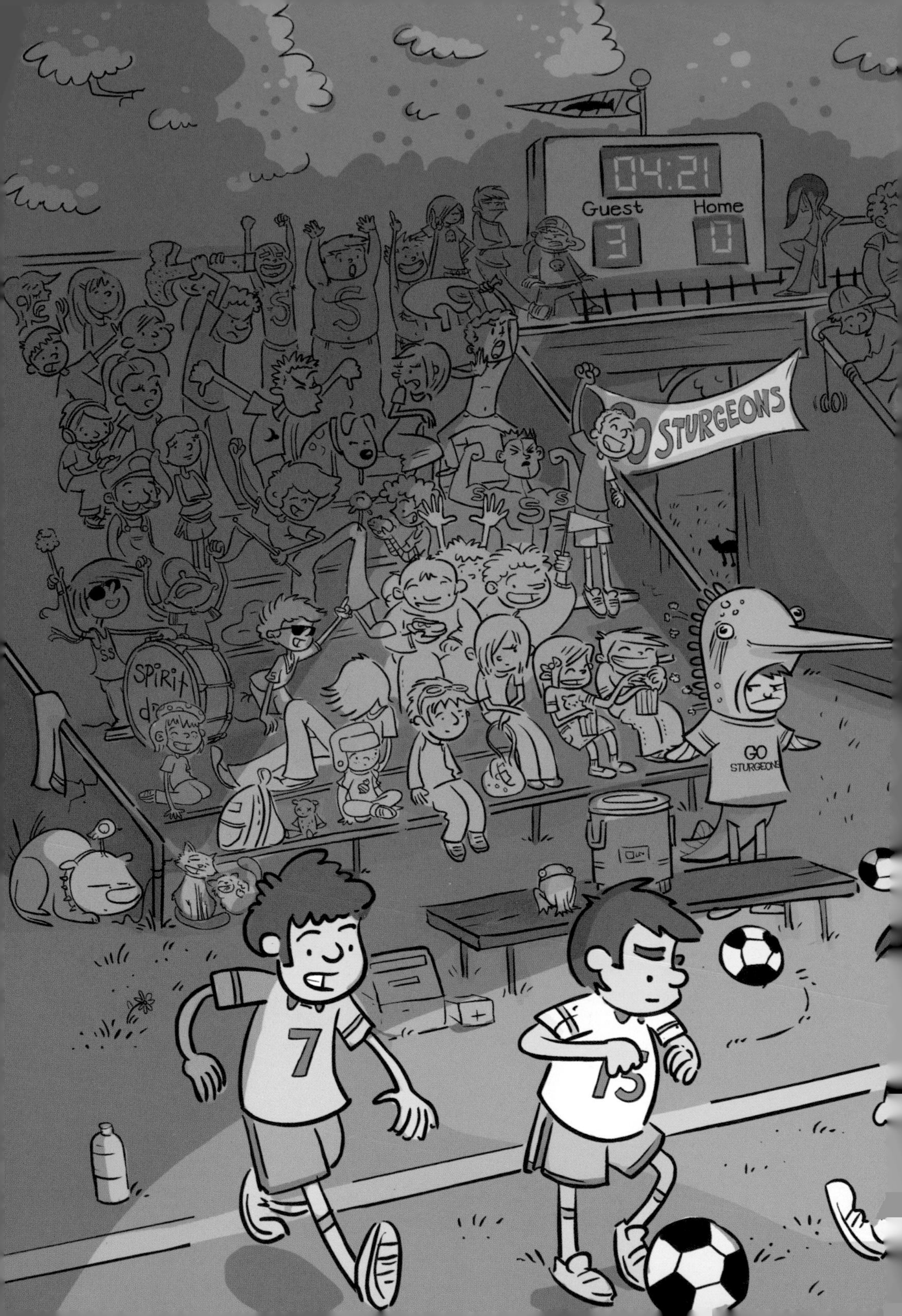
04:21
Guest
Home
3
0
GO STURGEONS
SPIRIT
GO
STURGEONS
7
13

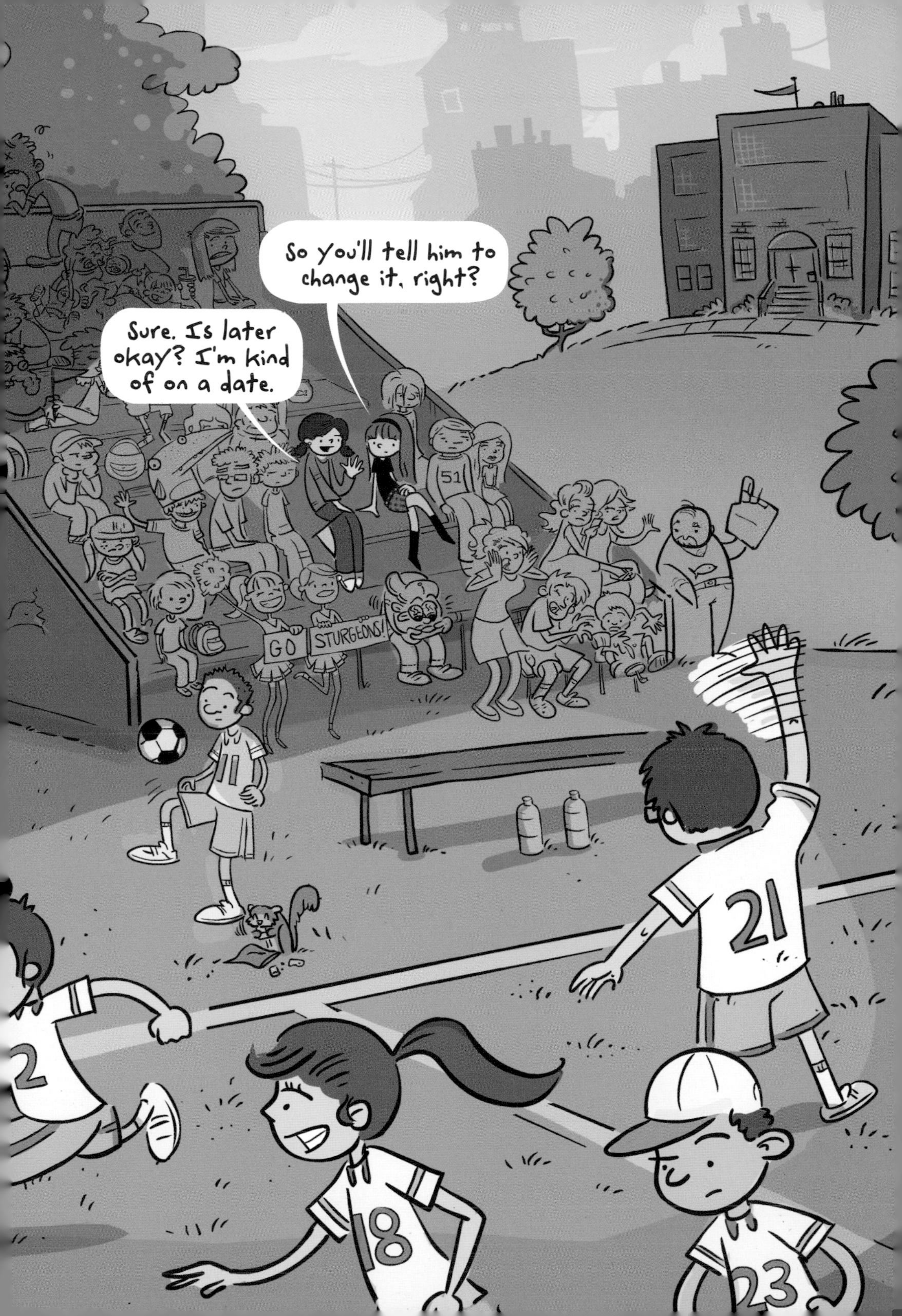
So you'll tell him to change it, right?
Sure. Is later okay? I'm kind of on a date.
GO STURGEONS!

10. One Song

I got a used guitar. My brother thought that I was nuts. But I know who I am...
Uh...
scribble
scribble
The sister of a handsome man.
Pablo! Quit it!
What? I'm just trying to help.
You can't help. Lyrics are very personal.
Don't make 'em too personal. You've got to sing them out loud.

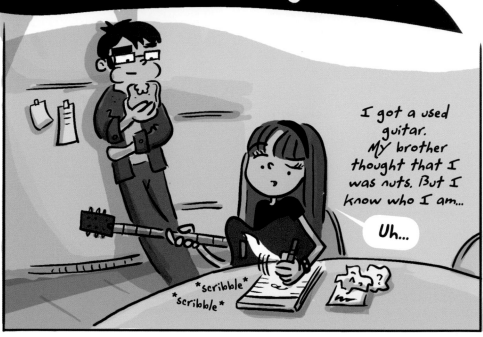

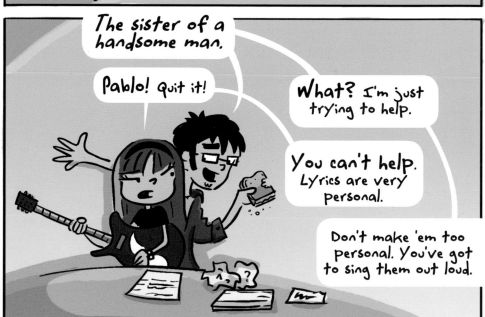

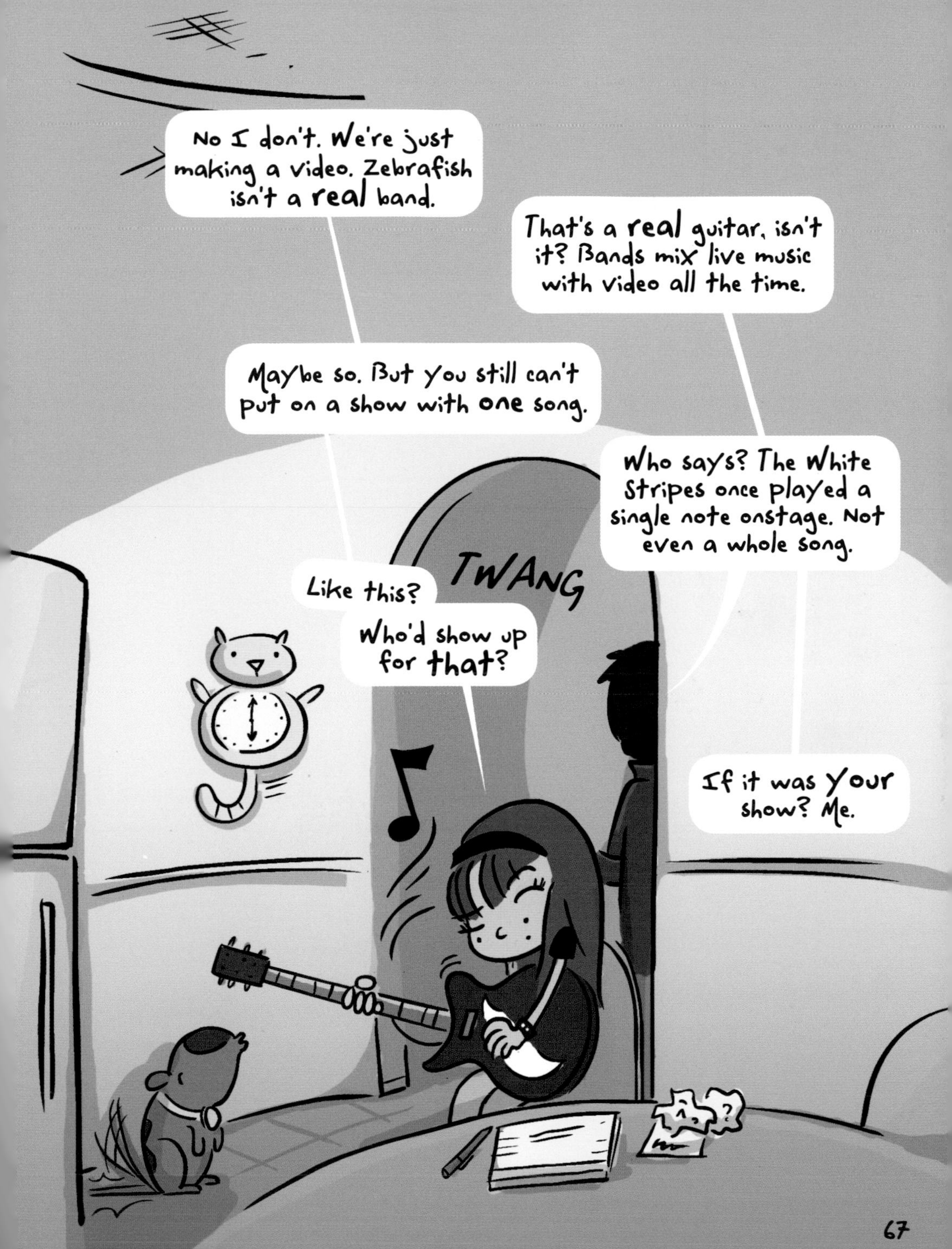
No I don't. We're just making a video. Zebrafish isn't a real band.
That's a real guitar, isn't it? Bands mix live music with video all the time.
Maybe so. But you still can't put on a show with one song.
Who says? The White Stripes once played a single note onstage. Not even a whole song.
Like this?
TWANG
Who'd show up for that?
If it was your show? Me.

11. Intensification

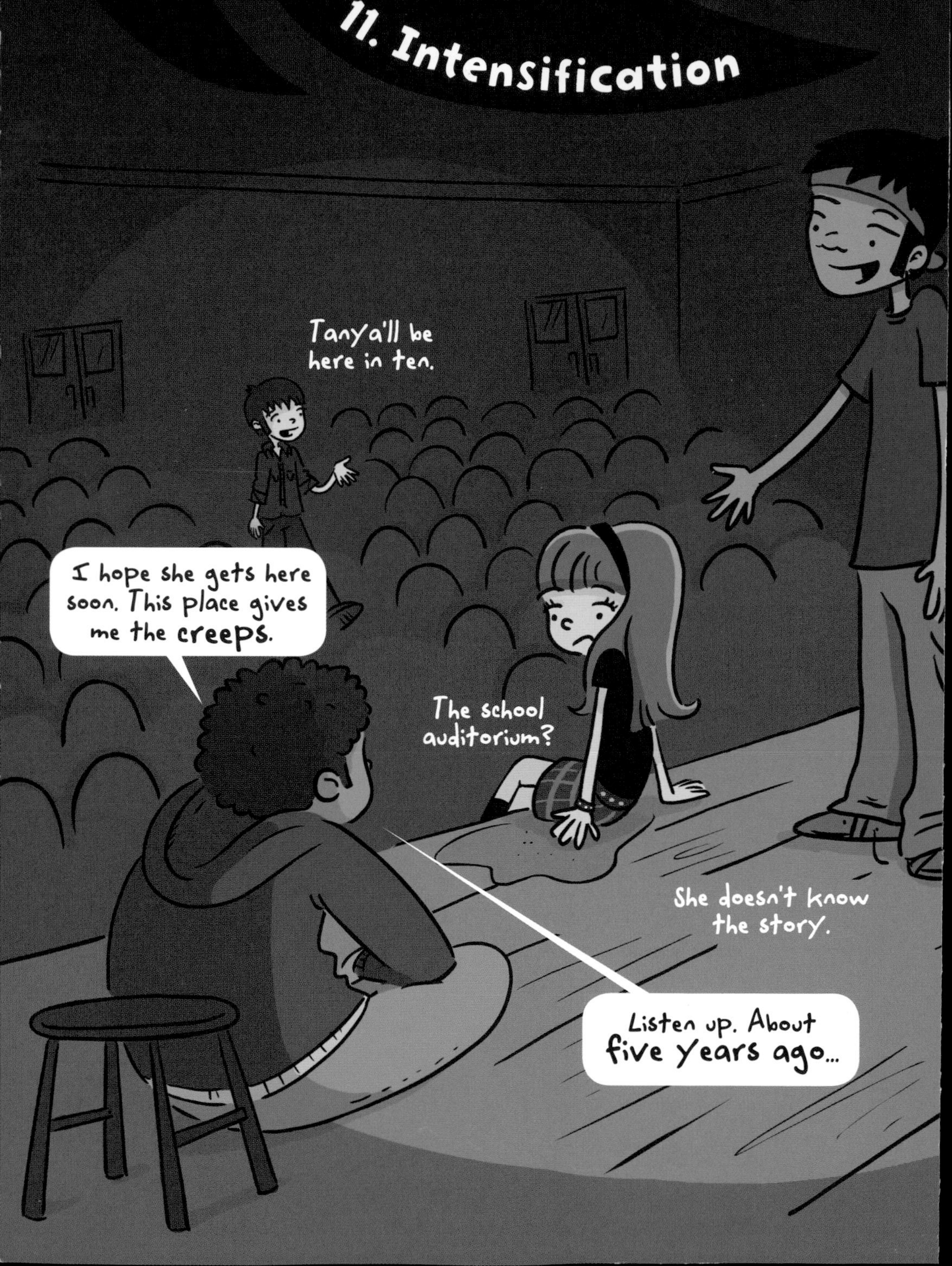

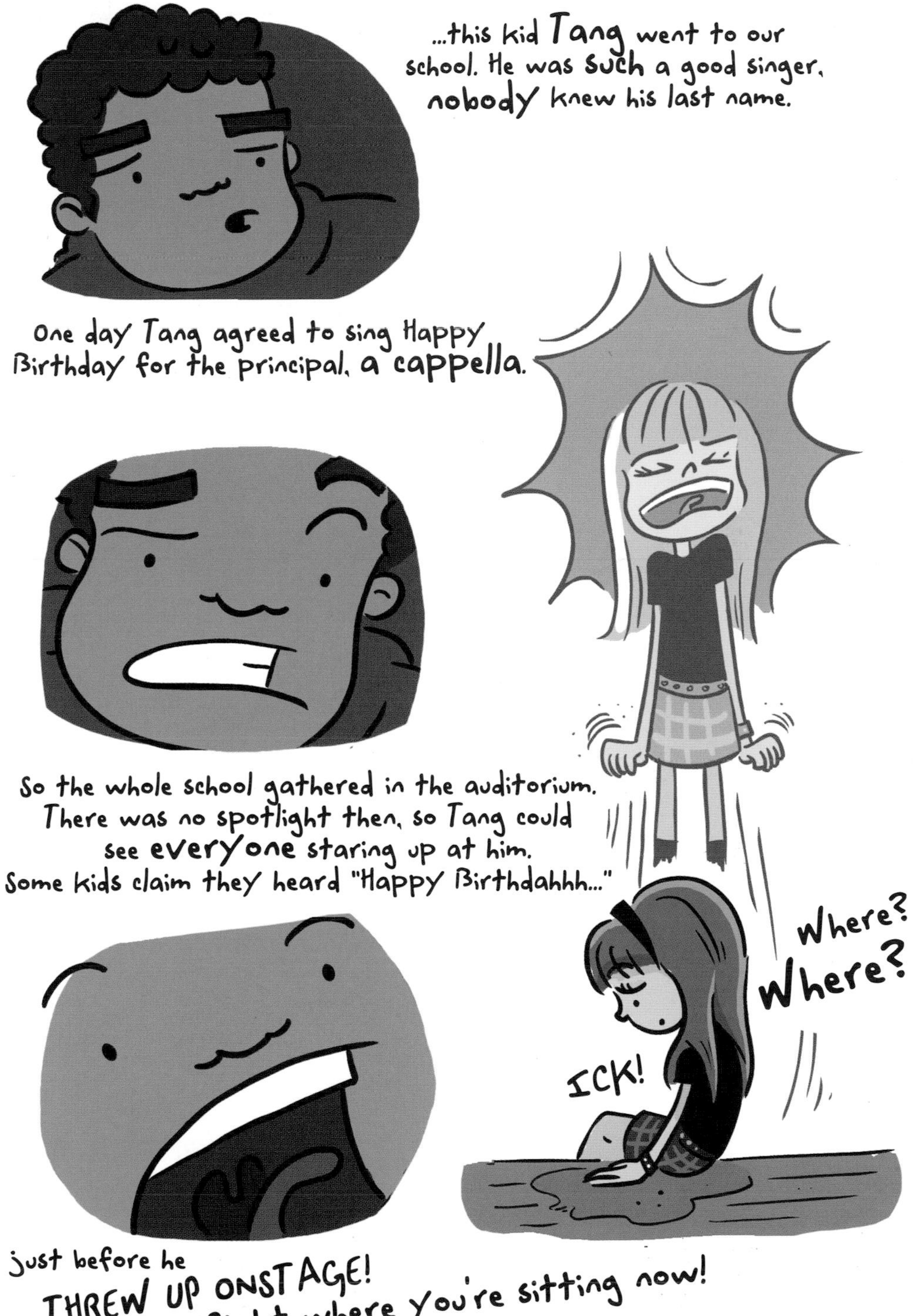

...this kid Tang went to our school. He was such a good singer, nobody knew his last name.
One day Tang agreed to sing Happy Birthday for the principal, a cappella.
So the whole school gathered in the auditorium. There was no spotlight then, so Tang could see everyone staring up at him. Some kids claim they heard "Happy Birthdahhh..."
Where? Where?
ICK!
just before he THREW UP ONSTAGE! Right where you're sitting now!

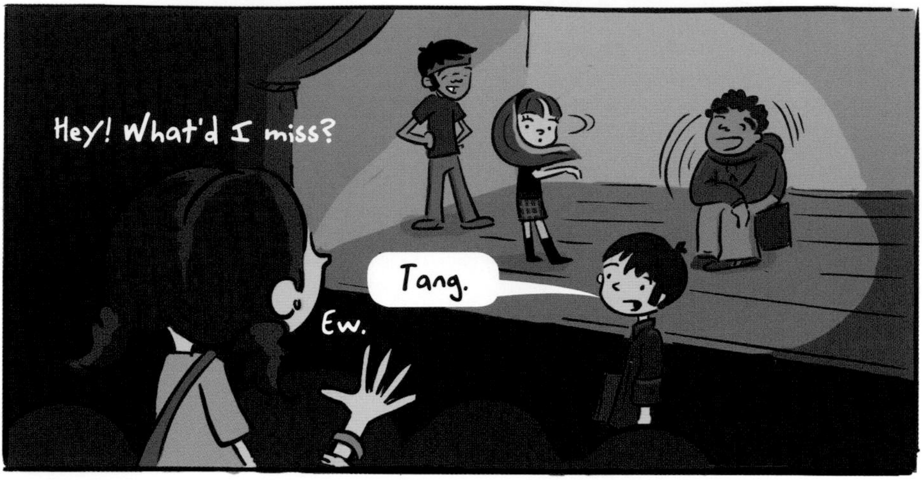
Hey! What'd I miss?
Tang.
Ew.

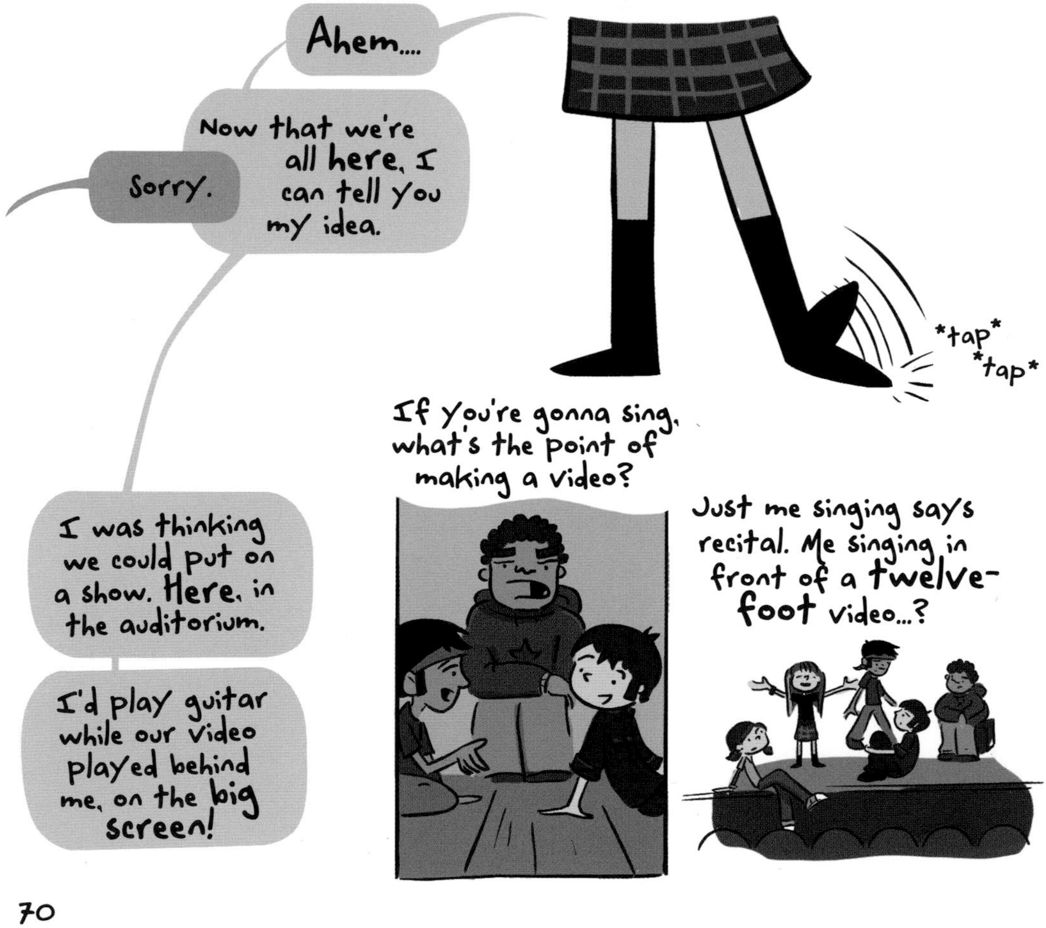
Ahem....
Now that we're all here, I can tell you my idea.
Sorry.
tap
tap
I was thinking we could put on a show. Here, in the auditorium.
I'd play guitar while our video played behind me, on the big screen!
If you're gonna sing, what's the point of making a video?
Just me singing says recital. Me singing in front of a twelve-foot video...?

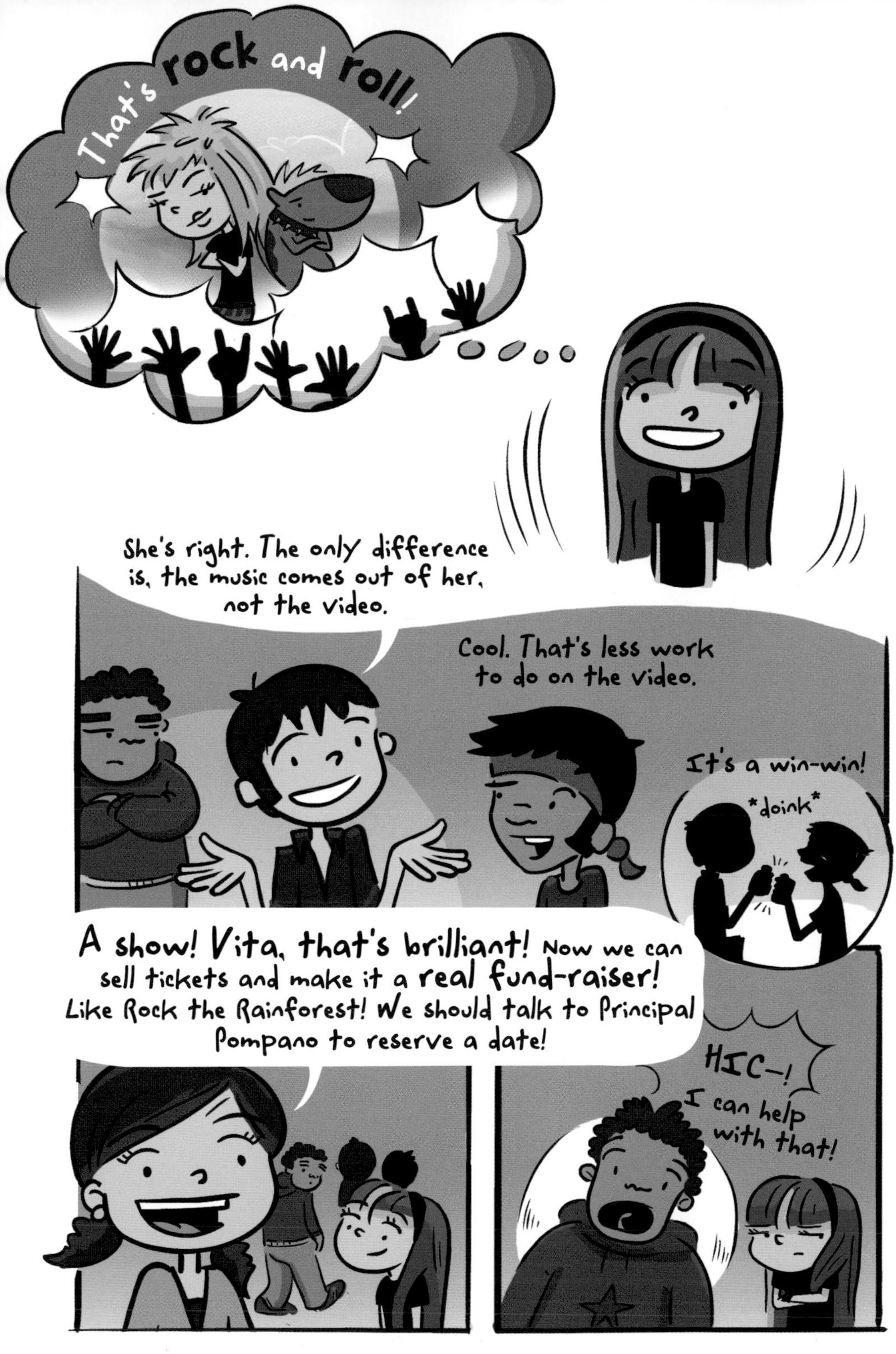
That's rock and roll!
She's right. The only difference is, the music comes out of her, not the video.
Cool. That's less work to do on the video.
It's a win-win!
doink
A show! Vita, that's brilliant! Now we can sell tickets and make it a real fund-raiser! Like Rock the Rainforest! We should talk to Principal Pompano to reserve a date!
HIC-!
I can help with that!

12. Impact

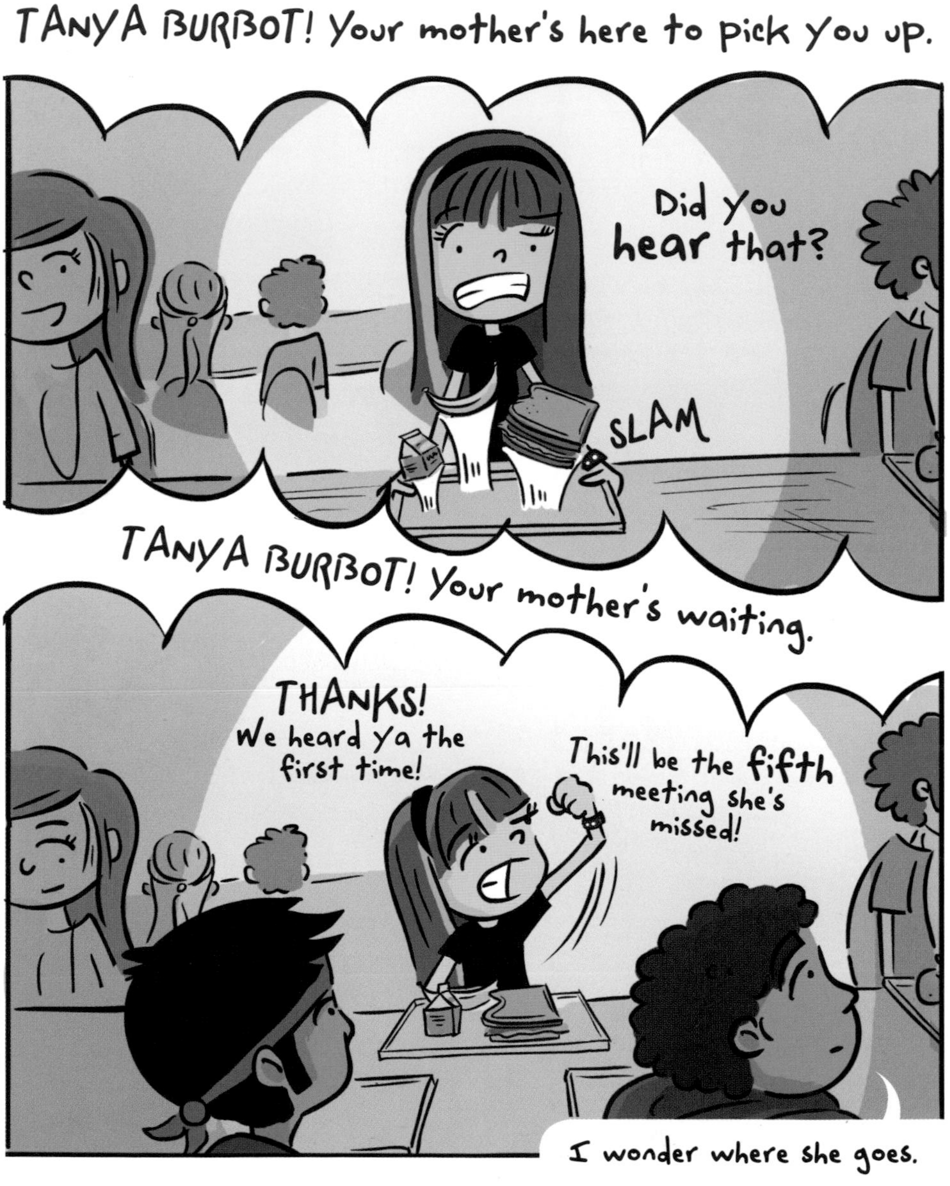
TANYA BURBOT! Your mother's here to pick you up.
Did you hear that?
SLAM
TANYA BURBOT! Your mother's waiting.
THANKS! We heard ya the first time!
This'll be the fifth meeting she's missed!
I wonder where she goes.

After School...

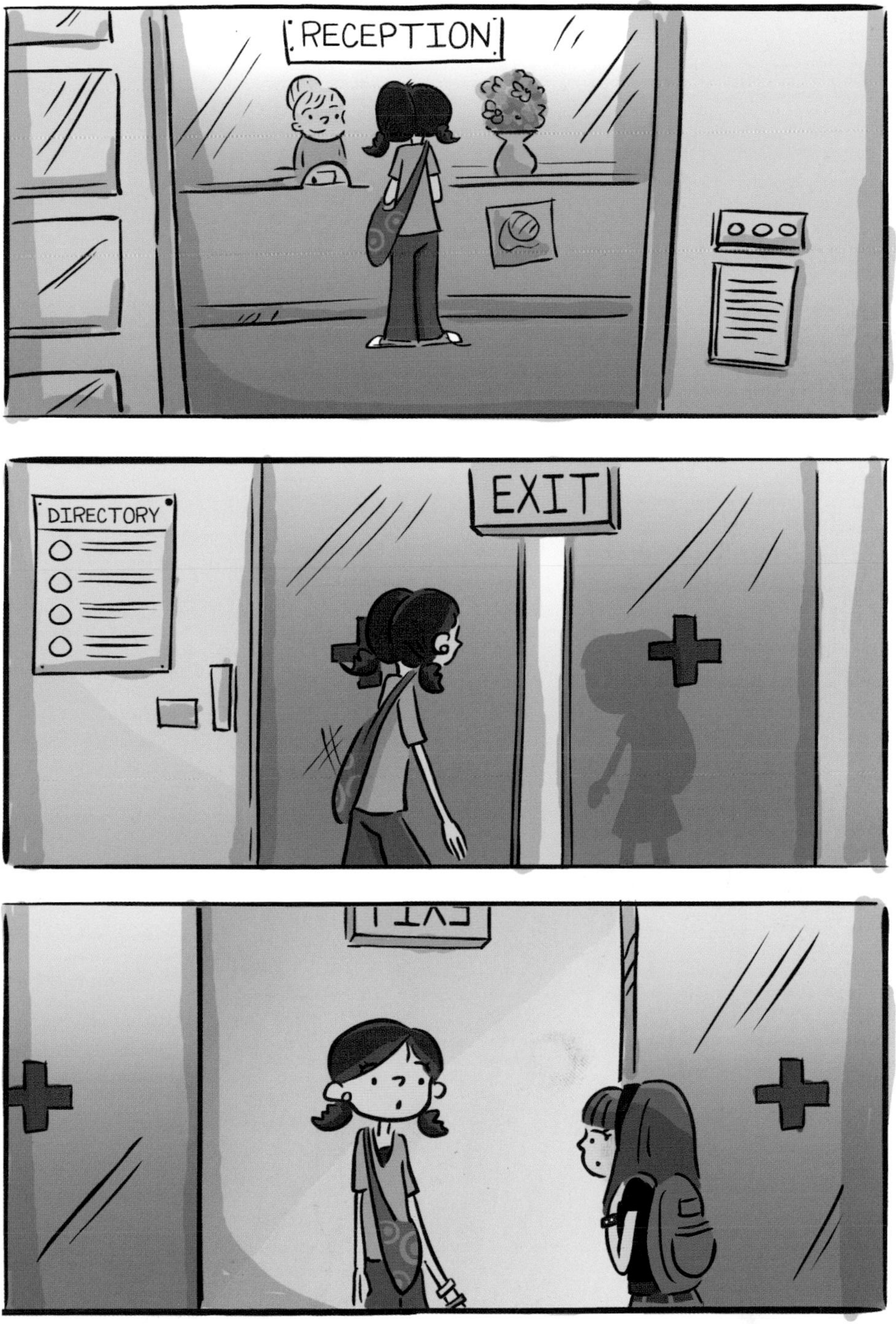
RECEPTION
DIRECTORY
EXIT

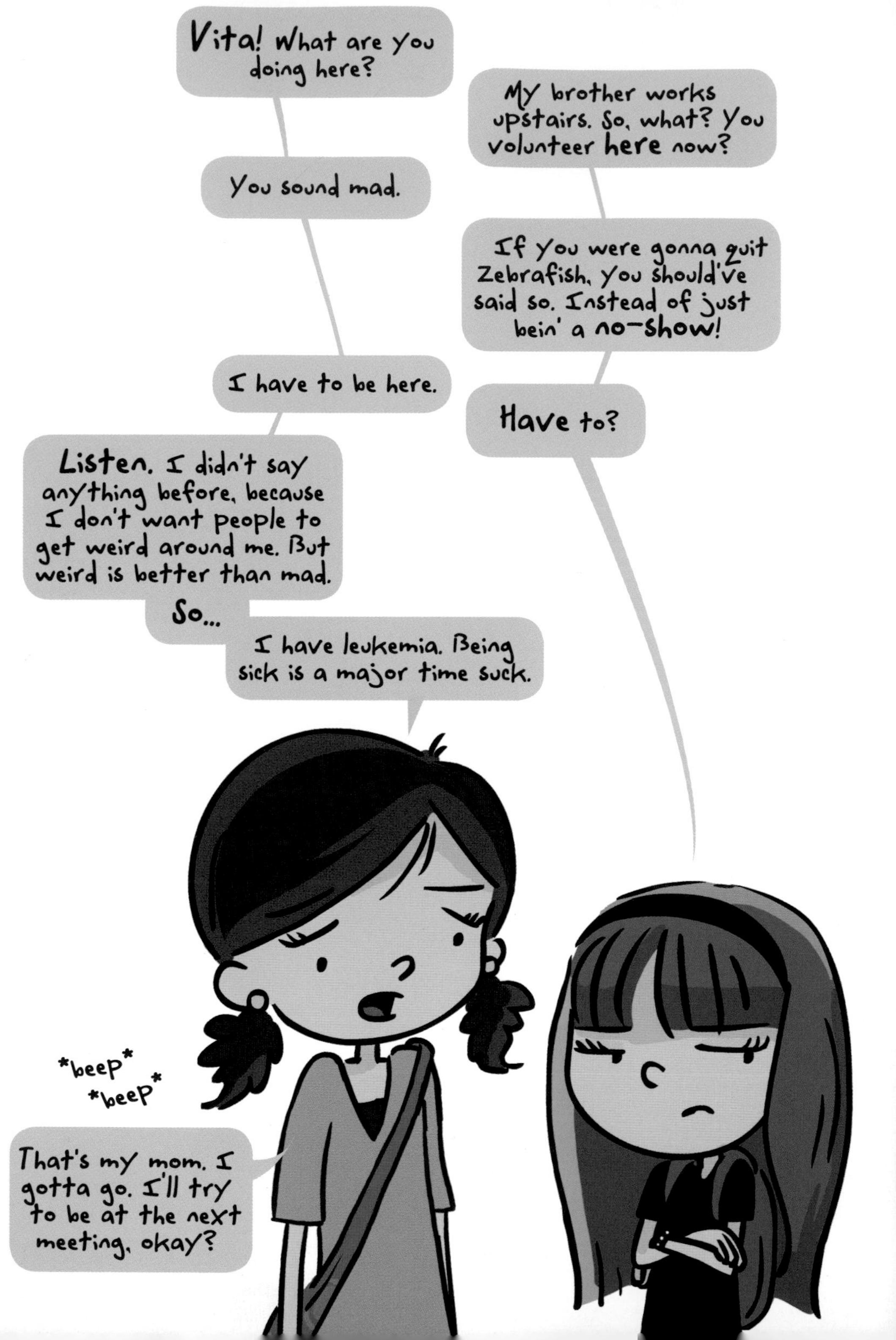
Vita! What are you doing here?
My brother works upstairs. So, what? You volunteer here now?
You sound mad.
If you were gonna quit Zebrafish, you should've said so. Instead of just bein' a no-show!
I have to be here.
Have to?
Listen. I didn't say anything before, because I don't want people to get weird around me. But weird is better than mad.
So...
I have leukemia. Being sick is a major time suck.
beep *beep*
That's my mom. I gotta go. I'll try to be at the next meeting, okay?

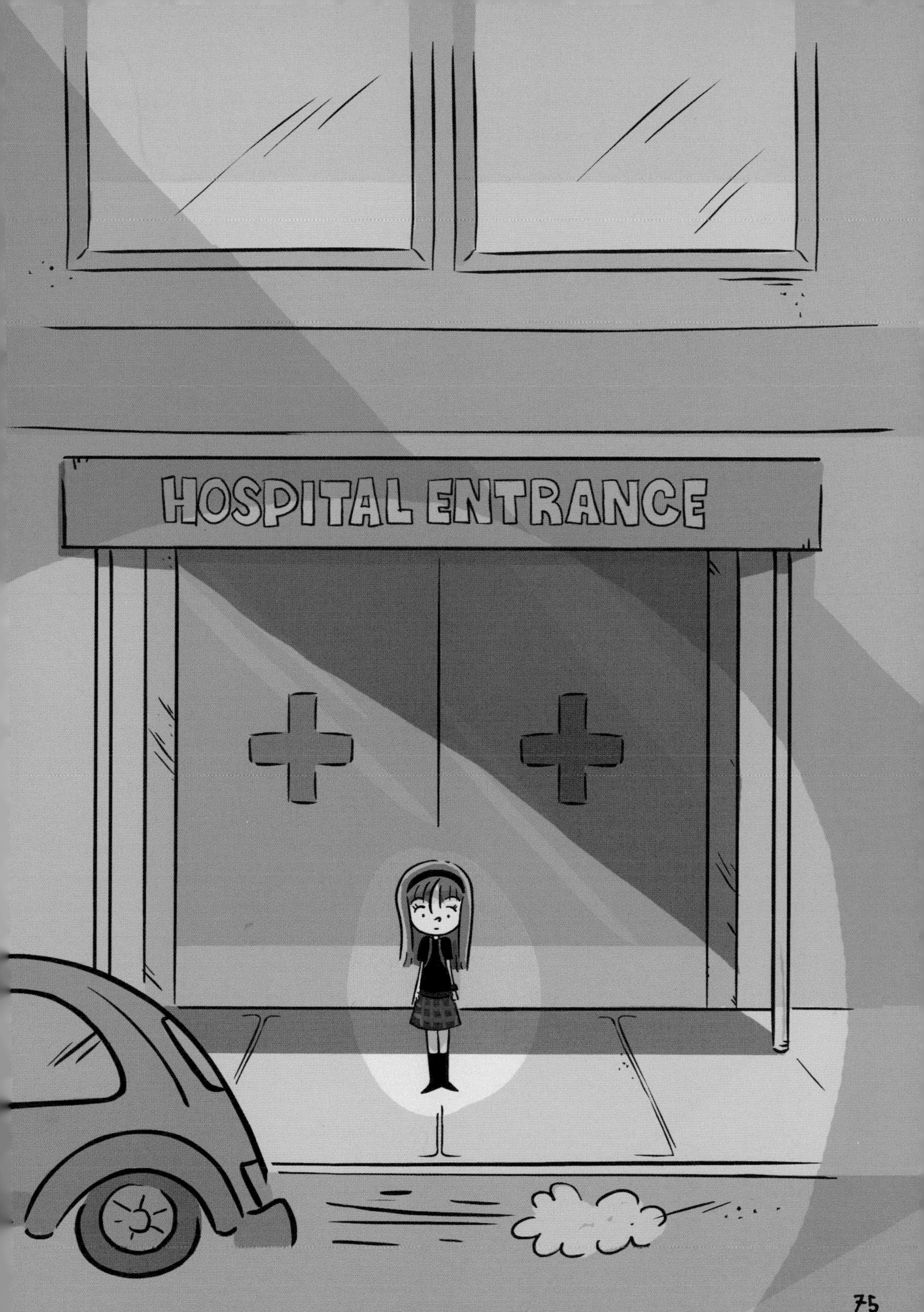
HOSPITAL ENTRANCE

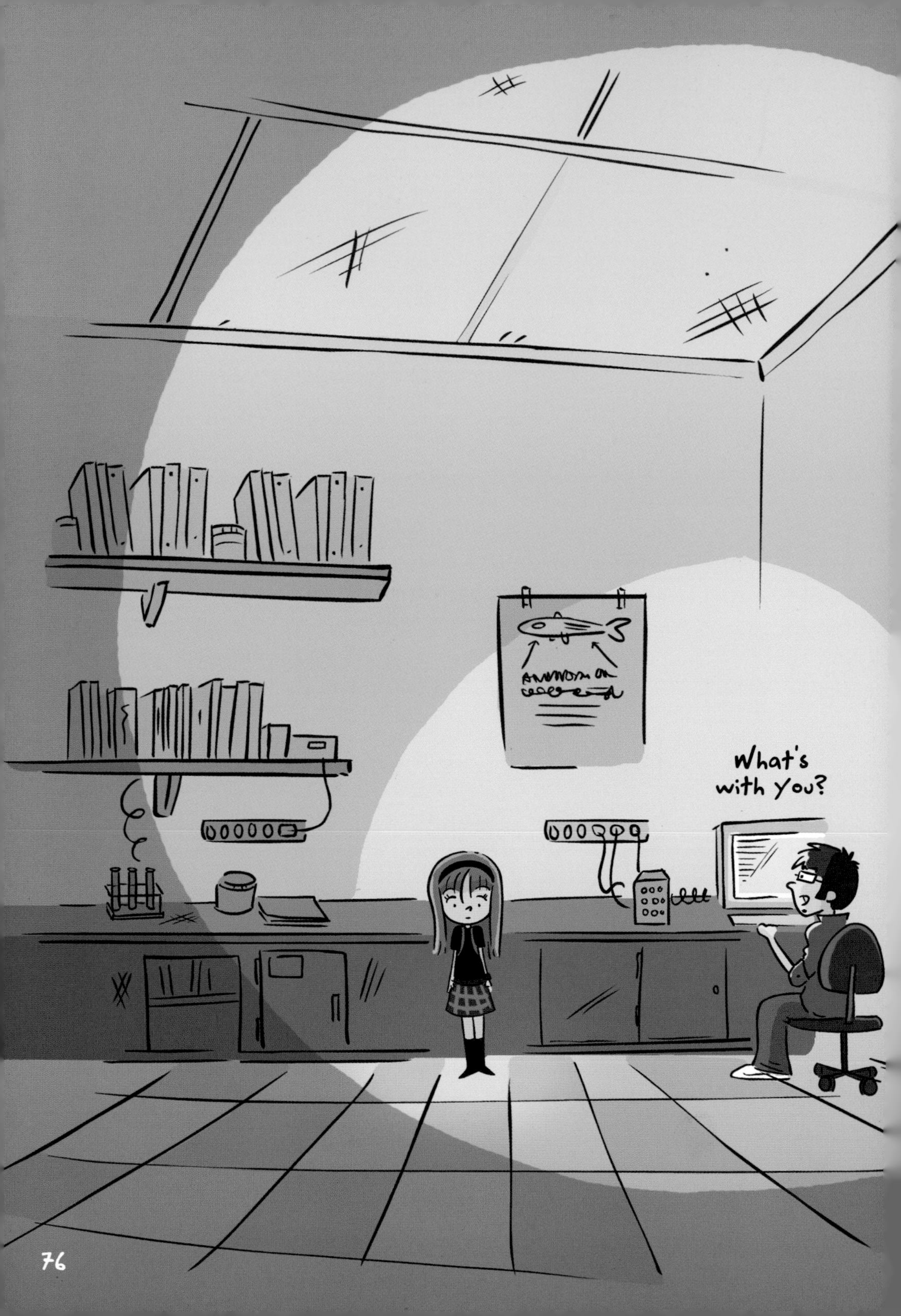
What's with you?

Leukemia's cancer,
right?

Yeah. Why?

Is it a bad one?

It's usually treatable.
But patients have to
go through a lot of
chemo. Sometimes for
up to two years.

Chemo didn't
work for Mom.

Well...chemo's not a cure.
It just kills cancer cells. The
problem is, the cells can
spread. With Mom's kind of
cancer, the cells spread faster
than the chemo could kill them.

sigh
C'mon, Vita. Let's take a walk.

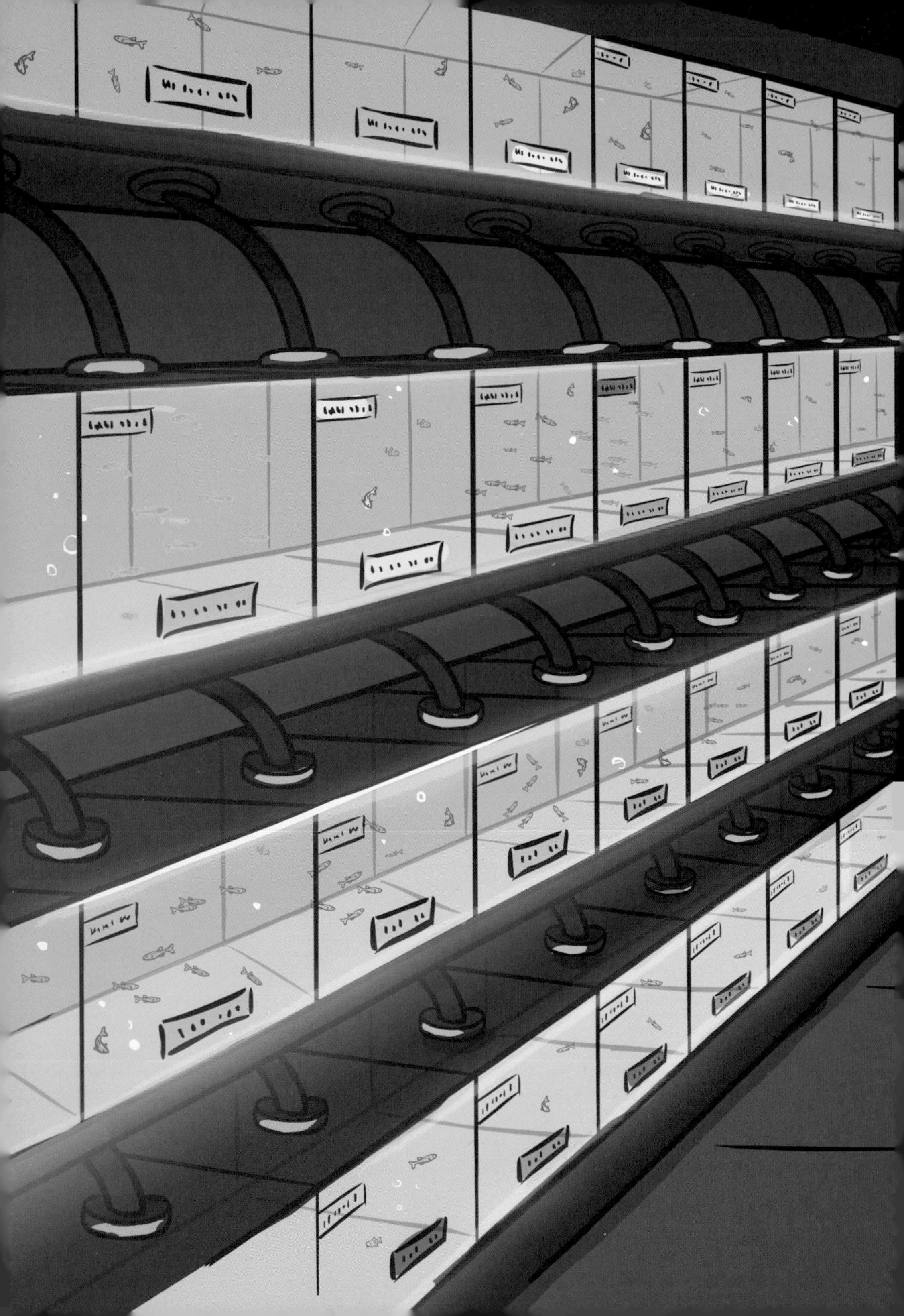

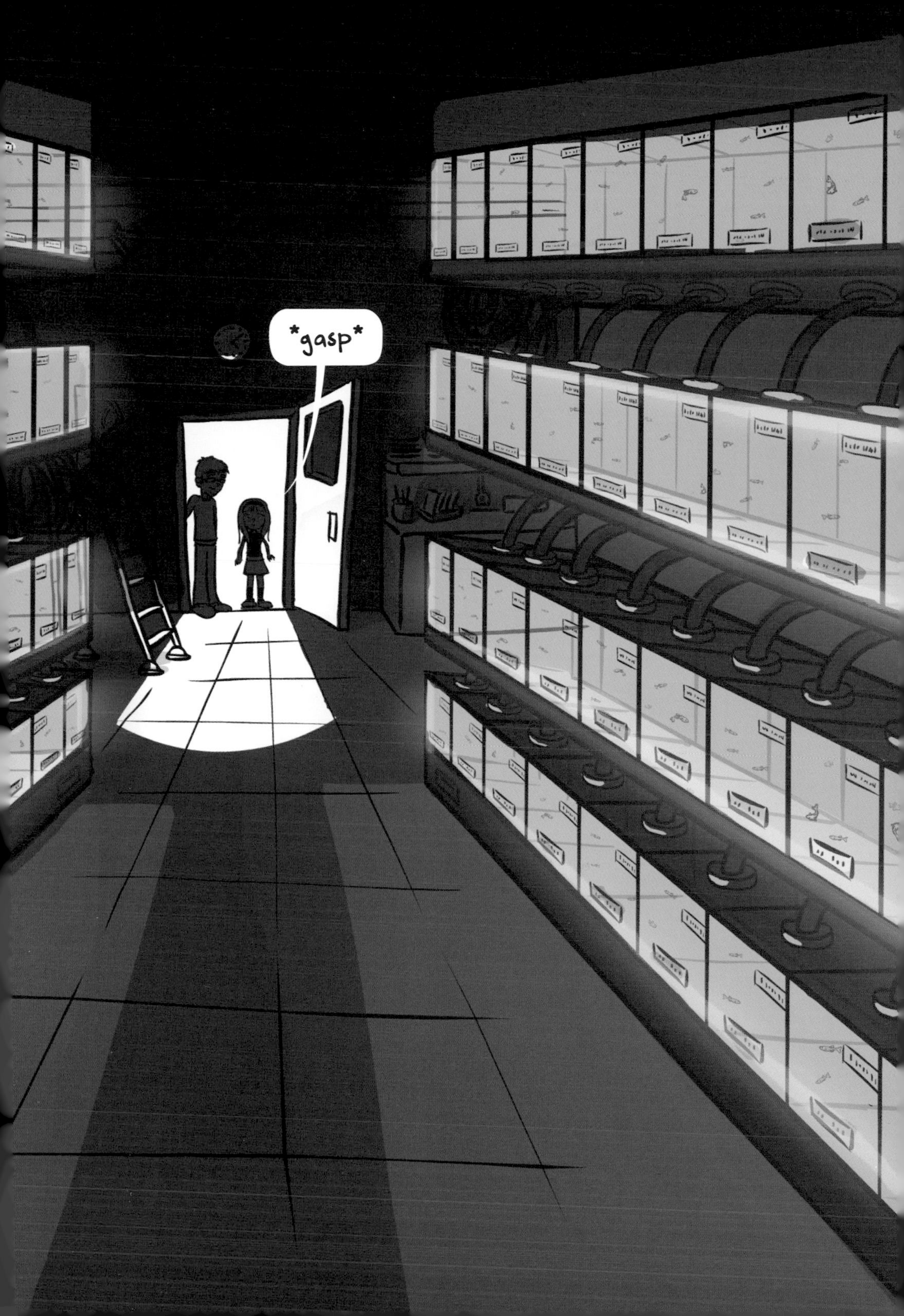
gasp

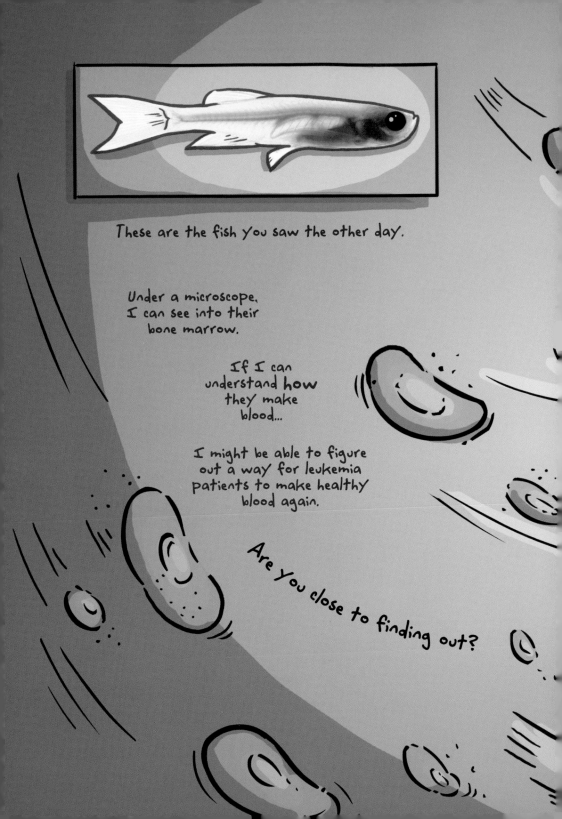

These are the fish you saw the other day.

Under a microscope, I can see into their bone marrow.

If I can understand how they make blood...

I might be able to figure out a way for leukemia patients to make healthy blood again.

Are you close to finding out?

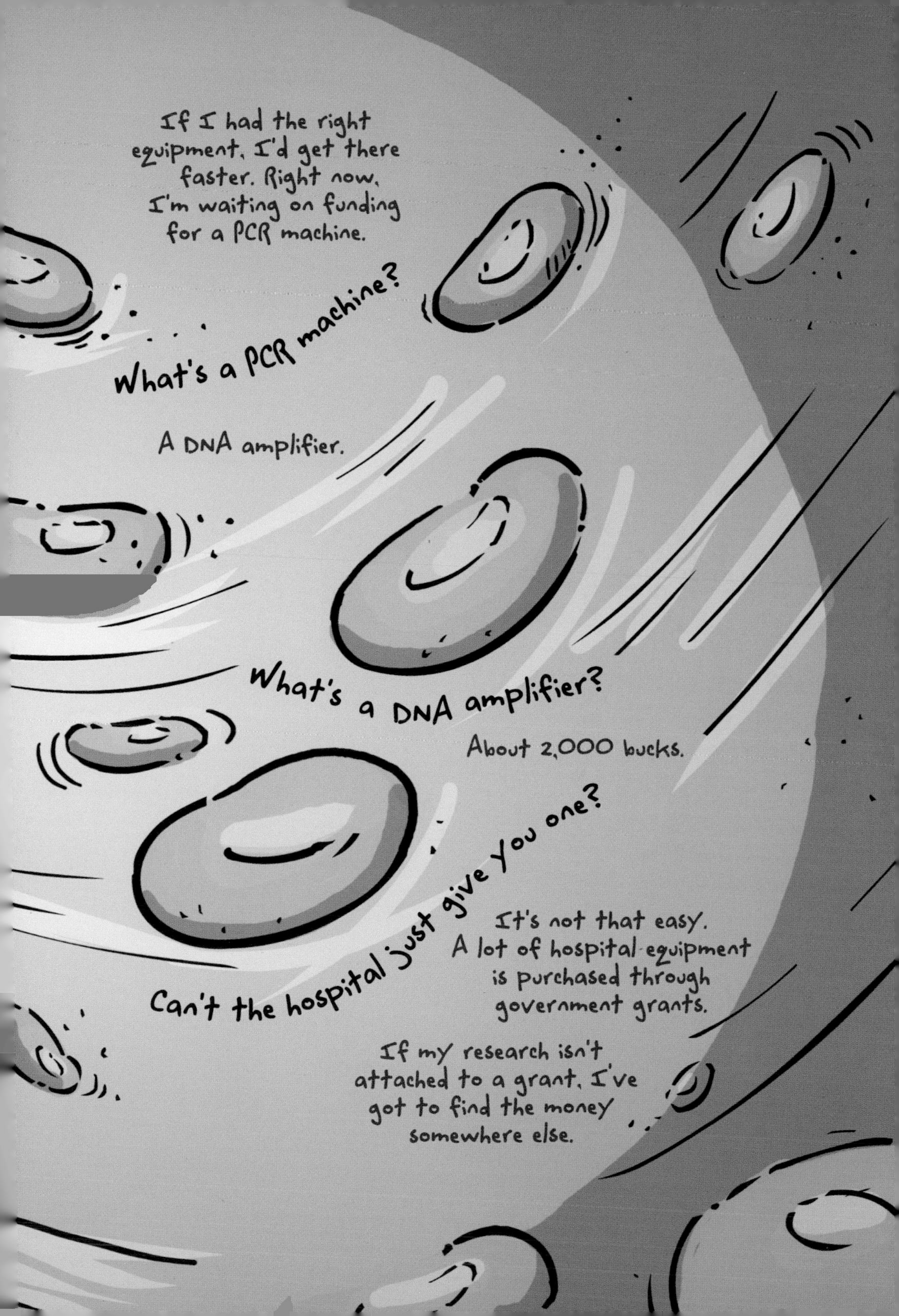
If I had the right equipment, I'd get there faster. Right now, I'm waiting on funding for a PCR machine.
What's a PCR machine?
A DNA amplifier.
What's a DNA amplifier?
About 2,000 bucks.
Can't the hospital just give you one?
It's not that easy. A lot of hospital equipment is purchased through government grants.
If my research isn't attached to a grant, I've got to find the money somewhere else.

13. Intervention

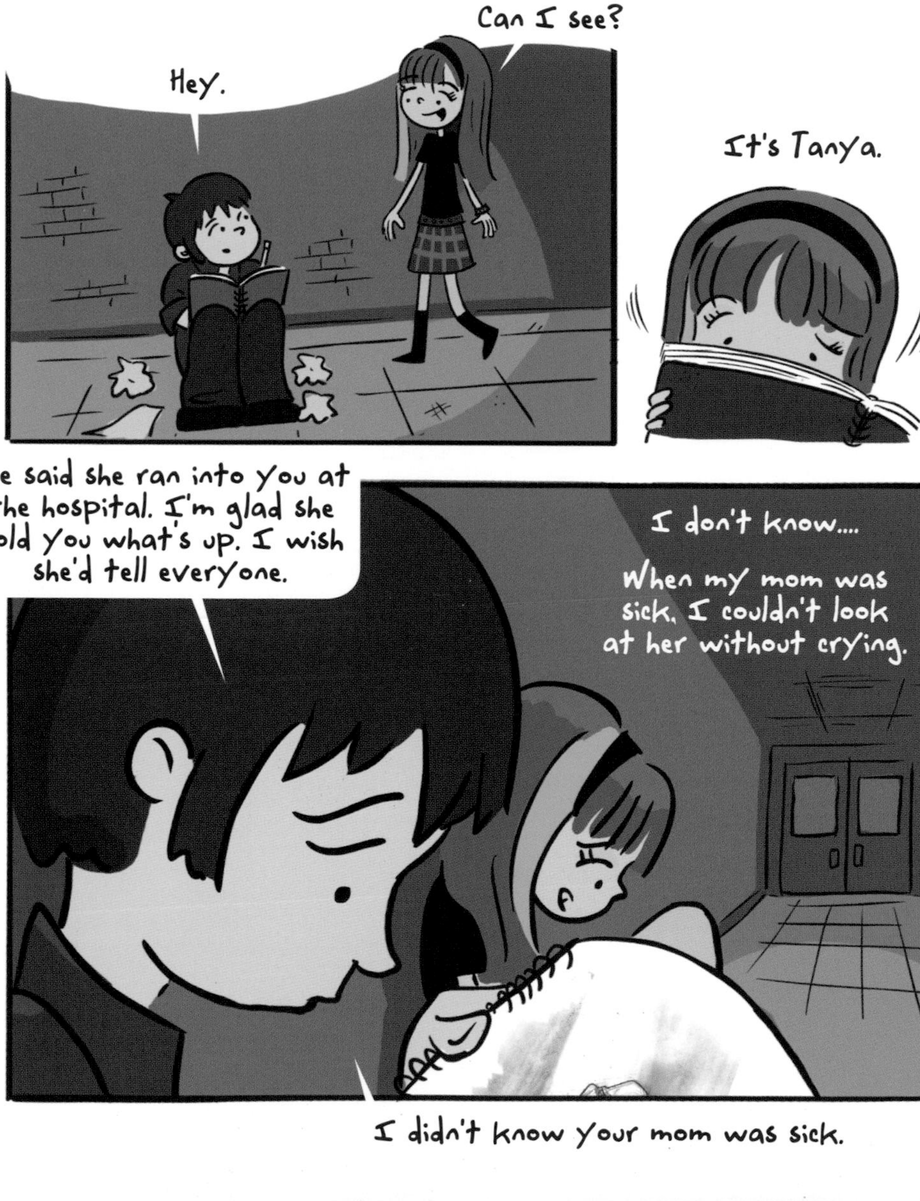
Hey.
Can I see?
It's Tanya.
She said she ran into you at the hospital. I'm glad she told you what's up. I wish she'd tell everyone.
I don't know....
When my mom was sick, I couldn't look at her without crying.
I didn't know your mom was sick.

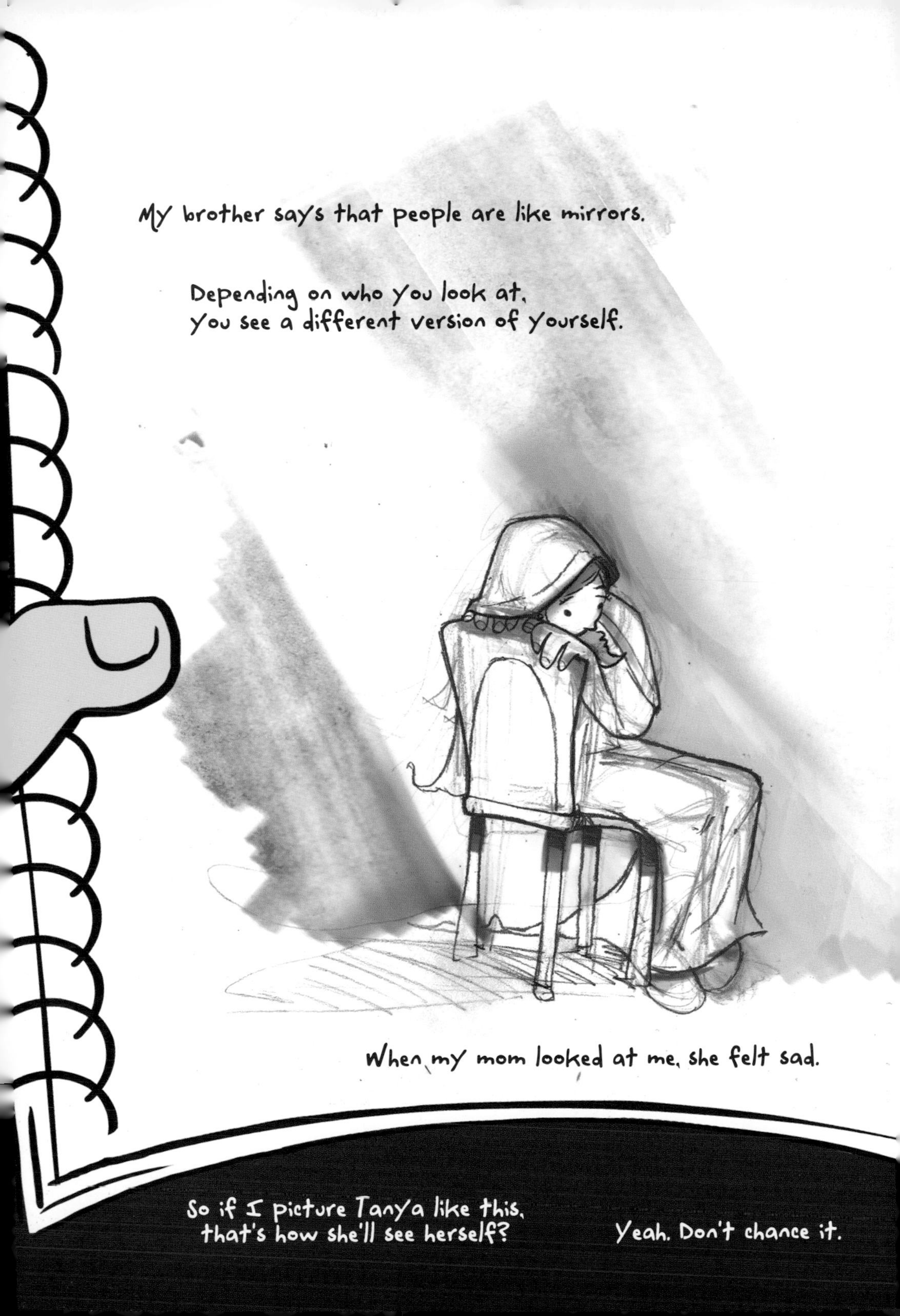
My brother says that people are like mirrors.
Depending on who you look at, you see a different version of yourself.
When my mom looked at me, she felt sad.
So if I picture Tanya like this, that's how she'll see herself?
Yeah. Don't chance it.

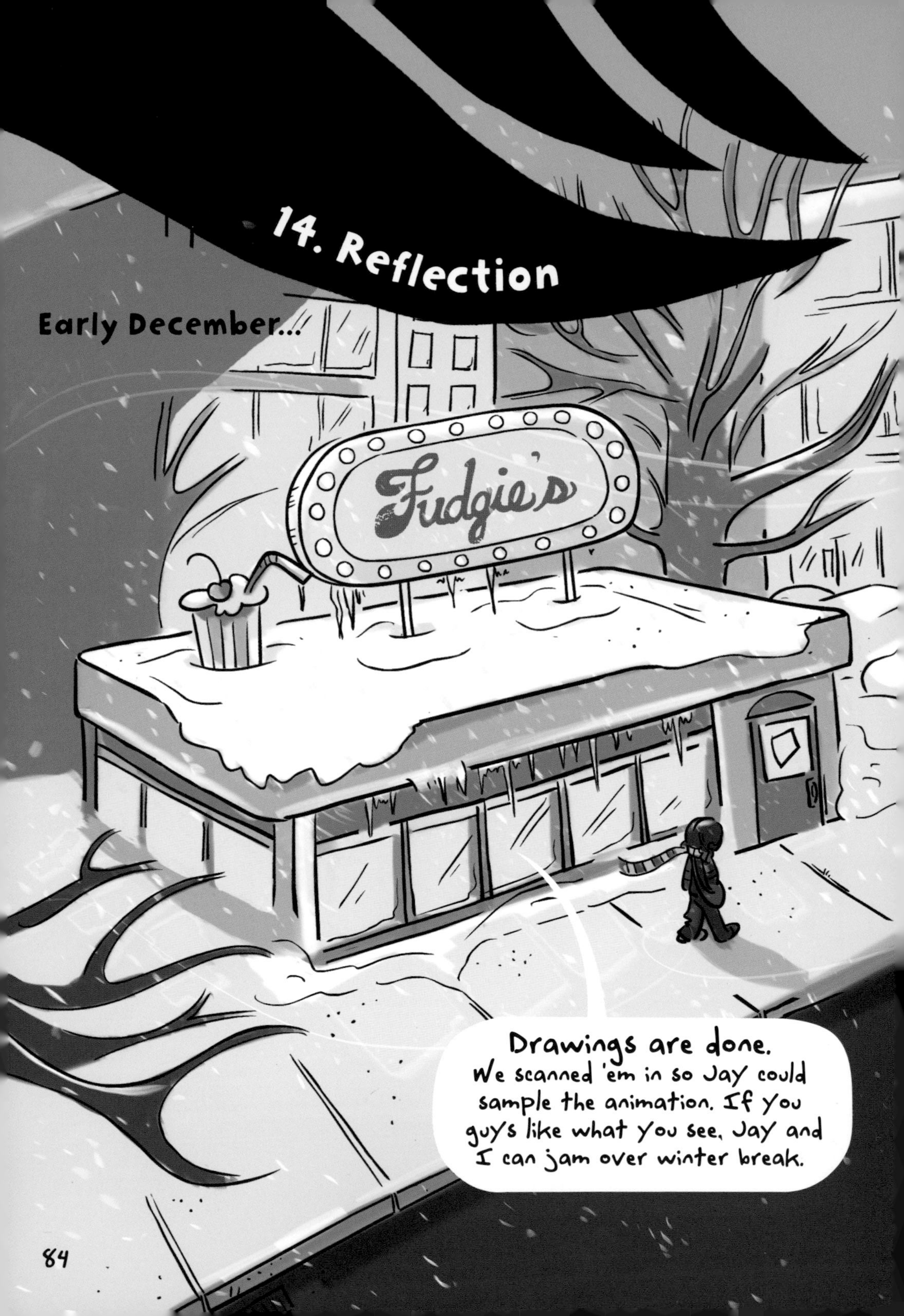

14. Reflection
Early December...
Fudgie's
Drawings are done. We scanned 'em in so Jay could sample the animation. If you guys like what you see, Jay and I can jam over winter break.

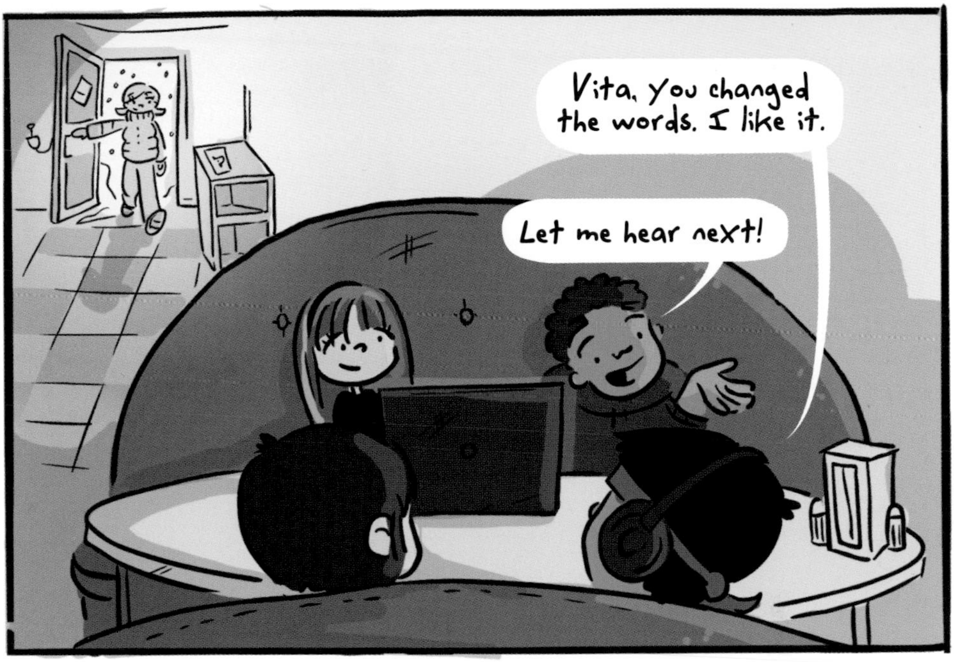
Vita, you changed the words. I like it.
Let me hear next!

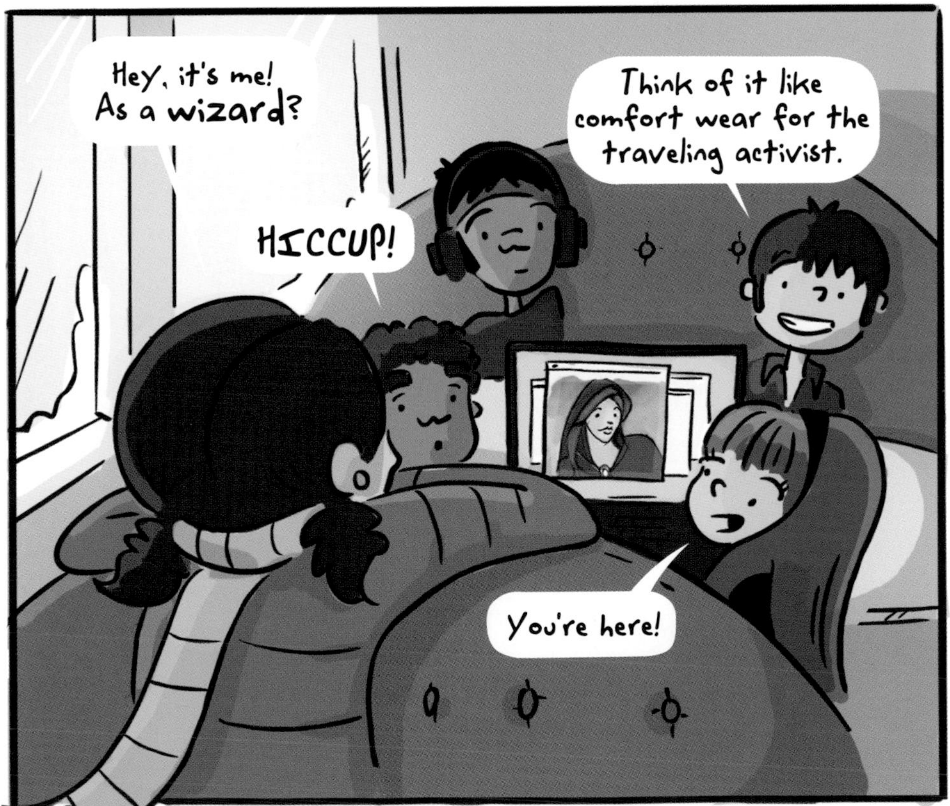
Hey, it's me! As a wizard?
Think of it like comfort wear for the traveling activist.
HICCUP!
You're here!

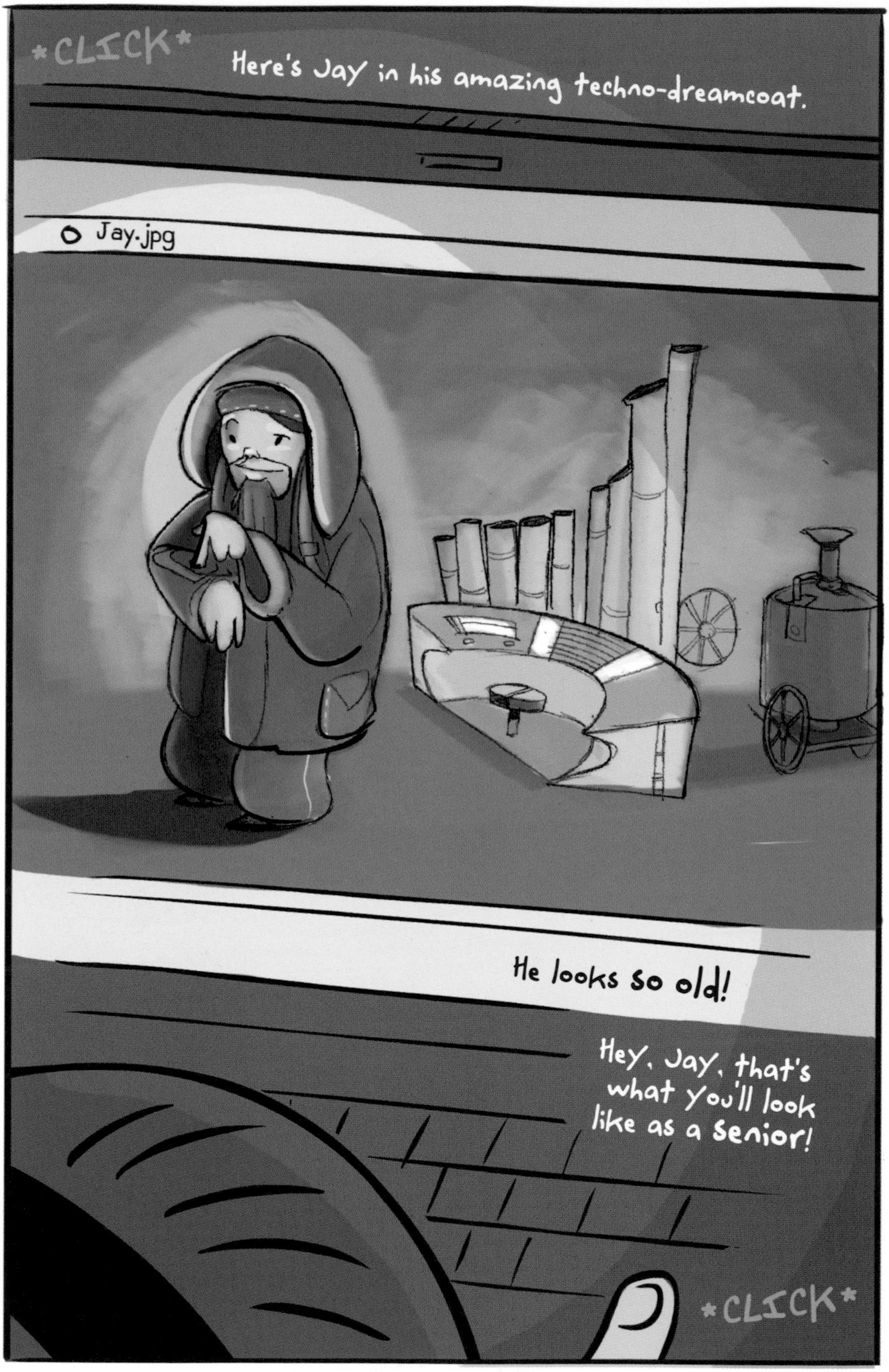
CLICK
Here's Jay in his amazing techno-dreamcoat.
Jay.jpg
He looks so old!
Hey, Jay, that's what you'll look like as a senior!
CLICK

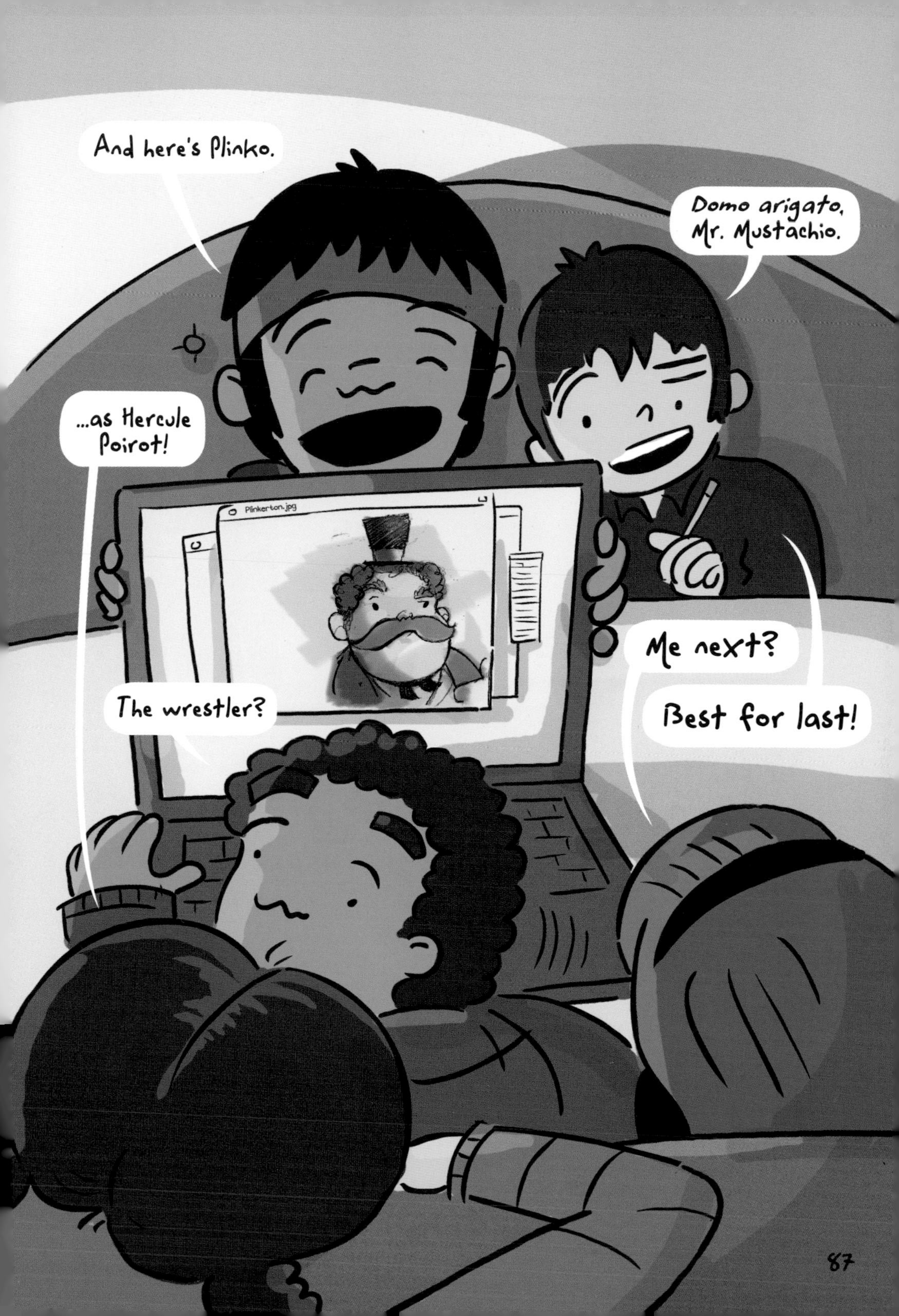
And here's Plinko.
Domo arigato, Mr. Mustachio.
...as Hercule Poirot!
Plinkerton.jpg
The wrestler?
Me next?
Best for last!

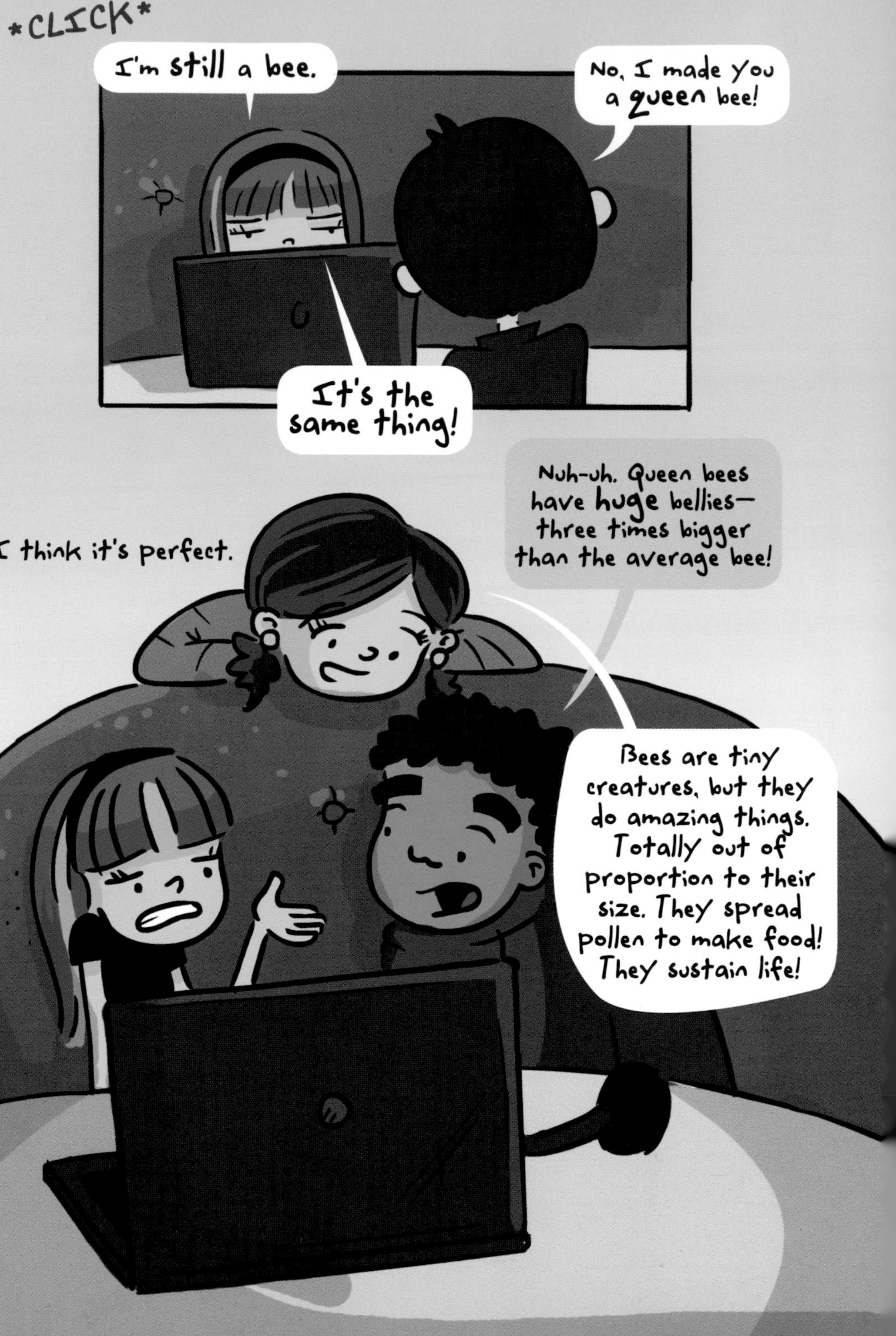
CLICK
I'm still a bee.
No, I made you a queen bee!
It's the same thing!
I think it's perfect.
Nuh-uh. Queen bees have huge bellies—three times bigger than the average bee!
Bees are tiny creatures, but they do amazing things. Totally out of proportion to their size. They spread pollen to make food! They sustain life!

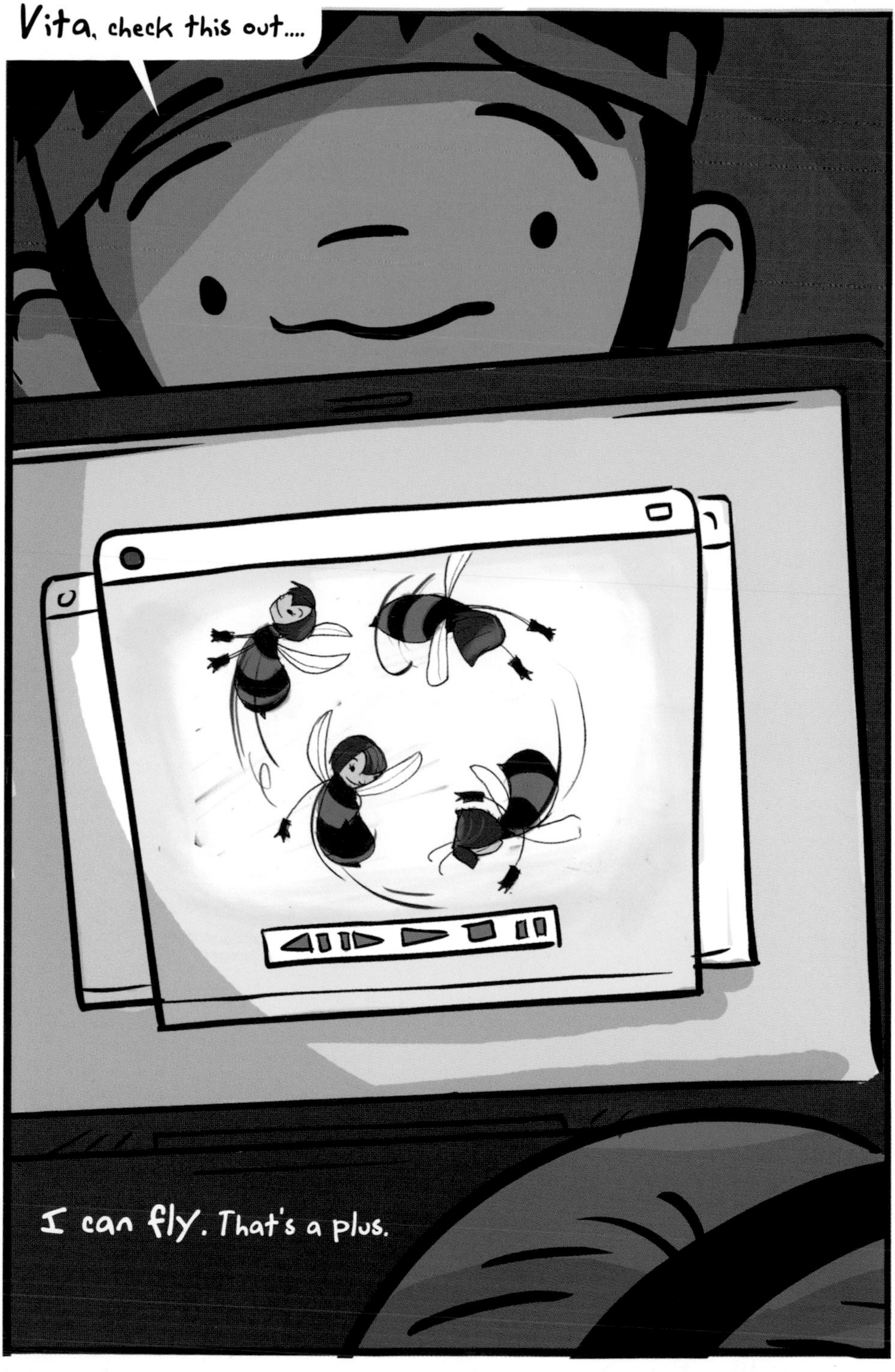

Vita, check this out....
I can fly. That's a plus.

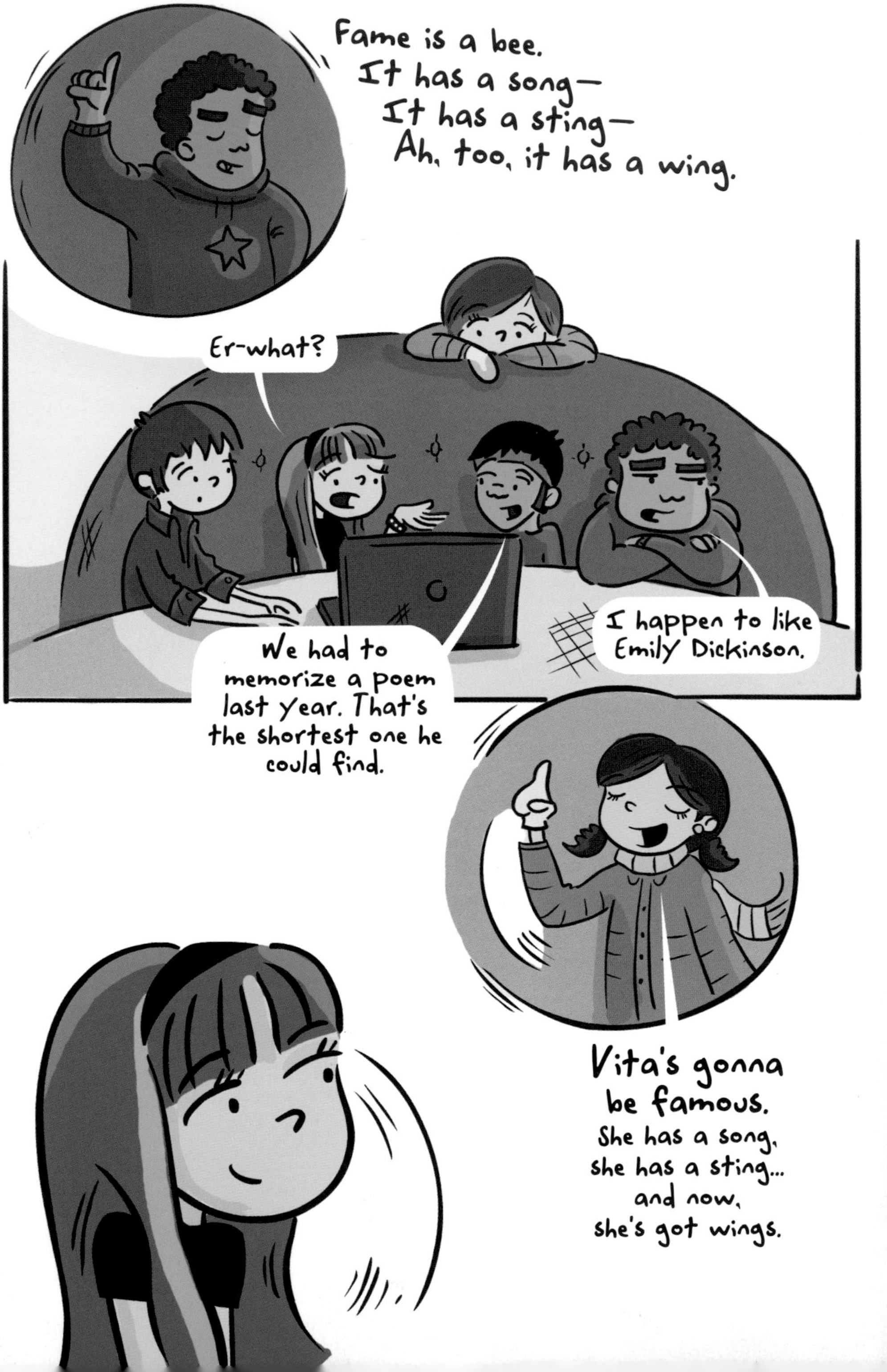

Fame is a bee.
It has a song—
It has a sting—
Ah, too, it has a wing.
Er-what?
We had to memorize a poem last year. That's the shortest one he could find.
I happen to like Emily Dickinson.
Vita's gonna be famous.
She has a song, she has a sting... and now, she's got wings.

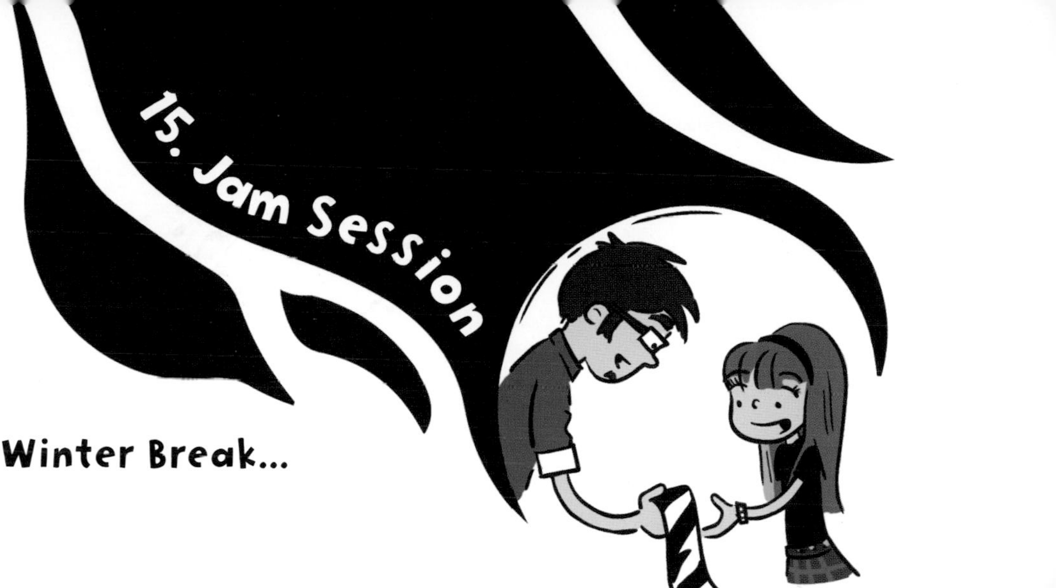
15. Jam Session

Winter Break...

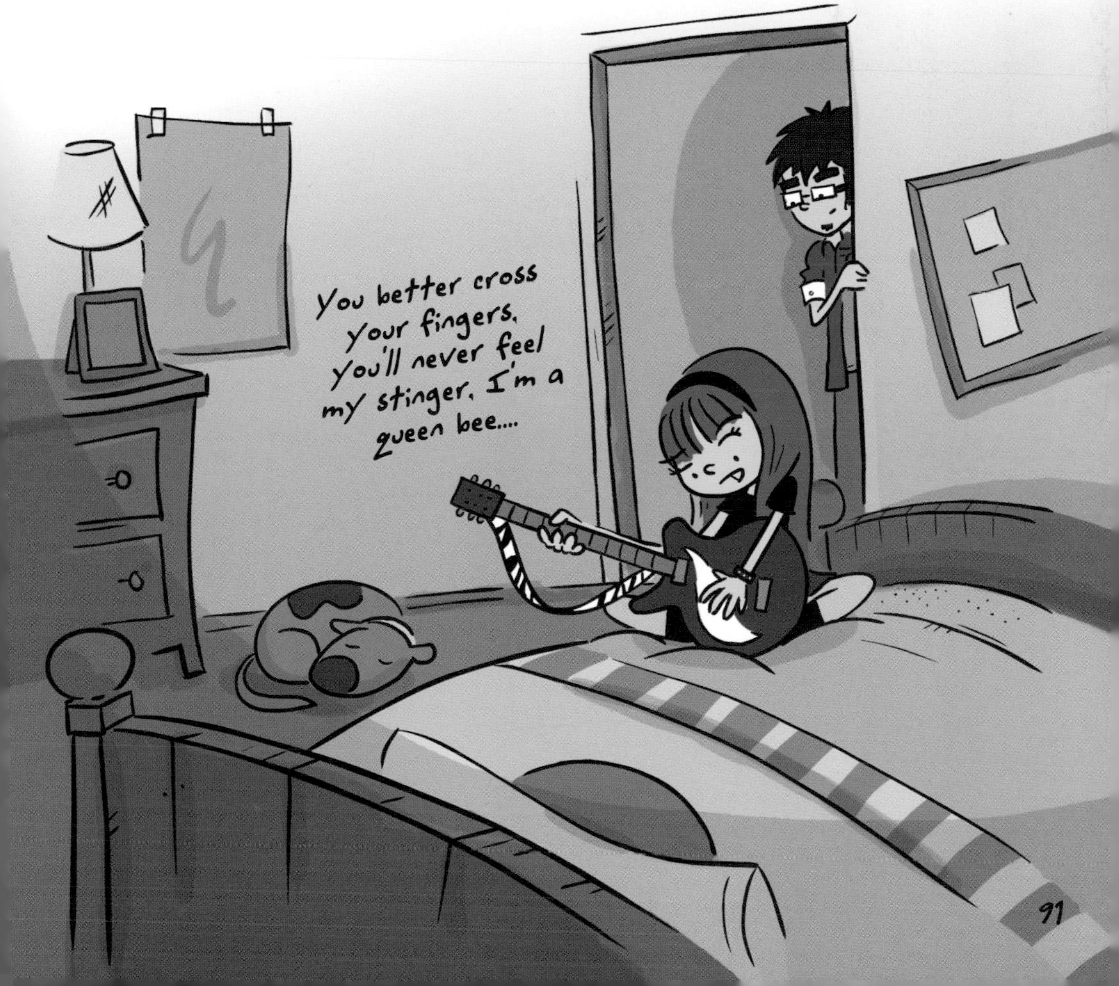
You better cross your fingers, you'll never feel my stinger. I'm a queen bee....

Across Town...

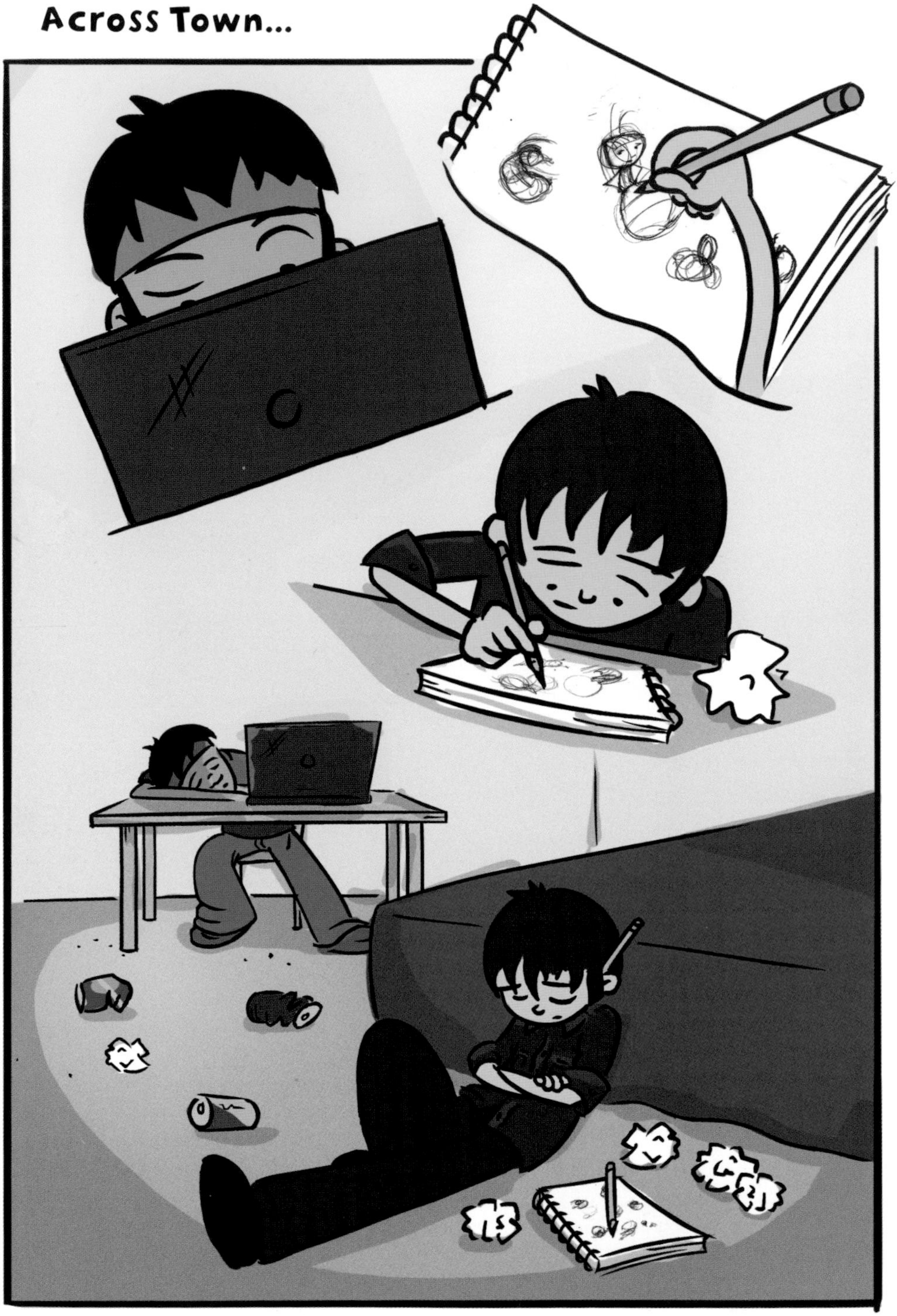

January. Back in School...

How does he expect us to sell 2,000 tickets?

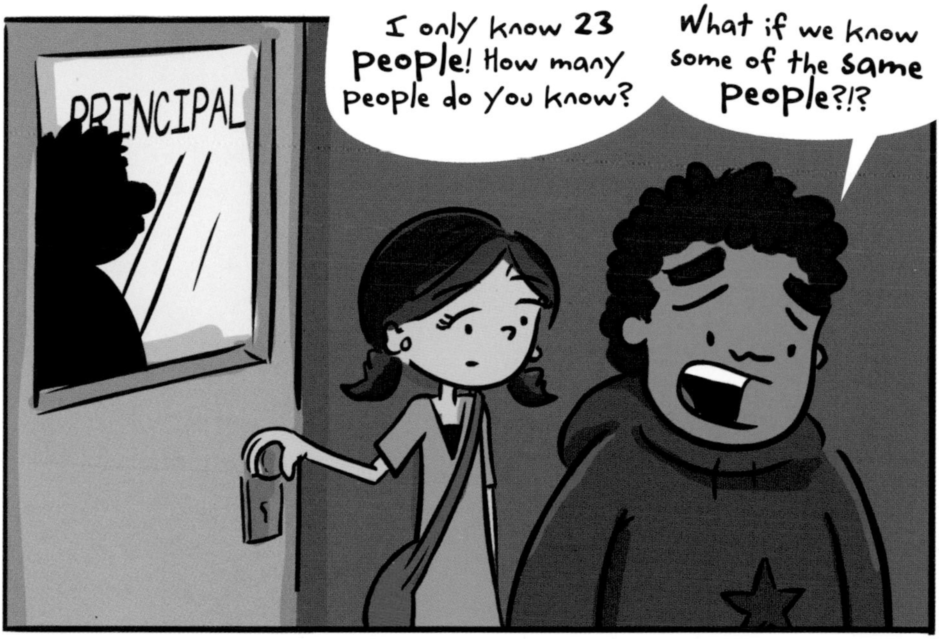
PRINCIPAL
I only know 23 people! How many people do you know?
What if we know some of the same people?!?

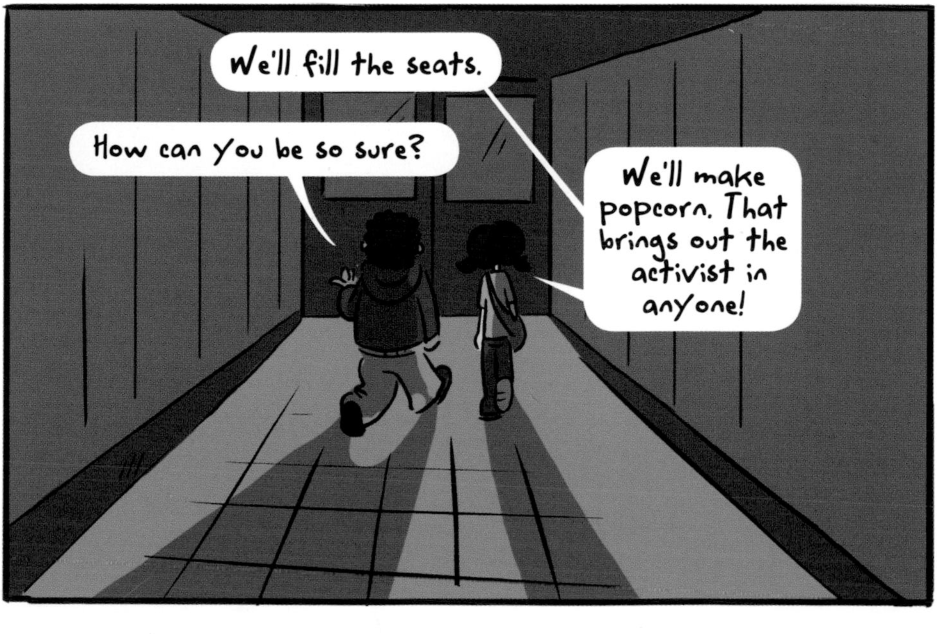
We'll fill the seats.
How can you be so sure?
We'll make popcorn. That brings out the activist in anyone!

16. Make It Better

February...

I hope we're not playing dodgeball again. When are we going to do something useful in gym? Like...

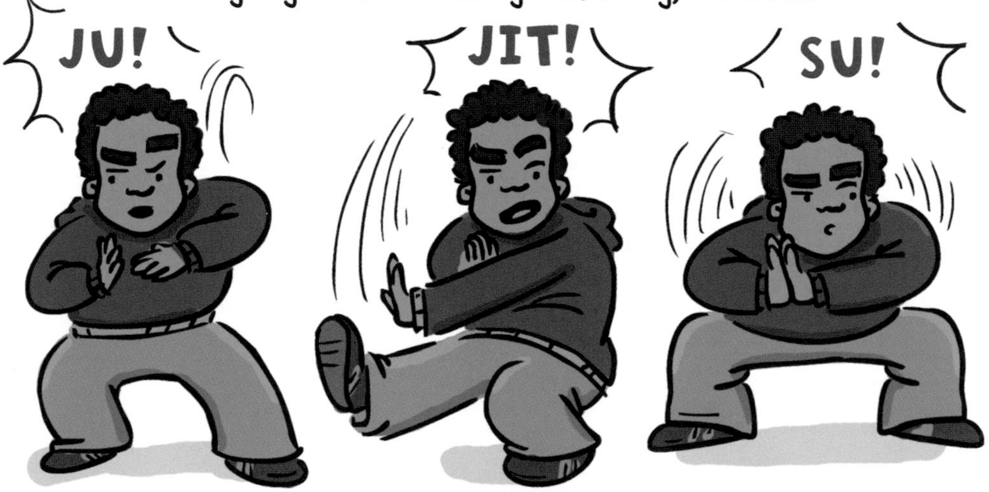
JU!
JIT!
SU!

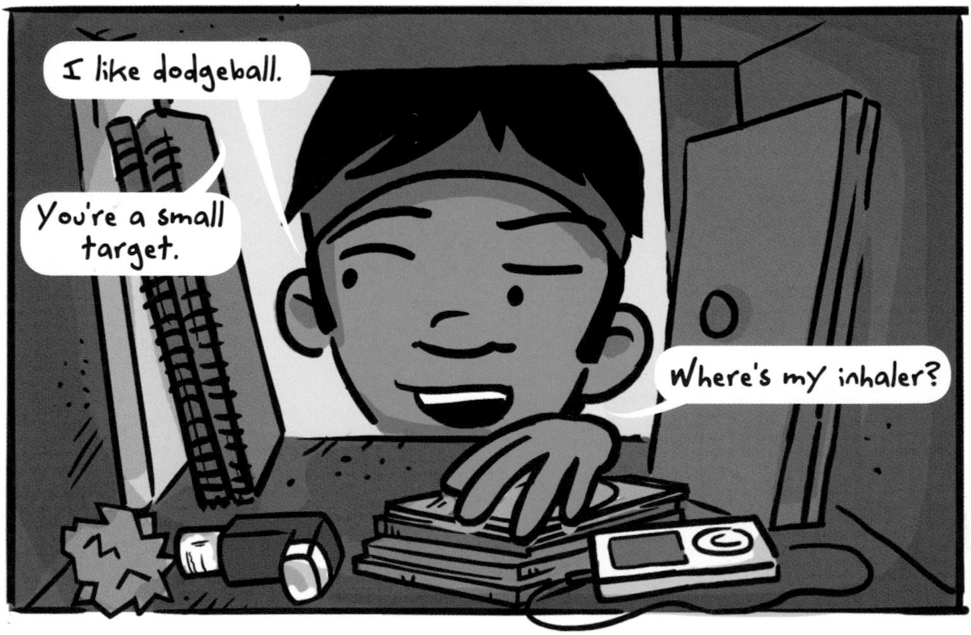
I like dodgeball.
You're a small target.
Where's my inhaler?

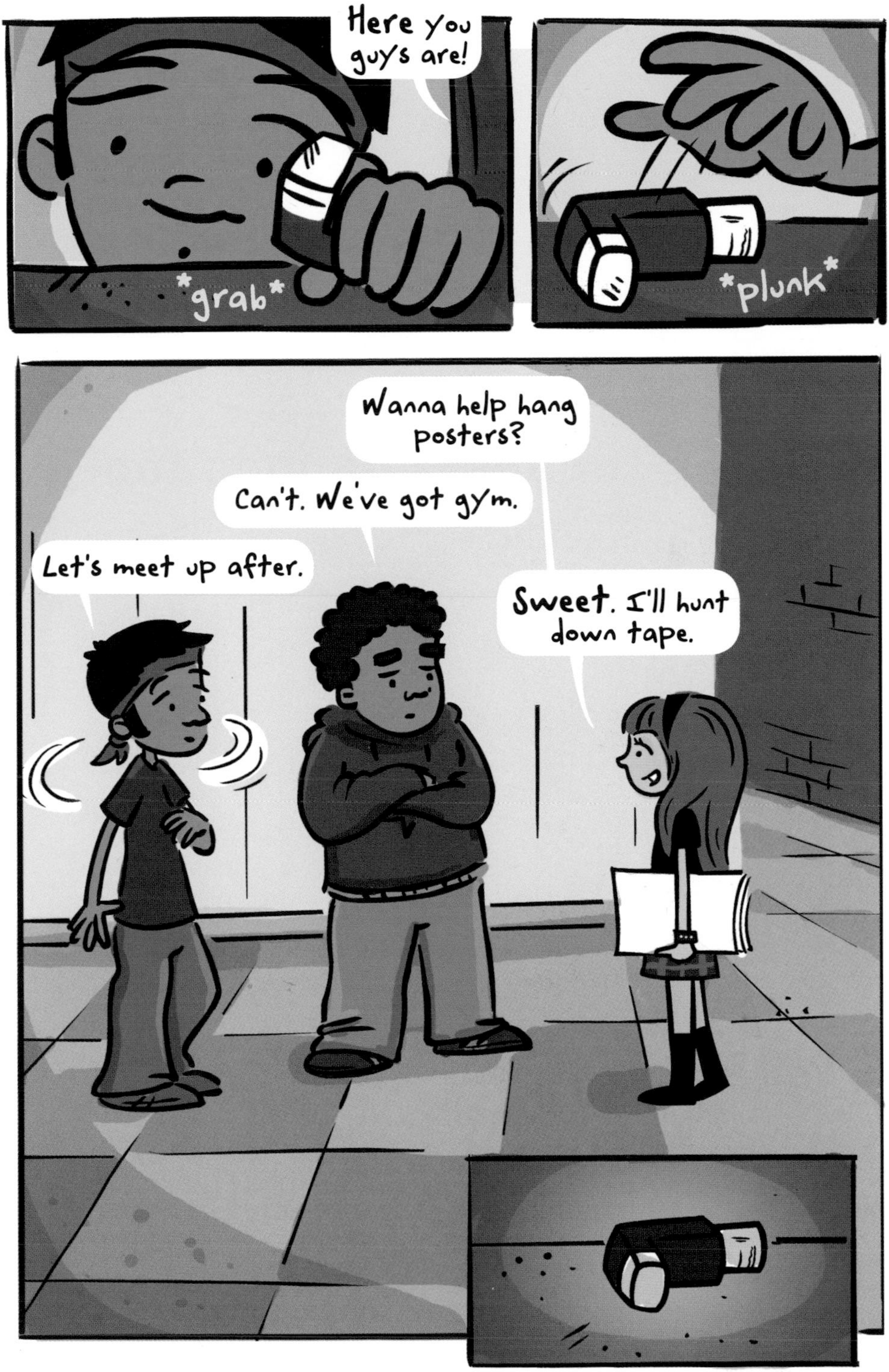
Here you guys are!
grab
plunk
Wanna help hang posters?
Can't. We've got gym.
Let's meet up after.
Sweet. I'll hunt down tape.

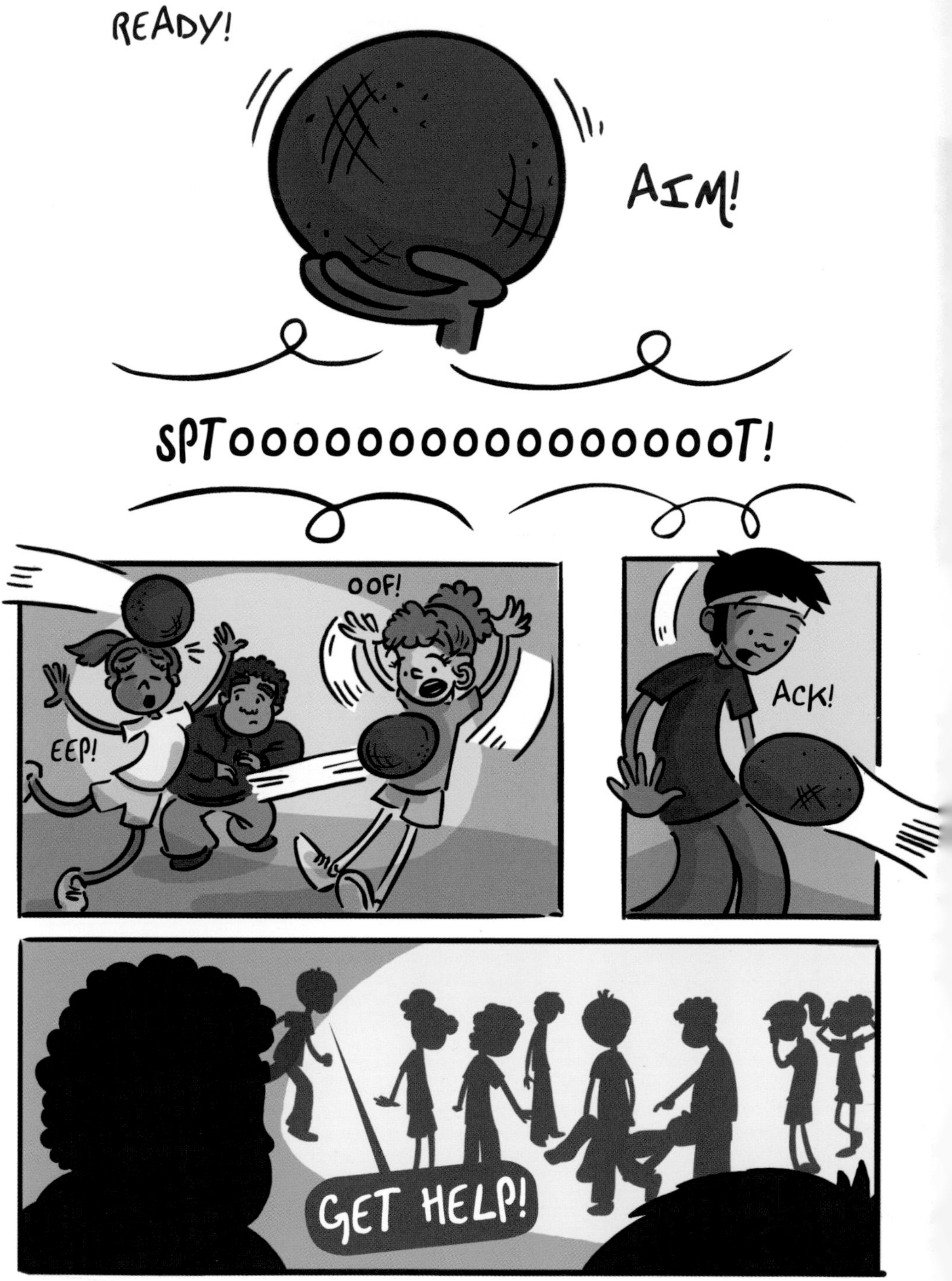
READY!
AIM!
SPTOOOOOOOOOOOOOOOOT!
OOF!
EEP!
ACK!
GET HELP!

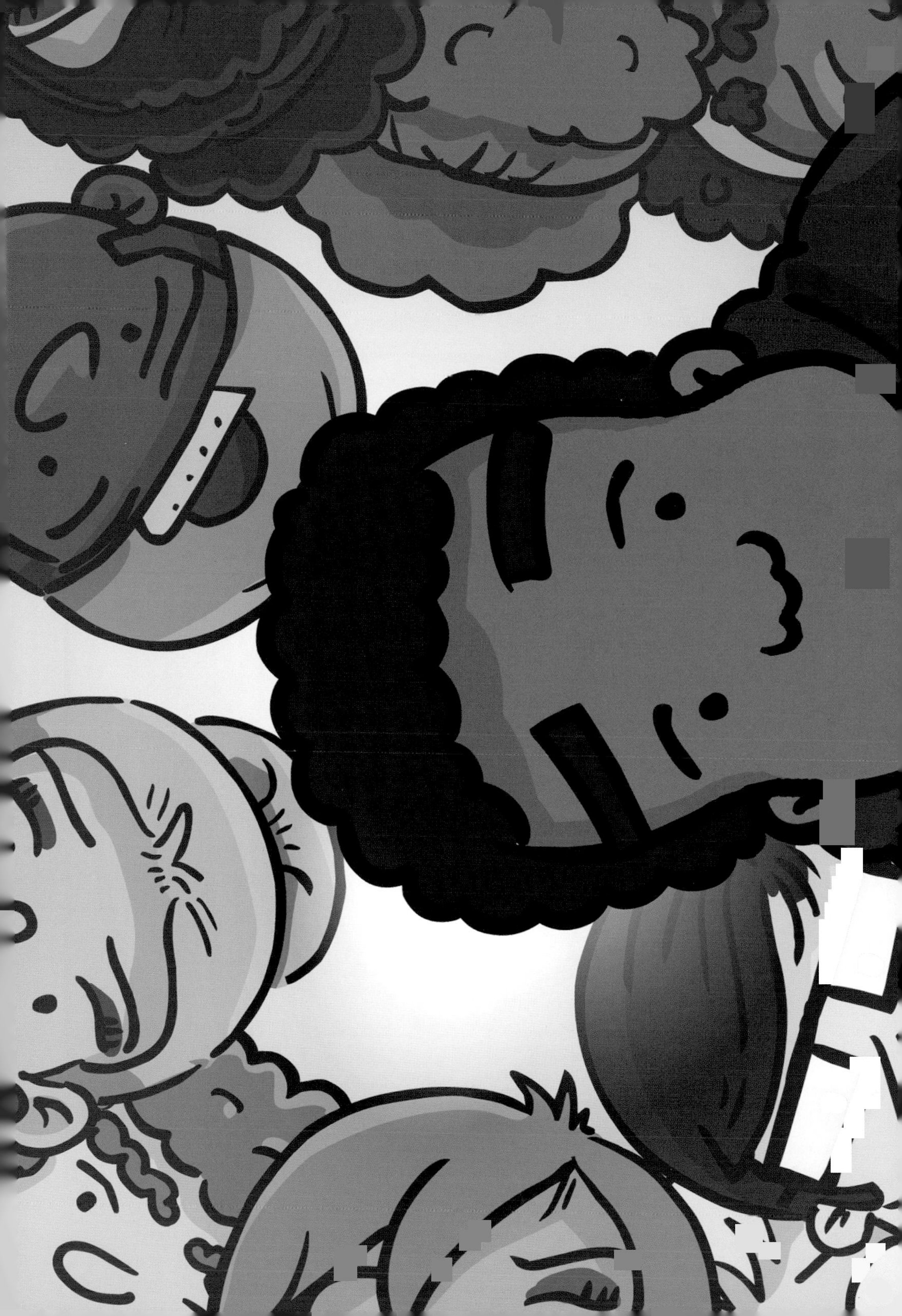

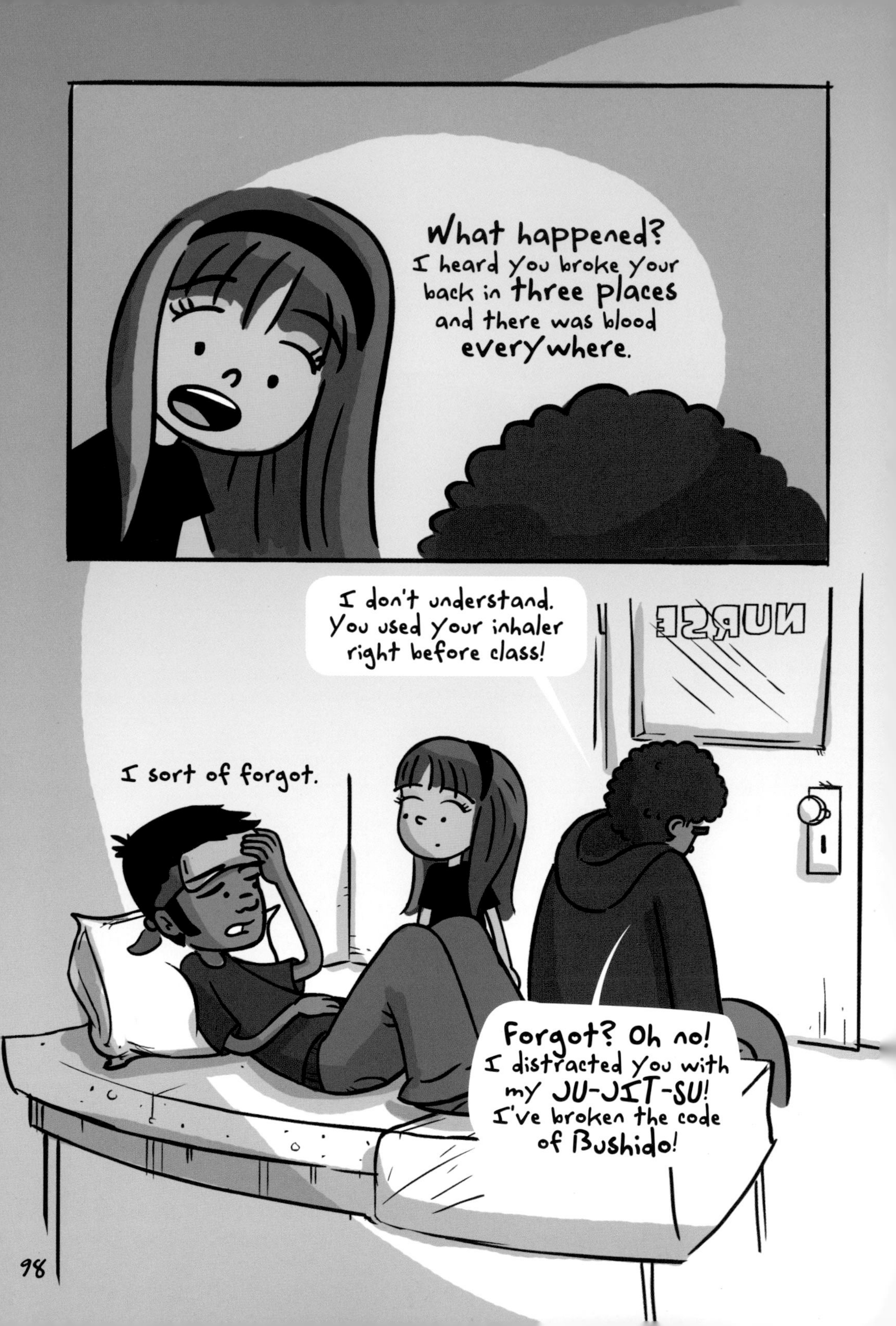
What happened? I heard you broke your back in three places and there was blood everywhere.
I don't understand. You used your inhaler right before class!
NURSE
I sort of forgot.
Forgot? Oh no! I distracted you with my JU-JIT-SU! I've broken the code of Bushido!

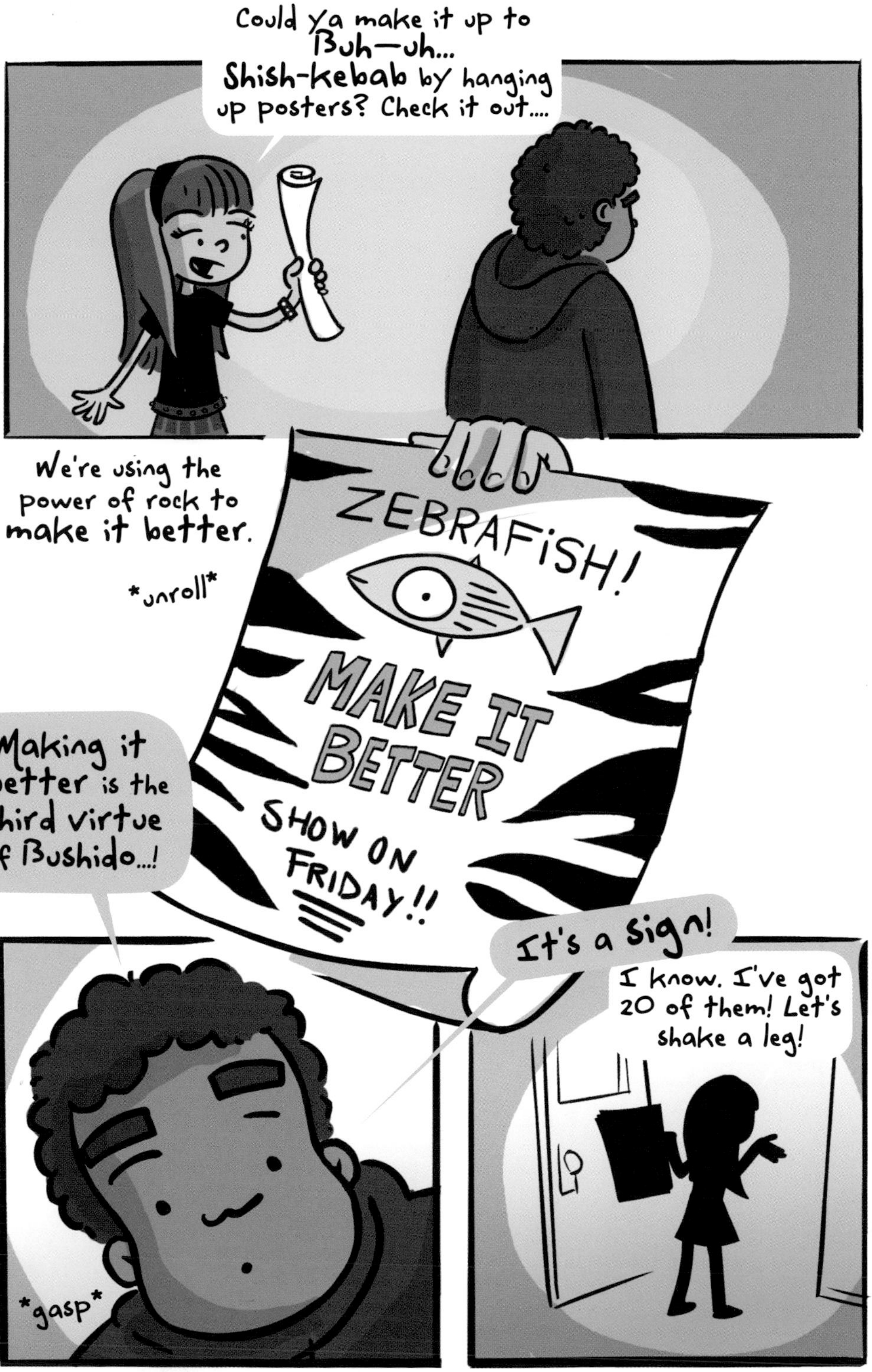

Could ya make it up to Buh—uh... Shish-kebab by hanging up posters? Check it out....
We're using the power of rock to make it better.
unroll
ZEBRAFISH!
MAKE IT BETTER
SHOW ON FRIDAY!!
Making it better is the third virtue of Bushido...!
It's a sign!
I know. I've got 20 of them! Let's shake a leg!
gasp

17. Preshow

March...

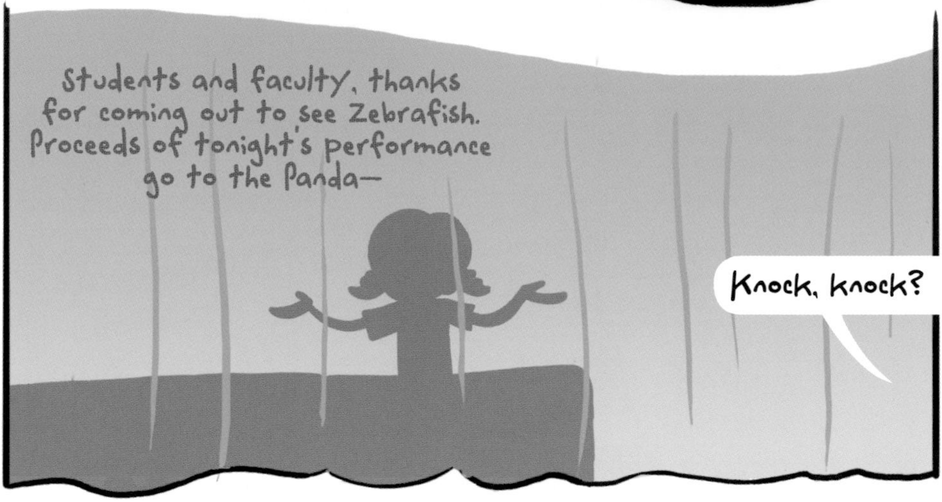
Students and faculty, thanks for coming out to see Zebrafish. Proceeds of tonight's performance go to the Panda—
Knock, knock?

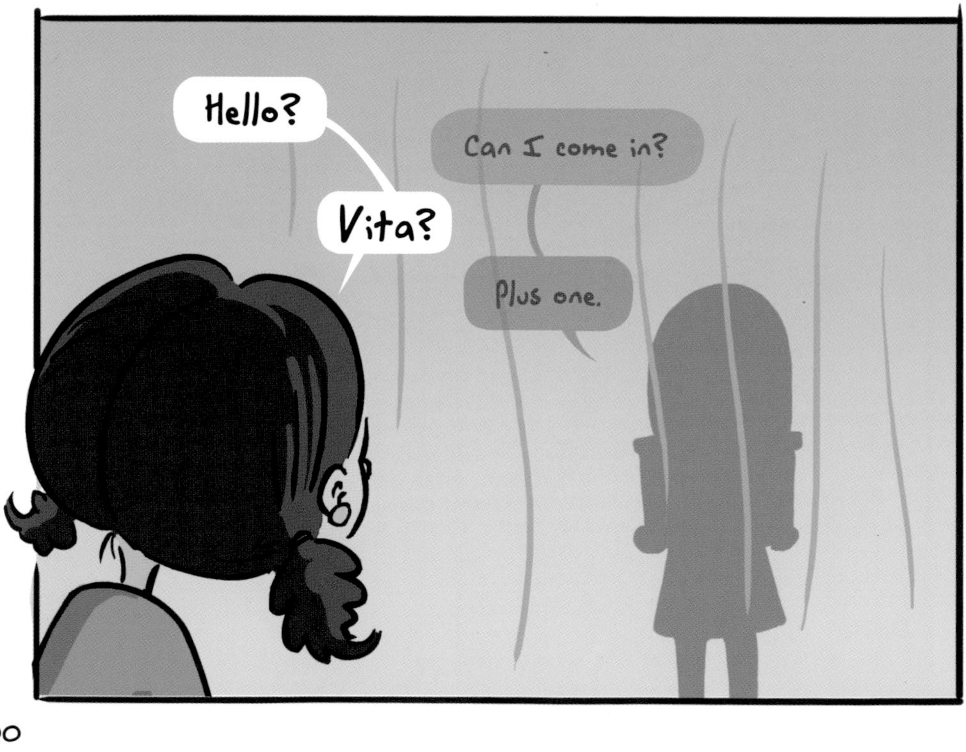
Hello?
Vita?
Can I come in?
Plus one.

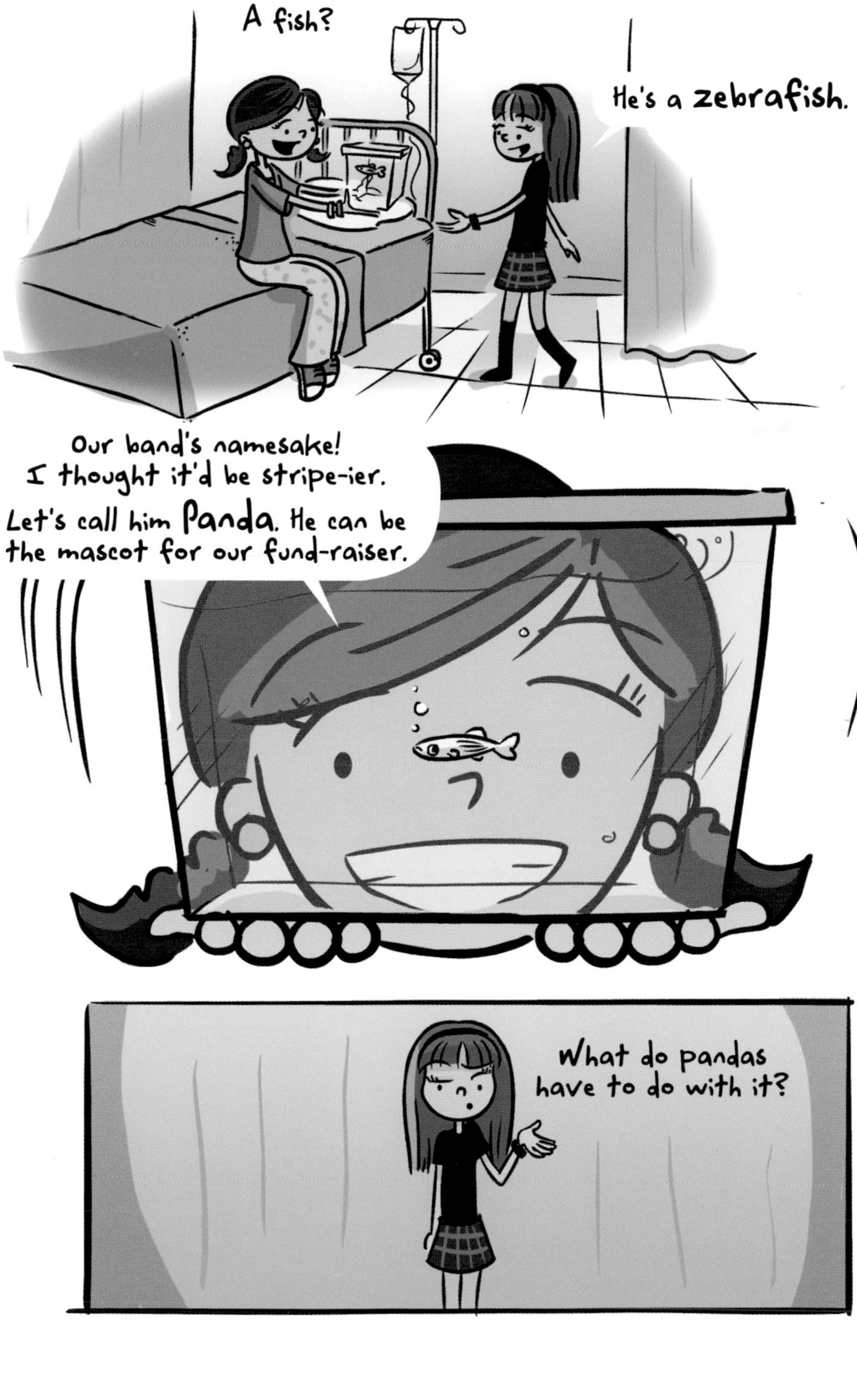
A fish?
He's a zebrafish.
Our band's namesake! I thought it'd be stripe-ier. Let's call him Panda. He can be the mascot for our fund-raiser.
What do pandas have to do with it?

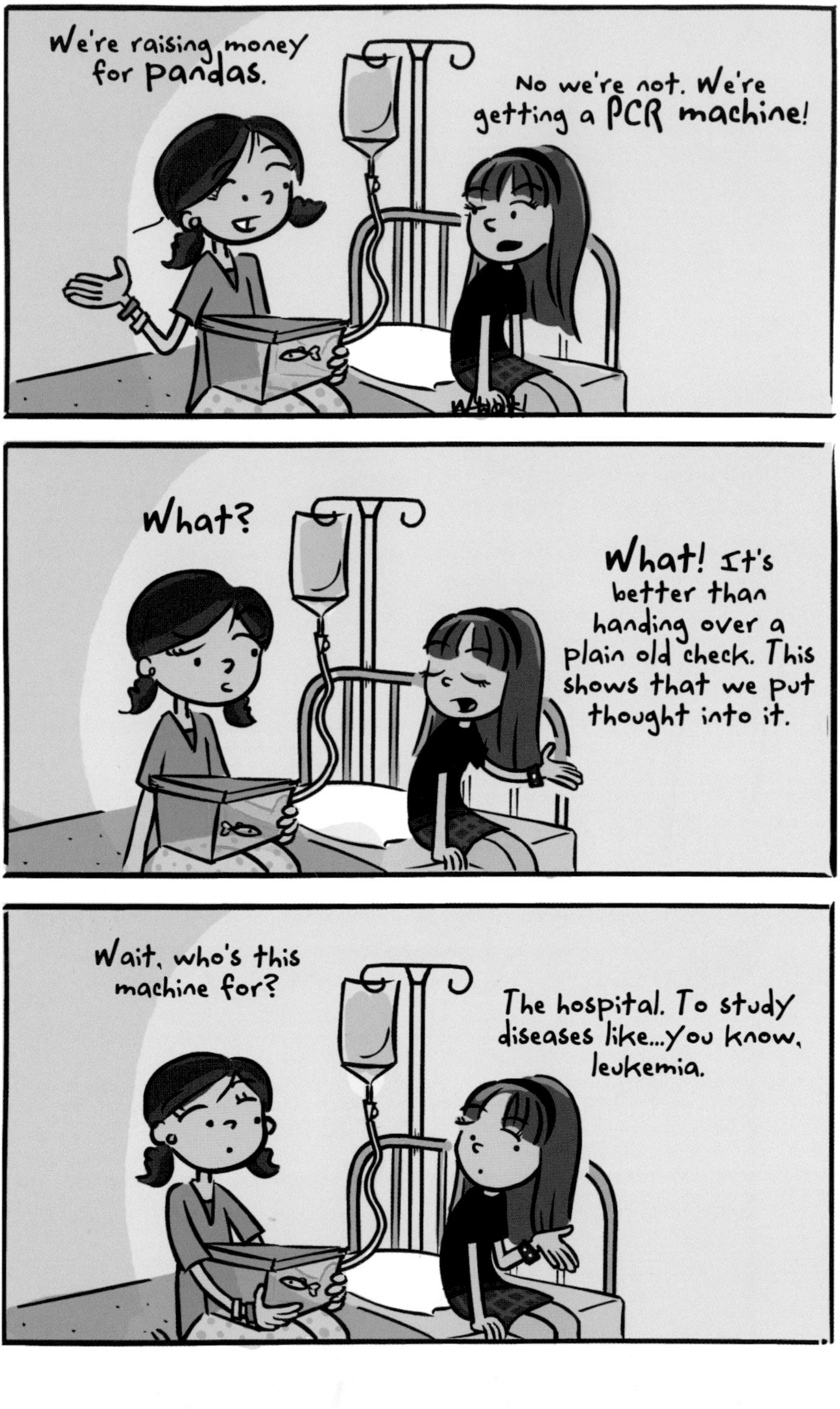
We're raising money for pandas.
No we're not. We're getting a PCR machine!
What?
What! It's better than handing over a plain old check. This shows that we put thought into it.
Wait, who's this machine for?
The hospital. To study diseases like...you know, leukemia.

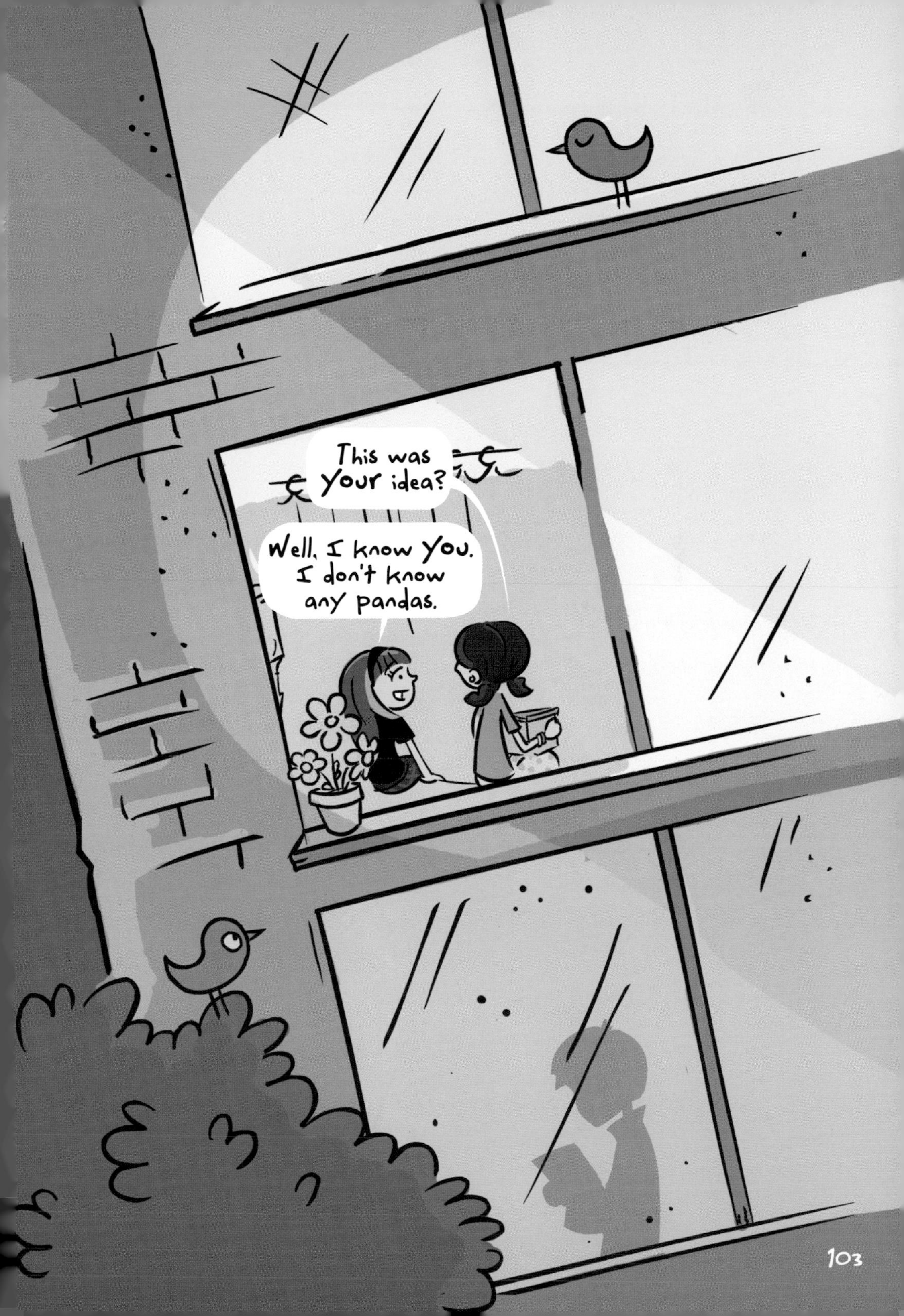
This was your idea?
Well, I know you. I don't know any pandas.

18. Zebrafish Effect

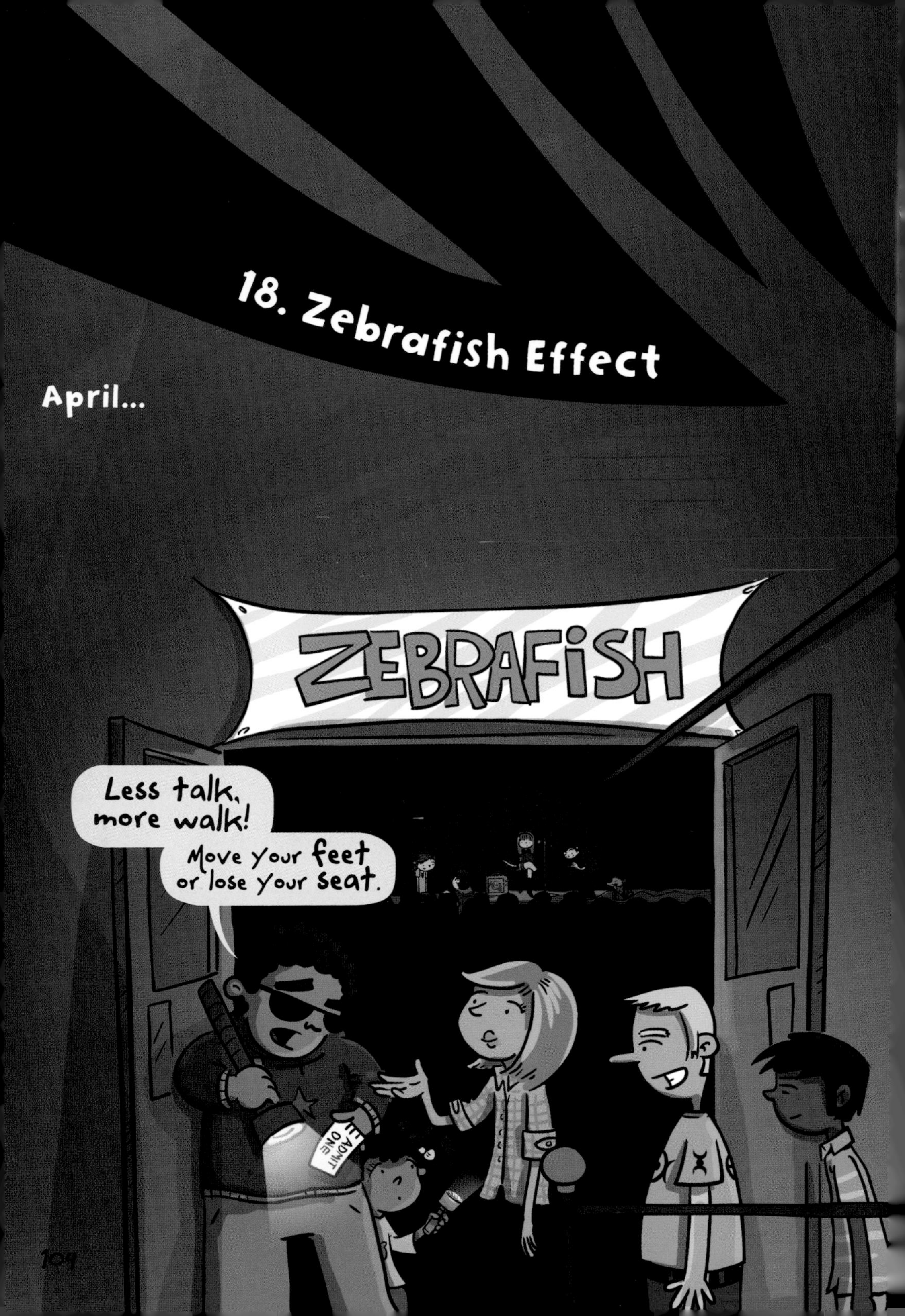
April...
ZEBRAFISH
Less talk, more walk!
Move your feet or lose your seat.
ADMIT ONE

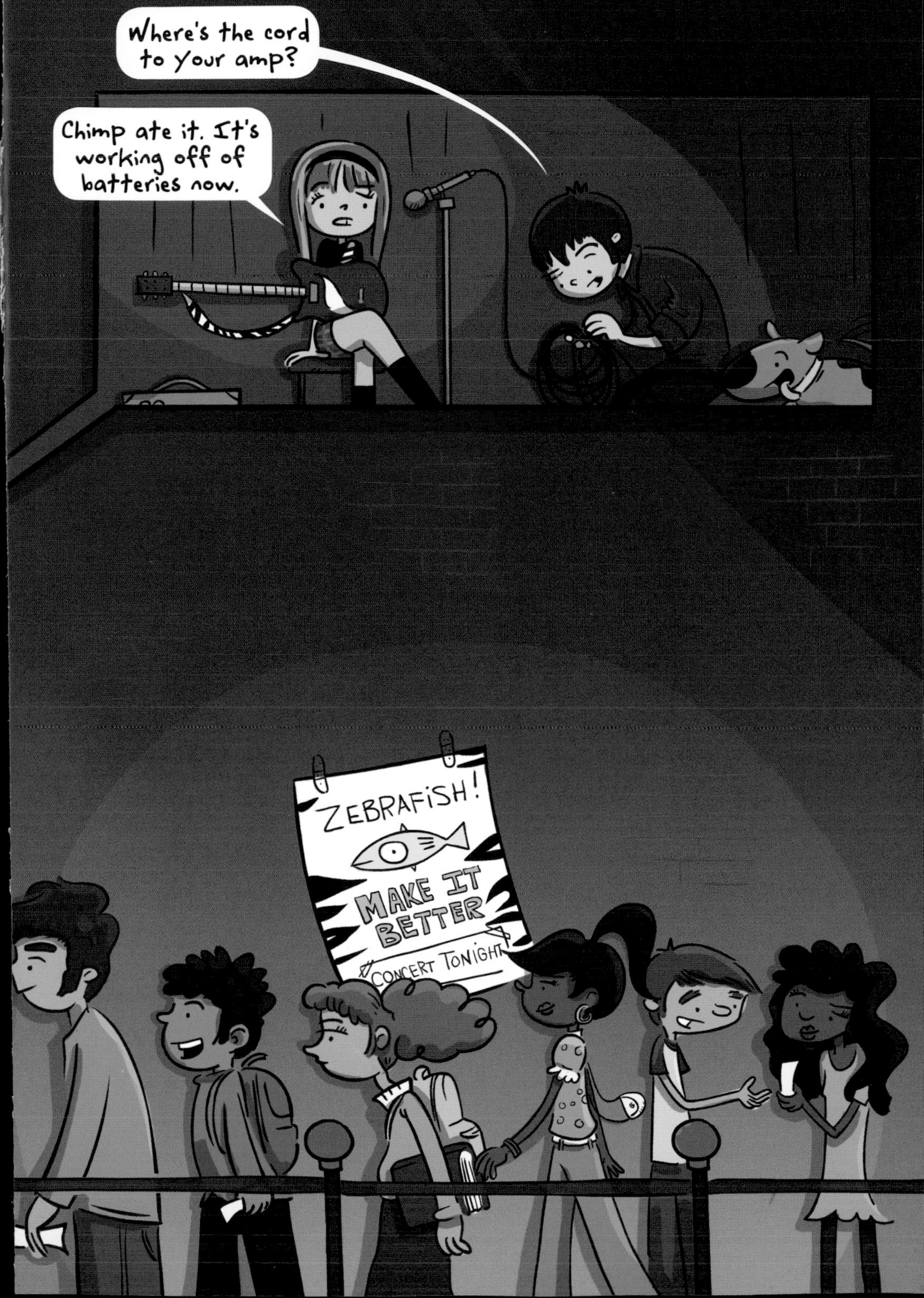
Where's the cord to your amp?
Chimp ate it. It's working off of batteries now.
ZEBRAFISH!
MAKE IT BETTER
CONCERT TONIGHT

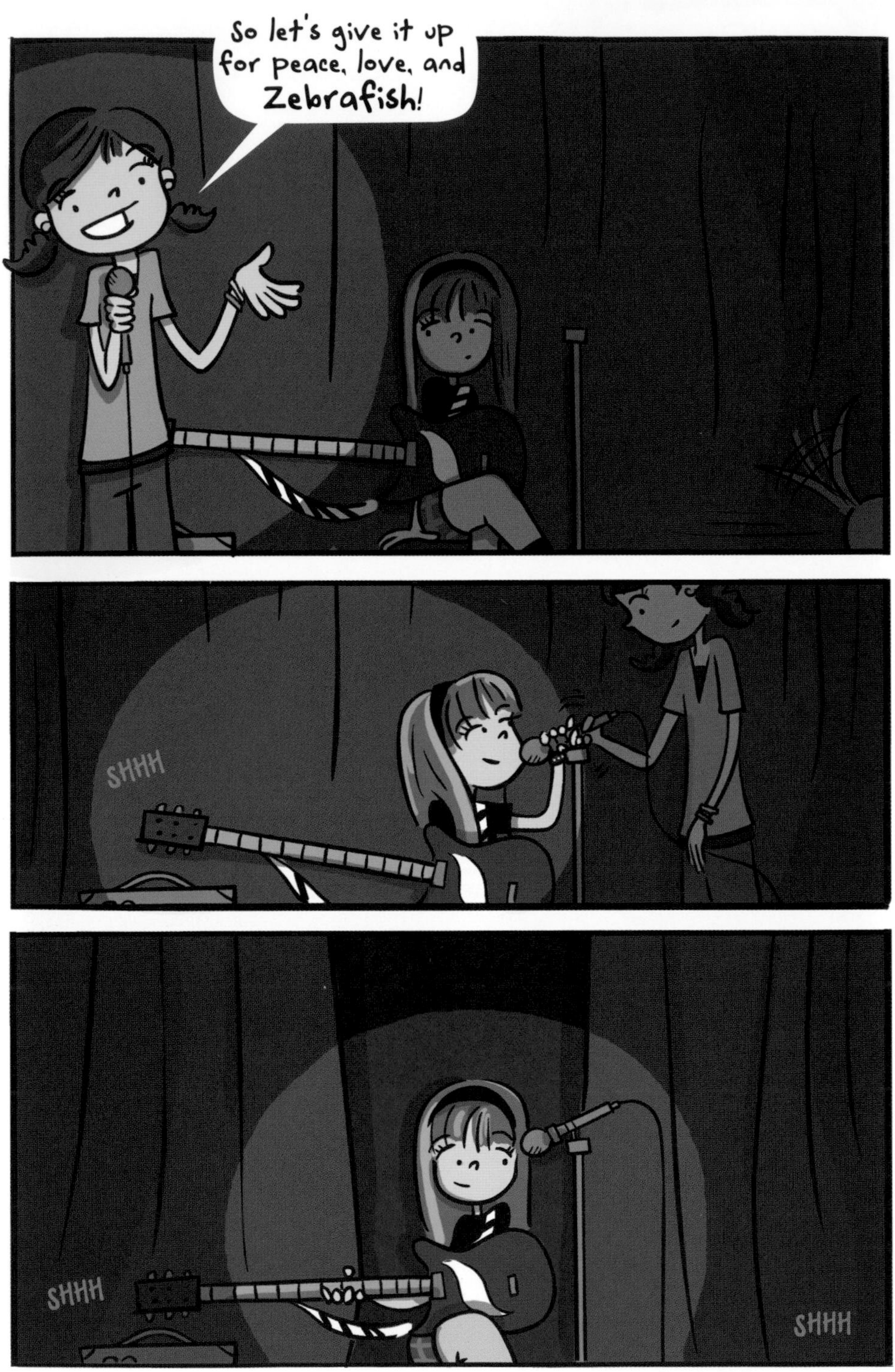
So let's give it up for peace, love, and Zebrafish!
SHHH
SHHH
SHHH

SHHH

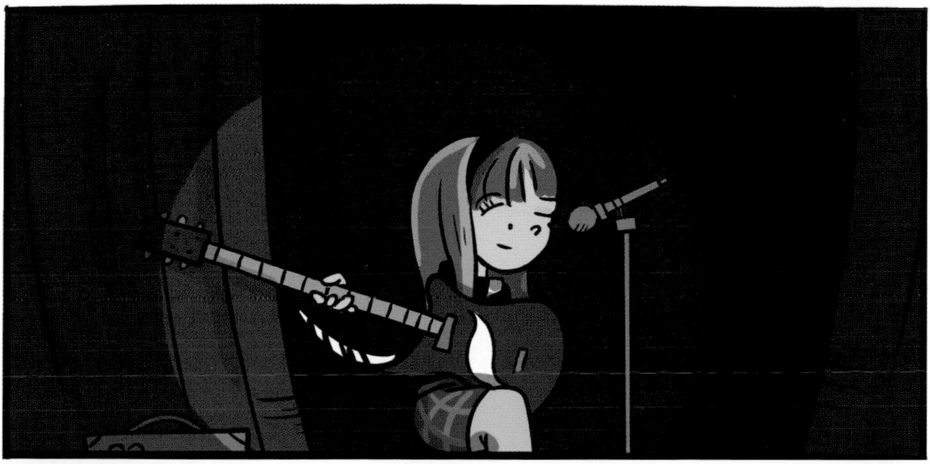

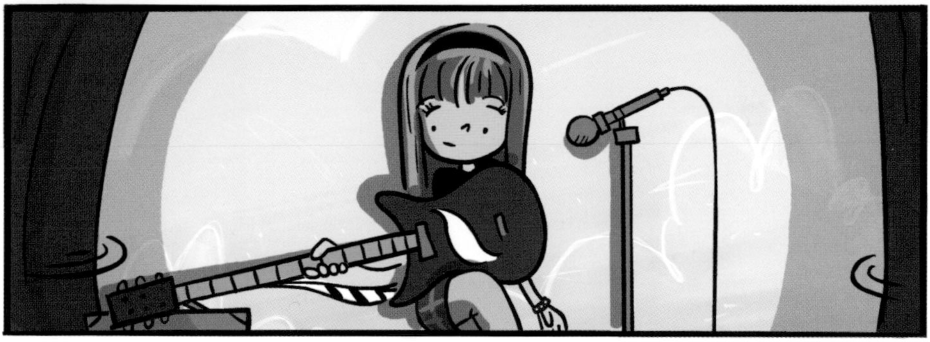

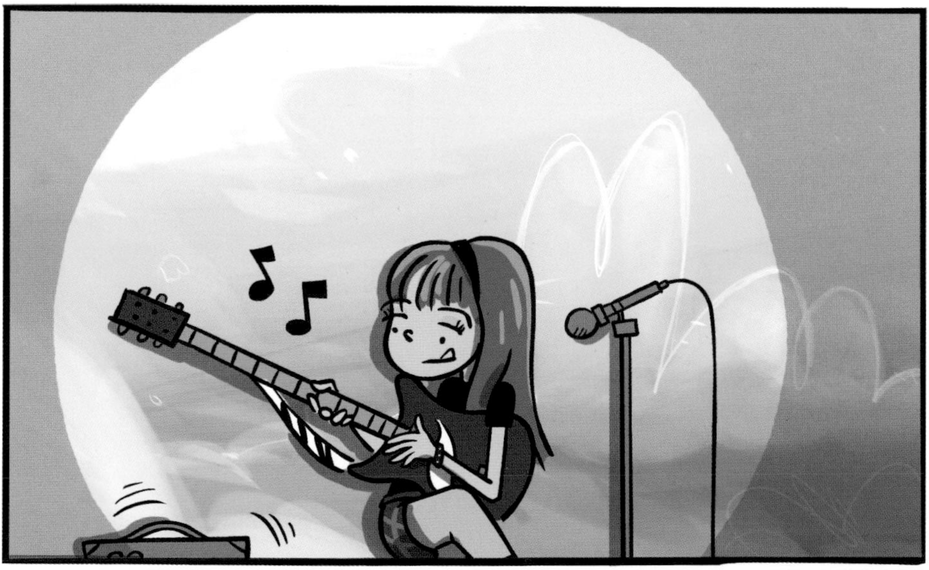

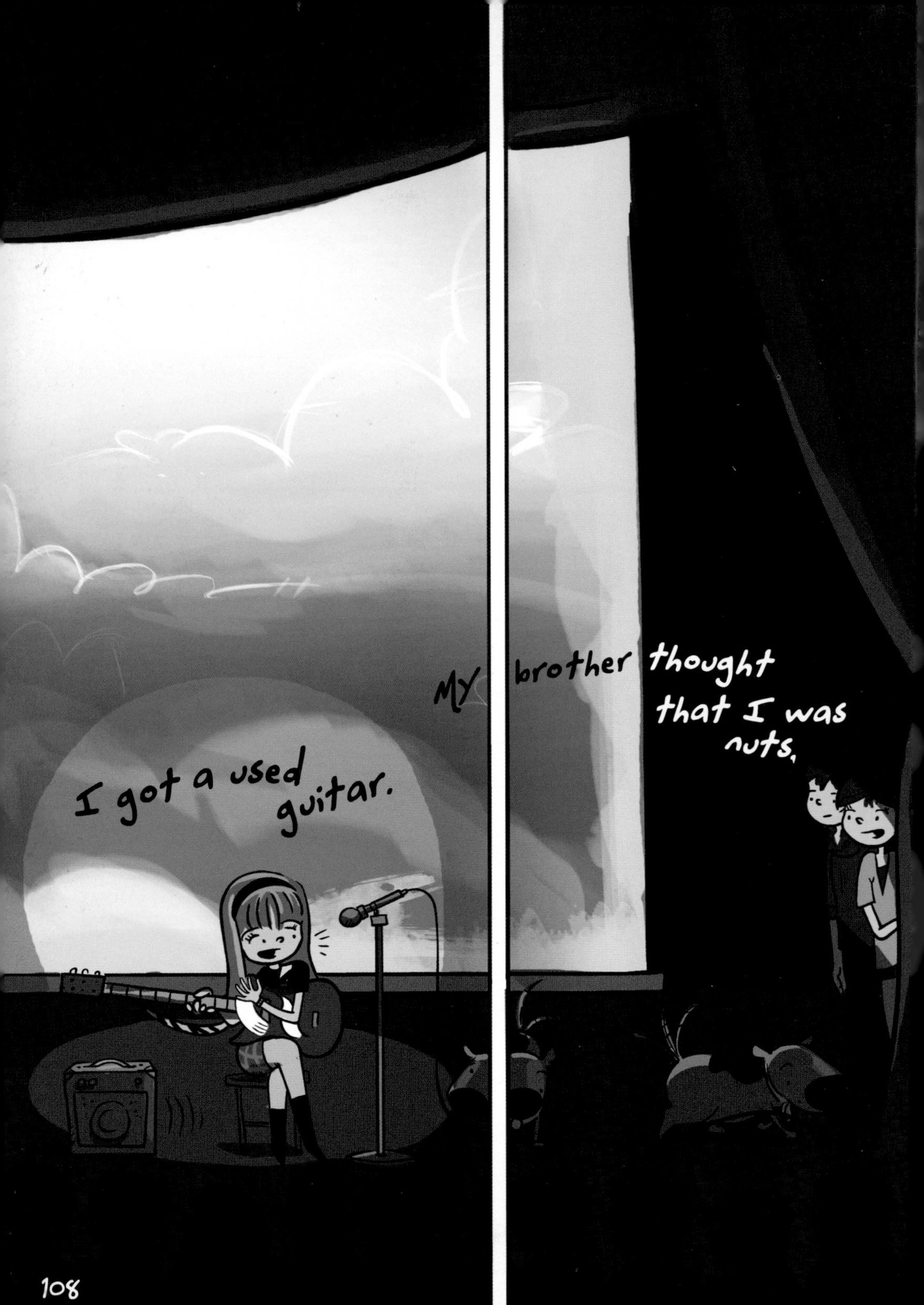
I got a used guitar.
My brother thought that I was nuts.

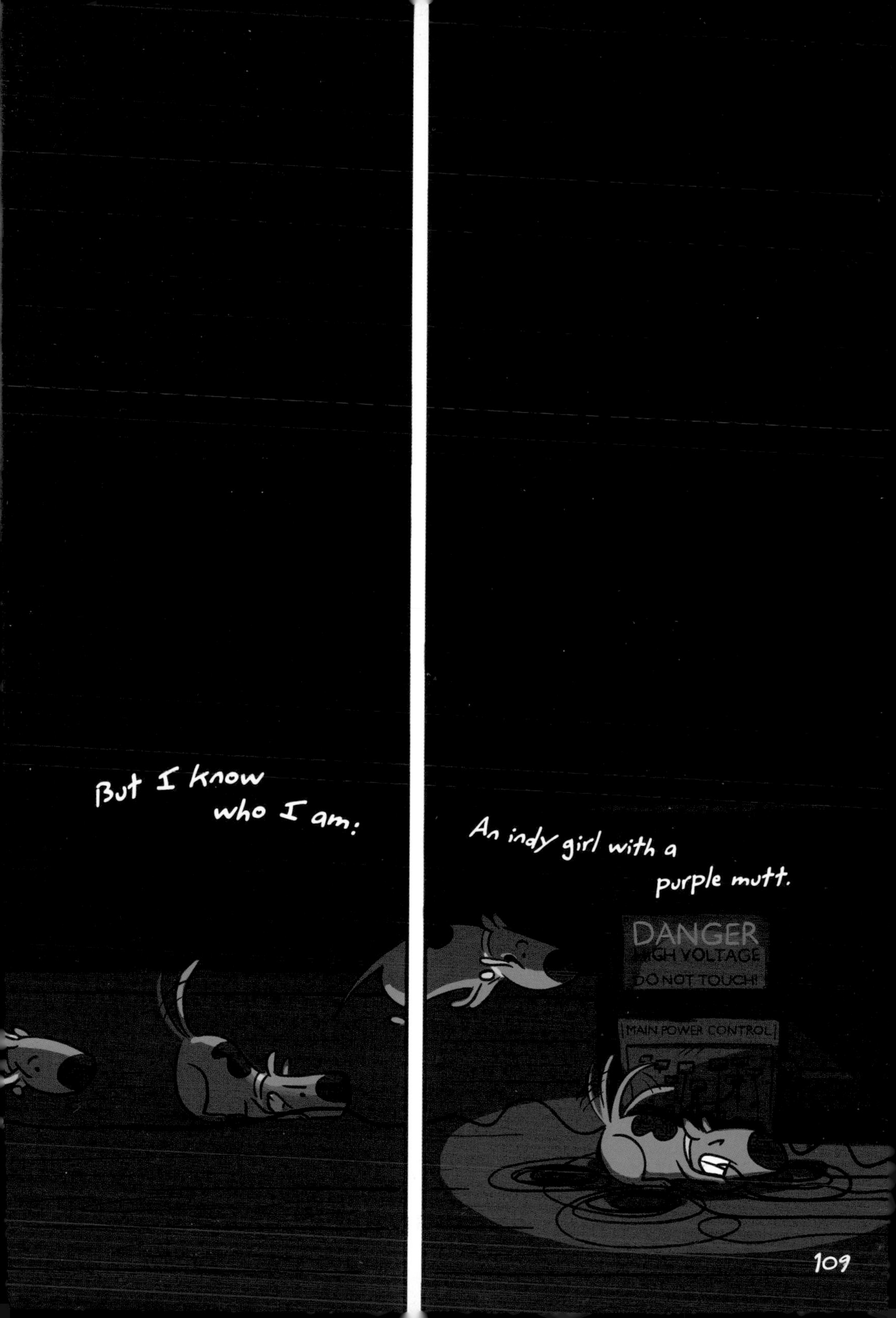
But I know who I am:
An indy girl with a purple mutt.
DANGER
HIGH VOLTAGE
DO NOT TOUCH!
MAIN POWER CONTROL

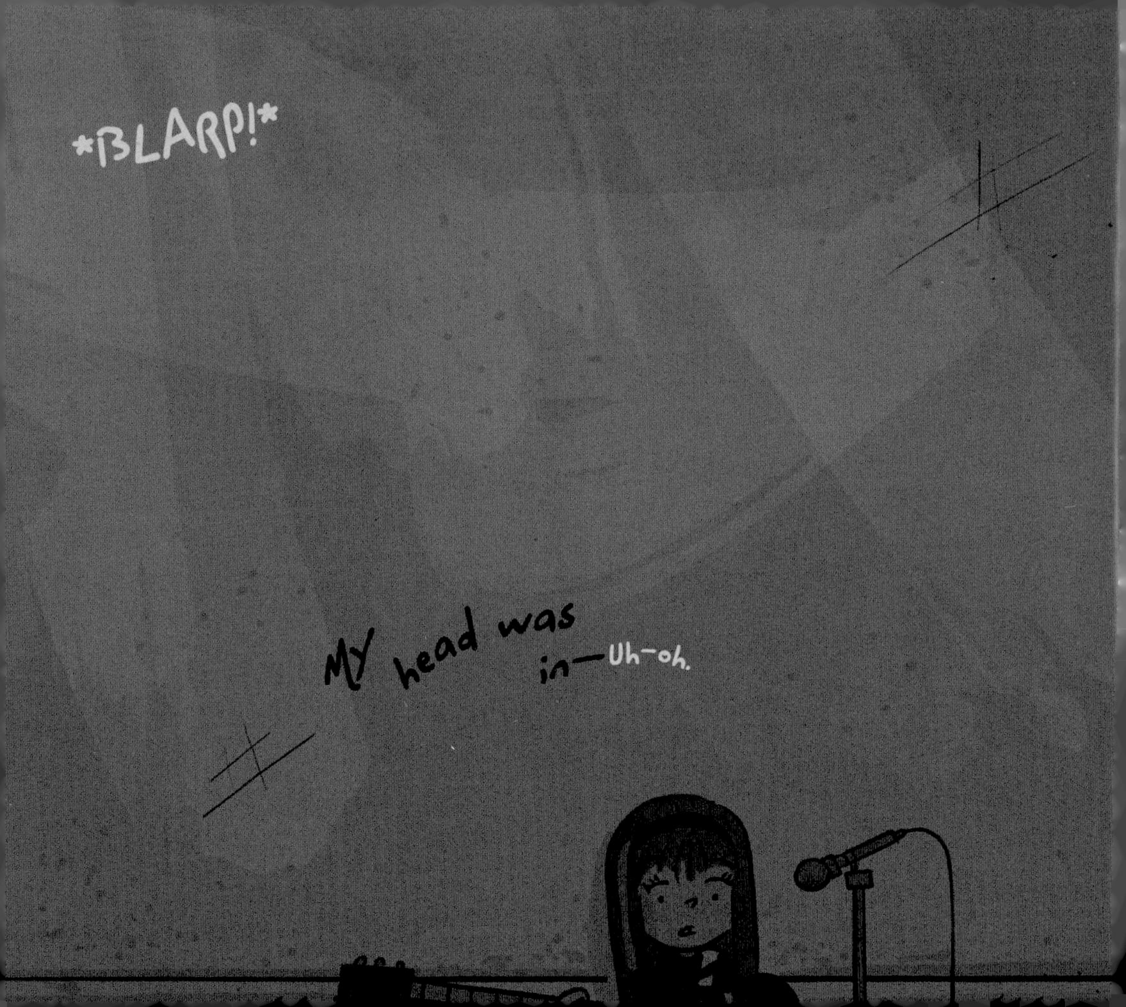
BLARP!
My head was in—
Uh-oh.

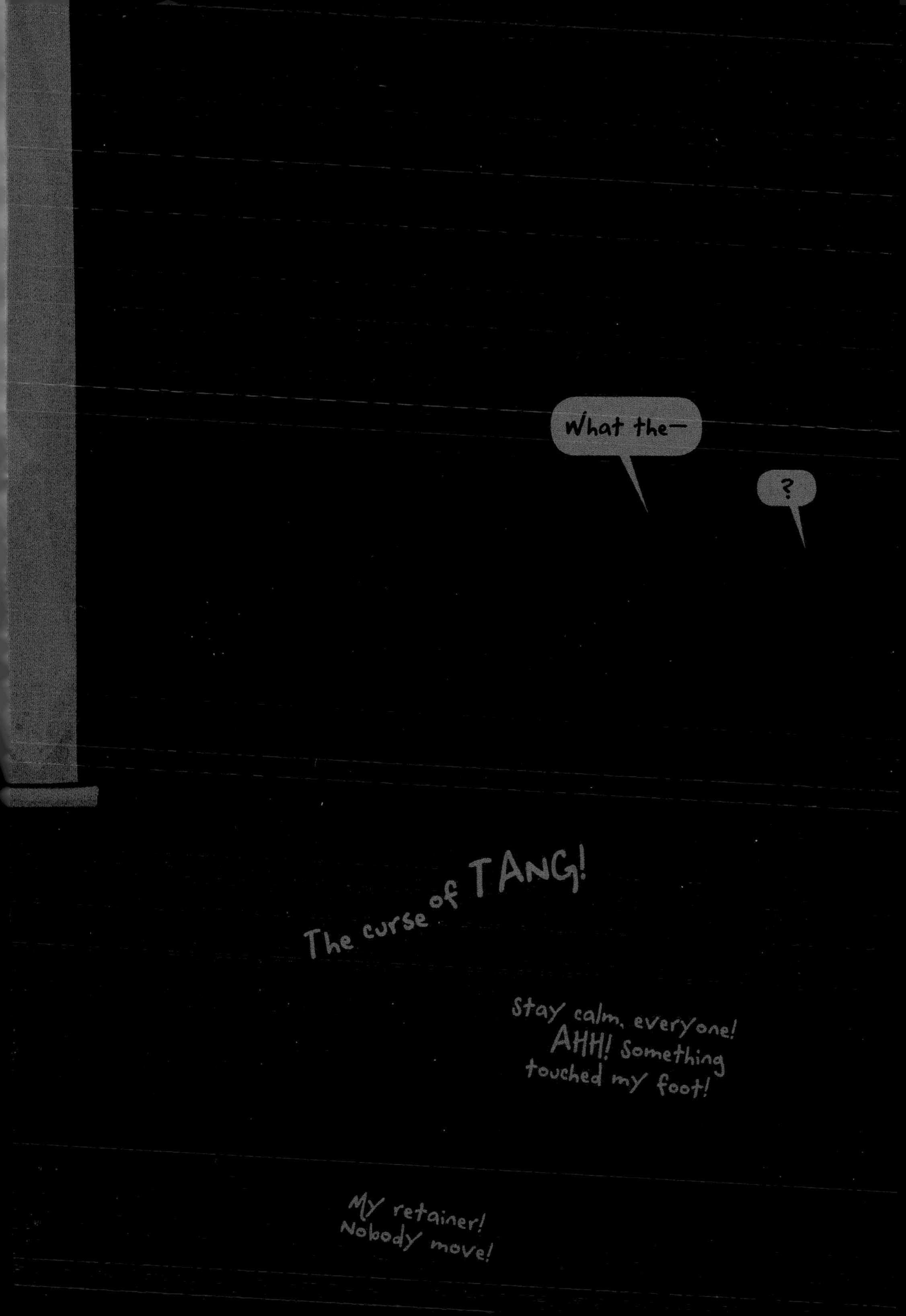
What the—
?
The curse of TANG!
Stay calm, everyone! AHH! Something touched my foot!
My retainer! Nobody move!

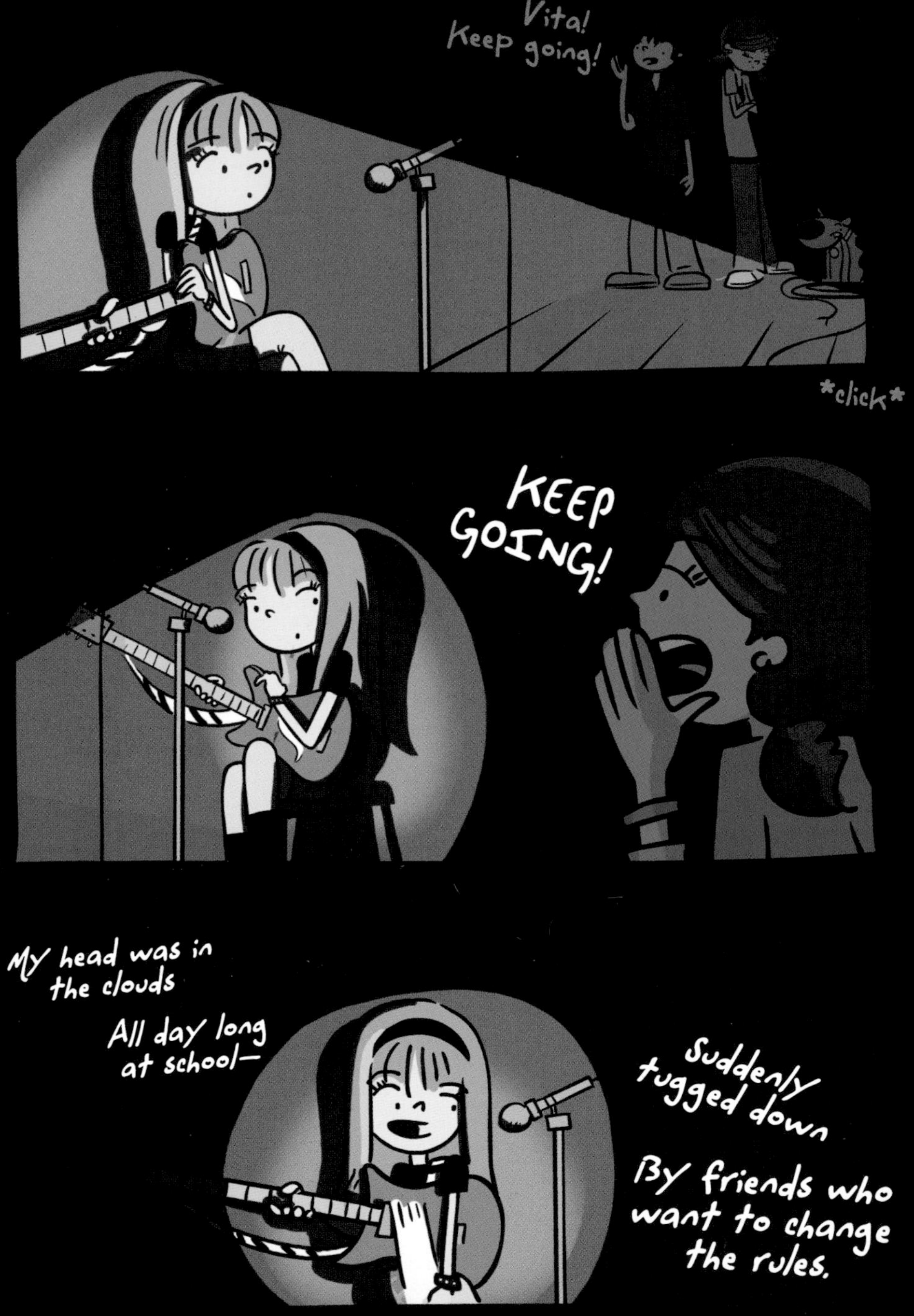

Vita! Keep going!
click
KEEP GOING!
My head was in the clouds
All day long at school—
Suddenly tugged down
By friends who want to change the rules.

Stick to it!
Success don't happen quick.
Stick to it!
Shake it up! Give life a
KICK!

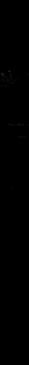

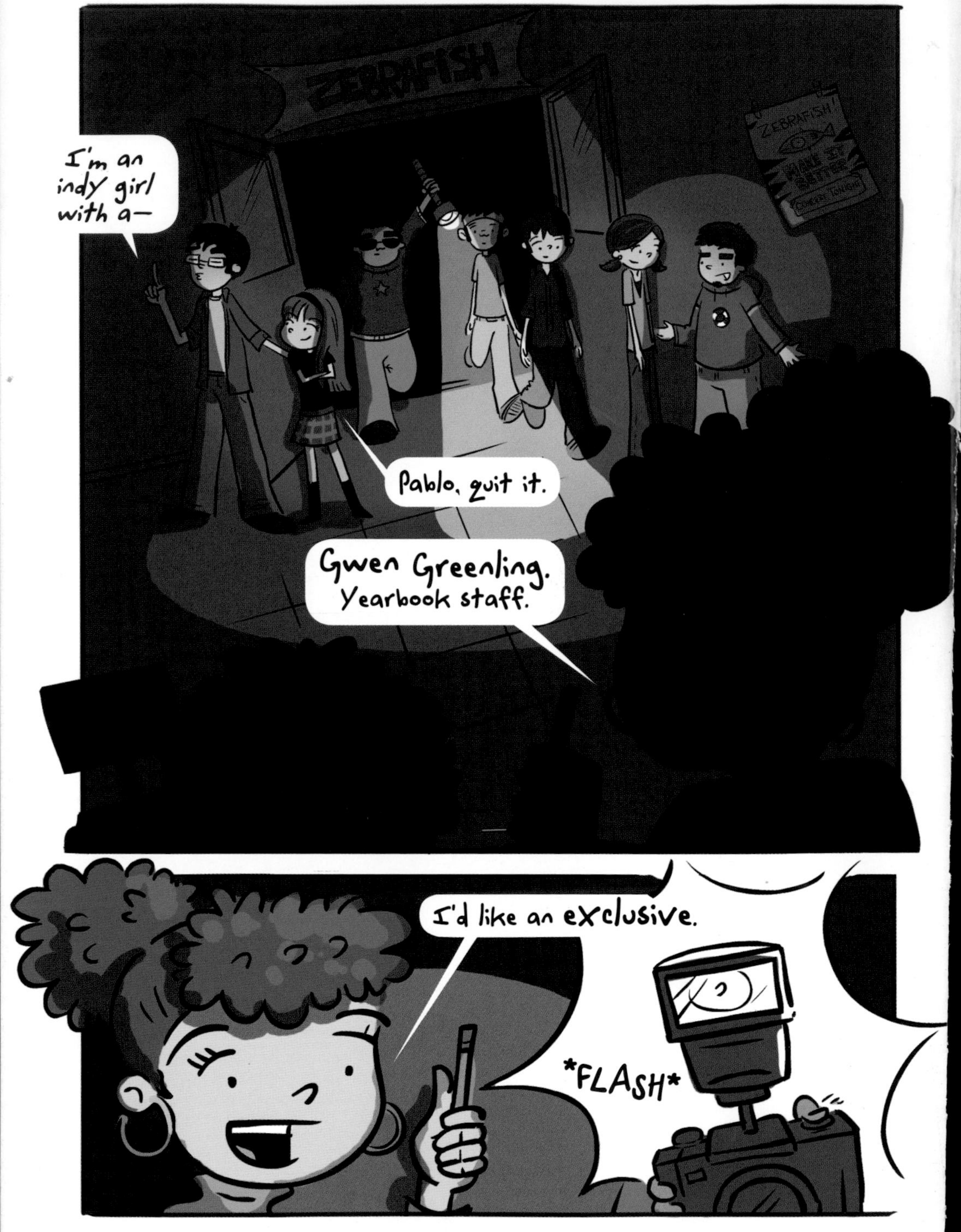
ZEBRAFISH
ZEBRAFISH!
MAKE IT BETTER
I'm an indy girl with a—
Pablo, quit it.
Gwen Greenling. Yearbook staff.
I'd like an exclusive.
FLASH

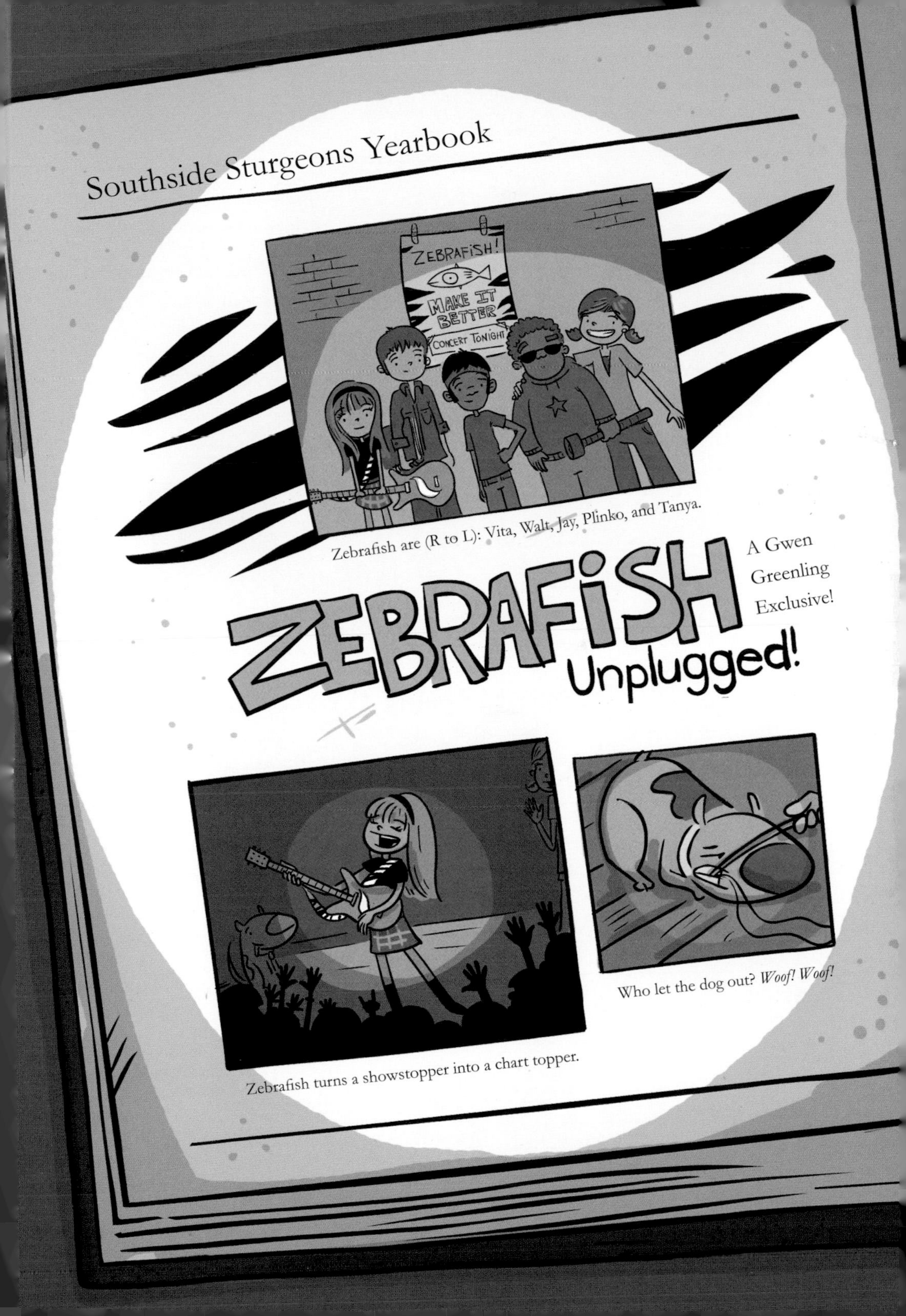
Southside Sturgeons Yearbook
ZEBRAFISH!
MAKE IT BETTER
CONCERT TONIGHT
Zebrafish are (R to L): Vita, Walt, Jay, Plinko, and Tanya.
ZEBRAFISH Unplugged!
A Gwen Greenling Exclusive!
Zebrafish turns a showstopper into a chart topper.
Who let the dog out? *Woof! Woof!*

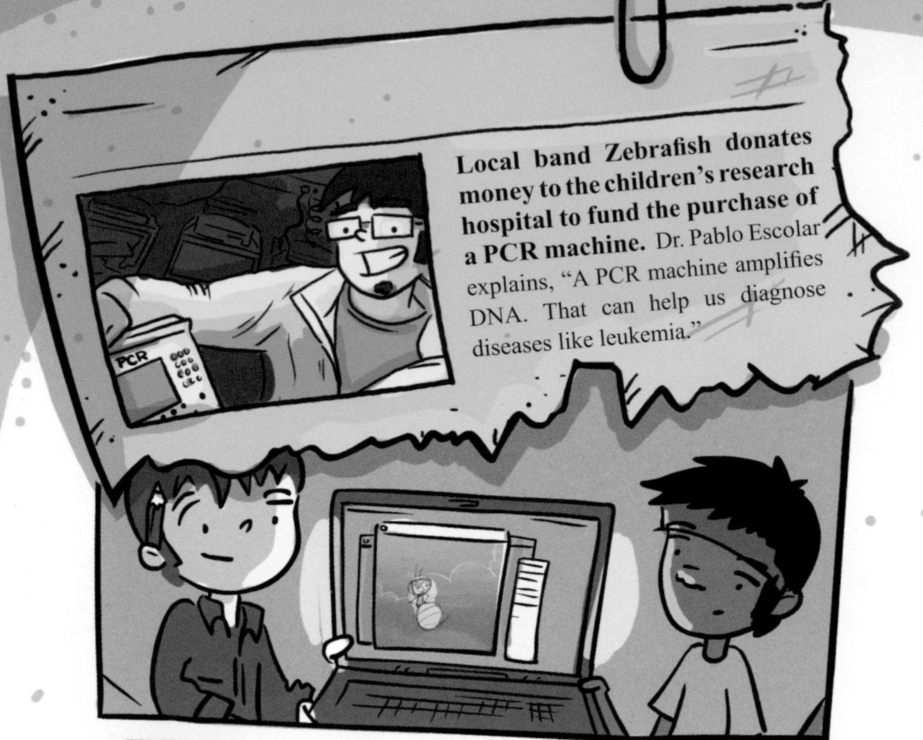
Local band Zebrafish donates money to the children's research hospital to fund the purchase of a PCR machine. Dr. Pablo Escolar explains, "A PCR machine amplifies DNA. That can help us diagnose diseases like leukemia."
PCR

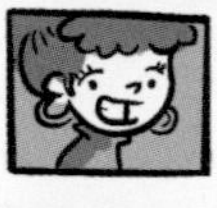

Zebrafish! Behind the Scenes!!!

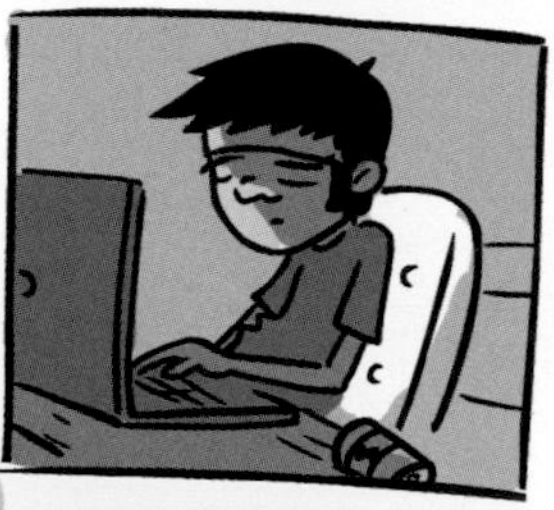

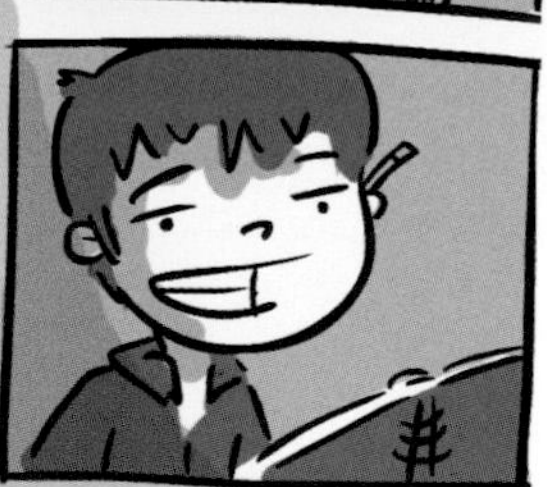

GWEN: *How long did it take to make the Zebrafish video?*
WALT: Roughly 100 cans of Boost cola.
JAY: Each.

GWEN: *Are you bummed that the video never saw the light of day?*
WALT: That was wrecked!
JAY: I almost Tang'ed on the spot.
WALT: That's gross, man.
JAY: Then 3 days later, it hit me. Let's get it online!
WALT: And 3 days after that, we launched zebrafish.com.
JAY: We've already got hits in the triple digits.

Vita,
The World knows you Rock,
'cause you Rocked the WORLD.
XO—
Jay

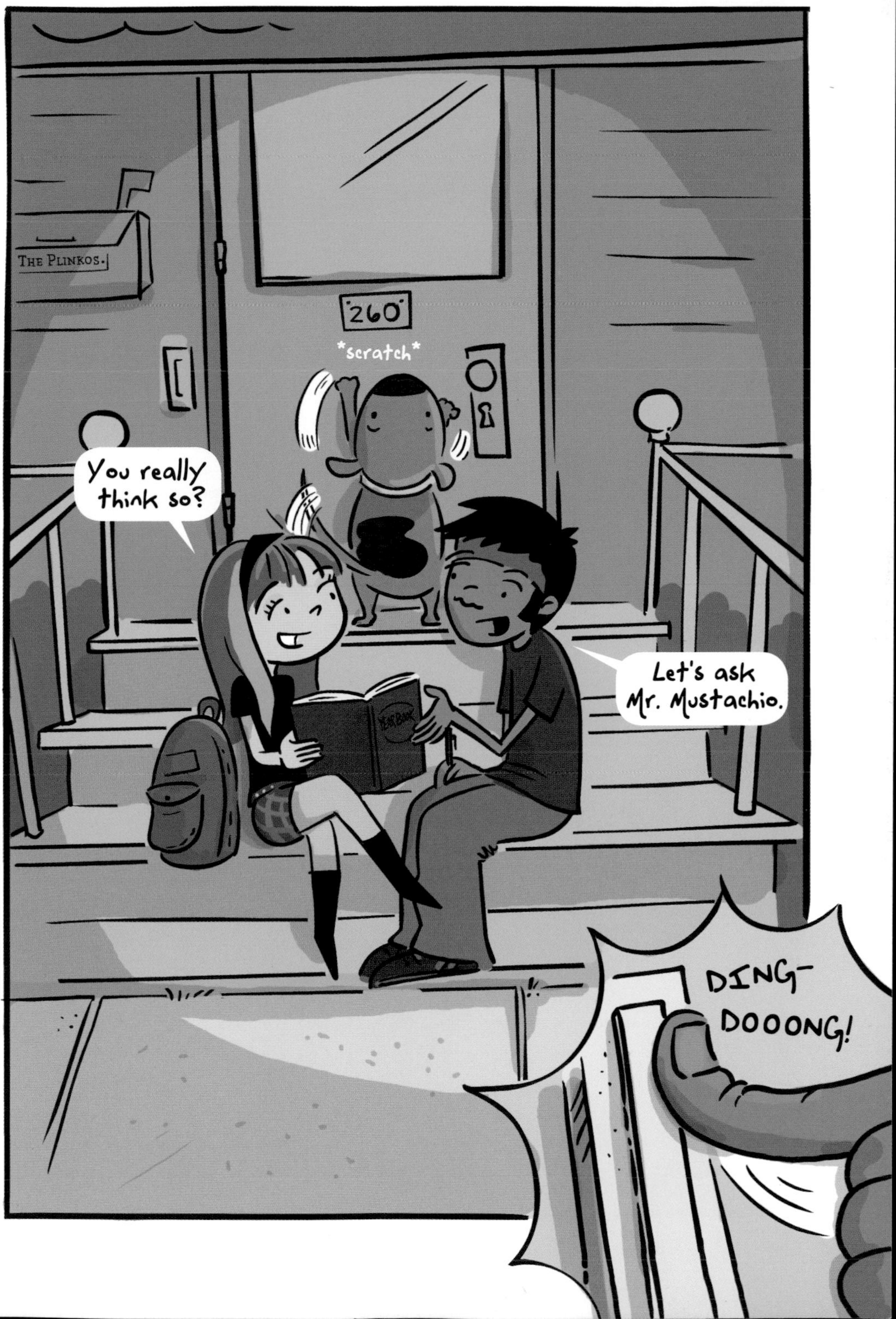
THE PLINKOS.
260
scratch
You really think so?
YEARBOOK
Let's ask Mr. Mustachio.
DING-DOOONG!

19. Encore

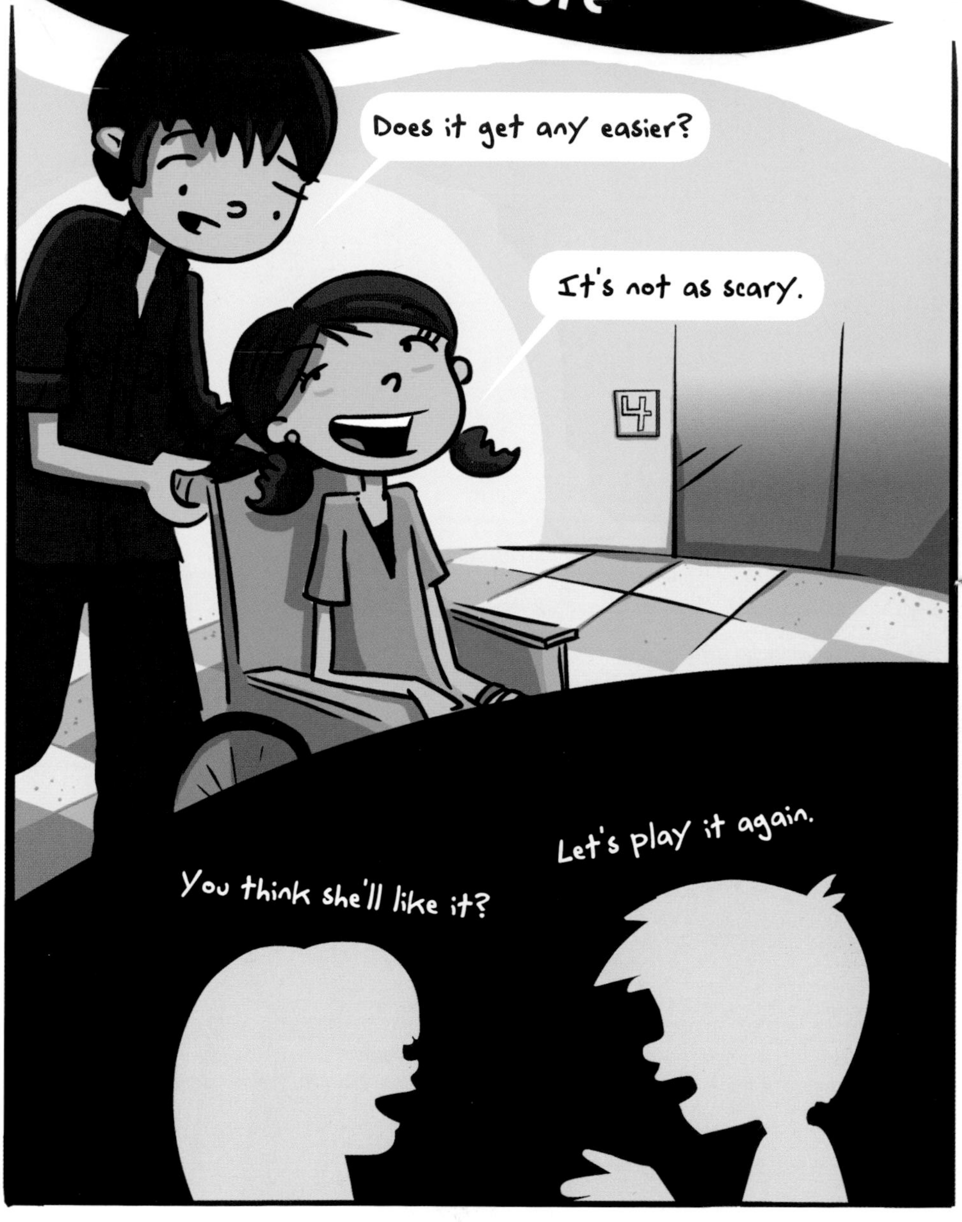
Does it get any easier?
It's not as scary.
You think she'll like it?
Let's play it again.

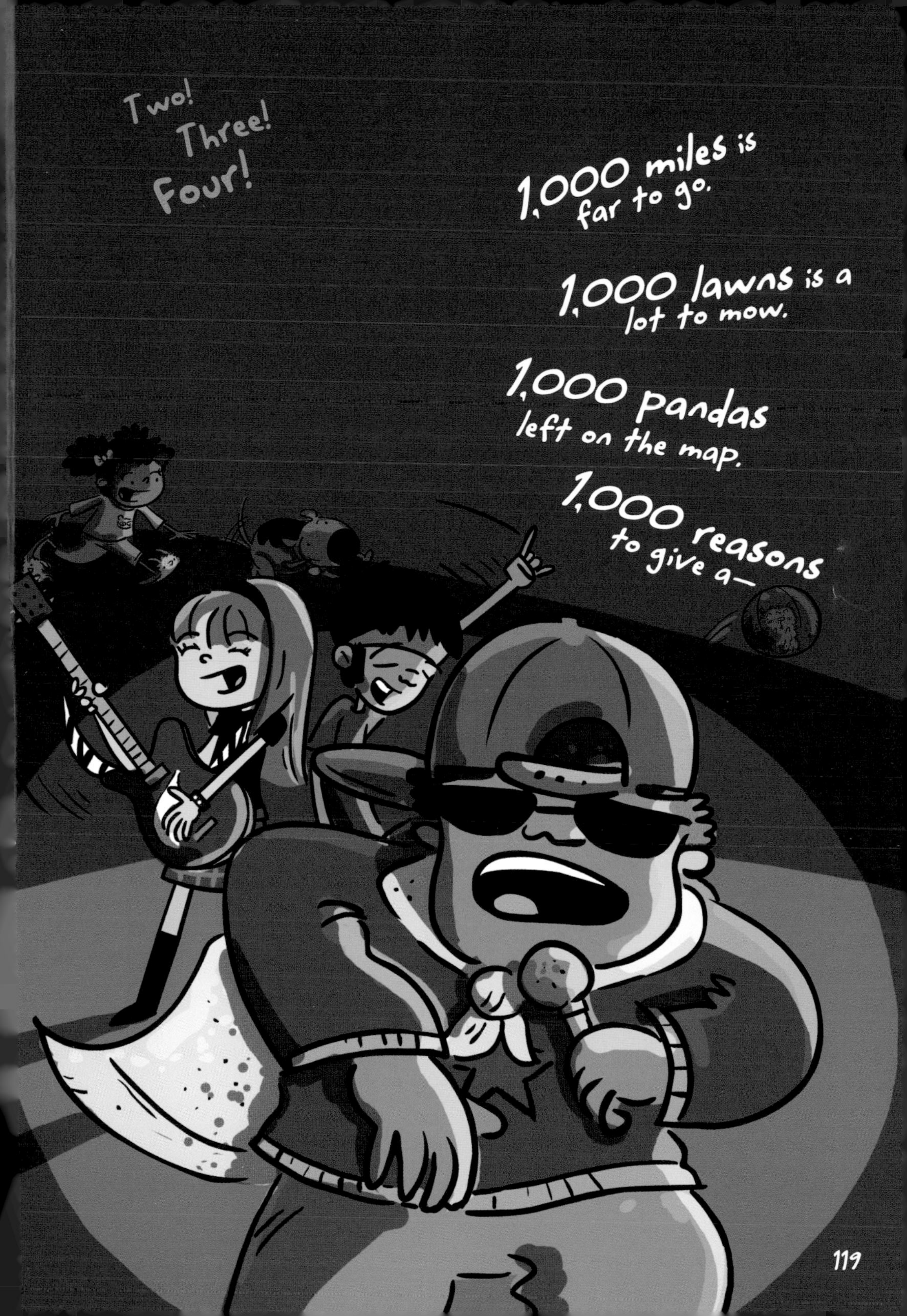
Two!
Three!
Four!
1,000 miles is far to go.
1,000 lawns is a lot to mow.
1,000 pandas left on the map.
1,000 reasons to give a—

START HERE

Many of my books end with the words: "The Beginning" because the end of a story can actually be the start of something **BIG.**

So in this space, where most books have those words "**THE END**," I wanted to let you know that in this book, on this page, you've hit the spot where things really start. This is where you get invited to get onboard.

Change happens in **2** ways – to you or by you. You can wait around for other people – adults, polilitician[s], college students – to make the **world a better place** or YOU – **YES, YOU** – can decide to **DO SOMETHING**. Tackle something small or something **HUGE**. Here's a tip: No matter how big the idea, you can start small. Like naming your project – designing a logo – telling a friend. So... find a cause you care about – there are plenty of problems in our world.

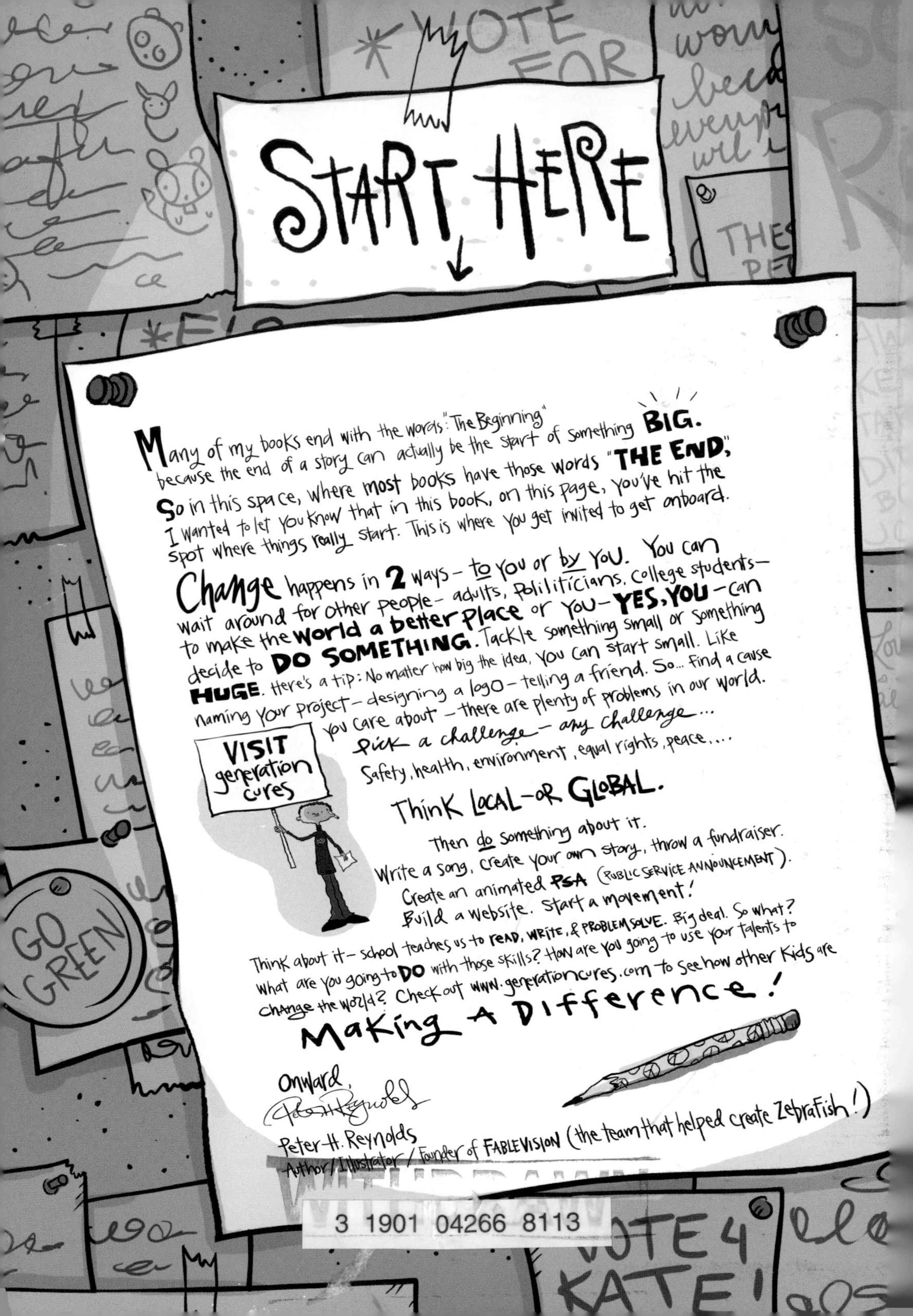
VISIT
generation cures

Pick a challenge – any challenge...
Safety, health, environment, equal rights, peace...

Think LOCAL – or GLOBAL.

Then do something about it.
Write a song, create your own story, throw a fundraiser.
Create an animated **PSA** (PUBLIC SERVICE ANNOUNCEMENT).
Build a website. Start a movement!

Think about it – school teaches us to **read, write, & PROBLEM SOLVE**. Big deal. So what? What are you going to **DO** with those skills? How are you going to use your talents to change the world? Check out www.generationcures.com to see how other kids are

Making A Difference!

Onward,

Peter H. Reynolds

Peter H. Reynolds
Author/Illustrator/Founder of FABLEVISION (the team that helped create ZebraFish!)